PLAY

YOU WOULDN'T STEAL A HOUSE?
WOULD YOU?
WOULD YOU PILFER SOMEONE'S DREAMS?
HANG ON, DID YOU JUST SAY YES?
WHAT KIND OF MONSTER ARE YOU?
BUT STILL...YOU WOULDN'T NICK MY LUCKY COIN.
WOULD YOU?
YOU WOULD?
HONESTLY?
WOW, YOU'RE A HORRIBLE PERSON.
EITHER WAY, DON'T DISTRIBUTE ILLICIT COPIES
OF THIS BOOK OKAY?

GRASS PEOPLE UP. IT'S THE ONLY WAY.

PIRACY IS THEFT

From cult director, Patrick Loveland, experience a return to true terror and imaginative cooking.

Two years ago, crazed maniac Jacob Burns burst onto your screens. First he captured the extended Hudson family from Texas. Then, over three days he prepared, cooked and ate his captives one by one. Have you been able to eat finger food at parties since you saw *that* scene?

Back then, only one man could stop him from putting the leftovers in the freezer and moving onto another hapless family. Detective Jack Putz pieced together the clues, and managed to save Julia - the only survivor of that terrible night - in a finale that left viewers reaching for the sick bags.

You thought that Jacob had been obliterated in an elaborate trap laid by Jack.

You were wrong.

Dead wrong.

Now, in the follow-up to the blockbuster hit that critics called, 'disgusting', 'primal', 'chilling' and 'brutal', watch with renewed horror as Jacob returns to the big screen.

This time, it's personal.

Putz took everything from him, including his dessert. This time Jacob will make him and his family the main course.

So pull up a chair.

Remember to say Grace.

And pray that you're not…second helpings.

JACOB'S BACK
THE
EATEN
II

Victorian detective Jack Nightingale was good at his job…too good. Having apprehended the members of a machinery breaking racket in the slums of London, he receives a chilling telegram; leave the capital by nightfall, or pay for his actions. Nightingale listens to no man, and heads to the nearest hostelry to celebrate his success.

He awakens to find the dead body of the Mayor of London in his wardrobe. Arrested and charged with murder, Nightingale trusts in Lady Justice to free him from this terrible predicament.

The trial is a fix.

The judge corrupt.

The verdict is in…

Death by hanging!

As he stares out at the Paddington crowd who have gathered to witness him swing from the hangman's noose, he prays for a miracle to figure out which of the many ne'er do wells he has put away, has booked him an appointment with death. The hatch opens and his body lurches down. There is a smattering of gasps and excited shouts as Jack's body dances at the end of the rope.

Yet the knot and fall did not kill him. He comes to hours later, to find that his broken bones have formed a thick necklace, sparing him from strangulation, but leaving him paralysed from the head down. As night falls, a solitary crow, carrion of the hanged dead, settles on the jib above, waiting for the first rays of light to hit the swinging body beneath his talons, so that he may feast upon the stricken man.

Jack has to work out who is to blame, in this terrifying tale of one man and his head, in a world where he can do nothing but think.

By dawn's early light, he'll hope to tell someone the true identity of the person that set him up, or the crow will have his fill.

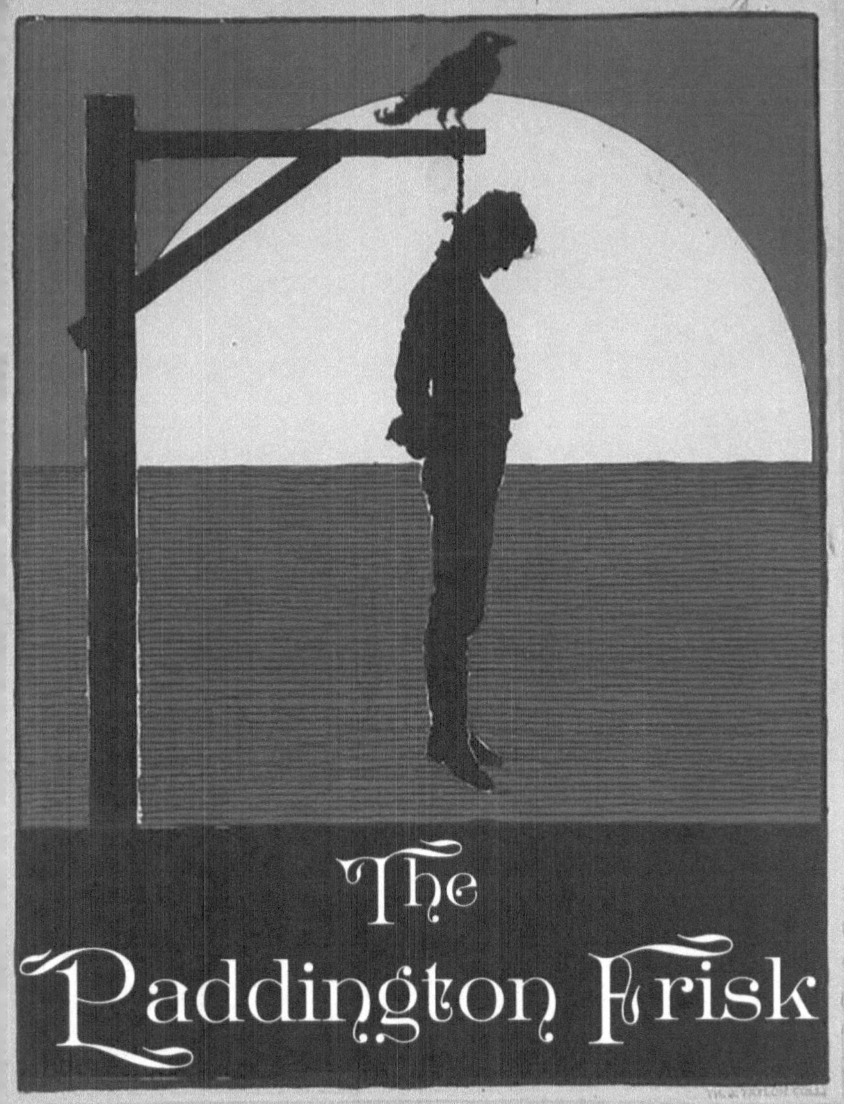

The Paddington Frisk

E BEST FOUR HOURS I 'VE SPENT WITH A
TALKING HEAD."
– THE DAILY VAJAZZLE

"TOUCHING, HEARTFELT AND RAW."
– VARIETY OF LIFE

BUDGET? WHAT BUDGET? AMAZING."
– CELLULOID DREAM

"JAW-DROPPING! A NOD TO FILMS OF A
SIMPLER AGE. WE WANT A SEQUEL!"
– FUDDY DUDDY REVIEWING INC.

The isle of Utopia is the last untouched paradise on earth. Man and ape live side by side in apparent harmony, working with simple tools to survive in a world trapped within the sands of time.

Their tranquillity is shattered one day when anthropological cult, Primate Dawn, land on Utopia's white sandy beaches, hellbent on capturing a rare albino monkey. The creature is said to be the divine being that, once sacrificed, will bring about the end of the world!

But this is no simple monkey that is ape-napped, it is the sacred ruler of Utopia, and his disappearance threatens to send the island into civil war. To stop man facing off against primate, the ruling castes agree to the creation of an elite force, made up from the best of the best.

With only seventy-two hours to save their way of life, human warriors Adam and Eve are forced to put aside their feelings for each other and their deep-seated mistrust of their monkey co-soldiers, to help save all of Utopia.

Using stunning state-of-the-art CGI, enjoy this ground-breaking film in the comfort of your own home.

Relive *that* fight scene, between staff-wielding religious zealots and Uzi-toting chimpanzees.

You'll laugh!

You'll cry!

You'll try to peek up the flimsy loin cloths!

But everyone will remember the day when the world was saved by…

EVOLUTION FORCE

WE TOOK THEIR MONKEY.

THEY WANT HIM BACK.

DUNCAN P BRADSHAW'S
CANNIBAL NUNS!
FROM OUTER SPACE!
PLAY MOVIE
SUBTITLES ON/OFF
BONUS MATERIAL

EYECUE PRODUCTIONS

IN ASSOCIATION WITH

A
GORE
.COM
PUBLICATION

1

"I hope they're not fucking dead already." Father Flynn looked up and down the road, before pointing at a house with light streaming from an upstairs window. "Is this us?"

Padraig, assistant to the priest, was currently attempting to repel a torrential downpour with a large golf umbrella. "That it is, Father, number twenty-three, black door."

The rain continued to hammer down on the nylon canopy, nearly drowning out their words. Flynn took another pull on his cigarette. Blowing the smoke out, he huffed. "Why does it always have to chuck it down when we do this? Just once, it'd be nice to have a spot of sunshine, you know?"

Padraig struggled to keep the umbrella level, whilst clutching a thick leather holdall to his chest. "Maybe it's the angels, Father, looking down on us this day. Shedding a tear of hope for the lost soul we're here to save."

Father Flynn turned slowly, taking in a lungful of smoke, and blowing it into Padraig's face. "What a load of bollocks, did you go all the way down on the Hallmark factory?"

"I…err….no, Father."

Taking in the last drag, Flynn flicked the cigarette butt, and watched as it spun end-over-end, finally coming to land in a puddle by the kerb. Flynn nodded towards the holdall. "And you're one-hundred-and-ten percent sure you brought everything this time? I don't want a repeat of last week, me, standing in the Entwistle's pantry dick in hand, as you rummaged around in your man bag for the elixir of enhanced willpower."

Padraig held the bag tighter. "Yes, Father, I remembered everything. I double-checked the inventory before we left."

"So you have the sheet?"

"Yes, Father."

"And the Holy shovel, you're absolutely sure you packed the Holy shovel?"

Padraig tapped the holdall. "Oh yes, Father. I put a spare in the car, just in case."

"I hope to hell you remembered my lucky cassock, Padraig, tell me you brought that."

Coughing, the weedy man nodded towards his boss. "You put it on this morning, Father, remember?"

Flynn patted himself down, and playfully slapped his assistant's cheek. "So I did. HA! I don't know what's with me today, my mind's all over the shop."

Padraig smiled sweetly, angling the brolly to counter a gust of wind that was trying to make the downpour go horizontal, and gestured towards the foreboding house. "It's understandable, Father, these occasions are never easy. Anyway, we best be getting on, the family are waiting, we should go and offer them solace."

"You're right. Here we are, standing in the pissing rain like a right pair of tits, and those poor sods in there are fretting about what's happening to their loved one. Come on, old friend, let's get this show on the road." Father Flynn ducked out from behind the cover of the umbrella and sploshed ankle-deep through a number of puddles. He arrived at the front door, legs drenched, Padraig a footstep behind, doing his best to try and shield his master from the brunt of the English summer rain.

Three hearty knocks boomed from the wrought iron door knocker. A series of hurried clanks, and chains unfurled, the door opened to reveal a middle-aged man, his face glazed with sweat. "Father, thank you for coming. He's…he's…"

Flynn landed a heavy palm on the man's shoulder. "Shhh, it's okay, I'm here now. We'll make sure that this troublesome process is handled with the dignity and respect that you expect from the church. That's what we do." He gave the man a wink and a playful shoot from a freshly-formed finger gun. He blew away the imaginary smoke and aimed the digit cannon skyward. "Now, if it's not too much trouble, can we come in? It's like the big guy upstairs is setting the scene to audition for a new Noah out here this evening."

Wiping away his tears, the man nodded solemnly, and ushered the two men inside. Padraig shook his umbrella then held it out in front of him, closed, but dripping profusely..

"Sorry, where are my manners?" The man closed the door behind the priests. "I'm Derek --it's my son, my little Timothy that you're here to see. He's upstairs, in his room. Has been since he was struck down with…you know…the unpleasantness."

Father Flynn was eyeing up a large oil painting that hung precariously from a rusting nail. "Of course, of course. Fear not, I have everything I need with me, Padraig here has double-checked everything. Whenever you're ready, we can go upstairs and see him. I take it…it's not too late, is it?"

Derek was silent and immobile for a few seconds before the words triggered a response. "No, no, he's a lot worse than he was when I called the hotline this morning, but with God's grace, he's still here. He's strong, is our Timothy. So strong!"

A shrill voice echoed down the hallway. "Cooee!"

Father Flynn jumped backwards, knocking his assistant against the front door. "Fuck me, what was that? It's not one of the fallen, is it? I don't think I packed my double strength crucifix. Quick, Padraig, to the belfry! Fetch me the Cross of Uttoxeter. I recognise the wail of a banshee…" The priest brought his balled fists up, Queensbury style, and pranced on the spot.

Placing his hands on top of Father Flynn's, Derek shook his head and lowered the punchy priest's dukes. "Don't worry, Father, that's no banshee. A harpy, perhaps…it's just Meredith. My wife."

A woman, with a smile that made Julia Roberts' wide grin look dull and lifeless, skipped down the hallway. An apron was wound around her waist so tightly that her arse cheeks were badly deprived of nourishing oxygen. She held a pair of scissors in one hand and a white orchid in the other. "I say, this is all rather jolly, eh? A real live priest in *my* house, the

Jamesons next door will be positively green with envy. They're proper full-on Catholics, you know? Seventeen kids, eight dogs and undoubtedly a mass-murder/suicide in the future when the mountain of debt engulfs them." She took a moment to breathe. "Did they see you arrive, Father?"

Flynn shrugged, smoothed his hair down, and plucked sugar puffs from his unkempt beard. "To be honest, Merry, can I call you Merry? It's chucking it down out there, so I could barely even see your house, let alone next door."

Meredith maintained her inane grin; if anything, she willed her facial muscles to exceed their suggested safety limits, the skin at the corner of her mouth beginning to crack. "Marvellous. So, I guess you're here about Timmy? I must say, I've never him look so pale, and because he's a ginger, he often hovers just above translucent on the colour spectrum. Then there's the vomiting…the endless, endless vomiting. Still, least it brought some colour to his face." She nudged the priest in the ribs. "All that splashback you see."

Father Flynn looked over to Padraig, who'd put on his best 'I don't know what you're talking about' face. Meredith seized on this. "With the flecks of sick. From the bucket? Anyway, here I am, prattling on about gingers and puke, you two must be parched. Can I get you a drink?"

Flynn rubbed his hands together. "Now you're talking, do you have-"

Padraig coughed. Having bagged the priest's attention, he tapped his wristwatch. Flynn ran his hands across his lips. "Oh…yes…I suppose. Don't want Archbishop Tena to use my face as a dartboard again, huh? What do you have on offer, Merry?"

With her mouth curled up so far that the corners of her lips were in the same district as her earlobes, Meredith said. "I have coffee? Or some hot cocoa?"

"I'm fine, thank you, Meredith," Padraig said, looking around for somewhere to put his umbrella. Derek guided him to a conveniently-placed coatrack.

Father Flynn tapped his inside pocket. "You know what? I

think I'll have a cocoa, thank you."

Meredith nodded, and sniffed the flower, nearly losing it in her open maw before turning and flouncing back to the kitchen.

"Would you like to see little Timothy now, Father?" Derek asked.

"You betcha, let's get this gig started. Padraig, best get the sheet out now, just in case."

Derek led the pair upstairs. Moving at a glacial pace, Flynn looked back at Padraig and hung his tongue out of his head. Finally reaching the summit, he pushed past the balding man, and blocked the landing. "Now, Dezza, is it alright if I call you Dezza? Derek is just a bit…drab. Excellent. I just want you to remember that Padraig and I are no strangers to the sights, sounds and indeed smells that linger within your son's room."

"He's not my son."

Father Flynn, halfway through enouncing his next word, stopped dead, slapping his gums shut. "He's not? What did you do? Steal him from a ginger's orphanage?"

Derek shook his head. "He's Meredith's, from a previous relationship."

"Ah, soiled goods, is he? Couldn't keep herself pure for you eh? No worries. As long as the nagging doubt in your balls that she compares the size of your dick to the other guy's isn't too overwhelming, then you're all good. Am I right, Dezza?"

"Sometimes…at night, I lie awake, thinking about things, wondering if…"

The priest stretched, pushing out a huge fake yawn. "Yeah, that's great, big guy. But if you don't mind? I've got a beverage on the way, and I'd quite like to get started with…ya know? So, which door is it?"

Unaware that he had been interrupted, Derek finished up, "…just maybe, that she would walk in front of a bus. BLAM. Dead. Or at least knock that terrible grin off her face. It was terribly sweet when we first got together, a real attraction, but now, ten years later? Day in, day out. It's like looking at a clown. Every. Single. Day. I didn't want to marry Pennywise, you know?" He looked at the priest's face, which was a mix of boredom and part-time enquiry.

"Which. Door?" Flynn repeated, jabbing his finger towards the assortment of closed doors lining the hallway.

Derek thumbed behind him. "The one with the frog's head on it. Timothy has…had…a penchant for amateur taxidermy."

Barging past, the priest peered closer at the frog skull, its skin long since flaked away, remnants of an eye hanging perilously via a dried string of optic nerve. "Charming lad…"

"Please, Father, do what you can. Even though he's not mine by blood, he's still my son, you know? Help ease his suffering, please."

Flynn rolled up his sleeves. "Dezza, I may come across as aloof and a little churlish, but rest assured, I'm the best at what I do. That's why they sent me. Not some two-bit Joe Shmoe who is more likely to cop a feel of your son whilst you're praying at his bedside and not paying any attention. Okay?"

Derek nodded, stifling a tear.

"Good, now, let's go see what we've got going down in Funkytown." Flynn pushed the door open. The stench hit him first: vomit mingled with damp clothing and pine air freshener, which had done a poor job of making the room smell like a spring glade. He retrieved a small pot of mint Vaseline from a pocket and dabbed a patch under his nose before offering it around.

The curtains hung limply from the pole, a thick wedge of lamplight bisecting the bed. The two priests tiptoed into the room, where a mass writhed gently beneath a heavily stained Power Rangers duvet. Father Flynn nodded to a chest of drawers, and Padraig headed towards it, carefully unpacking the contents of the holdall.

Flynn edged closer to the bed, noticing a pile of balled tissues on the floor, like a stack of white cannonballs. "Hey, little boy, I don't want you to be afraid, okay? I'm here for you. *We're* here for you." The duvet rustled. The Priest moved closer, wincing as he stood on a creaky floorboard. "It's okay, I know you've been through a lot already, and you've been suffering, it's okay. I'm going to help you. I'm going to set you free, do you understand?"

As the rustling intensified, the duvet rippled like a disturbed lake, limbs floundering beneath the starched cotton surface. Flynn reached the bedside table, pulling a face as he realised he had stepped in a fresh puddle of sick. Slowly, he moved his hand to the edge of the duvet. "Shhhh, it's okay, no more tears. No more bad things, but I'm going to need to have a look at you and see what I'm up against, okay, little fella?"

His fingers curled around the top of the duvet, Flynn crossed himself, looked to the sky, uttered a silent valediction, and peeled the sodden sheet down. It revealed a crop of matted hair, bits of sweetcorn woven into the fringe. Flynn ground his teeth together as he noticed the sores, dotted around the child's head as if he were a cratered moon.

Timothy's skin was grey and had the consistency of boiled broad beans. His eyes were open wide, their green irises aflame, pupils mere pinprick islands of black at the centre. Yellowing veins ran through the whites.

Flynn's finger caught on a pustule, taking it clean off, allowing a trickle of yellow goo to dribble from the crusty wound. The stench coming from the boy was unbearable, easily beating the smell of smeared spearmint into submission with its rotten odour. Timothy's chapped lips were parted, displaying rows of filthy teeth flecked with vomit and animal fur. Flynn released the duvet and pulled out his portable crucifix. "The power-"

Timothy's head cracked towards the sound, splintered bone grinding within his neck, and cackled in a voice that was not his own --unless he had been taking steroids on the sly. "Fuck off, Father, this little one belongs to me, and you can't have him back." To underline the claim, the boy began to convulse before letting out a fountain of green vomit which caught Father Flynn square in the face.

2

"So, Father, how bad is he?" Derek handed Flynn another towel.

Convinced he had something stuck inside his wiry beard, the priest picked and pulled at it with the towel, before turning to the man. "He's a category six."

"Six?"

"Six," Flynn smirked, before shouting. "THE NUMBER OF THE BEAST. Man, I never get tired of this gig."

"Is six bad?" Derek asked, hoping it wasn't.

Flynn began to laugh, and Meredith joined in, her mouth perfectly shaped to enjoy a brief bout of pointless laughter. After a few moments, the pair stopped. Flynn replied. "Yes, it's bad. The categorisation goes up to seven, but then you're talking about Lucy himself."

"Lucy?" Derek asked. "Himself? Is this Lucy a transvestite? He? She? It? Her? Sorry, I never know which pronoun I need to address them by."

Flynn chuckled. "Of course you don't. I wager your sheltered little life revolves around putting people into neat little boxes. I bet you don't go out much unless you run out of hummus. No, you hapless goon, Lucy, Lucifer. You know, the big cheese in the ol' charnel house down below. Where you go if you don't eat your greens, or if you like dismembering people and wearing their hollowed-out ribcage as a Sunday best waistcoat."

"Oh," Derek said.

"Yes," Flynn concurred. "*Oh,* indeed."

The priest coughed and made the internationally-recognised hand gesture for *drinking.* Meredith did nothing except clutch the steaming mug of cocoa tighter, and exhale loudly. He lost his patience. "For the love of God, woman, give that here." He snatched the mug from her, and turned his back. With one hand rummaging through the inside of his cassock, he fished out a stringy length of floss that the little possessed boy had yakked up over him, discarded it on the floor, and pulled out a small silver flask.

Padraig appeared at his side. "Father, what are you doing? You promised me you wouldn't."

"Padraig, I think you're pretty fucking awesome, you know that, don't you?"

Padraig's cheeks began to flush. "Why thank you, Father."

Unscrewing the cap of the hip flask, Flynn poured a healthy slug of brown liquid into the mug. "But in that room lays a demon, not out of Compton, but straight out of the Twelfth Circle of Vomit. They are a hardy bunch, and in order to defeat one, I will need to be suitably lubricated, for only a complete buffoon would attempt to exorcise one of those things whilst utterly sober."

Meredith stuck her head in between the two whispering priests. "I say, that little flask looks rather jolly!"

Flynn shook the receptacle, the dregs sloshing around within. "A gift from a Pagan druid I met on a team building exercise last year at Stonehenge." He gestured for Meredith to come closer. "So many people stick to whiskey when wishing to perk up a hot beverage. Me? I like to experiment. This here is Amaretto, works well with the chocolate, you see, accentuates the differing tones."

Jotting down a little note for herself, the woman asked. "So what would you say works well with Earl Grey?"

Looking her up and down, Flynn replied. "A small bottle of strong organic Belgian lager. Now, if you please, Merry, I need to prepare."

The woman nodded, The Joker's grin still affixed to her face. The others looked on as the priest began some reverse lunges on the landing, the strain of sinew and creaking knees killing the peace and quiet. After finishing his hot drink, he passed the mug back to Meredith, and did a quick burst of high knees, willing himself to beat his personal best. Flynn followed up with some tricep stretches, and eventually re-joined the cadre at the top of the stairs.

The priest beckoned them all into a huddle. He slapped his hands on their backs, pulling them in close, the smell of Amaretto and hot chocolate creating a potent aroma. "Now, by the law of the church, I can't stop you two wanting to go in there with me and my main man, Padraig here. But, if you do, there are some things you'll need to know first."

Husband and wife gulped and nodded as one.

"First off, if this demon is who I think it is, you should be aware that it is a master of cunning and confusion. In order to maintain its grip on your child, they will say anything to make you angry, to antagonise you and rile you up. It lives off fear, pain, short tempers and suffering."

Pushing his slipping glasses up his nose, Derek said. "Like Darth Vader?"

Flynn tutted, and slapped the man around the back of the head. "I swear to god, Dezza, if you butt in again, I will leave your son to be used as a demon's hand puppet. Did you ever hear what became of Elmo and the Cookie Monster after Big Bird helped broker the deal to sell their hand-sewed souls to Satan?"

Derek shook his head. Flynn grabbed hold of his cardigan and pulled him in closer. "They turned to prostitution. If you go down to St Pancras International train station, you'll see the pair of them, offering hand jobs for cookies and handkerchiefs, so trust me, you don't want your little boy to become a demon's plaything, capiche?"

"Okay. Sorry."

The priest patted Derek down, smoothing out the creases he had made. "That's fine, apology accepted. Now --as I was saying, this demon will say things to try and get a rise out of you, it will twist your words and prey on your darkest, deepest fears. I've even attended exorcisms where the demon has left the host body to momentarily possess small household animals, and forced them to defecate on people's favourite rugs and upholstered goods. If you think it's bad enough trying to get a demon out of a person, you have no idea how hard it is to get one out of a Cockapoo."

Meredith scrunched up her face. "Why is a cock in poo? Did the demon put it there? Seems odd to me, getting someone to pull their winky out only to shove it into poo-poo."

Flynn balled his fist and waved it under her chin. "Merry, your strong and defined jaw looks like it can take a punch, but if you interrupt me once more, I'm going to break my sole remaining oath, and strike a woman, okay? Now, I don't want to, but there's only one thing I hate more than being interrupted."

"Demons?" Derek offered.

Flynn closed his eyes. "No, Dezza. Not demons."

"Is it the Polish?" Meredith asked.

"No, it's not the bloody Poles. You really want to know?"

The pair nodded. "Fine. What I really loathe are xenophobes who won't let me finish telling them the motherfucking instructions and etiquette for an exorcism." He glared at the couple in turn, who both opted to remain mute.

"So, here's the deal. You two can come in, but you must stay near the door. Do not speak unless I tell you to, and under no circumstances must you engage the demon in conversation, are we clear? He might look like your sweet innocent Timothy, with added vomit, but that's not your little boy in there right now. It's an evil bastard wearing your kid's body like a birthday badge, remember that."

The parents nodded.

"Good. Now, relax, okay? Shake it out a little. You two are about to bear witness to something that most people will never get to experience. Ever. The resumption of the perpetual struggle between good and evil, light versus dark, man against demon, the holy against the unclean, the-"

Padraig coughed loudly. "Father, I think we need to…" he gestured towards the door.

Flynn clipped the man round the head, and glared at him. "Granted, it was no Independence Day speech, but fuck me, I felt like it was going somewhere. We'll discuss your attitude at your next monthly one-to-one, okay, Padraig?" He turned to the parents. "Come on, let's go. Stick behind me and remember everything I said. Your son's very life could depend on it."

Flynn put his hand into the space between them all. "Come on, I've seen sports teams do this. Everyone, put your hands on top of mine."

Nervous glances were shared amongst the huddle, but reluctantly, they agreed. "Aaaannnnnddd, BREAK!" Flynn flung his hand in the air and shadow-boxed his way down the corridor to Timothy's frog-skull-adorned door. Gently pushing it open with the toe of his shoe, he motioned for the others to creep inside the room.

The temperature within had risen markedly, the smell becoming more potent, the floor now squelchy underfoot, matching the consistency of a decent sized swamp. Once the others were inside, Flynn crossed himself and followed suit, closing the door behind him.

With Timothy's parents doing as they'd been told, and clutching hold of each other, Padraig went to the assortment of items he had laid out on the chest of drawers. Flynn cracked his knuckles one by one, each sounding like a bottle rocket going off. He walked up to his equerry. "Padraig, I don't like the look of him, he's glowing like a radioactive lollipop. I think we're going to have to get in there quick and finish this. I'm thinking…" Flynn clicked his fingers, "…the Brass Knuckles of Godiva, anoint them for me."

Padraig bowed his head and picked up the sacred weapon. Holding it aloft, he muttered the holy incantation of justice, then passed it to Flynn. The knuckles were a tight fit, and so they should be, having been used by Lady Godiva to give those blasted clothes thieves a good pasting once she'd caught up with them on horseback. Flynn flexed his fingers, allowing the metal to become one with his balled fist.

He stood over Timothy, his rheumy eyes fixed on a spot on the ceiling. "Oh, Lord, give me the strength this day to rid this innocent vessel of yours. To purge him of the foul monster that dwells within. Grant me the wisdom to mentally spar with this most foul of creatures, so that it does not befuddle my mind. Finally, bestow upon me the infinite patience I will require, so that the wicked barbs this denizen of the underworld will undoubtedly try to bait me with, fall on deaf ears. Amen."

Padraig boomed out an almighty. "AMEN," quickly followed by two far more muted offerings from Derek and Meredith.

Flynn leaned over the child, his face still festooned with boils and blisters, shining now with both sweat and pus. Timothy was grinning from ear to ear. *Definitely takes after his mother*, Flynn thought. Timothy's eyes flicked sideways as his neck cricked upwards, fixing the priest with a baleful stare. "The popular American TV series, 24, was a big pile of shit, you god-bothering nonce."

Flynn ground his teeth together, pulled back his fist, and shouted, "How dare you!"

3

Flynn continued to butt his head against the wall of the landing. "I'm sorry…I should not have risen to the demon's words."

"You have to admit, though, 24 did get a bit silly," Derek said.

The priest was on him in an instant, putting the man straight in a headlock. "What did you say?"

Trying to catch a breath, Derek squeaked. "It did get a bit silly. I mean, how many times did Kim get kidnapped? And seriously, Habib Marwan in the fourth series? He's either the world's best escape artist, or the lucky benefactor of the most inept security services in the world."

Flynn flipped Derek around, putting him into a Jack Bauer sleeper hold. "How dare you, you little shit. Take it back, TAKE IT BACK. I COMPEL YOU!"

Tapping against the priest's arm, Derek managed. "But how did they not see the headlights…when he…was driving a Humvee…through the desert…at…night…" before lapsing into unconsciousness. Flynn laid the man on the floor.

"He's right, you know," Padraig said, shielding his nether regions.

"That's as maybe, but no one disses 24, okay?"

"Father, please, the beast will have grown stronger from the beating you meted out. Your base actions will have only emboldened his black heart. We must tread lightly, else we will lose the boy to darkness. Forever."

"Fine, I know. I should've resisted, but that fey creature weaselled out my one true weakness…"

Padraig spluttered. "Just the *one* weakness, Father?"

Flynn tapped the side of his head. "Carry on, Padraig, I'm making a mental note of all of this. You forget that I know people, *powerful* people. All it would take is one word to El Pope, and you'll be repointing the gargoyles at Sacré-Cœur, sans safety harness I should add, in the time it would take me to crush your larynx with my bare hands. Choose wisely."

As he went to open the door, Flynn turned back to the others: those still conscious, at least. "I think I need to face the demon on my own, it will undoubtedly have grown in strength and cockiness since last time. You may not be strong enough to deal with its new found fortitude. It would not take too much more encouragement, before it'll escape from the wards we created, and be here with us in this realm. We will all then be in some serious doo-doo."

Padraig piped up. "Father, I think I should at least monitor events. Just to make sure there are no complications. If it were not for me prising you off the child last time, I fear your anger would've fully woken the demon."

"As you wish, but please, do not disturb me as I prepare." The two holy men re-entered the room. The heat had stripped the wallpaper, which pooled on the floor in great big piles of thick material. Mixing with the fetid water which had begun to spread across what used to be the carpet, it bobbed in time with every step made through the surface.

Padraig recoiled as he looked down at the afflicted child. He still had a smile plastered on his face, and his teeth had been filed down to form a mountain range of sharpened incisors. A bulbous tongue flicked out from his cavernous mouth, in between the chattering of pointy pegs.

A pair of horns were beginning to push through the corners of the boy's forehead. Nubs of bone strained to poke through the sallow skin, turning it almost translucent in places. The beast began to laugh. "Oh, foolish one, you are too quick to antagonise. I look forward to fully awakening, and bringing you…your DOOM."

Flynn stroked his beard, bringing it to a hairy point. "You may have tricked me into lashing out in a momentary lapse of concentration last time, but rest assured, you will not do the same again. I am a man of the cloth, I am His right hand, His weapon upon this earth, and you can provoke me no further."

There was a sound akin to keys being dragged down a freshly polished car bonnet, then the child began to quiver and shake. "My ascension is near, *priest*, and soon, you will not be able to stop me. I look forward to ravaging this pathetic planet of yours, for I have much vomit to expel this day. So many meat sacks to rend apart, to feast upon their still-steaming flesh." The child's limbs flung out, forming a star, and the rancid duvet flew across the room, splatting against the wall and sliding down like a discarded tissue full of snot.

Timothy began to rise, still horizontal, but no longer resting on the saturated sheets beneath him. "Impressive, most impressive," Flynn said. He walked up to the body, now hovering three feet from the bed. He ran a hand underneath the body. "No wires, full-on corporeal telekinesis, you're not messing about."

"Priest, I-"

Flynn pressed a finger against the child's mouth, instantly regretting it as the digit was covered in tacky goo. "Speak no more, vile creation, for it is time to end this. Padraig, fetch me the Holy Shears of Titchmarsh, we need to put paid to the energy field surrounding this bastard."

Padraig turned back to his holdall, umming and ahhing about where he had left the aforementioned trimming device. Timothy rotated in the air, now facing out sideways. Flynn flinched, wary of another potential puke barrage. "Priest, I know the true darkness inside of man, the reason you are so easy to tempt and tease. Why do you think we can so easily take over your puny tubes of flesh and bone?"

"Padraig…anytime today please…"

"I shall tell you…"

"PADRAIG, FOR THE LAST TIME, WHERE ARE MY MOTHERFUCKING HOLY SHEARS OF TITCHMARSH? I BESEECH YOU!"

Timothy jabbed a taloned finger into the priest's chest. "Though people may say so, you included, *holy one*, Ronan Keating didn't have the best voice in Boyzone, it was Mikey

Graham."

Flynn balled his fists. "You've gone too far this time, *demon*."

4

Derek and Meredith clung onto the door handle with every fibre of their being. Meredith in particular thanked Gino Tagliatelle, her Pilates coach, for building her core up to a pretty decent level for a woman in her mid-forties.

From within the depths of their son's room, there was a keen wailing sound. The room was being trashed, with furniture being reduced to its flat pack components as it was hurled against the walls and stomped into submission.

Flynn was on the verge of finishing another cigarette. "How did it know? I kept that one really well hidden. I don't even have the cassette in my Walkman anymore. I thought if I stuck to analogue, no pestilent demonic horde could figure out my love of Irish boy bands. Padraig, what the blazes are you doing?"

His assistant was pacing the landing. Having opened up his iBible, he cast a withering look at his boss, before continuing to whisper into the phone.

Stubbing the cigarette out on the bannister, Flynn retrieved another hip flask and began to down the contents. "I say, Father, I don't think this door is going to last very much longer," Meredith screamed.

Flynn waved them away as if they were an irritating wasp, instead opting to tip the remnants of the Advocaat down his throat. Finishing his call, Padraig checked the weather for the evening, before joining the husband and wife in holding the door shut. "You've really done it this time, Father. Archbishop Tena is not impressed. Not impressed at all."

"What have you done, Padraig? Have you stitched me up, you little snake?"

Padraig shook as he fought to hold onto the door handle. "I had to tell them what happened. The Order of the Crimson

Rosary hierarchy needed to be told of your failure."

Flynn took out his crimson rosary, and wound it round his fist. "My failure? What the hell are you babbling on about? I have everything under control. I think you overestimate the severity of the situation."

A horn the size of a forearm lanced through the door and speared Derek beneath his collarbone. The man screamed, scrabbling backwards along the landing whilst attempting to staunch the bleeding with a drying guest hand towel. The same towel which had been used previously to mop up the vomit that had drenched Father Flynn earlier on in the proceedings. Padraig pointed to the leering demon face, gurning through the hole in the door. "I think this constitutes a failure, don't you, Father?"

"I see you now, little man, I, Fattori Gutso, Prince of Puke, the Duke of Dry-Retching, have almost ascended, soon I will spill your guts and signal your DOOM!" The demon bellowed. The child's body stretched to near-breaking point, a thin skin pyjama set pulled to its limit over the heavily toned body of the demon.

Necking the last drops of booze, Flynn hiccupped and shouted back. "What is with you and the continual mention of DOOM? There are other words to use you know, you big red bastard."

"This hallway looks very pretty, dear," Derek said. His blood-slicked hands had slipped off the goring wound, and his pale face regarded the beige walls as if he were in the Sistine Chapel. Meredith shoved her arse against the door and kneeled down next to her husband, pulling her apron off and winding it round his body.

Padraig shouted over the din. "I've done what I had to, Father. They're sending–"

"Don't you say his name, you Judas bastard. Don't you dare say it."

Padraig ducked beneath another horn piercing the door, and managed to regain his composure. "They're sending…Father O'Malley."

Silence caused time itself to cease, just for the briefest of seconds. Even Fattori, revelling in his fully-grown head horns, peered through the breach in the door and mouthed. "Not Father O'Malley."

Events spun back to normal speed, and Gutso disappeared. Silence reigned until the thunder of hooves against floorboards rose in volume, and then what little remained of the door disappeared in chunks of wood and hinge. Padraig slammed against the wall, landing in a pile atop Derek and Meredith, which was the closest the pair had gotten to sex in the past four months.

Your only child's nightmarish attempts at taxidermy, and impromptu midnight art installations, where your attendance was compulsory, will do that to your love life, you see.

Flynn dropped the empty hip flask and hauled himself up to full unhunched height. "Not on my watch. I'm not having Mister Fucking O'Perfect waltz in here and snatch one out of my win column. You want a fight, you vomiting fuck, fine, come and get me." He took guard and beckoned the demon forward.

Fattori Gutso laughed, ripping the thin sheath of human skin from his muscled form as if it were an irritating sweet wrapper. "TIME FOR YOUR DOOM, PRIEST!"

"Seriously, are you sponsored by a company called DOOM? Do you get a percentage every time you say it?" Flynn whinged.

Fattori, like an angry bull, scuffed his hooves against the carpeted floor, ripping up chunks of fabric, and scraping it down to the bare boards. The demon began to huff and bray, the noise shaking the family pictures off the walls. Pictures of happier times, before Timmy had inadvertently become possessed from a misbehaving phone app and been ripped apart by the Prince of Puke.

Flynn pulled a drying towel from the top of the bannister, and shouted. "Olé!" Gutso charged the priest, who sidestepped at the last minute allowing the beast to rip the towel to shreds but career through the bathroom door, and smack into the sink. A fountain of water jetted from the broken taps, cleaning what remained of the child's guts from the demon.

"That will only hasten your d-"

"Yes, DOOM, I get it. Change the record, you demonic fiend."

Fattori sneered. "I was going to say *demise*, actually." He lunged forward, catching the swaying priest around the throat with one giant hand. He pulled the struggling man up to his bulbous snout, the smell of vomit overpowering. "I will enjoy feasting on your innards." The demon tried to fold the man up like a soiled pair of underpants, but the priest's skeletal structure held fast and refused to yield. Irked, Gutso picked up what remained of the heavy porcelain sink and hurled it at the window, sending the entire frame and double glazing spinning onto the front garden. Grabbing hold of the priest's arse, he chucked the man through the gap as if he were the last suitcase to be loaded on SleazyJet flight number B008I3S to Ibiza.

Father Flynn thought back to his years of training with the Order of the Crimson Rosary: in particular, the lesson about being hurled through a section of demolished wall by a demon and/or large beast. He balled himself up as best he could and prayed that there would be some kind of large shrubbery to break his fall.

Someone in the Listening-to-Desperate-Pleas department must've heard him as he landed head first in the bushy mass of Meredith's prize Thuja Occidentalis Danica. As Flynn extracted himself from the mass of twigs and leaves, Fattori Gutso leaped through the hole in the house and landed on the once-immaculate lawn. "I will make this quick, priest."

The demon began to gag and retch, his throat bubbling from within, the muscles contracting. His jaw dislocated, opening like a trapdoor, and Gutso let out a concentrated stream of spew. As soon as it came into contact with the air, it began to solidify, forming a long cane of vomit, encrusted with kernels of corn and other half-digested vegetables. With a skill, honed from millennia of being incarcerated in an antique jade pendant, Fattori began to whittle the bile baton down. Now basted in a layer of sap, Gutso crafted a puke-sword from the hardened effluence, and gave a triumphant roar as he held it aloft.

The demon began to work on his kata, swinging the sword around his toned red form, a scrap of pyjama bottoms managing to keep this paragraph safely in the 15 category. Flynn looked around for something he could use as a weapon, opting for a conveniently discarded hoe, returned by the Jamesons next door by being dumped in the adjoining hedgerow. "Now I have a weapon, hoe-hoe-hoe."

Holding his makeshift weapon en garde, Flynn began to circle the demon, taking a few tentative jabs, which were easily deflected by the remarkably sturdy puke-sword.

There was a hubbub building around the pair as they faced off. People up and down the street, having been woken up by the unadvised demolition work, shouted and hollered, taking selfies with the demon in the background.

Sensing a moment's hesitation by the beast, Flynn lunged towards him, bringing the metal end firmly up into his opponent's throat. The blow did nothing except get lodged in Gutso's Adams Apple. The demon grunted in annoyance, and brought his sword across his body, reducing the wooden pole to two halves and leaving the priest holding nothing but a ragged stick.

Flynn regarded the splintered pole and threw it behind him. "No matter, I shall defeat you with…the power of the Lord!" Rummaging around the inside of his cassock, he pulled out his favourite crucifix, the one given to him by his mentor, Father Mayeye. He held it out in front of him, the carved wood biting into his hand as he clutched tightly on to it. "By the power of Christ, your time on this earthly plane is done. I cast you out, demon, back to the summoning pits where you belong." He ducked under a lazy sword swipe, and pressed the cross against the beast's perfectly formed abs.

Silence.

Flynn looked forward, noting the absence of a sizzling sound, which he'd presumed would preface the holy object burning its way through the evil body of the summoned one. There was a throaty laugh from above him, and he dared to glance upwards, seeing that Fattori Gutso was wiping away demonic tears of merriment. "You really thought that would work? You had more chance with the garden implement."

"I…well, yes. I was pretty confident, actually. Saw it on the training video, it definitely worked."

Fattori wrapped a hand around the priest's, pinching the finger bones together so that he relinquished his hold on the cross. Bowing down, the demon clamped his teeth around the crucifix and knocked it back into his razor-teeth-lined maw. With a theatrical gulp, he swallowed it in one. "It'll do more damage coming out."

Flynn screamed, in part out of his hand being crushed, but mainly because Father Mayeye had given him that cross when he'd graduated top of class from the Crimson Rosary seminary.

Gutso let the priest go, depositing him into a crumpled heap on the damp lawn. The demon began to circle the holy man, who was nursing his hand and trying to click the bones back into place. "Wake up. Time to die, little man."

Fattori lifted a cloven hoof and pressed it against the priest's back, forcing his face into the lawn. Gutso lifted the sword above his head, ready to deliver the coup de grâce. Flynn struggled to breathe, trying to spit out the blades of grass which were going down the back of his throat.

There was a *whooshing* sound, but instead of Flynn experiencing the once-in-a-lifetime sensation of having his head separated from his body, he remained intact. Blinking away the dew, he could hear a hissing sound from behind him as the pressure on his back eased. Though his sappy fingers still caught on his clothing, the priest dusted himself down the best he could. Daring to turn around, he saw the demon lying on his back. A figure, clothed in black, was astride the beast's chest. The vomit sword lay on the ground, and Flynn limped towards it. "Ha! Trusty Padraig has laid you low. I knew he wouldn't abandon me! Now…let's finish you off. Time to bring you your…DOOM!"

"Not so fast, Father," a honey-soaked voice drawled.

Flynn spun around, witnessing the figure back-flip off the demon, who was disintegrating into a large puddle of vomit, the acid bound to render the desecrated earth infertile for at least three generations.

"O'Malley…"

"Looks like I arrived just in the nick of time too, Gutso here was about to chop your ugly head off, and then, no doubt, rip the entire neighbourhood apart, too."

People began to gasp, swoon and look aghast, the appropriate responses, all things considered. "How did you? I mean…I did…"

O'Malley slapped Flynn on the back, and held out a gore-covered, gold-plated fountain pen. "All demons, especially when freshly awoken, have a soft spot up their right nostril. With the correct application of force, they can be easily dispatched."

"But…I tried the cross, it didn't-"

O'Malley laughed, the kind of smug, self-centred laugh that comes just before a withering putdown. "You thought that would actually work?"

"But…the training video?"

"It was all staged. Didn't you recognise Father O'Roses under all those prosthetics?"

Flynn shook his head, the sound of bubbling vomit eating away at the ground rose above the screaming voice inside his own head. O'Malley nudged him, causing Flynn to drop the demon's fabricated weapon. "Hey, Father, I guess the pen *is* mightier than the sword, eh?"

Padraig appeared from the doorway, clapping wildly and even managing a few lusty wolf whistles. A small crowd of men clad in dressing gowns surged forwards, lifting O'Malley to the heavens, cheering and chanting his name. As he was carried away, O'Malley shouted. "Flynn, leave the mind-wiping to me, you run along to the mobile infirmary, go and get your hand taken care of."

The cheering became muted for a minute, as people exchanged odd looks at the mention of mind-wiping, before the crowd were caught up in the moment again and continued to exalt their saviour to the heavens.

Flynn watched on as the rabble moved away. His eye twitched, followed quickly by the rest of the left side of his face, his top lip curled up into a punky sneer.

"Cooee! I say, Father Flynn?"

He turned to see Meredith skipping out of the house, covered in blood. "What?"

The woman came to a halt in front of him. "I just wondered when little Timmy will be coming back? That's how it works, isn't it?"

Flynn snarled, shoved his good hand into his inner pocket, and pulled out his emergency shot of tequila. "Go and ask Mister Fucking Wonderful, I'm off to the pub." He put his hand into her face and pushed her away, before staggering down the path.

The demon's remains were fast disintegrating into the soil. A puddle of pink liquid and froth had formed from what remained of Fattori Gutso, the demon's facial features nothing more than a thin skin of drying mucus on the puddle's surface.

The mouth opened and spat a jet of vomit-broth onto Flynn's face. He retched as he swallowed some, quickly wiping the residue away. He gagged as the acrid taste stung the back of his throat, a disembodied voice echoing from the gloop. "I'll be back...*priest.*" Flynn lit a cigarette to take the taste away, and stamped on the foamy mulch, destroying the vestiges of the distended face as it sprayed over his trouser legs.

5

THREE MONTHS LATER

The crowd was at least six deep, and Sister Wilma's patience was all but expended. She chewed the inside of her mouth as she asked people to move aside, struggling to remain polite. Finally getting to the front of the horde, she stood behind a man who smelled of an open Parisian toilet. She wrinkled her nose and tapped him on the shoulder. "Excuse me, sir, but would you mind moving out of the way, please?"

The man turned around, revealing a beard so unkempt that Sister Wilma swore she saw something move within its bristling thatch. He shook a crimson rosary in her face, mumbling words to the effect of. "This would be an ecumenical matter."

"Ah, Father Flynn, isn't it? I didn't know you'd arrived."

The priest shrugged, and pointed towards the statue of Anthony the Lesser-Peeved, sitting amidst a sea of floral tributes and teddy bears. "Is that it?"

The smell of body odour, stale beer and urine assailed Wilma's olfactory senses. "It is, Father. Isn't he grand?"

The priest burped, a gust of fetid air billowing out of his mouth, before he turned back to regard the alabaster statue once more. The sculpture of Anthony saw him adopting his usual hunched-over demeanour, admonishing a figure unseen, his finger mid-wag, mouth open, eyes full of scorn. From the corner of each eye, a track of red liquid ran down the length of the statue, ending at the feet, making him look as though he was wearing a pair of comfy slippers. "How long has it been *crying* for?" Flynn fumbled through his earthly pocket possessions, hoping for a notepad and pen, but ending up instead with a ball of mixed lint, a half-sucked mint imperial, a receipt for a large bottle of vodka (recently imbibed), and the waving paw from a golden lucky fortune cat.

The smell started to affect the crowd, crammed groin-to-arse within the usually deserted church of St Barnabas. Noses twitched, and eyes darted around accusingly. Like slow-acting tear gas, people closest to the epicentre of the stinking priest began to edge away, content to a degree with having borne witness to the crying statue. Sister Wilma hooked an arm under the priest's armpit. "Come on, Father, why don't I make you a lovely cup of cocoa and we can have a chat about it?"

Flynn patted himself down. "But I don't have any Amaretto?"

"A lovely cup of Earl Grey then, Father?" Wilma offered.

The priest began to sob. "I can't even afford a small can of strong organic Belgian lager, either."

As the nun ushered him to a back room, the crowd wafted away the smell, and resumed their amateur photography of their local holy phenomenon. It had been highlighted in the weekly religious miracles publication, 'Cor Blimey, JC,' and a two-minute national news segment, tucked between a report on a random act of religious-based violence and grainy footage of a cute animal being rescued from a storm drain.

Wilma shook the man awake again. "Father, I thought that priests of the Order of the Crimson Rosary were accompanied at all times by an equerry?"

Trying his best to stand unassisted, Flynn jigged on the spot like an incontinent Elvis impersonator, jabbing a dirt-encrusted finger back down the aisle. "He's parking the car…I think…did I come by car? Come by car? Kumbaya? Kumbaya my lord, kumbaya-"

Sister Wilma jolted the priest, before he went full church karaoke. "It's okay, Father, I get the gist. Come on, let's sit you down and get you something to drink."

"Drink?" The priest's bloodshot eyes lit up.

"Not that kind of drink, Father, something to help sober you up. Come on." Clutching the disappointed priest to her bosom, Sister Wilma continued to lead him down a candlelit hallway, into a nondescript room at the back of the church. After depositing him in a chair and ensuring he wasn't going to list severely to one side or another, she disappeared into the adjacent kitchen.

"Father, Father, are you awake now?"

Flynn's eyelids alternated between the on and off positions, before settling on determining what, or who, the fuzzy shape in front of him was. It was a man, possibly. The voice's pitch was uncomfortably high, as if a delicate part of their anatomy had become trapped in a zip. Reaching out with his filthy digits, he ran them over the shadowy figure's face, and slumped back. "Oh…it's you. Did you manage to park your *car*, Gilbert?"

The equerry nodded furiously. "Oh I did, Father."

"It's not a real car though, is it? That silly little Smart thing you've got, it's more of a toy car. Padraig, you see…Padraig…now *he* had a *proper* car."

Gilbert fussed about the drunken priest, smoothing down his wild hair, steering well clear of the beard, and generally trying to stymy the creeping barrage his appearance and smell had on the human senses. "What car did he have?"

"It was a Volvo. A ruddy great big Volvo. Built like the Archbishop's shithouse, so it was. Bloody huge thing, with an aerial! Can you believe it? An actual telescopic aerial. Just think, in this day and age, with all the internet and…Netflickers…things, an aerial! For the radio. And not that digital bollocks, no, no, no. A good old-fashioned radio, with proper static, and a knob." Flynn turned his hands in mid-air, simulating the tactile sensation endured when trying to locate an analogue radio station. The priest tittered into his hands. "Not *that* kind of knob. You know? A radio knob. You know where you are with a good solid knob."

"Ah, a Volvo, you say? Well, my Smart car is far more

economical, so it is. And I wager that I can park it in places that his Volvo wouldn't get into," Gilbert continued to preen, although he quickly concluded that all he was doing was putting metaphorical lipstick on a particularly disgusting shit-encrusted pig.

"He used to keep a cooler in the back…had some sausage rolls in there, not the big ones, oh no, not Padraig. You know those little ones? Wee little things. You could pop one in your mouth and it wouldn't be no trouble at all. One time they even had bits of chorizo in. Imagine that. Pork sausage rolls with chorizo in. That's like being double teamed by a pair of fine looking pigs, their little hooves holding you down as they engulf you with their meaty swine wares. Sometimes…sometimes…he even had a pork pie."

Gilbert had zoned out by now, replying in oohs and ahhs at the right time. He stood back to take in his handiwork just as Flynn was recounting the tale of when Padraig had surprised him with a large Cornish pasty. "So, Father," he leaned in, conspiratorially, "have you had a chance to…you know?" Gilbert tapped the side of his large pointy Roman nose, winking in such auspicious fashion that one entire side of his face moved in unison.

Flynn looked back, vacant and dribbling.

"Have you…got to the bottom of this little mystery?" Gilbert began to elbow the priest gently, still winking, still looking like he was having some kind of brain malfunction.

"Not yet, but I know this kind of church," Flynn waved Gilbert in, who ventured as close as he dare, lest the alcoholic fumes pouring off the man render him over the drink-drive limit. "They are a nest of vipers, mark my words, Gilbert. You can never trust a nun. They've got these funny…beady…little…you know."

"Eyes?"

Flynn shook his head and let out a hiccup-burp, which made his beard shake and coo. "No, *habits*. They just follow you round the room." He attempted an appropriate mime with a finger, moving it around and following it with his eyes. This made him dizzy, though – and an equally appropriate bubble of vomit started to rise up the back of his throat.

"Are you still a little bilious, Father?" Gilbert asked, fishing around in his pocket for some indigestion tablets.

"Yeah, that damn demon…Fatty Guts, or something, he must've done something to me. Don't sleep either. Nope. Terrible dreams…terrible."

Gilbert moved in closer, putting a hand over his mouth and nose to blot out the stench. "Dreams about what, Father?"

Flynn's eyes grew wide, the veins bulging and the whites a pallid grey. He grabbed hold of Gilbert's collar and pulled him in like a rubbish bin on collection day. "Jack Bauer is looking into the room I'm in, through a porthole window. You know, those round ones on boats? Anyway, he's supposed to be trying to save poor Padraig from the evil machinations of Ronan Keating, but it's like he can't be arsed. Habib Marwan is with him too, grinning, just like he did in The Mummy. It's awful. Terrible film. Anyway, I want to help, but I'm tied upside down to a grandfather clock which is an hour slow. I'm forced to watch that bastard demon as he vomits up devilish implement after devilish implement, torturing poor little Padraig into giving up the location of my stash of Holy porn. You know, the good stuff. I wake up just as he pulls off his head with a pair of vomit forceps."

"I'm surprised you give *him* a second thought after what he did to you."

Flynn began to well up. "He was only doing what he thought was right. Can't knock him for that. No, he'll be back, I'm sure of it. Maybe he'll bring some mini Scotch eggs with him?"

"Here you go, Father," Wilma said, materialising out of nowhere, mug of cocoa in hand. Nodding his thanks, Flynn took it and began to blow on the froth, sending wisps of steam into the air. Wilma looked Gilbert up and down. "My my, I could just *eat* you all up."

Adjusting his man-bun, Gilbert blushed, before holding out a crooked hand. "Charmed, Sister."

Flynn slammed the mug on the table. "Sister, how many nunathys work here?"

"Three, Father."

"And the priest, what's his name?"

"Father Roger O'Hanrahan, but he's not here."

Flynn looked up as if he had just realised his undergarments were missing. "Really? How awfully convenient. How awfully convenient indeed. Disappearing on the very day that I turn up to investigate this little caper you've got going on here."

Sister Wilma's face pulled inwards, as if she were sucking on a mixed platter of citrus fruit. "I don't know what you're insinuating, Father, but may I remind you who you're speaking to."

"Oh…I know, *Sister*. A nun admitting her priest is on the run, as she admires a man bun, ain't no fun when you're…erm…where was I going with that?"

"You were going to tell me what you intend to do, Father. We are exceptionally busy here, even more so since the statue became a full-blown class three Holy relic."

Flynn stood up, the chair toppling behind him. "Hold your horses, Sister, I'm the one who determines if it's a Holy relic, and its classification. I saw the advertising sign you had prepared in the cloakroom, don't you be getting ahead of yourself. Something smells a little bit fishy." His finger waved in front of her, as if trying to complete an invisible dot-to-dot picture in thin air.

Sister Wilma folded her arms and puffed her chest out, "Actually, *Father*, I think you'll find that the only thing that smells fishy around here…is *you*." With that, she turned on her heels and floated out through the doorway, leaving Gilbert slack-jawed.

"O.M.G. Father, that was *in-tense*."

Father Flynn waved him away, and went in search of his mug of cocoa. "She's hiding something…I'll find it out."

Gilbert looked around, making sure they didn't have company, "So, Father, what *is* our next move?"

After sniffing his drink to make sure it wasn't made with

sour milk, Flynn took a big gulp, "Gilbert. I want you to go to your stupid little car, and get the following: a bucket, which you will fill with cold water, not tepid, cold. So cold that it would shrivel the heartiest of testicles."

"Affirmative."

"Then, I want you to get the spare flannel, you know the one, we used it to mop up the condensation from the hotel windows this morning."

Gilbert saluted, "Sir, yes sir."

"Open the boot and have a good rummage around by the spare tyre. I stashed some of the good rope there. You know it'll be good as the price sticker will still be on it." Flynn took another slug of cocoa, wincing as it burned its way down his oesophagus.

"Consider it done, Father. What are you going to do with all of that?"

Placing the mug on the table, Flynn pounded a fist into the palm of his other hand. "Gilbert, we've got some nuns to waterboard."

There was an awkward silence. Flynn was rearranging furniture, closing the blinds to prevent any potential witnesses catching a glimpse of the nefarious deed, and generally transforming the room to make it look a bit more menacing. Which, when a room is festooned with children's drawings of Jesus riding an Easter bunny, was easier said than done. All the while, Gilbert stood there as if he were the latest victim of Medusa. Finally, he coughed and asked. "Father, you're going to waterboard these nuns?"

Busying himself by sharpening strips of bamboo, and practising his favourite jamming-them-underneath-fingernails move, Flynn nodded, mumbling. "Oh yes. Give me ten minutes and they'll be telling me all the weird kinky stuff they do when the lights go out." He turned around, seeing that his equerry was still not moving, and tried to goad him into life by clapping loudly. "Well? What is it? These nuns aren't going to waterboard themselves you know? Though that *would* make my life a lot easier, could head back to that lovely little country pub we passed a few miles back. What was it called? The Mucky Spleen? Much better than that rubbish next door."

"Father, you know we can't torture them, remember St Roger's? With the homemade thumb screws? Even after I took them away from you, if I hadn't come back in time, I swear you were going to immolate Father Casper O'Docherty."

Flynn blew a raspberry. "He was lying to me. I didn't need to strip him down to his Mickey Mouse boxer shorts, douse him in kerosene and threaten him with a flare to know that he rigged the cross on top of the church to emit the Bat signal every time he heard a 999 call on the police scanner."

"Father, it wasn't just them, though, was it? You've been on a slippery path since *that* night. I don't mean to be a Debbie Downer, but you know what they'll do to you…if you mess up again. I can only cover your tracks so far. I'm not a miracle worker."

"Which is a good job, else I'd have to investigate you, too." Flynn glared at Gilbert with the larger of his two bulbous eyes. Finally, he caved. "So, Gilbey, are you going to follow my instructions or not? You know, like you're fucking supposed to. Commanded by God, you could say."

Gilbert shook his head. "I can't, Father, it's *my* job on the line too, you know."

"Fine, okay, I understand, I guess I can handle this another way." Flynn slapped a hand on Gilbert's back. "You're a good man, undoubtedly a liberal-snowflake-loving-pacifist, but a good man."

"Thank you, Father. So, what is your plan?"

Flynn sat down and stuck a finger in his beard, wiggling it, which made a chirruping sound echo from its wiry boughs. "I'll interrogate…I mean, *interview* them, one-by-one. I'll use their answers, cross reference them against each other, constructing an interconnected matrix of their alibis, which interlaces each and every facet of their stories. Then, when I've squeezed…I mean, coerced…shit…erm, *encouraged*, every last morsel of information from them, I'll be able to use the evidence before me and, with a steadfast determination, reveal the truth of the Case of the Crying Statue of Anthony the Lesser-Peeved."

Gilbert clapped his hands like a performing seal, enraptured by the words. "Father, that is like, totes amazeballs, so it is. That would be perfect, and an ideal way of proving to the Archbishop that you're over your blip and ready to get back on to the big cases again. I'll go and get the first Sister."

Father Flynn took in the praise, and waved Gilbert off as he left the room. Closing the door behind him so that it clicked gently in its frame, he padded his lumpy cassock, lit a cigarette and took a drag. "What an absolute fucking bellend. I'll get the truth out of these damn nuns, one way or another."

6

"Well, I think that's all of my questions. Thank you for your time, Sister Beryl." Flynn extended a hand which the nun examined cautiously before shaking it, all the while scrunching her face up in disgust.

"No problem, Father, may I go now?"

Flynn slammed his borrowed biro onto the table. "Not a chance. Tell me, Sister, who came up with the idea? If you tell me, it'll reflect better on you when they come to reassign the lot of you miscreants."

Beryl frowned. "I'm sorry, Father, what are you on about?"

Tutting loudly, Flynn pointed to the Polaroid picture of the statue of Anthony the Lesser-Peeved, his crimson tears glistening from the flash. "What do you think? The goddamn statue, you prissy witch. What did you make the tears out of? Ink? Ketchup? Printer toner? Strawberry daiquiris? Genuine human blood? Is the real reason Father Roger O'Hanrahan isn't around because you've got him trussed up in a dungeon somewhere whilst you slowly exsanguinate him?"

"How dare you, Father! I am a woman of God. I would never stoop so low as to defame my religion!" Beryl folded her arms and pouted.

Flynn grinned, his beard rustled, and a low *meep* sound came out of it. The priest nodded. "My thoughts exactly, Albie. My thoughts exactly. Sister Beryl, may I ask you a question, regarding your last posting?"

"Of course, though I fail to-"

"Your little sojourn at Saint Yvonne's, down in Eastbourne. Pray tell, *Sister*, why were you moved on from there? I've read your file, you won the South Eastern Golden Habit award two years in a row. Some of the parishioners likened you to Mother Teresa, so much so that you took to wearing open-toed sandals during Mass. So…Beryl, what happened? What could possibly have made the mighty fall so far from the Archbishop's grace?"

Sister Beryl shifted uncomfortably in her chair, and with her chin lowered, she mumbled into her handkerchief. Flynn cupped an ear, and shouted. "I'M SORRY? WHAT WAS THAT?"

"There was an incident…with a cake…at a summer fete."

Like a shark sensing the first drop of blood in the ocean brine, Flynn steepled his fingers and leaned in. "What kind of cake?"

"Father, I-"

Flynn stood up quickly, the table catching on his legs and toppling onto its side, the wooden border between interrogator and perp folding itself up neatly. The priest kicked the flattened table aside and pointed at Beryl, spittle flying from his mouth. "I asked you a goddamn question, Sister. What kind of cake was it? Coconut? Fairy? Black Forest Gateau? Perhaps a nice Battenberg?"

"It-"

He raised a finger, as if he had just worked out the answer to a tie break question in a pub quiz. "Oh, I've got it. It's so obvious to me now." He moved in closer, so close that his beard brushed against the bridge of her nose. "It was an angel cake, wasn't it?"

Sister Beryl closed her eyes, whimpered and brought her hands up to her face, trying to stymy the tears with her hankie. "It was, Father, it was!"

"What did you do to it? What did you do to that angel cake that was so bad, that they got rid of the Golden Wonder Nun of Eastbourne?"

"Father, please…"

"Was it dry, Beryl? Was it so dry that every parishioner who ate it, complained that all the spit in their head had been soaked into it?"

"No, please, I can't."

"The answer is in here, Sister." Flynn picked up a dossier of browning paper and shook it in her face. "Everyone already knows, from Bodmin to Ipswich, from Kidderminster to Alloa, Milton Keynes to the Isle of Skye, they *all* know. There are probably entire baking websites dedicated to your failure. So, go on, tell me. TELL ME!" He batted the woman around the head with the folder.

"The pink layer was too dark."

"Go on," Flynn was panting, his outburst being the most amount of exercise he had undertaken in quite some time.

"I put too much colouring in there, so it came out...well..."

"Come on now, tell me the truth."

"You can't handle the truth!"

Flynn pulled his hand back, ready to admonish the nun once more, and she sunk into her chair. "Why, I oughta..."

"Fine, the pink layer was red."

The priest flung his hands in the air, paper and photographs of the cake fluttering around him like chubby snowflakes, He shouted to the heavens. "AND THE TRUTH...SHALL SET YOU FREE!" Flynn sunk to his knees, allowing the sheaf of paper to pelt him as it fell back to earth, wallowing in a puddle of paperclips and the report of the angel cake red layer scandal.

Slowly, he rose to his feet. "Don't you think it's strange that you made the pink layer red, and the tears coming out of Anthony the Lesser-Peeved are *also* red? If you were me, wouldn't you think, 'hey, that sure is a coincidence right there!'?"

Sister Beryl hoiked back a thick wad of snot. "Honest, Father, if that statue has been tampered with, it wasn't me."

Flynn clapped his hands together. "Fine, you're free to go." As the nun sat there, unsure whether this was a ruse, the priest began to pick up the scattered papers and sort the table out again.

"I'm...in the clear?"

"Oh yes, off you pop. Thank you for your time." Father Flynn waved the woman away, and continued to tidy up the mess. As Beryl stood up, the priest hurled the mug at her, and she ducked under it with remarkable nimbleness. The empty beverage container smashed against the wall, sending shards of porcelain in a wide arc, one of the children's awful pictures fluttered to the floor.

"Why do you foul my ears with your lies? Your perfidy comes off you like a cheap pair of tights, they hang around your ankles like empty nylon bags of shame. You know what they do to nuns like you in the Centre for Re-Faith, don't you?"

Sheltering behind her hands, Beryl chanced a glimpse between her fingers. "I'm innocent, Father, you have to believe me."

Flynn moved in as if she were handing out free money. "A nun like you, with your reputation, and with your keenness for starching tunics to within an inch of their very existence. They'll get you to look after the baby nuns. The ones they grow in the vats in the laboratory."

"No, Father, please…"

He paced behind her. "You'll have to take hormones so you can breast feed the clutching spawn of the church. Their fingers all dewy, formed into claws, pawing at your bosom, drinking your haggard tit dry. Then, when you're nothing but a spent husk, they'll-"

"Don't say it, Father, please. I beg you."

Flynn peeled open her habit and pressed his chapped lips against her ear. "They'll make you go on TV talent shows. If you're lucky, you'll have a dog, a German Shepherd, called Colin, who you'll teach simple tricks to. Perhaps you can even convince the judges that it can speak, when all it really does, is bark funny."

Beryl burst into tears. "Please, Father, I beseech you."

"WOOF WOOF WOOF, becomes, *sausages*, if you can convince them, that is."

"I promise, Father, I had nothing to do with it."

Holding her chin, Flynn turned her head so that they were staring into each other's eyes. "Prove it."

"Gladly, tell me how, Father, tell me how I can convince

you of my innocence."

The priest took a step back and held out his hand which he had formed into half a Lego hand. "A game of thumb war."

"Is that legal?" Gilbert asked, skimming through the Terms and Conditions of investigation and the church.

Sister Beryl flexed her thumb. "But mine are too small, you'd easily beat me."

Flynn straightened out his hand. "Fine, Slapsies. You go first, don't you fucking dare take a run up or I'll chin ya."

"That's definitely out," Gilbert advised.

"Gilbey, fetch the playing cards, a round of Scabby Queen it is. First one to have all the skin shaved from their knuckles…loses."

"Now, Father Flynn, you know we can't do that, remember Oxford? The shopping centre fiasco?"

"Is that a car alarm going off?" Father Flynn cupped a hand to his ear. Gilbert snapped his neck to one side, hearing nothing, but, eager to make sure his insurance premiums weren't going to increase, he darted out of the room.

"Father, I don't think I-" Beryl began to say.

Flynn pushed the door to. "Okay, here's the deal, tell me where you keep the sacramental wine. Not the cheap shit, the good stuff. The stuff you keep for when the big fish are around."

Sister Beryl rolled her eyes. "I might've known, you're a base creature, at best. Over there, Father," she thumbed to a cupboard behind her.

The priest flung the door open and rooted around its innards. "Paint stripper…pipe cleaner…the garbage you use on Sunday Mass. Ah, here we go." He stood up and blew the dust from an old bottle. "A nice drop of *Château Lafite*, don't mind if I do." Retrieving a corkscrew from the cupboard, he opened the bottle and sniffed the cork.

Beryl edged towards the door. "Now, if you don't mind, I'm going to get back to work. Good day to you, may the Lord have mercy on your damaged soul."

"Whatever, don't go baking any more cakes now, ya hear

me?" Flynn called out after the nun-shaped hole in his vision. He sunk to the floor and wrapped his lips around the bottle, taking a big slug of wine. He let out another puff of stale air and relaxed even further, legs extended.

Looking around the room, he winced as he saw the damage; he was going to have to get Gilbert to find a dustpan and brush from somewhere. As if to confirm the fact, a shard of broken mug lanced into his thigh. "Fucking hell," he grumbled, as he picked it out of his trouser leg and skin. For a moment, he admired the blood smeared on the tip, looking at his upside-down, rose-tinted reflection.

Flynn sagged further, in danger of slipping horizontally. He righted himself and took another stomachful of wine. He skimmed over the crappy drawings on the wall, laughing at the implausibility of children's imaginations. He felt himself slip, and stuck his free hand out, stopping his descent. He chuckled, before feeling something gather up in the palm of his hand.

Placing the wine bottle on the stone floor, Flynn smoothed out the creased paper. "What the…?" In orange crayon, there was a figure he assumed was JC himself --the beard was a dead giveaway-- but the more he thought about it, the man could be anyone out of the Old Testament. Beards were very much in vogue back then.

Father Flynn pressed the bottle to his lips, and drank slowly, rolling his eyes at the depicted scene. The child had scrawled, 'The Marriage of John Cena'. "It's *Cana,* you dipshit, what the hell are these nuns teaching them?" The bearded man depicted in the drawing was turning puddles (at least, Flynn *guessed* they were puddles, they, like everything, were coloured orange,) into cans of energy drinks. He could almost smell the sickly sweet aroma, and took another glug of wine to wash the thought away.

There were also loads of stick people being given hamburgers and hot dogs. "Looks like Jesus is having himself a rare old time at this barbeque." As he looked at the paper, he sunk further, the swinging lightbulb eclipsing the artwork, showing thin lines of black through the drawing. Flynn turned the paper over, and the bottle parted from his lips, spilling wine into his beard, which was followed by a chirrup and a tiny belch. "Well, I'll be a motherfucker…"

Sister Wilma barged into the room. "What is all this commotion, Father?" She looked down at the near-supine priest and tutted. "I might've known. The apple doesn't fall far from the tree, does it?"

Flynn sat up, before managing to get to his feet. "Did I summon you? No. So what the fuck are you doing here? Hmmm? Guilty conscience, is it?"

"I heard shouting, and a monstrous din. You'll do well to remember that there are people in this church, pilgrims who have travelled far, some even from Wales, to see the Holy Relic that our church has been blessed with. They do *not* want to see a drunken priest."

Flynn looked at the sheet of paper, then nodded at the recently vacated chair. "Sister Wilma, it just so happens that I've borne witness to a true miracle."

"Really? I'm glad to hear it, I look forward to your patronage."

"Not at all, please, take a seat. We have much to discuss."

7

The pair stared at each other across the table, and the only thing missing was a finely poised game of chess laid out before them. Sister Wilma made the first move. "I'm glad you've finally been able to come around to the truth, Father. Why did you find it so hard to admit that what we have here, is a genuine miracle?"

Flynn smirked, before erupting into full-blown laughter. A tiny echo joined him from the depths of his facial hair. "I know, Albie, what the hell! Look here, Sister, do you know how many of these things I've been out to validate?"

Wilma shook her head. "No, is it many?"

"Enough to fill a statue kleptomaniac's house twice over. I've seen all sorts. This one, down in Havant, had tears streaking from its nostrils. The Holy snot of the South, they called it. People would come from miles around to kneel in front of it. After paying a tidy premium, some would even be allowed to sup on the tangy mucus, claiming they were being blessed by Margaret the Very Vain."

"That's...beautiful, money is truly irrelevant when compared to that kind of higher blessing."

Tapping out a cigarette from his packet, Flynn lit it, and held in the first drag, letting the smoke fall from his mouth. "Not really. You see, the room above the statue was utilised by various medical agencies. Every couple of months, people could go and donate blood. Unfortunately, the last people to use the room were the local sperm bank.

"The last *deposits* hadn't been collected and an enterprising member of the clergy realised the potential it had. After all, to most, the possible applications of spoilt spermatozoa are limited. Turns out, with a bit of forethought, it can form the foundation of an illicit money-making operation. All it took was a little bit of elbow grease, a few removed floorboards, a drill, and some patience. They would've got away with it if I hadn't turned up to verify its classification. So, not only had these people been conned out of thousands of pounds, they also got to kneel down and lap up rancid man milk."

Wilma's top lip wobbled. "That's disgusting, Father. Who would do such a thing?"

"Quite, who would?" Flynn took in another long drag, holding the nun's fierce stare. He snapped forward, causing the woman to flinch. "You see, Sister, I questioned the other two, and though Sister Beryl has some previous, even she wouldn't stoop this low. No. Instead, I found this. Divine intervention, you could say." The priest pushed the crumpled picture across the table. "Looks to me like you're having some financial difficulties here, eh?"

Sister Wilma took the sheet of paper, scanned its contents, and began to go red. "That damn woman…I told her to get rid of it."

"What better way to bolster the coffers than to get people flocking to your little church, eh? I mean, look at this place. You're the sole holdout in a multi-million-pound retail development. Your church services on Sunday mornings have to compete with the Wetherspoons pub next door. What are you going to choose? Salvation from eternal damnation or a cold pint of cider and a bacon buttie for a price less than fifteen minutes of marriage counselling?"

The nun crossed herself. "I told O'Hanrahan we should've sold up and moved, but he wouldn't listen to me, they *never* listen to me." She pulled herself up straight, ignoring a cloud of smoke blown in her face by Father Flynn. "Still, you can't prove anything, that's just a piece of paper, it, like you, can disappear. Besides, I know all about you, Flynn, who is going to believe a single word you say? You spend most of the time drunk. Innocent until proven guilty, Father. So why don't you, and your hipster equerry, get back in your little car, and feck off?"

Gilbert appeared in the doorway. "My car's fine…she

just…oh my, Father."

Flynn held a hand up. "It's okay, Gilbey, she's like a snared animal, lashing out whilst she's caught in a trap. She knows her little game is up."

Sister Wilma leaned across the table. "What are you going to do, Father? Cry? Go and get a proper priest down here to finish your job off again and take me in? Father O'Malley perhaps?"

The priest clenched his fist, crushing the cigarette. Gilbert swallowed and laid a hand on the man's bicep. "Father, leave it."

The nun smirked, and continued. "Better yet, why don't you go next door and drink yourself into oblivion? It's about the only thing you can do anymore. I heard about your last case, how you couldn't find those stolen bibles, even though they were right in front of you."

"They were…erm…" Flynn stuttered.

Wilma moved in closer, their noses all but touching. "You're a washout, a deadbeat, a bum. All you'll ever do now is deal with these nothing jobs, moved around from pillar to post, earning nothing but cirrhosis and a bad reputation. Get out. Get out of my church, you feeble excuse for a man."

Gilbert squeezed the priest's arm, both ignoring the burning from the table as the cigarette cherry smouldered atop the picture. Flynn's lip began to wobble, as if he was about to burst into tears. Then, a screeching sound broke the awkward silence, a tiny pinky-white hand with webbed fingers poked out of Father Flynn's beard, and slapped the nun across the cheek. The slap was little more than a tickle, but Sister Wilma held her face theatrically. "You…you…you hit me. I'm going to sue!"

The priest sniffed back his tears. "That wasn't me, you daft cow, that was Albie --you upset him."

"Who?" Wilma asked. Still nursing her face, like a footballer trying to get a free kick, she moved in closer to the priest's bushy beard. A smooth, pale pink face broke free from its cover, lidless eyes regarding her, impassively. Its little mouth slightly open, paws held open the thick thatch. The nun went into doting mode. "Awwww, hello there you little…" The head snapped forward, and its teeth nipped the woman's nose, Wilma shrieked, "…bastard." She pulled back, away from the clacking jaws, while the creature licked what passed for lips before retreating inside the itchy nest, its beady eyes still watching her.

"You made him angry now, you don't want to make Albie angry, he's got a bit of a persecution complex." Flynn had already furnished himself with a fresh cigarette, seemingly oblivious to the still-smoking artwork beneath his face on the table.

"What is it? That foul monster?"

"It's my pet axolotl, I rescued him from a cult I investigated out in the sticks. What were they called, Gilbey?"

"The Children of Ishtar, your holiness." Gilbert began to massage the priest's shoulders.

"That's them. They were an odd bunch of dicks, believed the zombie apocalypse was inevitable. Went around in white sheets and red hoodies. Got them all rounded up and sent off to the Scientologists, thought if they were going to do the whole cult thing, they may as well do it properly. When I went through their camp after, I found this little fella. He was scared, his tank had cracked, and he was all but out of water. When I picked him up, he darted into my beard and stayed there. Couldn't get him out. Guess the mix of sweat, food and naturally occurring oils has helped him to metamorphose. Anyway, whilst it was a little odd at first, I've got quite used to him, haven't I?" He poked a finger into his beard and wiggled it around, eliciting a happy squeaking sound.

Wilma centred herself, folded her arms, and stuck her chin out. "Still, my point remains. You can't prove anything, so sling your hook before I report you for molesting me." The nun went to tear her clothing.

The threat was met with a peal of hearty laughter; Flynn stood up, shrugging off Gilbert's hands. "You honestly think they'd believe you? I'd probably need a canary in a cage to go down *there*. No, Sister, here's what we're going to do…I'm going to need a full confession from you now."

The nun glowered back. "I don't think so."

"Fine, let's do this the old-fashioned way." The priest grabbed hold of the table and threw it against the far wall, where it exploded in a shower of wood. He reached inside his cassock, pulled out a First World War service revolver, and pointed it at the woman's head.

Gilbert shrieked, Sister Wilma retreated into her chair before regaining her poise. "You wouldn't dare, you sad little man!"

Flynn cocked the hammer. "Confess! Confess, you conniving harlot."

"Never! You're going to have to shoot me."

Sister Wilma stared back at Father Flynn. Defiant, the priest's aim wavered, before he lowered the gun. "I...I..."

"I knew it, you coward."

"You bitch!" Flynn pulled the revolver up, and with it aimed at her leg, pulled the trigger. The loud retort deafened the three occupants of the room. Albie retreated inside the beard as a thin pall of cordite wafted up from the barrel.

The nun clutched her leg, her white fingers wrapped around the top of her knee, trying to form a crude tourniquet. She screamed like a baby being baptised in lava. The priest looked on impassively, before shoving the smoking gun back inside his tunic. He picked up the half-empty bottle of Château Lafite and staggered out into the hallway, which was awash with the screaming and wailing of terrified pilgrims.

8

YESTERDAY LUNCHTIME

The Archbishop drummed his fingers on the leather-covered desk. He glared at Father Flynn, who sat in the plastic chair reserved for guests, a pair of sunglasses doing their best to keep out the hangover which was playing a meaty percussion beat inside his skull. Finally, Archbishop Tena ceased the tapping, and asked. "Well? What do you have to say for yourself?"

Shifting uncomfortably on the hard chair, Flynn fought against a sense of vertigo. "Archbishop, I can explain…you see, I had just uncovered their little plan. They were hell-bent on making the church look like a right bunch of mugs. Unfortunately, during one of the interviews, things went a tad awry."

"A *tad* awry? You kneecapped a nun, Father. I have heard of many things during my tenure in charge of the Order of the Crimson Rosary, but not once in those sixteen years, have I heard of a nun being shot. Would you care to explain?"

Flynn pushed the sunglasses back up his nose. "She was busting my balls, so I got my revolver out. I just wanted to scare her, you know?"

Tena picked up a sheet of paper, and waved it in front of the priest. "Sister Wilma will get to keep her leg."

"Oh, that's good."

"But her days of leading the Church's lacrosse team are numbered. She'll have to use a walking stick now. Where did you get the gun from in the first place? And why on earth did you threaten a nun with it? You know that most of them are sensitive souls, they don't need to be held at gunpoint, as some mad priest loses his cool." Tena slammed the paper down on the desk.

"It was my grandad's. He had it in the Somme, shot a few Jerries with it, if his tall tales are to be believed. On his death bed, he told us that he killed JFK and invented crunchy peanut butter. Poor old sod got a bit confused later on in life, so neither is a given. Still, he left me his service revolver in his will, so silver lining and all that."

Archbishop Tena brushed his paperwork together into a pile. "I don't care. Look, Flynn, you used to be one of the best. I've seen you do exorcisms with one hand tied behind your back, and in Esperanto, but you've been getting sloppy lately. You're a maverick, a loose cannon, and the church doesn't like its artillery on a ragged leash."

Father Flynn nodded. "It's just been a run of bad luck, that's all. It hasn't helped you benching me."

Tena opened up a drawer and pulled out a glossy brochure. "You know why I did. I hate to do this to you, especially given your aversion to nuns, but this is for the best. Last chance saloon, you understand?" He flipped the brochure around and slid it across the desktop to the priest.

Removing his sunglasses, which revealed bloodshot eyes, Flynn froze as he read the header, 'SAINT JUDAS CENTRE FOR REAFFIRMATION OF FAITH AND TRAINING CONVENT.' He picked it up limply and flicked through the pages, each adorned with beaming faces of priests and nuns playing an array of sports, or studying in a library. Some even looked like they were engaged in conversation and laughing. Flynn could feel his heart pounding within his ribcage. Each page revealed new horrors: the absence of a bar, communal sleeping areas, timetabled activities, RAMBLING! FUCKING RAMBLING!

He slung the brochure onto the desk. "There is no way you're getting me to go to that fucking happy-clappy camp. No way at all. Sodom and Gomorrah have more chance of being added to the suggested holiday list."

Tena lined the brochure up straight on his desk. "Flynn,

this isn't a request, it's an order. Thirty days. Thirty nights. You must stay there for the duration. By the end of it, you'll be evaluated, and if you don't pass the assessment, then I'm afraid…"

"Don't say it, Archbishop."

Tena cleared his throat. "I'm afraid you'll be busted back down to library assistant, in the Great Scripture Repository down in Romsey, where I found you all those years ago."

Flynn melted onto the floor, his limbs seemingly losing their skeletal integrity, removed by a mysterious source. "I can't do it. Thirty days? No booze? Nuns? You may as well kill me now."

"You need to get sober. You need to buck up and get your act together. We can't afford any more incidents --if the press got wind of this, they'd have a field day. We'd be shut down, and all the important work we carry out would be stopped. We can't allow this to happen. *I* can't allow this to happen. So the choice is a simple one." Archbishop Tena pulled out two coloured envelopes from his in-tray, and held one in each hand.

"You want to keep on drinking, threatening nuns and risking everything we've worked hard to counter, then you take this blue envelope. You'll be on your way to Romsey on the morning train and you'll wake up in your old bed. If you want to be a key member of the Order once more, then you take the red one, and the therapists over at the Centre will show you how deep your rabbit hole of self-loathing goes. Metaphorically speaking, of course, being that there aren't any rabbits on the grounds--they were chased out of there a few centuries ago by a bunny-hating bishop named Ted." Tena held out the envelopes.

Father Flynn rubbed his sideburns and reached a hand forward. The Archbishop withdrew the two envelopes. "Remember, all I'm offering is the possibility of redemption, no more, no less. The rest…is down to you."

9

LAST NIGHT.
JUST AFTER HALF ELEVEN.
11:32 TO BE PRECISE.

Chris spat out a wad of toothpaste, and rinsed his toothbrush. After completing his evening ablutions, he switched off the bathroom light and padded through to the bedroom, looking very dapper in his fluffy bunny slippers. Jennifer was still propped up in bed, flicking through a catalogue selling military grade night vision goggles. "You going to be long?" she asked.

"No, not loads in today. I'm just going to have a quick scan, see what's happening out there tonight." Chris opened up the French doors to the balcony, and perched on a plastic patio chair.

Twiddling with the focus, he peered through the binoculars, checking over his campsite.

He started, as always, with the sign, 'Hall Campsite, Come One, Come Hall!' At least, that was how it proudly read in his mind. In reality, one of the local teenagers, bored, and armed with a spray can, had changed it to, 'Cum one, Cum in Hall'. Chris tutted --he really did need to get some white spirit and sort that out.

Working his way down from the gravel drive to a rectangular car park, Chris counted the vehicles that were parked up. He opened his guest book and ticked off the registration numbers, checking that no one from town was taking the piss again. Satisfied that all was well, he flitted between the tents which were pitched up and down the grounds.

Unbeknownst to most of its guests, Hall Campsite was

founded on an old landfill site which had been put out to seed. In the eight years Chris had owned it, he had been forced to make a number of off-book payments to former guests who had taken ill after their tent pegs had broken into pockets of gas, releasing a variety of noxious fumes.

"What about the Pattersons?" Jennifer asked.

Chris turned his head and looked for the tell-tale triangular tent. "Mr Patterson is still up. Oohhh, he's in. Nope…he slipped out. Ooh, he's back in again."

"Wonder if he'll last more than two minutes tonight," Jennifer mused.

"Ah, bugger."

"Is he done already?"

"No, they've turned the lamp off, I can't see them going at it anymore. Ah well, there's always tomorrow, have those cameras arrived yet?"

Jennifer shook a jiffy bag. "Yep, I tried one out earlier at the salad bar."

Chris rubbed his hands together. "Excellent, have you solved the case of the limp lettuce?"

"No, but I did witness Mr Timmins knock one out into your homemade salad dressing, in full, glorious high definition."

"But…I ate that."

Jennifer laughed. "Yeah, I know. Was going to tell you, but you were wolfing it down as if there was no tomorrow, thought I'd mention it at a more appropriate juncture. Still, we know one thing."

Running his tongue over his teeth, Chris replied. "That Mr Timmins is more sweet than sour?"

His still-giggling wife hurled the catalogue at his head. "No, you plum. We know that the sneeze guard is at the wrong height for anyone intent on wanking off into the free buffet. Do you think we should put a sign up?"

"What? Please don't masturbate into the free provisions? Hardly think that'll work, perhaps we can get the rats to gnaw through his face? I've been training them. They can respond to simple verbal commands now, as the local Health and Safety inspectorate can testify to. Well, if they find him in time." He passed a cursory glance over the septic tank lid, and zoomed in, checking the padlocks were still in place. "Try wriggling out of *that* one, you bastard."

Jennifer shrugged and began her nightly routine of applying a myriad of wholly unnecessary creams and lotions to various parts of exposed skin. "I dunno, we need to do something, though. It's one thing resorting to kidnap and false imprisonment, and quite another allowing someone to foul the food for the other campers."

Chris turned back to the campsite, scouring the other tents and vans. "Nah, he's out of here in a few days. If he does decide to stay on, perhaps we can *invite* him to stay with the others in the chest freezer over by the sunken electrical appliance dunes. I've got his personalised invitation in the back of the wardrobe."

Kicking back in the chair, Chris took in a deep breath, enjoying the cool summer breeze. As he allowed his eyelids to droop over tired eyes, there was a bright flash of light over to his right.

"What the hell was that?" He jumped to his feet and leaned over the balcony, trying to crane his neck towards the epicentre. The small copse which bordered the ex-dump was still illuminated from the afterglow, making the verdant treetops look like broccoli florets covered in fine spider webs. From within the branches of the tightly-packed canopy, a ball of light contracted in on itself, before dying completely, delivering the campsite and surrounding area unto darkness once more.

Pretending to care - although any interruption in her evening schedule was not appreciated - Jennifer sighed loudly, signalling that whatever answer was to be offered, should result in no actions being assigned to her. "What was that, dear?"

With his binoculars, Chris tried to get a good look through the boughs and into the murky bowels of the woods. His finger feverishly worked the zoom wheel like he was trying to beat a previous high score. Finally he uttered. "Don't know, whatever it was, it's not there now."

Jennifer sighed again, rolling her eyes as Chris looked across to the bed. "So, what was it?"

"I dunno, this big light, then it just…went. There's no fire, so it couldn't have been a pocket of bog gas going up --not like last year, anyway."

"Best go and check though. Last time *you* ignored it, the entire south side nearly went up."

Chris kicked off his bunny slippers and began to shove his feet into his boots. "Yes, dear. Don't you trouble yourself, I'm sure I'll be fine."

Jennifer closed up one tub of lotion and unscrewed the lid of another. "Of course you will, what's going to be out there, an axe-wielding maniac? A family of misshapen mutant hicks, up from the valleys?"

Ignoring her sarcasm, Chris reached into the wardrobe and pulled out his baseball bat, swinging it to build up some courage. "Right, I'm off."

He stood stock still on the carpet while Jennifer dabbed pea-sized amounts of chemically-infused goo onto the dry spots of her face. "Okay, dear, don't be long."

Chris pulled a face, before stomping out of the bedroom and down the stairs. To help keep his spirits up, he whistled a cheery song as he went.

Malingering owls, skiving off their evening shelf-stacking jobs were hooting on distant perches, while a freshly-escaped chupacabra climbed a slag heap, its outline silhouetted by the full moon adding its howls to the late evening soundtrack. Chris kept an eye on the ground; once already his foot had disappeared into a hollow, created by moles digging their way through a subterranean plastic garden toy disposal site. Their excavations had left pockets of nothingness lying just below the surface, like spikeless punji traps.

The evening dew caught the moonlight and lit the way like emergency lighting on the floor of a stricken aeroplane. Scattered around were tiny flickers of flame, sparking little geysers of dump gas into glowing nightlights, setting a romantic scene. These small buds of fire tracked a path which led from the old campsite ground to Shipp Copse, where the mysterious flash had originated.

As he got closer, Chris saw a glow nestling within the undergrowth, like a pair of glaring hot coals. He stumbled into another underfoot void and held his hands out in front to ease his fall. Pushing himself back up using his baseball bat as a crutch, he cursed, and plodded onwards.

The copse was now only around twelve feet away, the grass cloaked by a low-level mist, which wrapped itself around Chris' ankles like a wraith with a foot fetish. There was a green tinge to the fog, coupled with hints of sulphur and burnt rubber. The ground beneath the soles of his feet felt slick. Chris slowed down, ensuring that every footfall met with solid earth, before continuing onwards.

He brushed a clutch of low-hanging branches to one side. The beam of light had changed to a baleful red, the yellow glow now casting out towards the other side of the forest, barely visible through the mass of twisted wood and leaves.

The bat felt heavy now. Chris hefted it to one shoulder, and used his free hand to move dangling vines and foliage out of his way.

There was a growling sound on the wind, as if a fearsome beast had awoken from a sumptuous feast the previous evening, and was lying in wait. With every footstep, the sound became louder and louder. It began to set his teeth on edge; the hair on the back of his neck jumped to attention, and he could feel his skin sheening with sweat.

Just in front of him was a dense curtain of undergrowth. The red light shone through the leaves, displaying the tiny tributaries within the greenery, making them look like distorted maps of the London Underground.

Chris could feel his heart raving within his chest, thumping against his ribs like an unmanned jackhammer. With a hand out in front, he was bathed in red light as he slowly lifted the natural sheet.

"Hello, my lovely," a woman's voice said.

Chris emitted a shrill scream, waving his arms in the air, the weight of the bat forgotten. His pupils began to dilate as they took in the scene beyond. A nun took a step forward, a chunky gold chain swung around her neck as she walked, its crucifix revealing a large, yet oddly-proportioned figure nailed to it.

A perfectly-placed hole in the canopy allowed a beam of moonlight to illuminate her, like a torch from the big OG in the sky himself. Her face was weather-worn, yet kindly, her skin almost translucent in the moonlight. Her thin, pursed lips were fixed in a gentle smile, hands clasped in front of her. She took another step forward, seeming to float above the fog which still blanketed the ground. "Do not be alarmed, we have travelled so very far. All we require is a brief period of rest and recharge, and we will be on our way. Could you assist us, my lovely?"

Chris' face was still twisted in a gargoyle stare of shock and fear, but he slowly began to lower his arms.

The nun stood a few feet in front of him now, and just beyond her was a large, old-fashioned coach. It reminded him of childhood holidays dashing to the coast, his dad undercutting the slow behemoths full of tourists, all racing to the beach. The orange side panels were carbon-scored and dirty, with huge black smudges running down the bodywork from fore to aft. The brake lights glowed red, and the exhaust spluttered and coughed before the engine gently revved up. Allowing his facial muscles to relax, Chris took a big gulp, and mustered a squeaky. "Huh?"

The nun continued to smile. "My lovely. I am Mother Superior Francesca, these are my fellow sisters, we have been on a journey for some time-"

"Some time," a chorus of voices echoed from the coach. Chris looked beyond the Mother Superior to see window-upon-window of nuns looking back at him, each a picture postcard of divinity.

With the bat, he pointed at the coach. "How did...? With the...and the...I mean, you're parked up in the middle of a..."

Francesca placed a hand on the fat end of the bat and lowered it slowly. Despite Chris' limbs being rigid with fear, she managed to push the weapon down with no fuss at all. She stepped into the freshly created gap and placed her other hand on his cheek. As soon as her fingers came into contact with his skin, he felt a wave of euphoria flood right through him. He felt lightheaded. Without form. He tittered, as a rogue thought ran across his mind: he was a red balloon, and in danger of simply drifting off into the atmosphere.

The nun released her hold on both bat and man, clasping her hands in front of her again. The nuns on the coach continued to look out, unblinking, mouths closed as if in silent contemplation. "My lovely, you see, we are nothing but simple creatures of the Path. All we require is somewhere to rest, to recover, then we will be on our way. Pray tell, is there a place nearby where we can stay? We are short on currency, but we won't be any bother. We'll run through the place at first light and make sure that no one will be able to tell that we were ever there. I promise." The last two words were delivered with the quickest of winks, so cunning that for a moment, Chris doubted it had even happened.

Finally, the English language came flooding back to him. "Of course, of course. The campsite is nowhere near full at the moment. You ladies can stay by the shower block, if you want?" He looked the coach up and down. "Though I'm not sure how you're going to get that out of he-"

Francesca placed both of her hands on Chris' face, cupping his chin, pulled him in close, and looked into his eyes. "Don't you worry about us --our driver, Sister Caitlin, has been to the ends of the universe and back, she'll be able to get this old thing out of here." There was a chorus of laughter from the coach; Chris joined in, nervously.

The Mother Superior began to spin Chris round on his heels. As he turned, his eyes caught the woman's habit, which flapped. For the briefest of moments, he thought he saw a forked pink tongue run across the join between black and white, before disappearing into the woman's chest. Francesca pointed the man back towards the house. "Thank you for your concern, my lovely, you get going now --we'll be just fine."

With a gentle shove, he stumbled forward. Finding his feet working autonomously, he took a few steps back towards the house. Casting a look behind, he saw the Mother Superior wave him off. In the coach beyond, he could just make out the other nuns whispering and pointing. He called out. "Park up wherever you can, breakfast is served in the morning from seven."

"Excellent, thank you, my lovely."

Chris furrowed his brow. "You're not…vegetarians are you? I don't think I've got much in apart from bacon and sausages."

"Vegetarian?" The Mother Superior ran the syllables around her mouth as if it were a particularly tangy pickled egg. She looked utterly perplexed, as if her life support had been disconnected and she had been left to fade away into obsolescence.

Chris ventured. "You know, people that only eat vegetables, non-meat eaters. "

Francesca's head realigned to the horizon, and her smile reappeared. "Good lord, my lovely, we're not vegetarians. We eat meat. Lovely, lovely, meat."

"Phew, that's a relief. I've got some mushrooms and beans in, but-"

"Nothing but meat in fact."

"…okay…thanks?"

"The bloodier, the better. Got to be fresh, too," Francesca winked.

"Fresh meat," the nuns cooed behind her.

"Yes. Fresh meat. We don't even mind having to catch it ourselves," Mother Superior added.

Realising his mouth was open, Chris snapped it shut, managing a nervous laugh. "You won't have to *catch* the meat, don't worry about that, it's already dead."

Francesca and the nuns clapped their hands with glee. "Oh you are awfully efficient, that will do nicely. See you in the morning then, my lovely. At seven." Waving him off, Chris picked his way home through the copse, the sound of a coach engine growing dimmer behind him.

10

The alarm did nothing except irritate an already awake Chris. Since meeting the nuns the night before, he had attempted -- and failed-- to get some much needed sleep. The sheer incredulity of them appearing in the middle of a dense forest, at night, with no road, no supplies and little to no sense of direction was certainly a puzzler.

It wasn't just that. Mother Superior Francesca was an odd sort. She reminded him of his grandmother, a kindly woman who, on the day of her retirement from British Telecom, had climbed the one-hundred-and-seventeen steps in the local church tower, checked the wind direction, and picked off twenty-three members of the local community --and seven cats-- with a sniper rifle. The only thing to lay her low wasn't a police marksman's bullet, but her pacemaker, which had overloaded and fried her alive. In fact, if it wasn't for this force majeure, Police estimated that the death toll might've reached three figures. The coroner's report backed this up with their rather blunt appraisal of the inhabitants of Lower Pickleworth, most of whom were in the twilight of their lives. Those that could actually hear the gunshots to try and flee, had the turning circle and raw speed of a milk float.

Up until the moment Nana had gone on her killing spree, she had greeted every day with the same fixed grin. Even when granddad had run off with the sub-postmistress, and moved in next door, the headboard smacking against the thin dividing wall, barely covering up the feral howls of lovemaking, she smiled. Even when her house burned down to a fine carpet of ash and destroyed every one of her treasured memories and heirlooms, she kept that inane grin on her face. Even when she was ensconced at the top of that church spire, picking off elderly members of the community with that high-powered rifle, many of whom she had played at bridge, she kept those pearly whites on show. The poor cow had insisted on an open coffin, and as sure as salmon throw themselves upstream over rocks, trying to help people win photography competitions, Nana had the biggest rictus on her face.

That absurd mix of softness, blended with a hint of possible mania, had kept him awake since meeting the Mother Superior a few hours earlier. Despite trying to assure himself that he was being silly, he couldn't shake the notion that the old girl was trouble.

His internal ramblings were interrupted by a sharp dig to the ribs, and he looked across to see Jennifer eyeballing him through a mat of ruffled hair. "Turn the alarm off, you idiot. It's your turn to do breakfast this morning. I want to have a lie-in."

Chris turned over, muted the din, and gazed at the ceiling. "Yes, dear." He managed to pull on a ratty t-shirt and pair of shorts, along with his bunny slippers, before sleepily stumbling down the stairs. The kitchen and dining room were in a large conservatory at the back of the house, overlooking the sprawling estate. It was open to any campers who wished to chance their arm at botulism roulette, and, more importantly, to those who had paid in advance.

The sun was already streaking through the conservatory windows. Chris unlocked the patio doors and kicked them open, the catch rusting up with age and disrepair. The breeze which blew in was a welcome one, helping him wake up a bit. He stroked his closely-shaved beard, before heading into the kitchen.

He rooted around in the fridge, hoping he'd have enough to feed all the holy newcomers. "Least this should help in buttering my way through Saint Pete's gates up top," he mumbled to himself. Chris opened up a pack of bacon and gave it the sniff test. Having only recoiled mildly, he nodded and stacked up some ropey-looking sausages, and mushrooms he'd found growing on a patch of earth he suspected had a firm foundation of human waste beneath.

Dropping the bounty on the worktop, he looked up at the clock; it was ten-past seven. Jennifer, the daft cow, had set their alarm later. Must've done it to try and weasel a few more precious minutes to herself in bed. Chris cursed himself: if he had bothered to look at the clock instead of conjuring up nightmare scenarios involving his new guests, he would've been up at six and had a head start on it all.

He fired up the gas hob and dropped a sizeable lump of lard into a large frying pan. As it began to melt, he looked into the dining room. The tables had been laid out the day before; napkins, which were supposed to have been made into the shape of barnyard animals, but instead looked like white dungballs, sat between dull silver cutlery.

"Mr Tomkins?" Chris looked over to the toilet door, and saw that it was ajar. Stepping into the dining room, he did a quick double-take, before calling out again. "Mr Tomkins, are you there? You're not hiding again, are you?"

Silence, save for the sound of spitting fat from the frying pan.

He ducked into the kitchen, and, on tiptoes, reached behind a mass of Fanny Craddock cookbooks to retrieve a folded telescope. His bunny-covered feet padded their way to the welcome mat outside the patio doors, now faded away to a mournful 'COME'. He pulled the telescope out to its full length, and began to scan the still-slumbering campers.

Nothing.

He looked under the tables, ensuring no one was hiding beneath them. Mr Tomkins had been a regular visitor to the Hall Campsite, and one thing was as true then as now --he had always been the first downstairs for breakfast. Rain, shine, hail, snow, accidental firestorm or quasi-natural disaster, Mr Tomkins had either been standing outside, or sitting down waiting, when the doors hadn't been secured properly.

Chris felt woozy, as if a central tenet to his being had been deleted, scrubbed from a blackboard. He steadied himself on a chair, before taking in a number of quick breaths. Resolved, he ventured outside with his telescope, and worked his way across the view to Mr Tomkins' tent.

Although he had always been on his own, the man had a massive, white, four-person tent. Chris squinted as he tried to make out what the shadow on the canvas side panel was.

"Is that him?" He asked aloud, the telescope at its maximum zoom. The black silhouette dissolved, from a dark purple to a deep red, as if it were a fresh beetroot stain being given a good soaking.

Just as he was about to give up and get back to his frying, he saw a nun crouch down, and go into the tent. Chris slammed the telescope shut, for as much as Mr Tomkins was religious about his breakfast habits, he didn't tolerate any degree of idolatry, be it fake or organised. He had once witnessed the man, shorn of clothing, chase the local Jehovah's Witnesses into the pit of old CRT televisions, for daring to bother him when he was pitching up one day. Chris shuddered at the memory of the naked man, his flaccid leathery penis slapping against milky white thighs, corral the startled men into a large blue Samsonite flight case.

Storming across the expanse of grass, Chris headed straight for the tent, his fists balled. Whatever these nuns were up to, it was no good. Perhaps they were a group of international tent thieves? No matter. They were going to be getting served their permanent eviction notice from Hall Campsite, right about now.

As he approached the tent, he saw that the silhouette wasn't the shadow of a person. It was a large stain. With the sun shining straight through the canvas, it took on a bright red hue, reminding him of the brake lights from the night before. He began to slow, his tunnel vision rescinded, and he looked left and right at the other paying guests.

The Pattersons' tent had been ripped open at the rear, the shredded green canvas flapping lazily in the breeze. Looking inside, he could see a couple of nuns, kneeling, shoving fistfuls of *something* into their midriffs. The scene was repeated as he clocked each tent or campervan. Entry had been effected, and a holy woman was there, looming over someone, as if administering some arcane rite.

Chris stumbled as his feet snagged on a guide rope and he fought to stay upright. He came to a halt level with the tent entrance, the panel unzipped, a pair of boots neatly arranged outside under the small porch. He could see a nun leaning over Mr Tomkins' sleeping bag, which appeared to wriggle like a freshly-hatched pupae. Chris coughed loudly. "Excuse me, what do you think you're doing?"

The twitching stopped, and Chris craned his neck to try and get a better look inside. At the top of the sleeping bag, he could make out Mr Tomkins' head. It looked odd, as if it had been blanched of colour, its mouth twisted in a gnarly yelp, eyes glazed wide open and panic stricken. As the nun began to swivel, he saw that the stains on the tent were blood and guts. Stringy pieces of flesh and veins hung down, like fibrous stalactites.

A gust of wind from the other side blew through the tent, and an aroma of raw meat assailed his nostrils. The nun turned to regard him, Mr Tomkins' head rolling off his blood-stained pillow as she did so, coming to a halt against Chris' fluffy slippers. He shrieked. Where the nun's habit joined her tunic, there was a large razor-tooth-lined maw, like an upside-down shark's head. The nun's face tilted backwards, as this large mouth opened and closed, smacking what must have been its lips. A serpent-like tongue flicked out, tasting the air, anticipating a new meal.

Still emitting a high-pitched wailing, Chris edged out of the tent, and spun around, determined to head back to the house, get a nice cup of tea, retrieve his baseball bat, and bash the hell out of whatever the nun-thing was. Just as one shriek died in his lungs, a fresh one rose anew, as he turned straight into the formidable form of Mother Superior Francesca, her peculiar smile still etched on her face. She unclasped her hands and placed a solitary finger on Chris' lips, which silenced him instantly. "Morning, my lovely."

Chris, mouth still open, made a scratchy sound with the back of his throat which had dried up quicker than trying to beat the cream cracker chomping world record. He eventually mustered up some saliva, swallowed, and asked. "What the fuck is going on here?"

Francesca pulled up one of her sleeves and tapped the glass of an antique wristwatch. "You said breakfast was at seven."

Chris nodded dumbly.

"It's nearly quarter past. I said yesterday, that we've had a very long journey, we need to build our strength up, it takes its toll, you know."

"What does? Eating people?"

Francesca giggled. "No, silly, intergalactic travel. For every ten light years, we need to feast, else we'll dissolve away into a lumpy paste. No one wants that, do they?"

Chris thumbed to the tent behind him. "Are you fucking kidding me? I'm pretty sure Mr Tomkins would love you and your wimple-wearing brethren to have disintegrated into lumpy paste, just look at him!" He pulled the flap open, exposing the ripped-open sleeping bag. The man's guts had been pulled out of their usual place of habitation, and were strewn across the groundsheet. The nun who had been snacking on his gizzard ducked through the entrance and ran the back of her hand across the join of her habit. A length of intestine snaked from where it was still connected to Mr Tomkins' internal physiology and to the nun's free hand. She yanked on it as if it were a toy dog on wheels, dragging the body along with her as she walked towards Chris.

"But look, it's fresh meat. That's something you couldn't give us, is it?"

"Well...no...but I had some bacon and it was relatively okay...ish."

"Bacon," the nun repeated the word aloud, trying to make sense of it.

"What the hell *are* you people anyway? Some kind of freaks?"

Chris looked around, as nuns began to exit the portable abattoirs which had been erected, the white of their habits stained red with blood. A few of the mouths still chewed on chunks of tough gristle or aged organ. They came to a halt, having encircled him, all avenues of egress cut off.

He felt as though he was potholing and had worked himself into a bit of a bind, unable to turn around and head for sanctuary. As the blood-encrusted nuns approached, their chest-mouths opening and closing, he held his hands out as if he were King Canute trying to keep the murderous tide from enveloping him. "Okay, back away, you don't need to do this, you know."

The words were met with the clack of teeth, as giant mouths masticated on thin air, the nun's human heads wobbling like defective dolls. Eyes continued to regard him, which was probably the freakiest thing about their appearance, flesh-tinged teeth aside. The head and shoulders looked like trapdoors made of flesh and bone.

The outstretched arms did little to stem the surge of the nuns, who closed ranks on their prey, the Mother Superior front and centre, still smiling, still clasping her hands in front as if she were praying for the homeless.

There was a scream from the house, Chris stood on tiptoes to see that a stumpy nun had tackled Jennifer to the ground. She had her dressing gown pulled tightly around her, but even from a distance, he could see that it was soaked with blood.

"Hold on love, I'll…" Chris looked around, seeing that the chance of escape was slim to none. The point was rendered moot, as stumpy sumo-nun pinned his wife to the patio. The nun's monstrous mouth opened up like a bin lid, showing off the pristine white teeth. Pitching forward, the maw snapped shut over Jennifer's head. After a brief struggle, the nun wrenched backwards, taking his wife's head clean off, and releasing a jet of blood which would utterly ruin the sandstone patio slabs.

"You bastards!" Chris eyed up the nuns, who had come to a halt, just out of reach. He kept his arms out, trying to create a circle of death from which he could operate. Sumo-nun continued to chew on his wife's head, which looked at him dispassionately as it bobbed up and down with every crunchy bite.

"Anyway, you won't want to eat me, I'm really stringy-" the last word was delivered two octaves up, as sisters Leah and Alicia stepped forward and bit through his arms, just above the elbow. Chris arched his back to the heavens, allowing a fitting howl to bellow from his lungs. The nuns sank their teeth in, before wiggling from side to side, helping the hinged jaws apply more pressure.

There was a sickening snap, followed quickly by another, and the two nuns tottered backwards. Each of their chest-mouths sucked and slurped on one of Chris' forearms. He sunk to his knees, blood squirting from severed veins and arteries. His vision began to swim, as if the world was being melted by a high-powered hairdryer. Francesca took a step forward, looming over him, blocking out the morning sun. He forced his eyes open, trying to maintain a degree of defiance. "Get off my land, you bunch of freaks."

Mother Superior ran a finger down his cheek, it made him feel all funny again. "Oh, my lovely, I can assure you, we're not freaks. Shhhh."

Fighting through the mixed feeling of bliss and excessive blood loss, Chris asked softly. "Then what the hell *are* you then?"

Francesca's smile grew wider. "Hungry."

11

"Not long now, pal," the taxi driver glared into the rear view mirror as he spoke, checking to see if his passenger was still conscious.

Father Flynn struggled within the seatbelt. Rubbing his eyes open, he looked through the window, taking in the idyllic countryside views beyond the safety of the glass. A field of cows idly chewed on cud, as a kestrel hung in the air, its gaze fixed on some morsel or other. In the distance, on the edge of a burgeoning forest, a deer left the safety of cover and watched as the car drove past. The priest caught the driver's stare, their eyes hidden behind black-lensed sunglasses. "Are we there yet?"

"No. We're just outside of Knighton, on the Welsh border, we'll go no further than that." The man tore his gaze from the mirror and back onto the road, and yelled a brief expletive as he yanked the wheel to the side. There was a slight bump and a barely audible crunch of bone. "Oops, sorry, wee squirrel."

Flynn looked back to see a bloodied smear on the tarmac, a bushy tail waving on the gentle breeze, the rest of the body pressed into the ground. "What do you mean, we'll go no further? I have to get to St Judas."

"The nunnery?"

"That's one word for it, it's in Dyn…Dyninbuttybach Leia…something."

The taxi driver chuckled. "Not from around these parts, are you? It's Dynynbwtya Lleian, one of the oldest settlements in Wales. That place has seen a few things, I tell ye."

"Like what? The advent of electricity? Broadband?"

"Nae, ye bawbag, things that would make that beard of yours go grey."

There was a nervous chirp from Albie. Flynn poked a

finger in the thatch, and stroked the creature's chin. "Bullshit. Typical taxi driver bollocks. This area is as interesting as rebinding psalm books, you're lying."

The driver looked back into the mirror, and slowly took his glasses off, revealing one eye which was completely white, a small semi colon of black at its centre. "Oh, really, pal? Why…I've got a wee tale that will terrify ye to within an inch of your demise. The things this forest has seen, the beastie that lived within…"

Flynn sat forwards, and on examining the reflection, he tutted and sat back. "Nice contact lens you've got there, *pal*, it might work on American tourists, but it won't work on me."

"Shit," the taxi driver wrenched the wheel again, this time there was a solid thunk, and a sheep cartwheeled over the car, landing on the road behind.

"Are you the Jeffrey Dahmer of the road? Any chance you could pay a bit more attention to it?"

Shifting in his seat, and checking that the road ahead was clear, the taxi driver coughed. "It was an October afternoon, many years ago…"

"Oh, for fuck's sake, we're really doing this? Fine, it might take my mind off the roadkill."

12

Do you remember Jive Bunny? It was 1989, and they'd just had had *another* number one hit single, "That's What I Like," I think. Anyway - we were young, carefree, and above all else, utterly bored. It was half term, and we had already had enough of mild arson and knock-down ginger. Everyone on our estate guarded their doors, waiting for one of us to slip up and try ringing their doorbell one more time. The only thing we'd be seeing after that is stars, and the inside of a hospital ward.

Now, I'm not one to blame, but if I had to name one person who got us into that big mess, it would be Dylan.

He came up to me after football. He'd seen the news, about the latest food craze that was sweeping the nation. Truffles. He said across the ring road from our estate was a sprawling forest, absolutely brimming with the things. I was like, "big deal," but then he told me how much money we could make from it.

When he laid it all out, he made it sound so easy. We just had to get in the forest, dig up the truffles, and get out of there. He said it'd be a few hours, tops, and more importantly, we would split the cash. My eyes must've lit up. The few remaining days of freedom we had left before school, we could spend blowing the cash on cheap cider and even cheaper cigarettes.

Ah, halcyon days back then, I tell ya. Me and my mates were thick as thieves, grew up together, we did. They called me 'Scotch' after my Celtic roots. There was Mack, who had a St John's in First Aid, he was always on hand to deal with any mishaps.

Then there was Dwayne, our gunner and weapons expert, he insisted on bringing along his air rifle. We said we didn't need it for a simple pick-up-and-collect job, but he was adamant. Truth is, he loved that damn gun, used to take pot shots at squirrels from his bedroom window. Even gave it a name, 'Ol' Paneless', on account of all the windows he'd shot out.

Cagoule was so-called because he wore that damn anorak day and night, rain or shine. But he was a dab hand with a bottle rocket, so we reckoned he might come in handy with some distress fireworks if we ever got lost. Dick Hawkins raided his big brother's CB radio stash, so we could all stay in contact. The forest was pretty dense, so it made sense to bring something along to stay in touch with everyone. The last thing we wanted was to get separated and lost.

Our gang was well-known throughout the estate, but of all our members, it was my best mate, Billy, and his unique 'gift', that was of particular interest to Dylan.

You see, he had been born with a hyper-sensitive olfactory sense. He could sniff out a hidden Snickers bar from a hundred paces, and it was this little trick that got Dylan's attention. Using that expert conk as a truffle bloodhound, he would easily lead us to the precious bounty, and we'd be rolling around in oodles of cash in no time. That was the plan.

Thing is, Dylan knew as well as I did that Billy wouldn't agree to anything without me being there, which is why he came straight to the organ grinder, like. I agreed, but I insisted on letting all the gang in on the deal. If one was to profit, then we *all* should.

We loaded up on stuff: crisps, pop, and Choc Dips, and made our way down to the edge of the estate. It was just after lunch, and with it being autumn, we were all glad the rain was holding off. For now, at least. Still, the forest looked pretty murky. I did wonder whether we should just turn back, go and find the boys from Munnings Court, and give them another lesson in football.

Sometimes, at night, when I'm alone in bed, and all I have

are the screams keeping me awake, I wish we had.

It was all so easy to begin with. Billy's nose was in fine fettle, and we were steadily filling a carrier bag with the earthy bounty. Yet in order to get the biggest ones, we'd gone further into the woods than we'd planned to.

His nose was twitching like a meerkat trying to work out where the snake was. He shushed us, before whispering that there was someone out there, probably hiding behind the rotting tree trunk that was a short way in front of us. With luck, we'd be able to lure out whoever it was.

Sure enough, after probably fifteen minutes or so, we heard a scream, and rushed towards it. Cagoule had his arms round a girl, who was struggling and swearing something fierce. Dwayne was waving Ol' Paneless at her, telling her to spill her guts, or he'd shoot her in the temple. He'd heard some dubious school yarn that a kid in the year above us had died after being shot in the temple with an air gun. Since then, it had become his default threat. I told them all to cool it, and after making sure that she was given some room, I asked her name. "Hannah," she said.

I pressed her on what she was doing, skulking around, following us. She didn't give much up, except that she lived on an estate the other side of the forest. We'd all heard of it, but the kids there went to a different school, so we never had any dealings with them.

Still, something didn't seem right. She was nervous, kept looking at the carrier bag of truffles, then at each of us, as if she was sizing us up. She had an accent, too. I couldn't place it at first. I asked her a question in my shaky French, and even shakier German. She laughed. "I'm Spanish, pendejo," which I assumed was something good, as she laughed afterwards. Knowing our stalker wasn't a threat, we said bye, but she insisted on tagging along. What could I do? She walked off ahead of us. I knew it was pointless to argue, so I told Dylan to stick close to her. Something wasn't adding up. At *all*.

We were taking a break under a mighty oak, the branches were near exposed, the leaves forming a mulchy carpet beneath our feet. As we passed round cans of shandy, there was a yell, and we ran over to see Dylan holding the side of his face. "That crazy bitch ran off into the woods. She snatched the bag of truffles." Without waiting to hear any more, Dick went after her, ducking under branches and skidding across the mossy ground. After giving Dylan some grief about being hit by a girl, we all chased after them.

We hadn't made it very far when we heard a scream, an ungodly feral howl. It made us pick up our pace and make a beeline for it. We got to a clearing, expecting to see the pair of them, but there was only Hannah. She was slumped to her knees on the ground, her back to us, not caring that the damp was soaking into her jeans. I looked around, something was wrong --why did she run off and then come to a dead stop? Dylan picked up the bag of truffles and checked to make sure none were missing. He gave a thumbs-up. Then it hit me. Where was Dick? As I stumbled past the girl, I looked down, nearly weeing myself with what I saw.

She was covered head to toe in blood.

The poor cow was near catatonic, and rendered mute following her ordeal. I did my best to wipe the blood off her face, but it was caked on like paint. Cagoule was trying to get some sense from her, trying to find out where Hawkins was, and why there was so much blood. It wasn't hers, that much we knew for certain, cos she had no obvious injuries. She turned to him, and whispered a terse reply. The words made Cagoule go white. He looked back at us, gulped and told us. "She said it was the woman who lives in the woods. It came for him. It claimed him whole."

Everyone was yelling at her then, trying to get her to tell us where Hawkins had gone. Her story was patchy, at best, I mean --Dick wasn't the biggest guy, but still, how the hell was his entire body missing? He had to be *somewhere*. As the others shouted and screamed, I looked around the group, and saw

Billy standing on his own, scanning the forest, his nostrils flaring, trying to pick up the scent. I went up and asked him, could he track down Hawkins?

He turned to me, looked me bang in the eyes and said. "There's something out there, and it ain't no man. It's old, dead old…" I contemplated slapping him, like they do in the movies, but he was bigger than me, and, best mate or not, I didn't think he would take too kindly to that. So I opted to ask him if he had a bead on Hawkins' trail. He raised a finger and pointed off into the distance.

I told everyone to knock it off, and got them on their feet. With Dylan keeping an eye on Hannah, properly this time, so she didn't bitch-slap him and run, we started to follow the trail. Billy was out in front. From time-to-time, he'd stop, take a big sniff, before offering a slight course correction. Dotted on the few leaves that still clung to their owners, were drops of blood, still wet and tacky.

After a while, I can't say how long, Billy held up a fist, and pointed off to a large tree in another clearing. As we approached it, its vastness became apparent. It was wide, and at its base, had a hollow carved into the wood. There was a low droning, as if someone was on the end of a distant landline, and then we saw them. Piled up in the guts of the tree … were bones. Hundreds of 'em. Most looked old. They had been left to the elements, and nature had claimed some of 'em, fusing them together with roots and branches. Moss covered a lot of 'em like a furry green skin, dirt and grit clinging to the insides of fibulas and bones I didn't even know the names of. There were skulls, big ones, small ones, broken ones. Sure enough, at the crest of this cairn, taking pride of place, was a fresh skull. Strips of glistening flesh hung from the cheekbone like meaty tears, and an eye still looked out from its socket.

Cagoule walked off and threw up, never did have the strongest of stomachs. As I patted his back, I heard a rustling in the branches, and looked up. For a moment, I thought I saw something looking down at us. At me. A human figure. A woman. Yet she looked…odd. Changed, as if something about her face wasn't quite right. Then Cagoule spewed up, covering my trainers in sick, and by the time I looked back, she'd gone.

They all asked me what we should do. In my mind, the answer was simple: we'd done all we could. The only recourse was to get the hell out of there and call the fuzz. No good could possibly come from staying. Everyone agreed, all except for Dwayne, who was nowhere to be found. The dumb shit had gone off for a piss, had a bladder the size of a ping pong ball, that one. We were all shouting his name, looking for him, when we heard him scream.

One thing you have to appreciate about Dwayne, is that he was a big bastard. Not just tall, but wide, too. Not fat, well-built you'd say. He was a one-man wrecking machine at rugby, and every other sport he tried his hand at, he excelled in. It made him a bit up his own arse, like, but the main thing about Dwayne is…*was*… if you were his friend, he had your back.

In the first year of school, I caught the attention of a pair of twin brothers, three years above us. For weeks, they'd corner me at lunch, and nick my dinner money, using a variety of methods. Flushing the newbies' heads down toilets was their favourite.

When Dwayne walked into the bogs that day and saw what was going on, he took them out in the blink of an eye. After ending up with matching shiners, they left me alone after that, which made the scene that was about to greet me even more galling.

Mack got to him first, found Dwayne cored clean through. His guts, or what was left of 'em, hung out where his belly button should've been. The only thing left intact was his spine, which you could see through the gaping hole. Mack went mental, they'd been best buds since primary school. He picked up Ol' Paneless and started firing off shots into the undergrowth, before chasing after a noise.

The others caught up and found what was left of Dwayne's body. Though we couldn't see Mack, we could sure as hell hear him, as he was still unloading pellet after pellet. I ran after him and managed to calm him down. That's when we found it. On a leaf, broken by someone fleeing from the scene, was a streak of bright green liquid. It could only be one thing. Blood. I pointed at it, and I remember saying "if it bleeds, we can kill it."

"But we're just a bunch of kids!" Mack screamed. "How the hell are we going to kill *anything*? It hollowed Dwayne out like he was a goddamn apple."

He had a point, but we had to do something, whatever was out there was picking us off, one-by-one. If there was one thing I was certain of, it was that I didn't want to be added to that pile of bones.

Heading back to where we'd found Dwayne, Cagoule was wrapping up the body with some bin liners, before we all sat down and had a chat about what we should do. The whole time we talked? Mack was sitting hunched over the body, talking to it. It was freaky.

Eventually, but not unanimously, we agreed we should try and trap whatever it was that was hunting us. We would go back to the hollow tree, make our stand there, using the one thing it wanted as bait.

Us.

Billy was a dab hand at setting traps, so he took the others away to block off all the main routes to us, whilst I sat down with Hannah, making sure she didn't do another runner. She had calmed down a bit, so I asked her if she could tell me what she'd seen. She looked at me like a frightened deer, then turned to stare into the forest, as if seeking permission. Eventually, she turned to me and said. "The people on my estate call her *la mujer santa que come la carne del hombre* - do you know what that means?"

I shook my head --I could barely ask for Tapas in Spanish, there was no way I could understand what the hell she was babbling on about.

She said it meant holy woman who eats the flesh of man. She said that for years, when the summers were warm, and the leaves fell early in the autumn, people would go missing from the streets. And everyone that went looking for those who had disappeared, went missing too. They never came back. She said her mother had seen her once. Not long after the disappearances started. She said it was a nun, but that she looked lonely. Her face was like ours, she said, but it had bits missing.

So her mother ran and ran, and never came back into the woods again.

I looked at her, to see if she was lying to me, but if she was, she was a hell of a good poker player. I was just about to ask another question, when I saw a luminous green streak on her sodden jeans. I asked her why she had done it. She just shrugged, and said. "If I can't have the truffle oil to mask my scent, the creature's blood does a good a job as any to tell the hunter which of the hunt*ed* can be spared." I was about to ask her what she was going on about, when there was a screeching sound and the rustling of leaves. A trap off to the left of the tree had been tripped, and something was thrashing around.

I couldn't believe what I saw --there she was, the nun. Hanging upside down, trying to pull the rope from her ankle. Except, she did look odd. Her entire head looked as though it was a mask, a good one, don't get me wrong, but fake all the same. There was something primal underneath, though with it struggling so much, I couldn't get a good look. Still, it made no difference, we had it trapped, there was no way it could escape.

Dylan forced his way through the group, and began to laugh, cracking some joke about the size of his catch. The rest of us weren't laughing, though. The nun fell slack, then twisted up. I thought she was going to try and unpick the knot, but instead, the entire top of her body, from where the grubby white bit of her habit started, just…opened up. Inside were razor-sharp teeth, and chunks of half-chewed meat hung in between them. She reached up and bit through the rope in one bite.

The next bit happened so fast. She flipped through the air and landed perfectly, Dylan was flapping his arms about, acting the fool. The nun took a step forward, flipped that massive jaw of hers backward, bit down, and ripped both his arms off in one go. He fell to the floor, screaming. She just stood there, her clothes, which seemed more like a layer of skin than anything, covered with dirt and twigs. That giant mouth of hers chewed on the arms before she darted off, quick as anything, back into the undergrowth.

Everyone panicked, Mack ran after her, Ol' Paneless in hand, yelling obscenities, vowing to avenge his friends. Cagoule went to check on the other traps, whilst me and Billy tried to see if we could do anything to save Dylan. There was blood everywhere. We managed to apply some tourniquets to his stumps, which turned the gushing streams of blood into mere trickles, but it was too little, too late. His eyes rolled back in his head, and he was gone.

I don't know how long Hannah had been shaking me, but eventually I must've realised, and turned to face her. She was speaking so fast, I couldn't understand a word she was saying. I struggled to get her to repeat what she'd said, but slower. She took a deep breath, and said "there are some bikes, not far from here. We left them by an old abandoned cabin one day when we were exploring. We could get them, use them to get out of here, escape this living hell."

It wasn't the worst plan ever, but with the floor slick with mulch and blood, it would be hard work to pedal. Given everything that had happened, though, it was probably our only chance of survival. I asked her where they were stashed and she waved off into the distance. They were old hand-me-down bikes, she said -Tomahawks. It was the lowrider of bikes, one small wheel at the front, and a larger one at the back, with a ridiculously well-proportioned cushioned seat. I myself had two, both given to me by my auntie, who used to raid charity shops. Sometimes with the aid of a sawn-off shotgun and a penchant for violence.

I waved Cagoule and Billy in closer and explained Hannah's plan. Once everyone was clear, I bellowed. "Get to the choppers!"

The trees began to thin out, and that's when we saw her. She was kneeling over Mack's body, his head missing. As we ran past, she snapped her jaws at us, raking Cagoule down the forearm. I managed to fend her off by swinging the bag of truffles at her, buying us enough time to escape.

We could hear her, though. I asked Hannah how much further. "Not far," she said, "just round the next corner." But we were in a forest. There were no damn corners. One thing we both knew for certain, Cagoule was slowing us down, but leaving him behind wasn't even an option.

Then the damnedest thing happened. As I wrapped a strip of jumper around Cagoule's wounds, Billy mumbled something and started walking back the way we'd just come from. He stripped down to his bare torso, and pulled out a Swiss Army knife his dad had bought him for his birthday. He turned to us, told us that we should go, and said he was going to face his destiny. Which was news to me, as he'd once told me in private that his destiny was to die being melted slowly from head to toe by a small mutant lizard. But anyway, Billy was a stubborn so-and-so, and I knew arguing would be pointless, so I just nodded at him and Hannah and I managed to half carry, half drag Cagoule between us. I managed one last look back through the trees, and saw Billy drag the blade across his body.

To this day, I have no idea why he did that.

Around ten minutes later, we heard him screaming. It continued for a good few minutes. The birds were squawking in the trees, but no matter how many of them joined in, they couldn't drown out that awful noise.

I asked Hannah again. "How far?" She pointed to the distance, doubled over, unable to speak, the exertion of carrying my wounded friend removing her ability to converse. This was hopeless and we all knew it, we needed more time. She was near-spent, and poor Cagoule was fading in and out, his face totally white. There was only one thing I could do: I'd stay behind, try and slow down the predator that was treating us as some kind of blood sport. They both tried to argue, but I shushed them, and sent them on their way. With luck, they would get to the bikes, get back to civilisation, and get me the help I knew I would undoubtedly need.

I watched as they disappeared into the undergrowth, before heading off in a different direction, hoping to lure this wretched nun away from them, and towards me.

Cut, ragged and weary, I pressed on. Any time I sought a moment of respite, I would hear that shrill cry from behind, spurring me on. The only thing that lifted my spirits was the knowledge that she had ignored the others and was now just after me. Then the realisation of that hit home, forcing me to push myself harder. I needed to level the playing field, yet I had no idea how to.

I tried to jump over a small river but landed on a rock and slipped. I went flying through the air, and disappeared beneath the water. It carried me onwards before depositing me into a large collection of fading rubbish and leaves. There was a noise behind me --somehow the nun had caught up. I did my best to cover myself with the assortment of crap I was lying on top of. I held my breath and hoped for the best.

She came in so close I could clearly make her out. Her face was a ragged jumble of an approximation of humanity, its veneer rotting away. I could see a small pair of mandibles clacking away through a gap in her visage. That dreaded mouth of hers, the one on her chest, opened and closed, teeth chomped together, and a forked tongue flicked out and tasted the air. She pivoted on the spot, now no more than a few feet from where I lay, barely concealed. A distant sound made her human head jiggle towards the noise, like a novelty jelly. The mouth on her chest closed up and she darted off in its direction.

Night was beginning to close in. I had a fair idea that Hannah and Cagoule had gotten away, and while I hoped that they would get help, and find me quickly, I knew she wouldn't let me get away quite so easily.

I had to take the fight to her.

I had to end this.

I stumbled through the woods, and straight into a huge fallen tree. The trunk was split in two and covered in scorch marks. Maybe a lightning strike, maybe some kind of extraterrestrial tree-hugger, it didn't matter, it gave me an idea. Finding some strong vines, I managed to make some rope, and heaved half of the shorn wooden trunk high into the boughs of a nearby tree. After tying it off, I knew I had a means to try and put an end to her murderous rampage. After making some of the surrounding area impassable, I attempted to make a narrow run so I could channel her into my kill zone.

I built a huge bonfire, and after daubing myself in mud, I hollered and yelled, trying to get her attention. Before I even had a chance to find a suitable hiding place, she was on me. I lured her into the channel, but she was too close. Using a branch, I took a few swipes and managed to catch her around the face, which tore off the entire sallow mask in one go. Her true form regarded me, that insectoid head of hers in its full glory. Its mouth snapped open and closed, shaped like a trapezoid, long, dripping fangs on the upper corners.

She rushed me, and caught me flush on the chest with a flailing hand that sent me spinning through the air like a top. I landed heavily against a tree trunk, which pushed the wind from my lungs. Before I could shake away the force of impact, she was on me again. That huge chest mouth snapped at me, tearing against my arms, gouging away. She pinned me to the ground, sensing that victory was imminent. This delay worked to my advantage, I grabbed hold of a rock, and smacked her round the head, sending her into a pile of leaves. She howled, both of her jaws clacking together, before she arched backwards and let out an ear-piercing scream.

Seizing my opportunity, I kicked out at her, and scurried backwards, underneath my trap and into the dead-end hollow I'd created. She was enraged, thrashing about and trying to lash out. She flipped onto her feet and stalked towards me, that deadly mouth of hers chomping the air, eager to wolf down what she'd managed a brief taste of.

She didn't notice the tree trunk until it was too late. As she stepped underneath it, I smacked the wooden pin, which held the suspended block in gravity's pocket. Hearing the rustling, the nun looked up, something akin to surprise on its wretched face. The trunk smacked straight into her chest, and the sound of her broken teeth pinging against the bark of surrounding trees was quite something. She let out an almighty scream, before finally falling silent.

Barely believing my luck, I picked myself up, and stood over my vanquished foe, its face speckled with its foul green blood. My body ached all over, but I still managed to scream at it. "What the hell are you?" Its jaws opened, and something like laughter peeled out of its throat. With clawed fingers, it pulled down the cloth skin that covered one of its arms, revealing a silver band wrapped around its bestial forearm. It tapped in a series of commands, before collapsing backwards, the laughter building.

I looked down at the device and saw that there were lights blinking out of existence. This was not going to end well. I turned around and sprinted as hard as I could, ducking underneath branches, trying not to look back or come a cropper on a hidden rock or root. There was a rumbling to my rear, and I felt a shockwave wash over me. I was thrown forwards and struck my head on the floor. I turned over, and looked up at the stars twinkling through the skeletal canopy, before falling unconscious.

When I awoke, it was morning, and I was moving. Some of my mates from the estate had stumbled on my sparked-out body, after Hannah and Cagoule had got back to the estate and raised the alarm. They had put me on a trailer hitched to their Grifters. As I was hauled back home, I looked back at the woods, the place which had claimed so many of my friends and which nearly became my tomb.

I'd survived.

Who knows how long she had been out there, preying on those who dared enter her domain. It didn't matter any more, her reign of terror was over.

I was going home.

13

The taxi driver waited for a response, his eyes flitting from mirror to the road ahead. "Well?"

Flynn pinched the bridge of his nose. "That was utter bollocks."

"What do you mean? Those woods, they're a source of evil, I'm telling you."

The priest moved forward, arms resting on the back of the driver and passenger seat. "Well, for one, you lost your accent pretty quickly didn't you? I thought you said you were Scottish?"

"Och aye. I sure am, ye wee bawbag."

"You can drop the act, you're as Scottish as a banana. Second, what you've actually relayed to me was the abridged story of cult action film, Predator, wasn't it?"

"No..."

"If it was any closer to the actual plot and characters, I'm sure there would be an army of keyboard warriors out there, ready to flame you back to the dial-up age. Was *any* of it true?"

The taxi driver squirmed in his seat. He could feel the priest's accusation boring into his skull, finally conceding. "Fine, *some* elements of my story may have been embellished-"

"Some?"

"Yes, the odd morsel I mentioned may have happened slightly differently in reality."

"The explosion?"

"Not so much an explosion, as a splatter of leaves as the nun breathed her last and hit her head in a puddle of mucky rainwater."

"I really must commend you on making the journey here just fly by."

"Fine, so what? I made some bits up. But I did lose my

friends in that forest to that evil bitch."

Flynn laughed, slumping back into his seat, letting the seatbelt pull taut once more. "Of *course* you did. There was an evil insectoid nun living in the woods, feasting on human flesh. Look, I've seen some weird things in my time, trust me, but that tale of yours is a little on the tall side."

Turning in his seat, the driver fought to look the priest in the eyes. "I swear on the bones of my mates, that most of the story I relayed to you is true. A good eighty percent or so."

Father Flynn moved to the middle of the rear seat and pointed towards the windscreen, but the driver continued talking to him via the rear view mirror. "The bit about the big log thing at the end, yeah, that may not have happened, she sort of tripped up over her own feet, I just bashed her head in with a great big rock."

"Erm…" Flynn continued to point.

"But I assure you, all my chums *were* eaten, I had to go to therapy for some considerable time. Sometimes, when I see nature documentaries, especially ones set in large forests, I still hear that wailing. Both of that she-devil, and my friends as they got eviscerated." Satisfied that he'd said his piece, the driver turned back to the front, just as the bumper made contact with something in the road. "Shit, not again."

A black and white figure, slightly-built, more humanoid than general woodland animal, disappeared from sight. A crack ran down the windscreen, shearing off one of the wipers. Something connected with the roof, and Flynn ducked down as the impact pushed the metal down into the cabin itself. The two men flicked their heads to the rear instinctively, seeing a figure --a man at their first guess-- roll down the back of the car, an aerial embedded in his midriff. There was a thud as the figure smacked into the tarmac, where it twitched once, a hand clawing at thin air, before patting the ground.

"Shit! I hit the Slender Man!" The taxi driver shouted, belatedly slamming on the brakes. The cab screeched to a halt, smoke pouring from the buckled bonnet.

"It wasn't the Slender Man, you anus." Flynn reached inside

for his hip flask, retracting his hand in disappointment when he remembered that the Archbishop had confiscated it.

"The Babadook then? It looked a bit spindly."

"For fuck's sake, it was a man, just a normal man --what is *with* you? Back up, let's go and see if they're still alive. You're a one-man wrecking machine, you know that?"

Swelling with some degree of murderous pride, the taxi driver put the sputtering car into reverse and edged it backwards.

"Stop!" The priest shouted, the rear of the car bucked as the back tyres rolled over the prone figure. The driver switched to first gear and rolled the car forward. "Oops!" There was another bump.

"What are you doing? Is catapulting the poor bastard through the air not enough, that you have to run him over? Twice?"

The taxi driver killed the engine. "Sorry. I'm done now." The pair got out, and tiptoed to the back of the car. There, lying face-down in the middle of the road, in a pool of growing green blood, was a man, wearing black. Not wasting any time on medical procedure, the driver grabbed hold of the body and turned it over, wincing at the damage.

The face was flecked with small stones, which were pressed into the skin, making it look like he had some very strange spots coming up. The nose was broken, and had been pushed into the skull, forming two small fleshy caves where the nostrils were. One eye was closed, whilst the other looked back, like Popeye. The eyelid had been ripped off, and was stuck to the man's forehead, like a sticker from an apple.

"Oh, Christ," the driver said, crossing himself, he pointed at the body's chest. Tucked into the shirt collar was a white band. "He's one of your lot, he's a priest."

Father Flynn kneeled down. "Not sure what he is, look at his head."

The taxi driver stifled upchuck. "Not sure I want to, thanks."

Flynn turned the head, a flap of skin and bone opened up

like a secret drawer, letting lumps of gristly brain plop out of the hole. Using a piece of ripped shirt, Flynn picked up the chunk of spongified brain. "Notice anything odd?" Instead of the atypical pink colour, it was a lurid green, more at home during the eighties than nowadays.

From the various wounds, and the gaping hole in the dead priest's head, green gunk continued to pump onto the asphalt. Flynn held the piece of brain out for the driver to look at, who declined the offer by turning away. "I'm not going near that. That blood though, it looks the same as that damn nun's. You know, the one who-"

"Yes, ate all of your mates, you have mentioned that once or twice." Daring to give the brain a bit of a sniff, Flynn winced as the smell of rotting fish and egg threatened to test his steely resolve. He wrapped it up with the cloth and shoved it into his inside pocket, the one he usually reserved for booze. The priest stood up and scratched at his fingers, trying to get the dried bits of tissue and blood off. "We need to call someone."

"Not a chance, they'll take away my license. They said after the fourth one-"

"The fourth one?"

"Erm…yeah, but I swear, none of them were my fault, honest. They just sort of keep…jumping out at me."

"This is number five? Technically, this makes you a serial killer. You've got to stop, okay? Pay some attention, take a course, have a break, stretch your legs, put the radio on, open a window, something, anything, just stop mowing people and animals down in cold blood. Okay?"

The taxi driver gave a double thumbs-up. "I'm on it. Could you do me a solid, though?"

"What?"

"Help me get him in the boot? I know a man in town, he can get rid of this, no questions asked. As long as you keep mum."

Father Flynn shook his head. "I don't know, this doesn't feel right to me."

"Look at him, he ain't human, is he? If he is, then his insides are sure as hell messed up. If we call the cops, they're just going to ask loads of awkward questions. Before you know it, we'll be in prison, dodging shower time, and trying not to be used as currency."

Flynn patted the dead body down, retrieving a small silver whistle, twenty pounds in one-pound coins, and a business card for a gentlemen's club in Knighton, called 'The Last Resort.' On the back was a name. "This handwriting is terrible. For a good time ask for…Melanie? Melania?" He pocketed his findings. "Fine, let's get him in the boot, I just want to get to this damn retreat. I chose the wrong day to be strong-armed into giving up drinking."

Smiling, the driver picked up the dead body's legs and waited for Flynn to lift the other half of the body up, and into the boot. After slamming the lid shut, and after it bounced open a few times, the taxi driver realised the catch was broken.

He rummaged underneath the still twitching corpse, trying to find some bungee cord. "Nearly done here, I can give you a lift to Dynynbwtya Lleian, then."

Flynn took off his jacket and slung it over his shoulder. "Not a chance."

"Eh? It's not far, just get through Knighton and it's a few miles on from there."

"Doesn't matter, I've had enough fun for one day, I'll walk into town and get a bus the rest of the way."

"If you're sure, appreciate you lending a hand with the dead body, though --much obliged, me ol' mucka. Oh, interesting fact of the day, might make you believe my story a bit more, come to think of it, do you know what *Dynynbwtya Lleian* means in English?"

Flynn trudged down the road, and stuck his fingers up to the man behind him. "Unless it stands for *free booze*, I couldn't give a rat's arse."

The taxi driver shrugged. "Suit yourself, mate, no need to be rude." Daring one look at the twisted body in the boot, the driver shuddered, then began to unwind the cord, working out how he was going to keep the lid from flying up whilst in transit.

14

Lee-Anne's day was not going to go down in the annals of history as being the best ever. The alarm clock failing to go off - following an overnight power cut - meant that every part of her carefully-choreographed morning routine had melted like an ice sculpture on a hot air vent. After finally cajoling her five-year-old daughter to get out of bed, they had arrived an hour late at school. Her decision to convince Lily that a half-eaten jar of salsa and near stale tortilla chips, remnants of the previous day's dinner, constituted a well-rounded lunch, was torpedoed on the stroke of midday. A phone call from the school, informing her that Lily had projectile-vomited over a number of classmates, caught Lee-Anne the instant she had finally managed to put her feet, with a nice cup of tea in hand and Loose Women on the telly.

Now, as the pair trudged through the streets of Knighton, their new puppy, Pom, had discovered a new pastime. "What have you got in your hands, Lily?" Lee-Anne asked, part of her not wanting to know the answer.

As if brandishing the mighty Excalibur, Lily held the gift aloft. "It's a present, Mummy, Pom found it all by herself."

"I can see that, but what is it?"

"A twig. I think. Though it smells a bit funny." Lily held the object underneath her nostrils and breathed in deep. Her cheeks began to turn green again. "It smells like bum mud, mummy."

Lee-Anne, her fingers indentured to years of picking up disgusting things, snatched the latest dog's discovery from her daughter, and sniffed it. "Lily! It's cat poo! Why are you playing with cat poo?"

Lily had stopped in the street, her cheeks puffed out, lips clamped shut, trying to hold the latest torrent of sick down.

Her eyelids blinked longer than they should, and she swallowed what remained of the contents of her stomach, her face deflating like a balloon with a slow puncture. After letting out a sicky burp, she shrugged. "Pom got it for me."

"But it's disgusting, Lily, you shouldn't pick up things from the street, okay?"

"Okay mummy, I'm sorry."

"That's alright, let me get something to clean your fingers with," Lee-Anne began to root through her handbag, its depths containing a multitude of antiseptic and detergent wipes.

"Mummy?"

"Yes, darling?"

"If things smell bad, can they taste nice?"

Lee-Anne's face dropped, and she sunk to her knees, her fingers opening up her daughter's mouth. "You haven't, have you?" Lily shook her head, and pointed behind her mum. Lee-Anne turned around, to find Pom lying on the ground, chewing her way through a fresh pile of recently-retrieved cat poo. "Pom, for heaven's sake, just leave it. Give me strength, between the pair of you…" Standing up, Lee-Anne grabbed hold of Lily's wrist with one hand, Pom's lead in the other, and yanked the pair into movement; they struggled to keep up with the enforced pace.

"Let's just get home, okay? No more poo," Lee-Anne said to the pair in her wake. Pom was still licking her snout, Lily's little legs marching ten to the dozen, trying to keep up.

"Mummy?"

"Yes, darling?"

"I need the toilet."

Lee-Anne looked to the heavens. "Of course you do. Fine, we'll pop in the shop on the way back, okay?"

The trio rounded the corner into Ignatius Lane at a clip. Lily made a suitable tyre-screeching sound, eliciting a happy yip from Pom, who trotted merrily next to her. The Quantico Zoom-Mart was halfway up the road, one of the smaller versions of supermarkets which pepper towns like unsightly pimples. Something was amiss. Lee-Anne looked up and down the road, seeing that, aside from one person outside the supermarket itself, there was no one else around. Given that it was lunchtime, it should've been teeming with office workers eager to take advantage of the bargain meal deals, even if the sandwich quality was somewhat dubious.

Still, fewer people meant she could get this little emergency pit stop taken care of quicker, and get back home to try and have one cup of tea before it went cold. As they approached the shop, the woman outside clocked them, and rang a small hand bell, one slow bong, followed by a quicker, snappier ting. As she turned to face them, Lee-Anne saw that she was dressed as a nun.

"Good afternoon, my dear, I-"

Lee-Anne held up a hand. "I don't have any change on me."

"Sorry?"

"I'm just taking my daughter to use the toilet, I don't have any money on me."

"That's okay, dear, I'm not after your money, I'm here to wish you a happy afternoon." The woman pealed the bell enthusiastically. "I think they're having some kind of electrical problem inside, though --nearly all the staff are out back."

Lee-Anne tutted. "Just marvellous. Will anything go right today?"

"It's okay, dear, some of my fellow sisters are inside, they will be able to take care of you both." The nun kneeled down to meet Lily at head-height. "Mmm, you look so yummy, I could eat you up right now, little girl."

Lily laughed. "You're a silly lady." The nun's habit twitched, the white oval curling up slightly. Lily giggled and went to poke it with a finger. The habit mouth began to open, sensing that an aperitif of finger food was incoming.

"Lily, don't!" Lee-Anne smacked Lily's hand. "What have I told you about touching things? I'm sorry, she needs to wash her hands properly. Are you sure it's okay to go in?"

The nun's habit closed up. "Oh, yes, go straight inside." Pom barked and stamped her front feet, and the nun stood up and glared at the animal, who continued to yip. "That...*thing*, will have to wait outside though."

"Of course, I'll just tie him to the post, unless you want to look after him?"

The nun shied away as if she had come into contact with an abrasive cleaner. "Not a chance. Horrible things. Give me furballs." She shuddered at the thought.

"What? How do they give *you* furballs?"

The nun stood up straight, her head wobbling, cheeks rippling like a wave machine in a pool. "Allow me to finish, I meant...give me Furbies any day of the week."

"Furbies?"

"Yes. Furbies. You still have them on this plan...settlement, don't you?"

"Yeah...but why would *you* want one? Actually, I don't want to know, I'm going to go inside now, okay?"

The nun acquiesced. "Of course, my dear. As I said, go right to the back, my sisters will take care of you."

Lee-Anne tied Pom to a post, before grabbing hold of Lily's hand, "fine, come on, Lils."

Watching the pair as they went in, the nun looked down at the dog. "Just you wait till the Furbies do hatch, this planet won't know what's hit it. Disgusting things, the lot of you."

The shop interior was in near darkness, emergency lighting casting a sickly glow down the aisles. It looked like there had been a struggle: items were strewn over the floor, as if someone had played a very energetic round of Supermarket Sweep. Squeezing each other's hands, the pair wound their way through the mess and towards the back of the shop. It was eerie. Though Lee-Anne could hear voices, they were a way off, and they were all women. There was not one member of staff around, standing in their iconic Quantico grey tunics, and sporting their trademark 'I don't give a shit *what* you want' sneer.

After skirting round a lake of own-brand cola, the pair reached the toilets, where another nun stood sentry. "Where is everyone?" Lee-Anne asked. This nun was short and squat, the perfect build for sumo or shot-put. Her eyes were long slits etched onto her face, and she, apparently, was less gregarious than the one they had seen outside.

"Out back," the nun said gruffly, thumbing to a dark corridor, a rectangle of light at the end signalling its terminus.

"Okay, well --we're just going to use the toilet and then we'll be on our way."

Sumo nun stepped in front of the doors. "Can't. Broken."

"Well this is just brilliant, isn't it? Why did that other one send me in here, if the toilets are broken?"

Silence.

"Hello?" Lee-Anne asked.

The bottom half of the nun's face went up and down, like a slow-moving piston. "Toilets out back. Go there." Sumo nun thumbed to the bleak corridor.

"And there are definitely toilets down there?"

Sumo nun nodded, though the movement made her entire face move, as if the skin was not connected to the bone underneath.

"Fine, come on, let's go." Inching their way down the corridor, they took care to avoid tripping over the various boxes which were piled up along the route. The light at the back of the shop grew bigger as they picked a path through the racking and recent deliveries. Another nun stood sentinel by the door, which led out to the loading bay. As they walked out into the open, they saw that a large, old-fashioned coach was parked in the middle of the concrete. Big black scorch marks ran down its umber body. There were dings and dents on the bodywork too, as if it had been pelted by rocks.

No sooner had they stepped outside than the nun guarding the door pulled it shut, sealing them outside. Lee-Anne shielded her eyes from the bright sun. As her vision returned, she took a step back, straight into the chest of the nun.

Lined up neatly were five rows of people, around ten deep. Some wore suits, others in Quantico attire, all of them standing to attention. Eyes forward, mouths closed, perfectly still and ordered. A few other nuns stood around the people, acting like shepherds, though it was clear that none of the group were going to make a move. They all just stood there. "Like cattle," the words escaping Lee-Anne's mouth before she could trap them inside.

"What are they doing, Mummy?" Lily asked, her face a knot of confusion.

"I'm not sure, darling." Lee-Anne walked towards the herd. As she got closer, she saw that they all had something protruding from their necks. It looked like an aerial, though it was made from some kind of brown organic material, like a stem from a rose. One of the nuns stepped back, allowing them closer. The object was around four inches long, and thrummed rhythmically in time with the person's heartbeat, which she could see from the pulse thudding in their necks.

The tendril had fine black hairs running up and down its length; it looked like a sickly insect leg. Lee-Anne raised her hand, her fingers unable to ignore her brain telling her to leave it alone.

"Ah, a few more for the tasting session, splendid. Tell Sister Felicity we have enough, and that she should seal the barrier closed," a woman's voice said.

The pair turned to see another nun walking towards them. Unlike her associates, she had a big gold crucifix on, it swung slightly as she crossed the gap between the coach door and where they were standing.

"What's happened to them?"

"All in good time, my lovely. Now, I am Mother Superior Francesca, and these people have very kindly offered to help us," the nun said, her fingers toying with the golden cross. She bowed over and addressed Lily. "Would you like to help us, little one?"

Lily shied away behind her mother. "Help you how? And what is that thing that's coming out of them?" Lee-Anne said, fighting the urge to touch that thing.

Francesca stepped in closer, now only a foot away. "It makes the process, more…kindly, *humane*, you could say." This got a round of chuckles from the nuns. "You see, meat tastes a lot more tender when the animal isn't struggling, isn't that right, ladies?"

There was a murmur of approval from the nuns dotted around the bay, and from a couple who were inside the coach, moving a large object towards the emergency doors.

"Meat? I don't understand?" Lee-Anne said.

Mother Superior raised the cross up, and jabbed it against Lee-Anne's neck. "You don't have to, my lovely, you're dinner, and food doesn't need to understand." Francesca pressed down on the golden figure's head, there was a PFFT, and Lee-Anne slapped a hand against her neck.

Francesca withdrew the cross carefully, leaving the sappy green stem jutting out of Lee-Anne's throat. As it writhed, it darkened, and dried out to a pale shade of brown. "There, much better, this will help you."

"Mummy?" Lily screamed.

The Mother Superior loomed over the little girl, crucifix in hand. "Oh, don't you worry, my lovely, I've got one for you, too."

15

Lee-Anne tried to will her limbs to move, even just a tiny amount.

Nothing.

Okay, so how about just one finger? Just move one finger.

Nothing.

She continued to stand there at the back of the third row, just in front of her daughter, looking out as the nuns busied themselves around the coach. The back window was propped open, and they were manoeuvring a large metal and glass chest through the gap. It looked like a telephone box.

After some careful wiggling, they managed to get it through the gap and rested it upright on the floor. It had a polished metal frame, with three glass panels on each side. At the top and bottom was a thick band of metal which ran around the circumference of the object. As one of the nuns opened the container door, another unfurled a thick length of cable from the back of the coach.

Lee-Anne managed a peek inside the engine bay, but instead of an old rusting engine, she saw a gleaming silver machine with blinking futuristic lights and things that went PING.

Opening a port on the back of the box, the nun plugged in the cable, and twisted it, giving it a quick tug to make sure that it was securely fastened. Smiling, she gave a thumbs-up to Francesca, who crossed herself and clutched the golden crucifix.

With the other nuns forming a backdrop, the Mother Superior addressed the rows of people. "Hello, my lovelies, so nice of you to all *volunteer* for our first pressing this year. There really is nothing like landing on your planet and starting off the collection process. I must say that many of you look positively ripe."

Francesca patted the side of the upright glass and metal chest. "This little machine is called the Zinnki Meat Processor 2000, it's received many top reviews, and…well, very shortly, you'll see the wonderful job it does. Sister Ophelia, what would you like us to make first?"

Ophelia ummed and ahhed, several of the nuns whispered in her ear, before she shooed them away, and said. "I want to make some potted human. With extra jelly."

Mother Superior clapped her hands together. "An excellent suggestion, the versatility of the human being really does lend itself to a wide variety of meat-based products."

A nun from one of the flanks broke rank and walked towards the Zinnki, holding a metal canister about the size of a petrol can. She opened up a side panel, unscrewed the canister's nozzle and began to pour the liquid inside a hidden reservoir. The stuff was thick and gloopy; as it caught the sun, it shone like a puddle fouled by petrol, the colours of the rainbow rippling through it. The nun tipped the canister, ensuring that every last stringy globule was inside. She closed the panel, and disappeared back within the massed ranks of black and white.

"Excellent, now, time is of the essence, so let's begin. 1A, come on down, my lovely," Francesca flipped open the body of the crucifix, revealing a small, smooth, silicone panel beneath. It had brightly-lit coloured pads, which she operated like a pro. At the head of the first row, Lee-Anne saw a twitch from the thing that was in the person's neck, and watched as it pointed towards the Mother Superior. It let out a little puff of air, saturated with fine particulate, as if it were a dandelion, its seeds blown by an errant child. The person began to move.

As they came into full view, Lee-Anne could see that they were wearing a shiny tracksuit. They marched like a clunky robot to the front of the machine. As they goose-stepped front and centre, another nun opened up a small control panel on the Zinnki 2000, and pressed a button which made the door concertina open. Francesca tapped another pad on her crucifix, and the man came to a halt just before the vacant machine.

"Now, we don't want your wrapping, do we? Nothing worse than having to peel that off. That won't do at all." She tapped another button, and the man began to undress. It took less time than expected, as he was wearing no underwear or socks.

With his clothes lying in a heap, the man took one step forward into the machine. Without a hint of embarrassment about his sudden nudity, he lifted his other foot in and turned to face the assembled ranks.

His eyes were flitting about in his sockets. They were strained, desperate, trying to find some semblance of control over his body. The nun pressed the button again, and the doors closed, sealing him inside. Francesca smiled. "Ah, we have waited many cycles for this day, there is nothing like the first pressing of a new batch. Animal, we salute you, may your flesh be firm yet yielding, rich but not sickly."

She nodded at the door operator, who tapped in a series of button presses, before taking a couple of steps back. The machine began to thrum. Lee-Anne could feel the vibrations running up through her feet, into her legs and shaking her entire body. Three lights lit up at the top of the Processor.

There was a loud hiss from the rear of the device, as two jet nozzles flipped out inside the machine and squirted a healthy slug of the viscous goo over the man's legs and feet. It looked like it had been diluted, but had become gloopier. As the nozzles retracted, the first light went out.

The noise began to build. Then, there was a loud WOOMPH, and a square block of metal, hidden within the top recess, slammed downwards. One minute there had stood a naked man, the next, there was nothing but a piston ram in his place. The bottom panels of glass were covered in red paste, thick gobbets of meat sliding down like blood-filled slugs.

The sheet of metal affixed to the roof ram, which had crushed the man, began to unfurl. Rubber-edged lips slid down the bloodstained glass panels to the bottom of the Meat

Processor, wiping it clean and collecting the human remains at the bottom. The sound changed as if it had shifted gear, and instead of pressing down, the now-open panels began to contract inwards. The second light went out.

There was a grinding noise, followed by what could only be described as a wet fart sound. The panel retracted, restoring itself to its original dimensions.

Lee-Anne strained to see what was inside the device, as the third light went out. The nun opened the door and crouched inside. Turning to the captive audience deliberately, she held aloft a jellied cube of meat and bone. As she studied the consistency and texture, it wobbled slightly. Lee-Anne could just about make out an eyeball suspended in the amorphous mass, looking out at the ordered rows of people standing to attention. The nun turned to a colleague, who held open a box. The nun placed the cube inside, a perfect fit, and sealed it up. The nun then placed it on a palette.

Mother Superior Francesca clapped her hands excitedly. "Mmmm, I can't wait to tuck into him later. Now, I think we'll make the first row into potted human, then I say we make some jam." There was enthusiastic clapping, but Francesca quietened her team. "Calm down, ladies, focus on the task at hand, we have lots to get through. Let's get this congregation processed without delay."

16

Father Flynn found that both pubs, the Royal Usurper and the Paralysed King George VII, were utterly deserted. In the pair of them, he found well-thumbed copies of the Racing Post, and bars filled with unfinished drinks. As he stood in the modern cavern of the Fiery Hipster, complete with exposed ducts and wiring that snaked across the ceiling, he contemplated whether he should just help himself to the wealth of craft ales on offer.

He was plagued by a nagging doubt. That this town was festooned with a network of hidden cameras, waiting to snare him in an elaborate honey trap. Any ensuing photographic evidence would be forwarded to the Archbishop, the final stamp in his passport speeding him on the journey back to being in charge of the last microfiche reader in the church.

He wandered back outside, aimlessly walking down the main High Street, which was completely bereft of humans. The shops were as deserted as the pubs, even the charity shops whose doorways were piled high with unwanted clothes and plastic toys. There were no old people rooting through the bargain bin, hoping to find something of worth. Newsagents were equally devoid of life, missing the key fiscal ingredient: customers. 'Specific interest' magazines sat on the top shelf, flaunting their wares to no-one but the fridges full of fizzy drinks.

Flynn ambled up the hill on the High Street, deciding to hit up one more boozer, before getting on the phone to see if someone was pranking him.

From the outside, the Obtuse Trappist was a good, old-fashioned pub. Sturdy black beams ran up the exterior walls. Lead-lined hatched windows offered nothing more than a murky glimpse into the bowels of the building. The sign, a monk, painted in the style of Picasso, swung gently in the breeze, each backswing eliciting a squeaking sound from the rusty hinge. The priest pushed the door open and walked inside.

The familiar smell of wet dog and spilt beer made his nose twitch. Albie stuck his head out from his beardy home, had a quick look around, before wriggling back inside. A now-familiar theme greeted Flynn. Amongst the scene of desertion, a fire was burning itself out, a thin wisp of smoke corkscrewing up from the glowing embers into the wide chimney.

The priest slumped against the bar, narrowly escaping glassing himself on a broken bottle. He propped himself up. "Hello? Is anyone there?" Silence greeted him, interspersed with a jolly beep-boop-beep sound from the fruit machine as it tried to tempt him into losing his spare change. The priest thumped the thick wooden bar with his balled fist. "If this is a joke, it ain't funny you know."

"Oi, god-botherer. Keep the bloody noise down will ya? Some of us have work to do," a Northern voice said from the murk.

Flynn squinted and managed to pick out a shadowy figure, sitting at a small table towards the back of the pub. The alcove in which he dwelled was crammed between the doors to the toilets. As he got closer, doing his best to avoid tripping in the gloom, he saw a man, hunched over the table, sat closest to the entrance of the ladies'. "Hello?"

In the act of trying not to smack into some furniture unseen, Father Flynn was ill-prepared to deal with the flying pencil, as it struck him on the forehead. "For fuck's sake, what are you doing?" He clamped a hand to the scratch, and rubbed it with his palm. "That really hurt, you know."

"You great big Jessie, if you thought *that* hurt, see how you get on with this."

At the last second, Flynn saw a half-pint glass materialise in front of his eyes. It smacked against his forehead, causing him to stumble backwards. As the glass smashed against the floor, Flynn pressed and poked his head with his fingers, trying to work out if he was bleeding. "What are you doing?"

"I said to keep the noise down, didn't I? You're interrupting me while I'm working, so you deserve a glass to the face. Now why don't you do me a favour, and sod off?"

The priest, content that he had not been subjected to serious injury, scampered across to the table, collapsing into the chair opposite. "Even so, you shouldn't be lobbing glasses at people, it's not very nice."

"Oh, boo-fucking-hoo. What's the matter, Princess, did I ruin your good looks?" The man's face appeared from the murk. His skin was pulled taut over his skull, forming shallow recesses in his cheeks, accentuating his wiry eyebrows, which seemed to point in seven directions at once. "You look like shit," the man offered.

Flynn dabbed his face again. "Yeah, well, I've had a somewhat interesting morning, topping off a rather crappy few days." The priest leaned forward, taking in the man's gaunt features. "Besides, you're a fine one to talk, you look like a necrophiliac has dug you up from a shallow grave. Don't open your mouth too wide, might have a millipede or something in there."

The man huffed. "Oh, you're absolutely fucking hilarious, aren't ya? I thought your lot had to be nice to everyone."

"Not today, not ever, and if I don't get to Saint Judas before nightfall, then the only people I'll have a chance of being nice to again are the old biddies that come into the library and ask for books they know you don't have. It's enough to drive a man to drink. And murder. Possibly both. Speaking of which, where the hell is everybody? I've been up and down this shitty town, and there's no one around. All the pubs and shops are deserted, what's the deal?"

The man placed both hands on the edge of the table, his eyes, sunken marbles within cavernous sockets, pinned the priest in place. "Everyone's gone to the Rapture." With that, he fished around in his long unkempt hair, retrieved a fresh pencil, licked the end, and flattened the newspaper out.

Flynn raised an eyebrow and checked the table; aside from

the newspaper and an empty bottle of tonic, there were no other alcoholic beverages around. Reluctantly, and still wired to think this was some kind of elaborate setup, he asked. "The Rapture? Are you sure?"

Sighing loudly, the man slammed his hand onto the table, splitting the pencil split in two. "That's what I said, isn't it? Do I speak with a st-st-stutter? No. The Rapture, they've all gone to it, and they're fucking welcome to as far as I'm concerned. Bloody do-gooders. Now, if you don't mind." The man nodded down at the paper, picked up a length of pencil lead, and ruminated over five down; *six letters – idiot, ridiculous person.* The man chuckled, looked at the priest and started to scribble his answer. "Wanker," he stopped, "oh, can't be, fourth letter is a P."

Flynn slumped back in his chair. "I don't believe it. The fucking rapture? I mean, Old Hag Tina in the Oracle cave said it would happen at some point, but I didn't think it would happen *now.* And why the fuck am I still here?"

"I'd say your inability to take a hint and piss off is a good enough reason to start with," the man suggested.

The priest tugged on his white collar. "You see this, yeah? This is…was, my fucking one hundred percent, bona fide invitation to the big party up top, you know? Forgive my sins and all that claptrap. I didn't go through all that bollocks for five years at the seminary only to be refused entry when the big day comes along. This is just ruddy fantastic, isn't it?"

"Numpty!"

"What did you just call me?"

The man emitted a growl of sorts and held up the newspaper. "It's the answer to five down, *numpty,* now do you mind? How about you wind your neck in and let me get on with my work in peace?"

"Work? You're doing a fucking crossword, not brain surgery." Flynn snatched the paper, opened it up, and tossed it back, laughing. "Correction, you're doing the crossword from the Daily Vajazzle, you'd have to be a complete moron to be unable to complete it."

A tad insulted, the man bristled and folded the pages open again. "Okay, Brainiac, nine across, a wiry dog --and it *ain't* a greyhound."

"How many letters?"

The man counted quietly, yet his lips moved with each number. "Seven."

"What does it start with?"

"Blank, h, blank, blank, p, blank, t." The man sat back in his chair, reached out for his glass, then tutted in annoyance as he realised he had used it as the opening fusillade against the newcomer.

Flynn raised a finger. "Easy, *whippet*."

The old man looked down at the crossword, and grudgingly filled in the letters. "Hmmm, lucky guess."

"I'd have thought you of all people would've got that."

"Why's that exactly?"

"You're northern, don't you lot get given a whippet each once you get to puberty? Along with your flat cap, gravy vouchers and woollen tank tops."

The old man bristled. "Oh, you're a comedian, eh? How about I pull out your funny bone and give it to my state-provided, non-existent whippet? Anyway, that question was just a warm up."

"Go on, give me another then."

"Fine, eight down, excessively proud of oneself, vain, nine letters."

"Easy, conceited."

"I know you are," the old man chuckled, "you walked straight into that, you dog-collar-wearing prick."

As the sound of laughter echoed around the dingy pub, the door opened and slammed shut. A lanky man, wearing a high vis jacket, approached the bar. He looked across to the pair and nodded. "Alright, Eddie, how you getting on with the old crossword today?"

The old man waved the paper. "Not too bad, only a few left. Though this 'un is getting right on my nerves."

Father Flynn closed his jaw, then pointed at the newcomer.

"Who's that?"

Returning to his puzzle, Eddie replied without looking up. "That's Trevor, works for the council, comes in here for his lunch break."

"So we're not alone then? Other people didn't go to the rapture either?"

"Course not, you think you're oh so special, don't you? With your stupid little white collar, and your great big bushy beard. I've seen harder grafters on the streets, painted in gold, you know, those living statues? They let pigeons crap on their heads, now that's dedication to your profession. This is before I even start on those crusty jugglers. All your lot do is bleat on about some invisible all-knowing god, and bringing everyone down by forcing people to repent their mortal sins. Why don't you just let us enjoy life, eh? What's wrong with a bit of robbing and false idol worshipping, eh? Never hurt anyone-"

"Where's Tina?" Trevor asked.

His diatribe interrupted, Eddie huffed and replied. "She's gone to the Rapture for a sandwich, said she'd be back in a bit."

Father Flynn coughed, then when that did nothing to garner a response, prodded the old timer. "Gone to the rapture for a sandwich? What are you on about?"

Eddie exhaled loudly, waving the pencil at the priest like it was a miniature spear. "The Rapture and Fiddle, it's up the top of Ignatius Road, one of those café bar things…you know the sort. Can grab a pint, and some of that focaccia bread, maybe a bran muffin," the old man spat on the floor, "course in my day-"

The priest began to laugh. "You dozy old bastard, I thought you meant the actual *rapture*, you know the end of days, fire and brimstone. If I'd known you meant some pretentious eaterie, I would've left you in peace."

Eddie thumbed towards the door. "Well now's your chance, off you pop, don't let the door smack you in the arse on the way out, you pretentious knobwrangler."

Standing up, Flynn went to leave, before turning back to

the old man, who balled his fist, cracking the last vestige of life from his writing implement. "What the fuck do you want now?"

"Do you know where the bus stop is? I need to get a ride up to Saint Judas, at Dynynbwtya Lleian," Flynn asked.

"It's past the Quantico Zoom-Mart, again, up Ignatius Road. You can't miss it. It's right at the end, by the Rapture, at the corner of Adrian Heath Lane. Now, if you don't mind?" Eddie glared down at his unfinished crossword.

"Not at all, thanks, I guess." Father Flynn, now accustomed to the gloom, began to head towards the exit. As he got to the door, he clicked his fingers and shouted to Eddie, "bastard."

"Well that's just charming, isn't it? I give you directions and you call me a bastard."

"No, you miserable git, *bastard*, sixteen across, a child born out of wedlock."

"Oh, why thank you so much. Are you going now? I was saving that one for later, I don't start the double-digit clues until the brain has warmed up a bit and the meat man turns up. Look, you've caused enough trouble, sling your hook, okay? Was hoping to do some overtime today, but you've put paid to that." There was the sound of breaking glass as a tonic bottle hit Trevor over the head.

"Ow, watch out, Eddie!" Trevor scratched his scalp, shards of glass flecking his safety jacket like crystallised dandruff.

Emerging from the pub, Flynn shielded his eyes, as daylight, even though it was a tad overcast, made the transition from near-darkness a painful affair.

After a few minutes wandering around the highways and byways of Knighton, he found Ignatius Road. The town centre was still making a good fist at achieving full-blown ghost town status. Aside from the odd car, the drivers giving him odd looks, Flynn encountered nothing except a cat, which hissed at him from atop a wall, and a seagull, which attempted to add a dash of colour to his cassock with some narrowly-avoided white and green faecal matter.

The doors to the supermarket were shut, the store itself

plunged in near darkness save for the dim emergency strip lights on the ceiling. Father Flynn cupped his hands and strained to look in, seeing nothing except for what looked like a nun darting through a door at the back of the shop. The figure disappeared quickly, and he was left with the distinct impression that his brain was beginning to reject him, and hallucinate.

YIP.

The priest looked down, to see a scruffy dog sitting on the pavement, its lead tethered loosely to a gas pipe. "Hello fella, how are you?" he asked, in that jovial voice that everyone affects whilst speaking to a dog.

YIP. YIP.

"Oh…you're a lady dog, are you?" Father Flynn petted its head, making its tongue loll out of its mouth, ropes of drool abseiling from its slobbery tongue down to the floor. The priest ran a finger under the gingham dog collar. "Of *course* you're a girl, why else would you be wearing this, huh?"

YIP.

Flynn kneeled down. "So, what are you doing out here on your own?"

YIP. YIP. YIP.

"What's that? Your owner left you?"

YIP.

"They went off to score a hundredweight of pure Afghani brown, and left you here as lookout?"

YIP. YIP. YIP.

"Thought so."

YIP.

"Eh? You thought you heard a noise?"

YIP. YIP.

Slobber overload.

"Don't worry, it's nothing, there's no fucker about, you see."

YIP.

"Really? And I'm supposed to trust you?"

YIP. YIP.

The dog cocked its head sideways, the way they do when they've left you a special surprise somewhere in the house, and can't wait for their best friend, *you*, to find it.

"Okay then, if you say so. But I must warn you, Mrs Dog, that if I let you go, and I find out that little Billy really isn't trapped down the bottom of a wishing well, there's going to be hell to pay, okay?"

YIP. YIP. YIP. YIP.

The dog stood up and began to prance on the spot like it was in a dressage competition.

"Fine, let's just untie this…" Flynn fumbled with the lead, his attempt at snatching the looped end thwarted, when, as soon as it could sense that freedom was on offer, the dog YIPPED once more and bolted down the street, back where the priest had just come from. It let out an apologetic bark, before rounding the corner and disappearing from view.

Father Flynn, still kneeling, began to rise slowly to his feet. "Well, that pretty much sums it all up, I can't even make friends with man's best friend." Trying the door once more, and finding that it had been shut up tight, he turned and headed up the road, towards a crossroads.

17

The first row had been crushed, cubed and packaged. The head of the second row had just disrobed and stepped into the cubicle, as the nun operating the controls turned a knob and flicked some switches. There were clicks from within the Zinnki, and a large circular blade began to build up speed at the top of the machine.

Lee-Anne looked on. The door closed, and the nun pressed the button. In the blink of an eye, the blade shot down through the woman who was standing there. Thick chunks of meat and bone flew up inside the processor, before landing in a higgledy-piggledy heap at the bottom. The blade idled at the top, before revving up and descending once more, chewing through the pile of flesh and offal beneath it. "How thick do you want it, Mother Superior?" The nun shouted over the din, keeping an eye on the consistency within the machine.

"Chunky, the same as we did on Ulopa Prime, I want to be able to spread it over some of the crackers they have here. Mmmm, simply divine!" Francesca replied.

Nodding excitedly, the nun turned a dial, which made the jagged metal disc spin faster and the teeth curl inwards. "Blessed Mother, I will make it so." She sent the blade down twice more. By the end of the second pass, the contents were barely recognisable as meat, more like a thick lumpy paste. Pressing another button, a tube lowered into the mulch, as the slowly-turning blade was raised to the roof. The giant straw sunk into the slop and began to pulse.

There was a sound like someone working to get the dregs out of a thick strawberry milkshake, before another PING signalled the end, the tube retracting back into the ceiling.

The operator nun opened a small panel on the side of the Zinnki, retrieved a large jar, and passed it to the Mother

Superior. There was an awed hush from the not-so-holy women, as Francesca carefully removed the lid and dunked a breadstick into the meat chutney.

The mouth on her chest opened slowly, as if reluctant to have a taste. Dropping the breadstick into the maw, the woman's face grinned. "Oh, my, this is delightful, perfect texture, the right mix of chewy meat and sweet juices. I commend you, Sister Tracey, please continue. Ophelia, you deal with the packing, it looks like we should get a good ten to twelve jars from each of the animals."

There was a round of polite applause from the gathered nuns, before they went back about their business. The next person in line stepped forward, and awaited their inevitable demise.

Lee-Anne looked down at her daughter, who, like the others, stood watching the entire thing, unable to run or scream. She wished she could reach out and comfort her, let her know that she wasn't alone, that it was her okay, mummy was here.

As the man took his clothes off and discarded them on top of the growing pile, she heard a scratching sound that was awfully familiar.

What the hell was it?

Just as her brain found the missing file, and played it - dog's claws scrabbling around on plastic lino as it bolted around the kitchen - she heard an unmistakeable sound.

YIP.

Though it hurt her eyes to look straight down, she could make out Pom's enthusiastic tail wagging away. The dog sat on its haunches and looked from Lee-Anne to Lily, letting out a low yowl. Lee-Anne tried to make her eyes as wide as possible, and as Pom looked up at her, she rolled her eyeballs from herself to Lily and back again. Pom cocked her head, and let out a big yawn.

"What's that noise?" Francesca called out. The nuns not involved with the various menial tasks assigned to them, scanned the area.

Pom stood up; the humans were being weird, unwilling to play with her. She was just about to find a patch of wall to sniff when something caught her attention. On the small human, she could see something strange, which had a peculiar smell.

Standing on her back legs, she placed her front paws on Lily's shoulders, and began to sniff the stem that was protruding from her neck. It smelt odd, yet familiar. Pom nudged it with her nose, seeing if it would move, but it stayed fast.

"There it is, one of those blasted bork doggos," Francesca shouted. "Ladies, go and deal with it immediately." Two nuns who had been trying to remove some of the scorch marks from the side of the coach put down their chamois leathers, and began to walk towards the amassed humans.

Pom's nose twitched. The thing, whatever it was, moved only in time with her prodding. Then it hit her. She knew what it was. Sure, it was smaller than the other ones, but it looked the same. It must be a new game the humans were playing. Normally they'd pick up a stick from the park and throw it as far as they could, pretending they didn't want it, but they did, because as soon as she brought it back, they lavished her with praise. Oh, this was going to be a good game. They had managed to grow sticks out of their own flesh! This would save so much time.

Sinking her teeth into the stem, Pom gently pulled. It resisted at first, but then it popped out of the small human's neck. As soon as it was out, the little girl fell to the floor, before standing up slowly, and rubbing the circular mark on her neck, a small dribble of blood trickling down her neck. Pom dropped the stick to the floor and began to yap, stamping her feet on the ground. "GO ON LITTLE HUMAN. PICK UP THE STICK. THROW IT FOR ME. I'LL GET IT AND RETURN IT TO YOU, OH LAZY AND CARELESS ONE. THEN, I CAN PUT IT BACK IN YOUR NECK AGAIN. BEST. DAY. EVER."

Lee-Anne heard Pom bark.

YIP YIP YIP YIP.

I wonder what she's saying?

Lily picked herself up slowly, and patted Pom, before looking up at her mum. "Mummy," she shouted. Using her mother like a climbing frame, she shimmied up and held onto the back of her head. She wrapped her little hand around the stem sticking out of her mum's neck and pulled it out, blood jetting over the dinner lady standing next to her. Lee-Anne sank to the floor.

"Get them, get them quickly. The little one will make a fine delicate pâté," Francesca screamed.

Lee-Anne's legs felt funny, but they were hers once more to command. She dabbed her neck, glad that she wasn't bleeding profusely, grabbed hold of Lily's hand, and spun on the spot, looking for an exit. The loading bay doors were ajar, and although Lily was sluggish to move, she did so, the pair beginning to stagger towards freedom.

One of the nuns peeled off, pushing her way through the neatly-ordered lines, and made a beeline for the two escapees. The other crouched down and plodded towards the still borking doggo.

Lee-Anne turned back, seeing that Pom was still sat on her back legs, waiting for something. "Come on, Pom." The pair began to whistle and verbally encourage the dog into moving. Both nuns were gaining on their respective targets.

Pom couldn't understand what was happening, what kind of bullshit game was this? She had pulled the stick out of the little human, and what had she done? Got the other stick, and not even picked up the one she'd dropped at her feet.

Ungrateful sods.

Then she looked at the little human's hand: hang on, she's still got that stick. That one was in the big human, the one that fed it. "OF COURSE. THAT STICK MUST BE THE BEST ONE. I'M GOING TO BE THE BEST DOGGO EVER. I'LL GET THE STICK, HUMAN."

YIP YIP YIP YIP.

Crouching nun, hidden behind a dragon-print jumpsuit leg pounced, and as she soared through the air, the doggo borked and ran off after the humans. The woman landed heavily on the floor, feeling one of the teeth in her chest chip. She pounded the floor as the doggo, resident to a number of planets in the solar system, bounded after the escapees.

Lee-Anne rounded the corner as fast as she could, still half-dragging Lily, whose little legs were struggling to keep up with the pace. Pom yipped away, and cantered by their sides. From behind them, the sound of shoe leather slapped against tarmac. Lee-Anne dared to look, and saw a nun bolting after them, head down, the tails of her habit flapping behind her. The mouth on her chest was open, its teeth glistening.

Up ahead, across the road, Lee-Anne saw an open shop, selling greetings cards by the looks of it. If she could make it, perhaps she could barricade herself in there. She had to buy some time, get her phone out, call the cops, get someone to rescue them and stop these homicidal nuns.

As the trio ran across the road, Lee-Anne heard the sound of a car gunning down the street. Jumping onto the kerb, the sound of stomping feet behind them had grown louder. At any moment, Lee-Anne expected to be tackled to the ground, and no doubt carted off back to the loading bay to be turned into some kind of meat-based foodstuff.

There was a screech of tyres as Lee-Anne reached the door of the card shop. She looked back to see the nun flying through the air, limbs flailing around as if she were a faulty Catherine wheel that had come loose from a tree trunk. Unable to look away, she watched as the nun landed on the asphalt on the other side of the crossroad. There was a sickening crunch, as bones shattered and punctured flesh and fabric. A squeaking sound followed, as her face took the brunt of the impact, and skidded down the tarmac, her skin and bone sanded by the road.

Then silence.

Short-lived silence, as it was interrupted by a man's voice shrieking. "Oh shit. Oh shit. OH FUCKITY SHITBALLS."

Lee-Anne saw that the car driver had brought his vehicle to a halt, and was standing on the street, head in his hands.

"Come on, let's see if he can help us," she said to Lily. The car was mostly yellow, though whether that was through intention or neglect, she could not discern. One of the doors was black, with the name of a minicab firm stencilled onto the panel.

Checking that there were no other cars using the road as a speedway, Lee-Anne looked left and right, before jogging across to the car, now stopped on the middle of the crossroads. "Oh shit, it's one of them, I told him, didn't I? That bloody priest. Told him there were more. Guess who was right? Yeah, that's right. Me. Thought you could come back here did you? Finish off what you started, huh?" The pair slowed down as they approached the man and the prostrate nun. The minicab driver, dressed in a black suit, with matching tie and a white shirt, took a few steps back, before taking a running kick at the nun. His boot connected with her padded buttocks, and her body bucked with the impact.

"They all thought I was mad when I told them what I saw, but it was all true, wasn't I? Well, don't you worry, missy, I've come prepared. I've been waiting. Old Ian has got a little something for you," the man who had administered the verbal dressing-down, leaned over the body, hoiked up a phlegmy ball of spit, and gobbed it onto the woman's back. Spinning on his heels, he pushed past Lee-Anne and Lily and headed back to his car.

"Stay here, Lily, okay? Keep hold of Pom, and do *not* go anywhere near that lady, you hear me?" Lee-Anne glared at her daughter, who nodded sullenly, sat down by the front wheel of the car, and hugged Pom, who didn't look best pleased at not having its stick to play with.

Lee-Anne stepped over a long streak of green goo smeared on the street, from where the nun had smacked into the road and skidded to her current position. It looked like someone had tried to spread mouldy butter over the road with a large knife. She shoved her hand into her back pocket and pulled out her phone. Checking it had life, she dialled 999.

The man pushed his way past her once more, holding something in his hand. Lee-Anne couldn't get a good glimpse, but the circular bottom glistened in the sunlight.

"Operator, which emergency service do you require?"

"Erm, police, I think, this nun, she tried to attack me and my daughter, though I think we'll need an ambulance too, she's quite badly-"

"A nun?"

"Yeah, she tried to-"

"Hold on please, connecting you now."

The line cut off, the woman's voice replaced by an old-fashioned dialling tone, and it rang and rang. Lee-Anne watched on as the man stood over the nun's body, cursing intermittently, one hand was shaking furiously. Lee-Anne saw that he was holding a spray can. After another bout of swearing, the driver grabbed hold of the nun's broken body, its limbs splayed at angles only seen on video games gone wrong. The man began to laugh, screaming. "I knew it was you, I knew it was you. Have some of this, you bastard."

The driver's feet straddled the nun's waist, as he bent over and began to spray the woman all over with the can. As the muffled phone ringing continued, Lee-Anne walked towards the odd scene, drawn to it like a mosquito to new arrivals on a tropical island. The man yelled. "SHIT, I knew I should've got the King size," and hurled the empty can down the street. "Don't you worry, you won't be able to eat anyone now, I've got a spare can in the car, you just wait there." Lee-Anne ducked to avoid being clattered.

She looked down at the body and put her hand over her mouth to try and hold on to the scream that had built up inside of her skull. The nun's face had been scoured away, and no vestige of humanity remained. Instead, there was the face of a bug. Two large round red eyes, formed from what looked like hundreds of smaller eyeballs, stared upwards at the clouds. A small pair of antennae twitched languidly just above them, in the middle of its face. Where its nose had been, a small snout snuffled the air, contracting and feebly coughing out a small cloud of green gas.

The dialling tone clicked twice, before a man's voice

demanded. "Hello, where are you calling from?"

"I…erm…"

"Where are you? What's your name?"

The driver pushed past Lee-Anne again, tutting at her. "No point phoning anyone, love, no one can help you, no one but me."

On the other end of the phone, Lee-Anne could hear a distant conversation, before the man's voice came back on again. "We have your location, stay where you are. Someone will be with you presently." The phone went dead.

The man shook another can and shoved the nozzle into the open snout nostril. With one foot on the nun's chest, he pressed the top of the spray can; the hissing sound was amplified through the thing's head. Lee-Anne turned her screen off and shoved the phone back in her pocket. "What the hell is that?"

"It's a bloody bastard, that's what it is, but I've got it this time. It won't eat any more of my mates, oh no," the man replied. The hissing sound stopped, Ian shook the can, and sprayed the remnants into the snout.

"What are you doing to it? What is that stuff?"

The driver tossed the can across, and bent down, grabbing hold of the nun's ankles. Lee-Anne read the label aloud. "Bug-Hunt, kills all known insects dead, 'If we can't kill it, then we suggest you take off and nuke the entire site from orbit. It'll be the only way to be sure'. Industrial strength. Warning, possibly hazardous to aquatic life."

The driver looked at the woman, as if they shared a hidden secret. Her face betraying that she knew nothing, he nodded towards the nun's body. "Come on then, love, don't just stand there, give us a hand."

"What? I don't understand what's going on, who are you? Who is she…it…whatever? Why are you shoving a can of bug spray into that nun's…I mean…*thing's* face? I'm very confused."

"Look, love, I'm Ian, and this *thing* is no nun. I met one of their kind once before, you see. I would gladly tell you the whole story, but it's a little longwinded, and to be perfectly honest, I'd be a lot happier if we got off the streets right now. So, be a doll, and grab her top half, will you?"

Lee-Anne followed the command and lifted the torso up. The head lolled back, its antennae brushing against her hand, causing her to shudder. Between them, they carried the lifeless body to the back of the car. With one knee propping up the body, Ian fumbled with a length of cord wrapped round the back of the chassis, eventually managing to open the boot. "Here we go, chuck her in. I'll give you two a lift wherever you want, okay? Free of charge."

Nodding, Lee-Anne pushed the boot open with her shoulder. As she went to swing her half in, she stopped. "Why is there a dead priest in there already?"

18

"Slow down, my lovely. Tell me what happened, Sister Tiffany." Francesca laid a comforting hand on the nun's forearm, which pitched in time with her sobbing.

Tiffany placed both hands on her head, and squeezed, making sure that the covering was lined up correctly. "After I tried to snatch the doggo, I got up and ran after the cattle. Sister Steffi was quite far away, but she was catching them, all she needed was a little bit more time and she would've…would've…" Tiffany sunk again into the Mother Superior's arms.

"There, there, it's okay, but Sister, you need to tell me what happened. We need to know."

Extracting herself from Francesca's bosom, Tiffany nodded. "Of course. So, the woman meatsack and the little one had just crossed the travel lane. By now, Steffi was in close pursuit, when this yellow and black conveyance came out of nowhere and hit her, head on."

The gathered nuns oohed and ahhed, some crossed themselves, others nibbled on small arm bones, freshly pulled from the still-standing humans. Francesca looked at the group and shook her head slowly. "Then what happened?"

"Steffi, she just…she didn't stand a chance. She hit the transport lane and slid across the surface, I came to a halt, and hid behind one of the metal light givers. I could see from where I was, that she was still alive, barely, but her human mask had been shredded, I could see her lovely little snufflecone, as it sucked and slurped her own blood up from the floor. Then, the driver of the conveyance got out, he was…he was wearing a black suit-"

The nuns, Francesca included, gasped.

"-white shirt-"

The gasping increased tenfold, some of the nuns fanning each other with dismembered hands.

"-and a thin black tie. He was wearing a pair of dark eyes, the ones with the little metal arms that rest on their disgusting bony aural receptors," Tiffany finished, beginning to sob again, the middle of her face sucking itself in so that it formed a rubbery shallow cave.

The loading bay was awash with theory and accusation, as nuns looked at each other, pointing, shouting. Francesca patted Tiffany on the back, and held up a hand for silence. "Ladies, quiet, we do not know that it was one of *them*."

Ophelia blurted out. "What else could he be? He must be one of the Men in Black."

This made the rest of the nuns cross themselves again, waving their hands and starting to tell each other stories, the ones they had heard since they were mere pupae in their cocoons. "SILENCE," Francesca's voice boomed around the enclosed space.

"We do not know for certain that this…*thing* was one of the Men in Black. Pray tell, Tiffany, what did it do after that?"

Tiffany shook her head. "It was terrible, the Man in Black…human stormed over to her, said something, I couldn't hear what, turned her over and…sprayed her with…the Poison Gas of Disintegration."

There was much shrieking, nun looked to nun, muttering, cursing, some even suggested that they should leave now while they had a chance. Francesca held her hands up once more. "Quiet down ladies, quiet down. Whilst it is terrible what that beast did to Sister Steffi, our little expedition remains unchanged. We have a job to do, a quota to meet, whether it is an MiB or not, it makes no difference, we have to continue the harvest."

Francesca walked up to the nearest human, a portly man dressed in jeans pulled up to his nipples, and a t-shirt drenched in sweat. "Look, the crop is the best we've had for years. We have big juicy ones, filled with fat, perfect for the budget markets." In a hand, she grabbed hold of a roll of stomach fat, squeezing it with her fingers. "Mmmm, not to my taste, but we could salt the obese one's skin, roast it and peel it off. There are whole hives of Ritchi on Klathu who would salivate through their many armpits for some human crackling."

She skipped down the row to a woman dressed in running gear. "Look here, we have ones that are positively corn fed, and not just that, they're lean, they've been taking care of themselves, imagine what the lucrative Ursa Minor sector would make of these, huh? We've been trying to break into their exclusive range for decades, and now we have an abundance of choice. If I were so inclined, this would be a time for song, for dancing, for merriment."

Some of the nuns, the younger ones, began to clap excitedly, Francesca fixed them a steely stare. "But I'm not." They tutted in disappointment.

Francesca squeezed, slapped, and pinched some more of the product as she made her way back to her sisters. "We stay on course, we finish up here, head to the base and send the samples back tonight. We cannot afford to keep the tasters waiting, else we will lose our credibility."

Ophelia coughed. "Mother Superior, do we not have to meet the worm first?"

"Yes, we do, the wretched creature will be waiting at a transport hub, not far from here. I hope they have some actionable information for us on possible settlements. The last one was positively useless. Though I did enjoy peeling him from head to toe."

"How will we recognise him?" Ophelia asked.

"He will be dressed in the usual way, but make sure you verify it by scent, we don't want any mistakes. He should also have an offering for us, something to tide us over on the journey. I'll let you decide what to do with him."

"I'm going to turn him into a honey-glazed meat popsicle," Ophelia said, licking her lips, while the other nuns clapped.

"Good, now get back to work, I want this lot of cattle butchered and packaged within the next half dimpling, time is of the essence," Francesca bowed shallowly, as the nuns peeled off and resumed their work.

"Oh, Sister Tiffany, can I have a word, please?" Francesca called out. As the nun got near, the Mother Superior put an arm around the woman, pulling her in close, walking them over to a dumpster.

Looking over her shoulder, Francesca moved the pair behind the metal bin. "Excellent, Sister Tiffany, I think we're alone now." She cast another glimpse behind them. "No, there isn't anyone else around. So, we have a small matter to discuss, do we not?"

Tiffany sagged in Francesca's arms. "Sorry, Mother Superior, it all happened so fast, I just froze...I..."

"Shhh, it's okay, my lovely, though you know the rules of engagement, it quite clearly states-"

"That no sister gets left behind, I know, your Grace. I'm sorry, I should've acted sooner."

Francesca's head flipped backwards, her chest mouth ravenous. Before Tiffany could react, the Mother Superior jumped in the air and snapped the upper jaw over the nun's head. There was a crunch as the teeth bit through the body with ease. Tipping backwards, Francesca shook the nun down into her gullet, Tiffany's lower arms hanging by slithers of skin. The vigorous shaking tore them off, and they landed on the floor. Sister Ophelia was on them like a flash, shoving the still-wriggling appendages into her eager maw.

Francesca grabbed hold of Tiffany's ankles, and pulled, tearing the legs off at the knee. She passed the legs to Ophelia whose eyes lit up with glee, gladly shoving the offerings into her mouth and crunching down on them. She rummaged around inside and pulled out a small bone, which had become lodged in her teeth.

Mother Superior's forked tongue licked the sticky green blood from her fingers. "Apology accepted, my lovely."

19

Father Flynn had wound his way through the hushed lanes of rural Knighton, the bus stop signs offering a series of metal-topped breadcrumbs to the last stop out of town. Behind him was a council estate, bustling with the sounds of kids playing football, skateboards grinding down handrails, and car alarms going off as unattended wallets and handbags were liberated.

The final bus stop was a curved shelter. A red metal frame held thick plastic sheets in place, their surfaces scored with compasses, knives and anything else the local populace could find to deface and mark their territory with. Through the yellowing plastic, Flynn rolled his eyes; there was another person waiting. One of the sole reasons for this trek was to sweat out the booze from the night before, see a bit of the town, and get to the last stop in the hope it would be deserted and social interaction would be avoided.

The closer he got, the stranger the view became. There was definitely someone in the shelter, but they weren't standing, and judging from the angle they were positioned at, they weren't in the sitting position either. Whatever it was they were doing, they were rocking back and forth rhythmically.

"What the fuck are you doing?" Flynn asked.

The man's head whipped round, causing him to wince and rub his neck. He looked from the priest to the bench in front of him, then back to the man. "Erm, it's not what it looks like."

"You've got your dick in a length of metal tubing. Tell me exactly, what it is you *are* doing, if you're not having sex with a bus stop bench?"

Extricating himself, carefully, from the hole, the man bent over as he tucked everything back inside his underpants. After a few awkward moments where he experienced difficulties with zipping his trousers back up, he smoothed his clothes down, and turned to face the priest. With his hand outstretched, he said. "Apologies, I've got a bit of a problem. Oops, hang on." The man reached up and retrieved a small digital video camera from the shelter stanchion. "It's for my website," he offered, as he waved the camera around, before shutting it down.

"Can we start again?" The man asked.

"If it consists of me on camera detail whilst you fuck a road sign, I'd rather not."

Laughing nervously, the man flicked his ponytail back behind his head. "I'm David Owain Hughes, but you might know me by another name?" The man began to wink, managing to look creepier than Jeffrey Dahmer wearing one of his human head hats.

Flynn took a step back, and took the man in, seeing if a spark of recognition would be willed to life. The man's face looked as if it belonged to a giant baby, but pony tail aside, the beard managed to remove any hint of cherubic innocence. After a few seconds, the priest shook his head. "Nope, not a Scooby Doo."

The man deflated.

"Hang on…"

"Yes, you remember me now?"

"Were you on Crimewatch last month? The Valleys Flasher? I thought they caught him? You. Whatever."

David shook his head. "No, that's my brother, Barry. He's on the run now, though, managed to escape from custody. Police say he's a menace to society."

"I couldn't for the life of me think why," Flynn muttered.

"Huh? No matter. No, you may recognise me from my series of videos on the internet."

"I'm going to regret discovering any of this information, aren't I?"

Oblivious, the man pulled a comb out of his pocket, unfurled his pony tail and began to groom himself in an attempt to look more normal. "I'm better known as Phil. Phil de Hole, online celebrity, and dark-net superstar."

"Dear god…Phil de Hole? You actually sat down and came up with that name?"

David nodded. "Oh yes. It fits perfectly, pardon the pun, for what I do."

"And that is? Again, please bear in mind that my enquiry is more to try and kill time ahead of the bus turning up, and on the off chance that you're a serial killer, who will murder me violently if I don't play along."

Ignoring the priest completely, David continued. "I've always been interested in it, ever since I was young. My mam used to tell me off all the time, 'Stop putting it in places it doesn't belong, our David', if only she could see me now."

"Fucking bus stops? Yeah, I'm sure she'd be deliriously happy with maternal joy."

"Anyway, a few years back, I thought --why not turn it from a hobby into a job? So I did. I bought my first camera, and made my first video. You see, if I can stick my dick in it, I will. You name it, I've porked it. Park benches, lamp posts, had to climb to the top and take the sensor off, that was a bit dicey, where do you put the camera?"

Realising the question wasn't rhetorical, as David was glaring at him with dewy eyes full of nostalgia, Flynn said. "I don't know, coerce a crow? You got me, how?"

"Head camera. I got a headband, and tied it to it, years before Go-Pro did, should've patented it really, but I've been busy."

"Yeah, screwing any static object with a diameter big enough for you to stick your fetid wang into."

"You should see how many hits I get nowadays. Started off small, only a handful of views, but then more and more people were subscribing. I was getting suggestions from all over the world. Uzbekistan. Holland. Papua New Guinea. Eritrea…"

Flynn patted himself down, retrieved his cigarettes and sparked one up. Albie poked his head out of his home, and chirruped. "That's right," said Flynn, "though if I were you, I'd stay hidden. Chances are that if he sees you, he's likely to offer to turn you into an internet star." The axolotl's eyes flared wide, before he turned and burrowed back inside his bushy home.

"…Somalia, North Korea. All over, really. So I thought I'd better come up with a name, you know? I thought about what I was doing and that's when it hit me! I fill a hole. Phil de Hole, you get it?"

Blowing smoke into David's face, in the hope it would make him leave, Flynn replied. "Yes, that's great, post-modern. Or something."

David stroked the shelter. "We've been through some rare old times, this bus stop and me. Starred in my first video as Phil. HA! That nearly ended in disaster. I snagged a bollock on a little lump of metal. One sudden movement and I would've become half a eunuch."

"What a shame that would've been."

"Exactly! I came back and filed it down a few days after. Since then, my man sausage slides in and out like a dream. The things this bus stop has seen…" David looked at it, wistfully.

"For fuck sake, it's a bus stop, with an inordinate amount of human semen having coalesced within its frame. It is incapable of retaining any of these so-called moments you think you've shared with it. Tell me one thing, Phil…David, have you ever had sex with a real woman?"

David sniggered like a child discovering a rude word. "Err yeah, of course I have. It's not the same, though."

"Why's that?"

"Well, my tastes are pretty specific. You of all people will think I'm a little freaky."

Coughing out a lungful of smoke, Flynn said. "You fuck inanimate objects, so trust me, I think you've got the weird angle covered. Go on, tell me."

David moved in closer, looking around. "I asked my last girlfriend if she would…you know…dress up for me."

"Oh sweet Jesus, you didn't ask her to dress up as a kiddie's climbing frame, did you?"

"Of course not, that's just sick. No, I asked her to dress up as a…this is weird…a nun."

Flynn shuddered. "A nun? If I were you, I'd stick to plunging your man meat into exhaust pipes, it's safer."

David smiled; his mouth was all teeth amongst his beard. "That's why I'm here. You know, in the hope they see me."

The penny dropped. "Of course, the nunnery up at Saint Judas. So, you think if they see you giving this bus stop a good seeing to, one of them will fall in love with you?"

Beaming with pride, David nodded. "Yep, it worked on Madonna, didn't it?"

Flynn dropped his smouldering cigarette butt on the floor and crushed it with the heel of his boot. "You have a twisted sense of logic, my friend, but best of luck to you. Ah, here we go."

The sound of a large engine working its way up the street broke the peace and quiet. An orange coach, with what looked like burn marks down its flanks rumbled up the road Father Flynn stuck his hand out.

"It's no good, they never stop," David said, kicking the ground.

Flynn tugged at his white collar. "I think you'll find I have the right ticket for this particular little trip."

Indicating, the coach growled to a halt in front of the two men. The doors hissed and opened up. A stern nun made her way down the steps, coming to a halt in front of Father Flynn. Leaning in, she began to sniff him up and down, like a dog giving another dog the once over. She paused by his chest, breathing in deeply. "Fine, on you get, worm." She thumbed to the open doors, then moved onto David, who was standing by the metal pole, picking out dirt from under his fingernails.

"Worm? That's a bit rich coming from a glorified penguin."

The nun glared, her eyes boring right through him.

"Christ on a bendy bus. Fine, but if you are going to insist on the *worm* thing, I'd prefer Mister Worm, or Sir Worm, adds a degree of gravitas."

"Are you going to get onto the bus, *worm*, or am I going to have to pull your so-called arms out of their sockets and beat you to death with them?"

"Wow…your people skills are second to none. I'll concede this round, but only because if I don't get to Saint Judas' soon, I'm in danger of being shipped back where I came from." Flynn took a step onto the coach, looking down the aisle at row-after-row of nuns, all of them looking at him as if he was something unpleasant they had trodden in.

"Worm, is this what you have brought us as an offering?" The nun asked, pointing at David, whose face had gone bright red.

Flynn turned back. "Erm…yes? Do you like him?"

The nun circled David, poking and prodding him as she went. She reached the front again, opened his mouth, and ran a finger around the inside of his cheek. "Hmm…it's not the best, but he should do, the journey is not far. Next time, worm, find one with less hair, you know it gets everywhere."

Completely puzzled, Flynn said. "Okay…"

"On you get," the nun said to David, patting his backside, and giving a thumbs-up to Sister Alicia, who loved nothing more than a good bit of rump.

Rare.

David's face lit up. "Oh, wow, thank you, thank you. You don't know what it means to me."

"Get on the coach, be quiet, and we'll make it quick," the nun answered.

"Oh, don't you worry, the one thing I guarantee you, is that it won't take very long." David grabbed hold of his crotch and swung from pole-to-pole down the aisle, until he plonked himself next to Father Flynn.

The priest was looking out of the window, the unkempt hedgerow whizzing by as the coach picked up speed. Verdant fields laden with crops were laid out as far as the eye could see.

With a bony elbow in the ribs, the peace and tranquillity was interrupted. Flynn turned slowly. "What?"

David's face was still plastered with his goofy smile, a single tear of joy tracking down his cheek. "I just want to say thank you, for getting me on here. This is amazing. Just look at them. They all seem really friendly. That one over there said she's looking forward to tasting me down the back of her throat. Kinky, eh?"

"Whatever, look --I'm going to try and have a quick power nap, the hangover is starting to kick in, and between these charming ladies-" Flynn glanced at the nun in the chair behind hissing at him, "-and you, I think I'm going to get my head down for forty winks."

The stern nun appeared by the two men. "It's time."

Flynn opened an eye and regarded the woman. "What for?"

"Not you, *worm*, it's time for him, the offering. Come with me." The nun whistled and there was a commotion at the back of the coach.

David pivoted on his bum cheeks, so his legs were in the aisle. "The offering, eh? That sounds kinda sexy. What is it time *for*? Are you keen to get your teeth into me?"

"We are, but we want to make something worthwhile of you first."

"My mam would be so pleased. She's always wanted me to become something dead tasty, you know?"

The nun pointed to a large metal and glass device at the back of the vehicle. Its doors were open invitingly, and one of the other woman was fiddling with a control panel. "We will make you into something *tasty,* just go to the back, Sister Fanny will look after you."

Sniggering, David elbowed Father Flynn once more, who balled his fist and shook it at the man. "Hey, Father, she'll 'look after me' huh? Eh? Eh? I bet she will. Bit of hanky-panky in the on-board toilet, eh? Don't mind if I do. Come to think of it, I don't think I've done it in a toilet before. Well, not with anyone else anyway. More of a Han-d Solo moment, you know what I mean?"

The gruff Sister grabbed hold of the scruff of his jacket. "I said *come on*, we don't have all day."

"You're right, we best crack on with it, Sister, there's an awful lot of you to get through." David rubbed his sweaty palms on his trousers, "wish me luck, Father."

Flynn waved the man off, and closed his eyes. "Whatever

you think is about to happen, won't. One thing I guarantee you, underestimate nuns at your peril. If I've learned one thing from my time around these harpies, it's that the instant you let your guard down, they'll make mincemeat of you."

20

As the coach banked round a sharp corner, Father Flynn was flung forwards into the metal bar of the chair in front of him. He scratched his head and rubbed his eyes. "Where am I?" Out of the window, he saw that they were passing between a pair of large sandstone columns. Half a metal gate went past, the bars painted black with corkscrew metal tips.

There was a crackling sound as the tyres crunched over the pea gravel. Winding round another bend, the priest managed to get his first look at St Judas that wasn't from a glossy brochure. It looked imposing, aloof, and musty. The gravel track snaked through an immaculately maintained lawn, where a pair of old nuns were uprooting rogue weeds. They held their backs as they stood, trying to stretch out their advancing years and ruing the unnecessary workload placed upon them.

The main building looked like a country house from a posh television show, where the house staff would line up at the bottom of the stone steps as the Lord and Lady returned from spelunking in the Mongolian steppes. Roman columns ran from ground to roof, free of moss and lichen, the groundskeeper a blatant pedant. The main house spawned two wings, one storey shorter than the main building, but no less imposing. Each had a pair of French doors opening to the front, and a number of wrought iron tables and chairs sat on stone patios. A nun reclined on one, hacking away at her calloused heels with a potato peeler.

Up a hill, and set away from the house, was another large building. At first glance, it looked like an observatory. It had rounded walls, which ended in a large dome at the top. Whilst similar in construction - the stone was at least the same colour - it was evident that it had been constructed far more recently. The masonry had a glossy sheen, like someone whose skin had been pulled too taut after cosmetic surgery. Whilst the craftsmanship was undoubtedly top notch, it was noticeably more modern. With its distance from the primary property, it looked like the main austere building had disowned it, like an orphaned child, shunned and stashed in a coal scuttle, ready for collection and reassignment.

There was another gut-churning lurch as the coach tilted round the next corner, stealing the view of the houses away. Flynn switched sights to the other side of the coach, but was met by more baleful stares from the nuns.

Two things then struck him; the first was a delicious smell, the second that their chests were rippling. "What is that?" He asked aloud. The nun's mouths were closed, but their bodies moved as though they were chewing on something.

Then it hit him: it was pastry, baked to perfection, mixed with something else, meat, bathed in a rich gravy. The smell made his salivary glands go into overdrive; he realised he was drooling as an annoyed chirp sounded from his facial hair. He felt Albie tug at some of the shorter hairs, making him itch.

The pair of nuns behind Flynn were dusting their hands clean. Crumbs flecked their habits, which undulated like the aftermath of the wave machine at the local pool. The motion was an odd one –it was as if their entire chests were pulsing. At one point, he thought he saw the edge of one of their habits curl up. One of the nuns, a younger woman, with a strand of blonde hair hanging from the top of her habit, looked back at him, daring a smile.

"Hi there, what's your name?" Flynn asked, holding out a hand.

"I'm Erica," the nun replied. She looked at the priest's hand and started to move hers. There was a slap, as the nun next to her interjected, knocking Flynn's hand aside. She fixed Erica a stern gaze. "Do not mingle with the worm, Sister, is that clear?"

Erica clasped her hands, and looked down into her lap, nodding gently. "Yes, Sister, I'm sorry."

"You will be," she switched attention to the priest, "as for you, eyes forward, *worm*."

As he went to turn away, Flynn saw the Mother Superior who had given him such a warm welcome making her way down the aisle. "Excuse me, what was that pie? It smells divine."

Francesca brushed past him. "Minced meat pie, I suppose we have you to thank for the idea."

"Eh?"

The woman stopped at the row ahead and turned slowly around, the entrance to the house appearing through the front windscreen. "I trust you have a suitable cover story arranged?"

"Well, yeah, it's not really a cover story, though, it's-"

Francesca held up a hand. "I don't care. When you are ready, signal us as per normal protocol. Someone will be with you presently, so that you can debrief us on the state of play in the wildlands. Make sure that you are alone, and go with her immediately, okay? We have a taster shipment to send off later, so it might be prudent to wait until the new day cycle has begun, am I clear?"

Flynn nodded, his brow furrowed in puzzlement. He opened his mouth, but before any words could escape, the coach ground to a halt, and hissed as the brakes kicked in. Francesca placed a hand under Flynn's elbow, leaned towards him and breathed him in before leading him towards the front door. "Just blend in, do what you're supposed to do, and don't give them a reason to be suspicious."

"Suspicious? Of what?"

"Exactly. Now go, you will need to check in with the normal ones." Francesca held her arm out, ushering him outside.

"Normal ones? Fine, whatever, I'll get signed in. Where will you be?"

The Mother Superior pointed to the cylindrical stone house. "Where we always are, at the main sanctum." She looked down the length of her nose at him. "You don't look familiar, how long have you been our guest in servitude?"

Flynn stood on the bottom step and looked back into the

coach; all the nuns were angling to get a good look at him. "For some time, a good ten years or so now, serving the big gaffer up in the sky," he pointed upwards.

Francesca bowed slightly. "Of course, we all serve the GAFFER. Forgive my questioning. We just have to be careful. We encountered a slight problem in the last population centre."

"That place was pretty strange. Dare I ask what the problem was?"

"Nothing we didn't take care of, I'm sure all will be fine. Providing we all work expediently, we should be gone before anyone knows we were even here."

21

"Padraig, is this the place?"

"That it is, Father O'Malley. Yellow car, black door, looked like a minicab, struck the nun at…this junction. With the assistance of a woman, the one who made the emergency call, I'm guessing, they put the body in the boot, then headed off in that direction." Padraig lowered the iBible, which continued to play the grainy CCTV images, and pointed off down Brown Street.

O'Malley walked up to the large green stain, which was drying now, and kneeled down. He dabbed his pinky into the goo and took a sniff. "A hint of metal, definitely organic, but unsure what astral plane it's from. We're going to need to get our hands on that body, Padraig. Let's roll."

As the pair headed back to their car - a converted Popemobile from the 1982 Papal state visit to the UK, and blessed by Pope John Paul II himself - O'Malley took a quick lick of the goo, his face scrunched up as if he had sucked on a lemon. "Are you okay, Father?" Padraig asked, pressing the key fob to unlock the doors with a BEEP-BEEP.

"I am, kind Padraig. That goo has got a bit of a kick to it."

Padraig swung open the driver's door, went to go in, and stopped. "Was it wholly necessary to have a taste?"

O'Malley's cheeks flushed. "I…erm…get onto HQ, Padraig, we need to locate that car. Get the asynchronous satellite up, I want real time data, stat." The priest ducked under the door frame and sat down, his face still gurning and twitching.

"Yes, sir." Padraig got in, slammed the door and set his iBible up on the hands-free docking station. After cycling through a wealth of menu options, he tapped the 'Surveillance' app, and waited as it tried to locate him via GPS. "I hate this bit, you'd think by now that it would be able to find us. I mean --it tells me how long it is to get back home when I'm sat at my workstation. Yet, when I actually need to use it, the little egg timer thing just keeps on going."

Padraig turned to Father O'Malley, who was scraping his tongue with his fingernails, each pass removing another film of frothy grey spit. "Thut up and dwithe."

"Dwithe?"

"Yeth. Be quieth. Dwithe. Thar away."

"Sorry, Father, I don't know what you mean."

O'Malley rolled his eyes, and with his foamy fingers, made the internationally-recognised hand signal for driving.

Padraig nodded. "Yes, Father, of course. Ah, we're up, satellite is in position. Looks like Edgar, back at HQ, has found our hit-and-run, they're not too far from here."

"Then geth going."

Firing the car up, Padraig stifled a chuckle, and began to follow the instructions.

"Turn around when able to," the speaker commanded.

Padraig tapped the iBible. "Damn thing."

"Turn around when able to," the emotionless voice intoned once more.

"I don't need to, you silly thing, I'm already-"

"Turn around when able to."

Padraig fiddled with the phone, the voice set to mute. "Yeah, I don't think we need to hear it, as I say, we're not too far."

Ian turned the key once more, even though, on this, the eighteenth time of doing so, the engine still refused to do anything except cough and splutter like an asthmatic robot. "Nearly got it." His face was a picture of concentration and steadfast determination, his teeth unknowingly chewing on his upper lip.

A pall of smoke had steadily been pouring from the bonnet

since they had left the scene of the hit-and-run. At one point, it had gotten so bad, that Ian had wound the window down and stuck his head through the gap. Every so often, he would spit out a bluebottle or a wasp. As they reached the outskirts of town, the engine had given up the ghost completely, the damage to its internal workings too much for it to bear any longer.

Taking the key out of the ignition, Ian held it up to the light, then blew on it. "Got a good feeling about this attempt, you'll see." He stuck the key back in, jangled the fob with its abundance of pointless totems, then twisted it once more. The engine coughed, growled, then spluttered its last, a loud metallic crunch and clank signalling that something important-sounding inside had shorn off. This was the signal for the smoke-to-clean air ratio to increase significantly. The air vents began to pump the noxious fumes into the cab.

Coughing, Lee-Anne wrenched open the door and pushed Lily out. Pom jumped onto the road and shook herself, before engaging in some hind-leg scratching action. Finally relenting, Ian pushed his door open, got out, and slammed it behind him. Without a hint of sarcasm, he stood by a still coughing Lee-Anne and thumbed to the car behind him. "I think I'll need to get the AA out, sounds like the bearings have gone."

Lee-Anne looked up at him, hands resting on her knees. "Of course…bearings…that's what it is."

Ian nodded knowingly, pulled out a soiled handkerchief, and began to buff up a door panel, trying to remove some of the green blood splashes which adorned the paintwork like infected pustules.

There was a WUMPH, which made them all jump. From the bonnet, in between the ventilation holes, small flags of horizontal flame began to flicker in the air. As it grew in intensity, waves of fire lapped over the windscreen. "Ah, bugger, this car was two payments away from being all mine, that's just marvellous."

Lee-Anne began to edge further away, grabbing hold of her daughter's hand as she did so, who in turn had hold of Pom's lead. Ian reluctantly joined them; the fire at the front of the car had grown so much that the upper tips of its flaming fingers rose above the height of the vehicle. Ian herded them further back, all the while, they maintained their gaze at the growing inferno. "Never turn your back on a fire," Ian mumbled. As if to underline that fact, a jet of flame shot out from the exhaust, like a WW2 flamethrower purging a foxhole of its inhabitants. Though short-lived, the fire and heat caught a pile of cardboard waiting to be picked up. After all, it was recycling bin day for the residents of Baptist Street.

Ian kept on edging backwards, moving his unwitting customers with him, trying to reassure them the best he could. "It's fine, cardboard burns itself out pretty quickly, we'll be fine."

Fate, not content with leaving it be, had other plans.

"Mummy, is it Bonfire night?"

"No, Lily, why do you ask?"

"I can hear sparklers."

Lee-Anne swivelled her head slowly, sure enough, from the small localised fire of the recycling pile, came a hissing sound, as if a firework taper had been lit. There was a bang, as a near-empty can of Panther deodorant combusted from the heat. The three of them watched open mouthed, as the metal can-turned-rocket was launched into the air. Pom began to bark and howl, straining against her lead. Unable to tear their eyes from the sight, the sparkling meteor looped over the houses, like a mortar, the screeching sound slowly fading away to nothingness. Pom settled down. The others still listened intently.

"Look," Ian pointed at the recycling pile, now nothing more than a pile of ash, already being spread across the street by a gentle breeze, "I told you it wouldn't last long."

"Your car, too." Lee-Anne nodded towards the charred giloppy, the fire abated, a thin wisp of black smoke the only sign of the recent conflagration.

"All's well that ends well, I mean, the car's a write-off. Could've done with it burning up the passengers in the boot…if you know what I'm saying, but hey, could be worse?"

There was a distant boom, and the ground shuddered beneath their feet. Car alarms began to go off, adding to the building cacophony. A mushroom cloud of thick black smoke rose slowly above the houses. "Mummy! It looks like a clown's face," Lily shouted, pointing to the blossoming after-effect of destruction looming over the usually quiet town.

"Oops?" Ian offered, before there was another WUMPH, closer to them. The trio looked back to the car, which had combusted once more. A paradoxical wave ran through Ian; part of him wanted the evidence to go up, it would save him a few quid from his original plan of getting Vinnie, the car scrapper, to squash the evidence and send it off to be turned into tin cans. But also, he had just gotten the car to how he liked it. The Magic Tree had removed the weird smell which had plagued it since he had bought it, nearly new, from a dealership down in Newport.

"Freeze, no-one move," a man's voice commanded them from behind, "turn around slowly, no sudden movements, or there'll be…trouble."

Lee-Anne moved first, managing to get Lily and Pom facing the man in one fluid balletic movement. Ian wiped away a tear at his loss, before following suit. Opposite them were two priests, one was holding a German Luger, his slicked-back hair giving him an air of mystery and authority. Behind him was a man clutching a large leather holdall to his chest, as if it contained a deadly secret, or a nest of vipers, the look on his face indicating that he couldn't decide which.

"I'm Father O'Malley, and I'm guessing you're the driver who took out the nun back in town?" Keeping his handgun trained on the suspects, the priest moved in closer.

"Where's your evidence, copper? Priest…man…person, what are you exactly?" Ian asked.

Padraig held up a flattened hedgehog, and with the Popemobile doors left open, moved forward. "Quiet! We followed your trail of murder. And the satellite, in truth, it was *mainly* the satellite, but seriously, there are a lot of dead pets in the streets today, going to be a lot of owners printing off missing posters later."

Lee-Anne stormed forward, stopping the pistol-wielding priest in his tracks. "No there won't, those damn nuns have turned god knows how many into rissoles and kebabs, if it wasn't for his bad driving, they would've got us too."

"They turned my friend Mandy's mum into marmalade," Lily added, helpfully.

O'Malley regained his composure. "Fine, we can sort it out later, first off, where is the body?"

"Which one?" Ian asked. No sooner had the words escaped from his mouth, than he slapped a hand over it, worried he would spill his guts over more hidden secrets.

"What do you mean, 'which one'?" Padraig asked.

Lee-Anne pointed behind her. "They're in the boot, but I'd be quick if I were you, eh?"

The two priests saw the minicab, now well and truly aflame. Shoving his pistol into the back of his belt, O'Malley raced over to the blaze. In one movement, he pulled his cassock off and wrapped it around his hands like a pair of holy oven mitts. "Padraig, are you just going to stand there? Help me, man."

Padraig jogged to O'Malley reluctantly, trying to shield himself from the heat with the holdall. Lee-Anne clutched her daughter's hand, and watched on, as the priests attempted to jimmy open the boot. Ian whistled nonchalantly, and with hands plunged deep in his pockets, edged away from the scene.

"There's bungee cord wrapped around it, do you have your multipurpose dog collar, Padraig?"

Nodding, the equerry pulled the multi-tool from around his neck and handed it to O'Malley. Rifling through the assortment of options, he mentally discarded the corkscrew, nail file and toothpick, settling on the small handsaw blade. Padraig placed the bag on the floor, and with his hands in his sleeves, pulled the cord taut.

O'Malley sawed through it as quickly as he could; the heat was building, sweat running down his temple, soaking into his shirt. "Nearly there…nearly there…" he muttered, "got it." He fell backwards onto his arse as the cord's hold was finally removed, the boot popping open.

Standing in front of it, the two priests nodded at each other, O'Malley said. "On three, one-"

"Wait."

"What?"

"Do we go on three? Or one-two-three and then go?"

"Does it matter? Padraig, this car could go up at any moment."

"Of course it matters, on one we go on three, the other we go on four."

"Fine, the first one."

"On three?"

"Yes."

"Okay."

"One, two…three," the pair lifted the boot up the best they could, and as they opened it, a tidal wave of smoke rolled out from the interior of the car, smothering the priests. Padraig waved frantically, clearing the cloying vapour away. "I'll take the nun, you take the other one." He shoved his hands under the nun's armpits and began to drag her from the boot.

"Other one?" O'Malley looked into the void and saw another pair of legs. Cursing, he grabbed hold of the trouser legs and heaved the body over his shoulder. The two priests turned and started to run away. They managed to get a few feet from the car, before it exploded, the entire vehicle lifting off the road as it went up. A small fireball was ejected into the air; somewhere, scientists monitoring greenhouse gas emissions noticed a spike over the English/Welsh border.

O'Malley lifted his head. The woman and child were lying on the road a little way off, both waving back, gingerly. The priest lifted the dead body's arm from the side of his head and poked Padraig. "You okay?"

"I think so, Father, although my fingers have gone into the nun's guts, it really is rather disgusting. It feels like uncooked black pudding."

Down the road, a horn tooted. Ian, in the driving seat of

the Popemobile, waved into the rear view mirror before turning right into Poacher Lane. There was a startled yelp as an urban fox became his latest victim, before near-silence descended, the only sound being the crackling of fire.

22

"So then what happened?" Father O'Hanrahan asked the question again, tapping his index finger against his lips.

Lee-Anne drummed her fingers against the table. "I don't know how many more times I can reword the same sentence."

O'Hanrahan pushed himself off the metal desk, landing on his feet with a solid slap. "Try me again, sister. How about you keep going until what you're saying makes some kind of sense."

Picking up one of the sandwiches, provided to her through the interrogation, Lee-Anne peeled off the top layer of bread and rooted around the filling. Discarding a sliced tomato, she peeled the slither of corned beef from the bottom, complete with chunks of piccalilli. She waved it under the priest's nose. "See this? This is what those bloody nuns did to those poor people."

He ceased tapping his lips and looked back, puzzled. "They opened up their own sandwich shop?"

"No, they turned them into food."

"Like corned beef?"

"Yes."

O'Hanrahan dipped his finger in the piccalilli, licking the tart sauce off. "And some kind of chutney, you said?"

"Yes, it was disgusting. My daughter had to stand there through it all, she's probably mentally scarred for life now."

"Because the Mother Superior injected some kind of worm into your neck which rendered you, your child, and all the other people unconscious?" O'Hanrahan rolled his eyes. "Why do I always get the nutjobs?"

"Excuse me, how dare you, we've been through-"

"Mummy, look, Pom has brought us another present!" Lily skipped from the corner where she had been playing, and presented her mother with a brown stick.

"Not more poo, is it? What did I tell you about picking stuff up?"

"No, Mummy, it's the stick that the nunnies put into us when they turned everyone into meat paste."

Lee-Anne took the proffered stem from her daughter and waved it under O'Hanrahan's nose. "What's this then?"

"A stick? Looks like the staple chasing tool of the humble domesticated dog, if you ask me."

"It's the thing the chief nun put in our necks, she could control people using it. I'm telling you the truth, why won't you believe me?"

An awkward silence fell. Lily shrugged and went back to play with Pom, who was taking it in turns to sniff each corner of the room, the bolted-down table and chair legs in a clockwise motion. O'Hanrahan gave the stick a sniff. "So, tell me one more time, what happened with the nun?" He turned his attention back to the stem, and was about to take a quick nibble when there was a loud buzz and the door swung into the room.

Father O'Malley entered with a flourish, a thick folder under his arm. He peeled off a thin cloth mask which covered his nose and mouth, and pushed it into his pocket. "Thank you, O'Hanrahan, I'll take it from here." The priest held the door open, with an intense stare that urged his colleague to leave. As he vacated the room, O'Malley snatched the stem from O'Hanrahan's hand "Yoink," and closed the door on him.

"I'm sorry about O'Hanrahan, he's…a little dim." O'Malley placed the folder on the desk, and walked to the corner of the room, where a small camera looked down on proceedings. He ran his hand around the back of the device and pulled out a wire, and the bright red light beneath the lens faded to black. "We won't be needing any Peeping Toms for this little chat of ours, eh?"

Lee-Anne nodded, pulling her hair back and tying it in a ponytail. "How long are we going to be here? This isn't fair, we've done nothing wrong --and from what I can see, you're not the police, so why are you holding us here?"

Reaching into his pocket, which made Lee-Anne flinch, O'Malley pulled out a crimson rosary and lowered it onto the table, the beads clicking and clacking against the polished surface. "I'm an operative within a special branch of the Catholic church. It is our job to deal with the…more unsavoury sides of the world. Exorcisms, wards, seals, fighting demons of all varieties-"

Lee-Anne let out a loud "HA."

"-we investigate supposed miracles, and places of spiritual mystery. I've pushed the very skein of existence, looked through the double-sided mirror of faith, and I can tell you this for nothing…it ain't pretty."

"Unlike your eyes…" the words escaped Lee-Anne's mouth before she had a chance to hold them hostage. She blushed.

Not batting an eyelid, O'Malley continued. "Something went down in that Quantico-Zoom-Mart loading bay. I know that. Do you know why I know that?"

"No, why?"

"Because you said it did, and there are two dead bodies in a minicab driver's boot which are like nothing I've ever seen before, and I've seen things that would make your bones bleed."

"That doesn't sound awfully pleasant."

"It's not…not at all. But still, you have to remember that for every case which ends in me stripped down to my holy vestments, fighting against the forces of evil…"

Lee-Anne rested her head on her hands and murmured.

"…there are cases which are nothing more than hoaxes, some more elaborate than others, but still, they waste our time and resources, and we're spread thin…so thin…" O'Malley looked off enigmatically into the middle distance, and Lee-Anne craned her head, wondering if he'd seen a spider.

When he spoke again, the sound of his voice made her jump. "So you see, we have to make sure that when we speak to someone with an incredulous tale such as yours, that they're telling the truth."

Lee-Anne blinked away the words. "But you have the bodies, don't you? Of the nun, and the priest? Surely you can see that what we told you was the truth?"

O'Malley stood up, and turned his back to the woman, staring into her eyes via the mirrored wall in front of him. "We do, but they were both badly burned. To be honest, we're not sure exactly *what* we've found, other than it's some*thing*. Our forensic department will keep dicing and slicing, whatever it is they do, but I need to get out there, pick up the trail, and get to the bottom of what's happened."

"Look, Father, I can only tell you what I told that idiot. Those nuns, and there were loads of them, a whole coachload of them, they had all those people lined up, where have *they* gone? They've got to be somewhere, haven't they? I know what I saw. That crazy bitch made those poor people take their clothes off-"

"By using a radio-controlled crucifix."

"-and walking them willingly into the Zinnki Food Processor, 2000 series, where they were basted, smashed, minced, jellified, preserved and packaged away. I don't know what else I can say."

O'Malley turned back to Lee-Anne. "Okay, I believe you."

"You do?"

"Yes, but the fact remains, we have nothing to go on. Do you remember the number plate?"

Lee-Anne shook her head.

"Did they say where they were going, where they've been?"

"No. Why don't you go down to the supermarket and search the loading bay?"

O'Malley unwound a length of string which was bound around the folder Opening it up, he picked up some photos and placed them in front of Lee-Anne. "We already have. Nothing there. The place was closed up, sure, there was a shiny tracksuit top sat in the open, and a few funny-looking bones that the scientists are going to look at, but nothing else."

Lee-Anne rifled through the photos. "This can't be, what

about CCTV? There's bound to be a video or something of those damn nuns, you can't take over a supermarket and go unnoticed."

"It stops at eleven thirty-seven. Looks like a localised power cut, which would explain the state of the shop when you went inside looking for the toilet."

"I'm not making this up!" Lee-Anne glared at the priest. "I may be many things, tired since 2012, deprived of tea, but I did not concoct this story. Explain that," she pointed to the stem.

O'Malley twirled the stem in his fingers. "The petri-dish-botherers will have a look at this, don't worry about it." He perched on the edge of the desk. "Hey, it's okay, we'll get to the bottom of this, I'll see to it…personally."

Lee-Anne mustered a weak smile, and looked across to Lily who was trying to plait Pom's hair, and failing. "You've got to, if it wasn't for that taxi driver…it was a miracle we got out of there alive!"

O'Malley cupped her chin and raised it so that they were looking into each other's eyes. "I think you'll find that miracles are my specialty. I'd cross the vast expanse of oceans, wrestle the angriest of bears, wear the stinging nettle onesie of the sensation-stripped Barutu clan, mentally spar with the cleverest of gurus, *anything* to get to the bottom of this little incident. Rest assured, I won't leave a stone unturned in finding out what really happened, you have my word on that, okay?"

Padraig bustled into the room, disturbing the building tension. "Father, I've found something."

O'Malley cast a withering stare at his equerry. "Really? So soon? You don't say. Isn't that just peachy. Come on then, what do you have for us?"

Pulling up a video, Padraig pressed play, showing stop-motion of a battered, scorched coach driving down a quiet road. "Look, sir--" he paused it and enhanced 224 to 176, the image stuttering and clicking, zooming onto the front of the window. He passed the iBible to O'Malley, who held the device out to Lee-Anne. "Nuns."

Lee-Anne gasped. "That was the leader, they all followed

her commands. She told me her name was, Francesca. Mother Superior Francesca."

O'Malley slapped the machine into Padraig's chest. "Where have they been?"

"We're not one hundred percent, but we have a field team at a campsite, a few miles out of town, they've…"

"What is it, man? Tell me."

Padraig tapped on the device, bringing up a slideshow of images of lacerated tents and upturned camping stoves. "They've not found any bodies, Father, but they've found blood…lots and lots of blood. The two might not be linked, but it seems an awfully big coincidence."

O'Malley pulled out a small cylindrical device from his pocket, held down a button and spoke into it, his voice echoing through the tannoy. "Alright, listen up, gentlemen. Our nuns have been on the run for one-hundred-and-eighty minutes. Average coach speed over potholed country lanes, barring damage to tyres, is thirty-three miles-per-hour. That gives us a radius of...", he looked to Padraig.

"Just under fifty miles, Father,"

"…around fifty miles. What I want from each one of you is a hard-target search of every petrol station, campsite, sheep pen, container box, rocky outcrop, garden shed and chapel in that area. Checkpoints go up at fifty miles. Your fugitive's name is Mother Superior Francesca, who is heading up a band of nuns. Go get them."

23

The nun behind the reception desk shushed Flynn before he'd even had a chance to form a word in his throat. She merely pointed to a long wooden bench, which ran along one of the side walls within the lobby. Sitting down, the priest examined the interior. The décor matched the outward appearance: white walls, high ceilings with intricate plasterwork, culminating in giant flower heads which looked down on the people within. Hanging from the centre of the ceiling was a wrought iron candelabra, replete with electric candles.

Flynn squidged his foot on the carpet, the thick ruby pile barely yielding to his cursory examination, springing back into place when he lifted his foot to survey the quality. Oil paintings of miserable priests, in a wide array of colourful and over-the-top garments were displayed prominently on the wall. Small bronze plaques, polished to within a millimetre of their existence were underneath, listing the many high ranking religious folk who had presided over the inhabitants of the building.

Behind the reception desk, the nun tapped away at a keyboard in a particular pattern: a flurry of keystrokes would end abruptly, followed by a loud tutting, and a fingernail hammering away at the backspace key. The air smelled of lavender and bleach. As Flynn struggled to make out the name of a painting of a man with the most dashing of moustaches, the phone rang.

The receptionist-nun cupped a hand over the receiver, and gave Flynn a quick darting look, before tutting once more and hanging up. "Someone will be with you shortly."

"Thank you."

The woman was on her feet, her height the same as when she was seated. She maintained her stare, as if her brain was negotiating a checklist of social interaction; her eyes flickered as she held up a cup and saucer. "Can I get you something to drink? A tea, maybe? Coffee?"

"I'm good, thanks, Sister, unless it's an Irish coffee?" Flynn winked and gave the nun a cheeky grin.

Placing the cup and saucer back on the desk, the nun lowered slightly as she sat down. After what seemed like an age, she exhaled loudly from her nose. "No, I don't have any Irish coffee, just this stuff from Quantico-Mart. Think it's from the slopes of Mount Nicaragua? Sorry." With that, she resumed her cycle of typing, tutting, and furious deletion.

"Worth a try, I guess," Flynn rubbed his sweaty palms against his trouser legs. It felt like a job interview, or at worst, some kind of medical inspection. There was nothing personable about this manor house so far. It seemed to have been designed to keep any visitors at arms-length, behind a façade of austere history and walls packed with paintings of dour men.

There was a loud buzzing, and a door clacked open. To his right, a nun bustled in through the open doorway, a smile etched on her face from ear-to-ear. Flynn hated her already. There was a loud clatter from the reception desk. The nun behind it edged away from the pair, speaking with hushed tones into the telephone, her eyes fixed on the new arrival. After a few seconds, she smacked the receiver down and dived behind the desk, her eyes resurfacing just above the lip of the desk, keeping watch.

"Hi-de-ho, camper, I hope you had a pleasant journey here today, Father? I'm Sister Roberta, but you can call me Sister Roberta," the woman chuckled into her hands, which were cupped to her mouth as if she was drinking out of them.

"Okay…"

Roberta offered Flynn her hand, who took it, reluctantly. The instant his hand was within range, the nun grabbed hold of it as if it were an escaped animal and she were the irate zookeeper. Amidst the sound of his bones cracking, he tried to pry Roberta's hand open with his free fingers, failing miserably.

"I'm the welcome nun. It's what I do, HA HA HA HA HA HA. I came downstairs from my little office, which doesn't have a window and where the roof leaks." She pulled Flynn in closer, ogling him with one beady eye. "Do you know which room is above me?"

Flynn shrugged. "I don't, the priest's massage and sauna room?"

"No. The disabled toilet."

"Oh."

Roberta pulled her hand down, yanking the priest even lower, so low that he could feel his back straining under the pressure. She put her lips to his ears. "We don't even have any disabled here."

"But you-"

"YES," the words echoed through his entire body, "I know, we *might* get a disabled person in one day. But…why is the disabled toilet on the first floor?"

"I don't know? Is that where they keep them?"

Roberta started to laugh, before stopping mid-cackle. "No. It doesn't make any sense. We don't even have…a lift." The nun pulled back with an incredulous gasp, angling for some sense of empathy.

"That's…a shame?" Flynn replied, unsure what possible sequence of words might free him from this woman's secure grip.

"Are you one?"

"One what?"

"A disabled. Are you one?"

"Not to my knowledge. I get a dodgy knee in the winter sometimes, but I guess that doesn't count."

"No. It doesn't. But every day, drip-drip-drip. Always in the same place, the same speed, the same sound. Drip-drip-drip. No matter what I do. I've tried putting a meringue underneath it. Nothing. I put some sellotape over the leak. Nothing. I used Neil's special pants. Nothing. All I get is that yellow-browny water drip-drip-dripping down on my desk. Right where I put my mug." The nun stuck her tongue out and shook it, spraying

Flynn with spit and halitosis.

"Why don't you move your mug?"

"What?"

"Move your mug. If you put it on another part of the desk, then it can't be drip-drip-dripped into, huh?"

Roberta pondered this by prodding a mole on her chin with her free wagging finger; with the computations complete, she shook her head. "No good. If I put my mug somewhere else, where would I put the other special things? The mug goes next to the phone, which goes next to the in-tray, which goes next to my name plate, 'Sister Roberta – Welcome Nun', that's what they call me, which goes next to the rat, which-"

"I'm sorry, *rat?*"

Roberta sniggered once more. "All the other nuns call it a mouse…it has a long tail which moves the arrow on the telly screen. But I think it looks more like a rat, especially since I covered it in my hair clippings."

Flynn opened and closed his mouth; reasoning that he couldn't add anything of note, he remained silent.

Roberta beckoned him closer, lifting her robe up slightly around her midriff. "From down there, Father…if you get my drift?" The woman began to cackle and hyperventilate, her entire body shuddering and spasming.

Trying to put the image of the woman's fabricated rat and freshly-mown lady garden to the back of his mind, Flynn tried to extricate himself from her grasp once more. The sweat which had built up from their clammy skin and her lack of social grace acted as hand lube, and facilitated his escape. Flexing his fingers, which had gone white from the crush, Roberta continued to cackle and raise her tunic. Flynn laid a hand on hers. "Please, Sister Roberta, I've had quite a long journey, perhaps you could regale me with stories of your shaven haven some other time? I'm quite looking forward to finding out what I'm supposed to do here, and see where I'm going to be staying, *could we?*" He gesticulated towards the doorway and the wide staircase beyond, which offered the tantalising prospect of getting away from the weirdo.

Disappointed, Roberta smoothed down her robe, and fiddled with the hairs which sprouted from her mole. "Of course, Father, follow me. Though if you ever wish to see my rat, you just ask." She finished with a wink, which was an attempt at being seductive but merely looked as though she was suffering from some kind of embolism.

Following the woman at a safe distance, Flynn watched as the door to reception closed behind him. The receptionist-nun still peered over her desk, eyeballing them as they went. In his head, the sound of a cell door slammed shut, even the faces of the paintings, which provided an audience up the stairwell, seemed to look at him with disdain, unworthy of being part of such a prestigious building.

"You can meet my friend who shares my office with me, he's called, Neil. Neil Byemouff, you'll like him, he's like me, but without the shaved bits. He probably won't say much to you first off, but I reckon you'll become best buds in no time at all. He's friends with everyone, but mostly me," Roberta continued to chatter as they strode up the stairs. The nun had pulled her tunic up, so Flynn made sure there were no reflective surfaces ahead of them lest he catch a glimpse of the mouse-covering factory.

As they walked down the first-floor corridor and through another security door, which Roberta opened by slapping the access card against a panel, a siren blared. "What is that?"

Roberta shrugged. "I can't hear anything. Come on. We're nearly at my office. It's great, you can wear my special coat if you want? It gives the *best* hugs."

Turning a corner, a near identical corridor ran into the distance; closed doors and a small observation window next to each lined the way, in place of the oil paintings. Outside one of the doors, the only one that was open, lay two priests, both face down in the thick carpet, both twitching gently, their feet inadvertently keeping time with the siren.

"My god, what's happened to them?" Flynn jogged over to the men, kneeling down and feeling for a pulse.

Roberta shuffled down towards him. "They wouldn't fix

the toilet. They made my tea taste funny. When they came to give me my medicine, I hit them. With this."

Roberta was holding a length of radiator pipe. "Where the hell did you stow that?" He looked the woman up and down, she was doing some squats. "Actually, I'm not sure I want to know."

"Freeze!"

From the end of the corridor came two heavily-armed priests, wearing body armour which incorporated their white collars --it was very tastefully done. A deft flick of their wrists extended their telescopic batons. "Okay, Roberta, get back in your room, no one else has to be rendered unconscious today." They edged towards her, hands and batons out in front, trying to convey both a sense of calm *and* outright hostility.

Roberta giggled. "Sillies, I only wanted to welcome the new guest. It's what I do, isn't it? Welcome people, else why am I called the Welcome Nun? Duuuhhhh." This made her laugh so hard that she blew snot-bubbles out of her nose.

Seeking to take advantage, the pair advanced, though this was halted when Roberta waved the pipe in front of her. "It's okay, Roberta, put down the pipe, we can sort this out amicably," one of the heavily armoured priests said, though the way he was swinging his truncheon hinted that he hoped he had a chance to try out his new backhand smash technique.

Flynn tiptoed backwards, coming to a halt as he felt a hand press into the small of his back. Spinning around, he was about to scream when a gloved hand was clamped over his mouth. He looked into the eyes of a masked man, dressed in the same body armour as the two priests ahead of him. The man raised a finger to his covered lips, and herded Father Flynn behind him.

With Roberta still occupied by the two men in front of her, she failed to see the newcomer creeping up behind her. "Just wait until he meets Neil, they're going to play Connect Four, and the winner will get a frontal lobotomy, it's going to be Funhouse Central!"

The man jabbed his hand out at the back of Roberta's neck, and there was a loud clacking, as if a plastic turnstile was rotated quickly. The radiator pipe landed on the thick carpet soundlessly, as Roberta jigged on the spot, her vocal cords managing nothing but a, "la-la-la-la-la." The buzzing stopped, and the nun collapsed to the floor as the priest checked the taser and placed it back on his utility belt.

"Check her for contraband, and put her back inside," he commanded. Turning back to Flynn, he rolled the balaclava up his face, exposing a face pockmarked by old acne, and a scar which ran from jawbone-to-temple. "The name's Yowder, Father Yowder, I'm guessing you're Flynn?" He folded his balaclava up and clipped it under a band on the shoulder of his armour.

"Yeah…I'm sorry, what the fuck is going on here? Who's she? Who are you? Who are they? Where's the exit?"

Yowder nodded towards Roberta, who was being searched thoroughly. Though unconscious, her lips curled into a smile as one of the guards ran a hand around her inner thigh. "Sister Roberta is one of the patients here, she has been for some time. She used to work at the main seminary up in Hull, but one-too-many handshakes and Monday morning induction courses made her a little loopy. We'll get her comfortable back in her room, it's modelled after her old reception. It makes her feel at home, more comfortable."

"She said something about a Neil…somebody? Who's he?"

Moving down towards Roberta's room, he pointed at a sign in the window. "No one, no one *real*, anyway."

Flynn caught up and read it aloud. "Nil by mouth…figures."

"Sister Roberta jumped the priests as they carried out their afternoon rounds. She does this every once in a while. We really should take more care, but hey, I guess when you're in our profession, you always look for the good in people, eh?"

Father Flynn looked on as the two guards lifted Roberta onto a single bed, tucking her in. Opposite the bed was a curved wooden desk. Set neatly on its surface was a telephone, PC monitor, a mouse covered in pubic hair clippings and a selection of office furniture, all secured to the desk by one means or another. The surface of the mug rippled, and Flynn looked up to see a large brown water stain on the ceiling tiles, another drop of dubious looking water dripping down into the mug.

"Okay…so you guys are running some kind of mental home, I can't wait to see what kind of cell you've got for me."

Yowder put an arm around Flynn and led him away. "Nonsense, this wing is for our long-term guests. Rest assured, Archbishop Tena told us to make sure you were comfortable, and that's not a euphemism for restraints and electro-convulsive therapy. No, we look after the few Crimson Rosary operatives we've had down these halls, trust me on that one."

"Fine, so, we've cleared all that out of the way, now who the hell are you?"

Coming to a standstill, Yowder unlocked a door, and pushed it open, revealing a plush suite within. "Me? I'm your therapist. Get your rest, Father Flynn, we start tomorrow, and trust me when I tell you, you're going to need every ounce of your strength to get through the next thirty days."

"I really can't wait…woo-hoo…et cetera."

Yowder looked up and down the corridor, checking for anyone within earshot. Satisfied that the only other people were busy dealing with unconscious patients or guards, he pulled Flynn in. "Look, I know that you want two things, to get out of here as quickly as possible and to be back doing what you love doing, kicking demon's arses, chewing gum and investigating the paranormal. Am I right?"

Flynn nodded. "Of course, but Archbishop-"

"-Tena pad can go to hell. Metaphorically speaking, of course. Look, I offer an under-the-counter, express service, if you catch my meaning?"

"Go on…"

"Instead of taking thirty days to unpeel you like the proverbial onion, slowly deconstruct you, before piecing you back together again, I offer an altogether more *direct* approach to therapy. It's not for everyone, trust me, the principles are banned in many establishments, but it gets results."

"You're saying that you can get me out of this place quicker?"

"Exactly that. As I said, it's not for the weak-willed, you will have to do exactly as I say, operate on your whims, your instincts. I will test you, take you apart if I need to, I only offer this to the strong."

Flynn puffed out his chest, before wheezing. After composing himself, he said. "This sounds a bit more up my street, the idea of sitting around here singing hymns and getting in touch with my feelings isn't really something that appeals."

Yowder slapped a hand on the priest's back. "Good man. In that case, I shall leave you to prepare, I shall pick you up tomorrow morning, and we will face your demons head on. I warn you now, the journey, though short, will be nothing short of terrifying. Some don't make it, their minds turn to rice pudding at my avant-garde methods. There is nothing gentle about what will happen, I will pit you against your evils in all their disgusting forms."

Flynn squared up to the man. "I'm not afraid."

The corner of Yowder's lips curled upwards in an approximation of mirth, and jabbed a finger at him. The nail was long and curved. "You will be…you will be."

24

Teams of priests, clad in transparent plastic aprons and wading boots that ended under their armpits, trounced around the campsite. Tent poles, still hammered into the rock-hard ground, acted as flagpoles. Tattered remnants of canvas fluttered from them, a memorial to a scene of devastation, missing one vital component of a massacre.

"Where are the bodies?" O'Malley asked. He lifted up a length of inner sheeting, which was smeared with bloodied handprints and small chunks of meat smudged onto the cloth. With fingers protected by thin latex gloves, he held the top of a sleeping bag and pulled the zip down. It resisted, the teeth getting stuck in dried-on flecks of gore, before eventually relenting to open up like a submarine roll. He peered inside.

A few flies, gorged on what little had remained, buzzed in annoyance and flew past his head, missing his swatting hand. A small chunk of dried kidney sat in the middle of the sleeping bag, as if it had had a bad dream, and was hiding from whatever night terror had forced it into its polyester sanctuary. "There's loads of…*bits*, but no bodies, are we even sure that this is human? Could be some kind of cult, heaven knows we've seen enough of them, especially in this part of the world." O'Malley let the top flap of the sleeping bag droop, leaving a small entrance into the dank, bloodstained cavern.

"Look, Father, a finger, or at least what's left of it." Padraig held up a transparent plastic bag. A small length of bone sat at the bottom, and the equerry turned it this way and that, trying to work out which finger it could be.

O'Malley tapped his finger against his mouth, regretting it almost immediately as he smudged claggy blood over his top lip, giving him a small, but easily-identifiable red Hitler moustache. With the back of his other hand he rubbed at it.

"I've not seen anything like this since the Coombes family, down in Dorset in '02, you remember that?"

Padraig shook his head. "I was still studying, Father. How is it similar?"

"Terrible business, an inbred family of local farmers believed they were receiving telephone calls from God, telling them they had to cleanse the county of non-believers. They were pig-farmers, and would lure hapless tourists and out-of-towners onto their turf. Under the guise of running a pig-racing afternoon, they would butcher their victims as if they were swine, slitting their throats and hanging them from their feet until they were bled dry. Then they cured the meat, keeping it for themselves and feeding the offal to their pigs." O'Malley prised another ravaged tent open with the toe of his boot.

"That's disgusting." Padraig wrinkled his nose.

"By the time we got there, they had an entire coachload of Belgians hanging from the rafters, I'll tell you one thing though, Padraig."

"What's that, Father?"

"We made a lot of money from those pigs. I don't know what's in human organs, but those porkers were well-fed." He pointed to the car park where a large armoured truck and trailer sat, its roof jam-packed with rotating satellite dishes and aerials which interfered with low-flying aircraft. "Managed to pay for that little beauty. Say what you will about nut-jobs, but they came in handy."

"What happened to the Coombes family?"

"The damnedest thing, just as we were rounding them up, the phone went. We all thought it was a wind up, I picked up the receiver and instantly felt at peace, you know? Like all my fears and worries just drifted away. I felt so serene…"

Padraig's jaw dropped. "Really, Father?"

O'Malley chuckled. "Of course not, it was some insurance company telling me they had found some money set aside for a car accident I'd supposedly had. I hung up and we locked the family up in the secure facility at York. I imagine they were sent to the fighting pits as lion fodder, they were too far gone."

"Father, we found something." Father Doolan marched across the open ground, nearly disappearing into a sinkhole formed by a large patch of airport boarding passes. Regaining his footing, he held his iBible Pro out to O'Malley.

After a few awkward seconds, O'Malley asked. "What is it I'm looking at, exactly?"

Doolan pinched the screen, zooming in on a patch of forest, photographed from above. "The Almighty 800 Drone picked this up on one of its passes. It's a small copse a few hundred metres away --look at the centre, Father."

O'Malley took the tablet from his colleague and squinted. Amongst the trees was a newly created clearing. The epicentre was charred, and trunks lay pointing out from the landing site. As the priest zoomed in even closer, there were a set of tyre tracks leading out of the dense woodland. Anything which had been in its path was bent over and snapped. The tracks eventually dissipated but were heading towards the car park that the Mobile Command Centre was currently dominating over.

"How the hell did a vehicle land in the middle of the woods?" O'Malley asked, rhetorically.

"That's not all, Father, we contacted NORAD, asking them if they had recorded anything unusual in the last couple of nights --look at this. The quality isn't great, but…well, see for yourself." Doolan tapped on a video icon in the top left of the screen and the picture changed to a night time shot of the UK.

The country was in darkness, save for the major urban areas which were lit up like luminescent algae in a pond. Doolan zoomed in on the Welsh border area, and fast forwarded to a little after half-past-eleven at night. 11:33, to be precise. The area was utterly black, save for a few lights from the house and the main road which ran off a little way away. The screen blossomed in light as a streak of fire appeared from one corner and came to a stop. A circle of light, about the same dimension as a milk-bottle-top hovered in a spot, before shrinking into nothingness.

"My god…" Padraig mumbled.

"Indeed," O'Malley replayed the video in slow motion, "and I'm guessing that this landing site is the same place as this forest?"

Doolan nodded. "From what we can work out, yes, Father."

As he pondered, Padraig's iBible rang; after exchanging pleasantries, he held the device out to O'Malley. "It's for you, Father. It's the boffins from forensics."

The priest took the phone and ambled around the gutted tent, nodding and saying. "Uh-huh." After two laps, he passed the phone back to Padraig.

"Well, what did they say? Do they have any news on the bodies they found?"

O'Malley took the bag with the finger bone from his equerry and held it up to the light. "They say that both bodies are quite badly burned, so they can't be one hundred percent, but they've been able to make some progress.

"The male dressed as a priest, is some kind of…Annelid. His arms and legs are prosthetics, and damn good ones at that. They've sent them to engineering to get some information on the compounds and alloys used."

"That dead priest was a *worm*?" Padraig asked. "How can that be? It was the same size as a man."

"Quite, they say that it was wearing the priest's body as some sort of disguise, like it was a suit of some kind. The nun, though…" O'Malley snapped a hand out, and pulled it back in, gently opening his fingers to reveal a bluebottle crawling across his palm before taking flight. "…they say it's a kind of insect, the head at least, looks like a fly, or a praying mantis. The eggheads said it has a large mouth in its chest, no doubt able to rip a man apart, that's not the damnedest thing, though."

"What is it, Father?" Padraig begged.

O'Malley turned to face him. "The nun's legs were…human. Which brings me to those strange bones they found in the Quantico-Zoom Mart loading bay. The scientists say that they belong to no known species on this planet.

"My god, you don't mean..."

"I think we're going to need the big fella on our side on this one, Padraig. You see, those bones, those alien bones, they had teeth marks on them. It looks like these nuns, whatever they are, eat both their own kind, and us."

"But that's…just…what are we dealing with here, Father?"

Padraig and a number of priests who had gathered around gasped in unison. O'Malley regarded them, one by one. "I don't know exactly what kind of unholy union has been formed, but I can tell you categorically what we're dealing with here.

"Cannibal nuns from outer space."

25

Mother Superior Francesca got to the end of the row of the five subjects, and turned on her heels, a smile beaming from her face. "Oh, my lovely sisters, you have done well indeed. I have received word that the tasters we provided were of excellent quality and appearance. All that remains now is to select the harvesting destination. Looking at what you have brought me to sample, I must say that you have excelled yourselves yet again."

The five nuns, stood behind their respective offerings, sagged with palpable relief, looking from one to another, exchanging small nods and grins. Sister Roberta broke the silence. "Thank you, Mother Superior, your principles and guidelines inspired us." The other nuns mumbled hurriedly in agreement.

Francesca stood by the last human, all of them naked. She surveyed the man, pinching his arms and pushing his abdomen. "This one in particular looks in perfect condition." She did a lap of the offering, squeezing the man's rump and opening his mouth, looking inside. Francesca stood in front of him, leaning in and reading the label which hung round his neck from a fine silver-linked chain. "Oswestry?" Francesca looked across at Sister Wanda. "Have we not been there before? It sounds familiar."

Wanda, head bowed, eyes fixed on a point on the floor, shook her head. "No, Mother Superior, it was not on the forbidden list of settlements."

Francesca pursed her lips, running her hands around the man's throat, skirting round the thorn of control which jutted from the base of his neck. "Yes, this specimen is of exceptional quality, are they all like this?"

"Most of them, your grace, they do not seem as puffy as the

ones from the larger settlements."

"Agreed, it would appear the lack of proximity to big nests leads to leaner subjects. Though, of course, one can never tell, it's all in the taste, wouldn't you agree?"

Wanda's eyes flicked up; beyond the imitation ones in her mask, something twinkled from behind, a bead of drool running from the corner of her mouth. "Definitely, your grace, it is *all* about the taste."

"Excellent," Francesca flipped open her crucifix, made a note of the frequency which had been stamped on the man's label, and pressed a button. His left arm raised from his side, coming to a halt perpendicular to his shoulder. Mother Superior looked into the man's eyes, she could see the panic and terror within. They flickered, trying to break the hold that was imposed on him, dispense with the shackles which limited his motor skills, and give him a chance to run away from these damned nuns, to freedom.

Francesca smiled, the warring eyes and body proving no contest at all for the thorn which had wormed its way into his central nervous system, paralysing him, making his functions compliant to only one person. She ran a finger down his cheek. "So soft, so smooth, this one took great pride in his appearance." She cupped his balls with her free hand, which shrunk on contact. "And of optimum breeding stock too, quite the catch indeed."

The nun ran her hands down the man's arms, feeling the contours of his biceps and triceps melt away to the forearm, still held out perfectly straight and true. "Well, let's see if he tastes as good as he looks." The top of Francesca's body pitched backwards as the chest maw opened up.

Sharp teeth glistened from the harsh lighting in the hall, angled to present the offerings in the best possible way. Francesca tipped forward, slowly enveloping the man's arm in her mouth, which remained open. Gently, slowly, she eased forward until her top teeth rested on the edge of the man's collarbone. Like a Venus flytrap, her mouth closed gradually. The teeth bit into the skin, easily piercing the wrapping.

Separating the limb from the body, there was a pop as the shoulder bone popped out of its socket. Francesca slammed her jaw shut and tugged backwards, ripping the arm off in one go. She tipped her head backwards, almost gagging on the limb. Her long throat convulsed, the back teeth grinding against skin and bone, managing to crush the morsel down into a more manageable portion. As she stood there, blood sprayed over her from severed vein and artery. It ran off her clothing, waxy like skin, and spilled onto the stone floor. Still the man stood there, his skin turning white, his eyes hooded and heavy.

Allowing herself to be soaked with blood, Francesca chewed idly, passing the meat, sinew and bone from one side of her mouth to the other. She swallowed down a big chunk and gargled on the remnants of blood and saliva, infused with the fragments of bone. The blood slowed to a trickle from the wound, pitter-pattering onto the hard floor. Francesca nodded slowly. "Hmmm, not too bad, not too bad at all. This one was a bit nutty, with hints of Wooty berry and Thurki bark. There's a definite aftertaste too..."

"Is it caramel?" Sister Polly asked.

"No..."

"Charcoal?" Wanda volunteered.

"No...it's a little like the Grzki fish from Clay 9, tangy, but not unpleasant." Francesca swallowed the juices she had swirled around her mouth and snatched the label from the man's neck. She pressed a button on the crucifix, which flicked out a hard nib from the bottom, she began to scratch onto the surface.

The other nuns looked on nervously, then the scratching stopped, and Francesca announced. "This one from Oswestry is a possibility, but I think we need to try the others first. Please, sisters, tuck in to this one, see what you think. We don't want him to spoil, now, he is on his last ounces of strength."

Mother Superior edged backwards, wiping gobbets of blood and flesh from her chest chin, which parted, the reptilian tongue lashing out and licking the dregs from her fingers.

As she backed away, the other five nuns closed in on the

man, barely alive. As Wanda bent him over, her chest mouth opened up and she ripped off his head with gusto. Before the body had a chance to fall, the others set upon him, biting and ripping into what was left. As they tried to get their fair portions, they would click loudly at each other.

A few minutes later, all that was left was a slick puddle of blood, and a few toes. The other four subjects in the row stood there stock still, each trying to look to the left to see what was happening. The few that did were unable to tear their gaze away from the grisly sight, and their inevitable demise.

Francesca fished out a length of ligament from between her teeth and wound it round her finger, then walked across to a table and placed the label down on it. Taking a jug of water, she poured it into her chest maw, which ran it around within, trying to take away the taste of Oswestry, in keen anticipation of the next sample.

"Well, sisters, what did you think?" Francesca asked.

Wanda let out a burp. "He was okay, not as nice as I thought he would be."

"That's the problem with these apes, appearances can be deceiving, I agree, he was okay, but I've had better," Kelly agreed.

Mother Superior clapped her hands. "Excellent, so, Sister Kelly, you're up next, what do you have for us today?"

Kelly wiped her mouth with the back of her hand, and stood behind her sample, a young woman. "This one is from Ludlow, and she was a tricky one to catch, very fast, I had to use the electro-net of snagging to capture her in the end."

Mother Superior walked around the stationary naked woman. As she came to a stop behind the subject, she tutted and pointed. "What's this?"

Sister Kelly hung her head, "She must've fallen…"

"You hit her with the club of compliance, didn't you?"

"No, your grace."

Francesca stood in front of Kelly, who refused to meet the Mother Superior's icy gaze. "Don't lie to me, my lovely. You know I don't like a liar."

164

"No, your grace."

"So, tell me the truth, did you hit her?"

"Yes, your grace."

"With the club of compliance?" Francesca raised an eyebrow.

"No, your grace."

"Then with what? Spit it out now, child, hold nothing back."

Kelly rummaged around within her tunic, before holding out a length of wood. "With this, your grace."

Francesca snatched the item from the nun, and studied it, her attention drawn to a fading bronze plaque affixed to the top end, which was flecked with dried blood. "In memory of Albert Braithwaite, he loved this place. So take a seat you breathing bastard and enjoy being alive, because I'm not."

"It was on one of the seating implements that the sample ran past. As I said, she was very fast, I had to subdue her before she got away, she could've warned someone."

"Why did you not use the club of compliance? You know that if we need to subjugate one of the cattle, that it is the best thing to use, it does not damage the meat, and is considered to be an organic way of stunning the food. Look at this contusion!" Mother Superior pointed to a large welt which had come up on the base of the woman's skull. Francesca smacked the bench slat against it, breaching the skull and causing a slurry of black congealed blood and chunks of brain to splat onto the floor.

The other nuns gasped in horror as Francesca bent down and fished through the gooey detritus with the piece of wood. "Look at this, you think we would get a decent price for this quality of meat?"

Sister Kelly shook her head. "No, your grace, just I-"

"SILENCE." Francesca's voice echoed around the multi-tiered room. The chamber was a square temple, set within the rotunda. Balconies looked over a large stone courtyard, which was bathed in light. Nuns who had been busying themselves with various packaging and quality control tasks wandered out onto the walkways to see what was going on.

Turning around to take in the audience, Francesca raised the piece of park bench and pointed at the audience. "Sisters, some of you are getting slack in your duties. We are here to find and prepare new delicacies for the universe, which means that we must take every care to ensure they are of the highest quality. I gave all of you exact instructions on what you should and shouldn't do, did I not?"

"Yes," rang out from the nuns as one, gathered on each level.

"We have been given this opportunity by the GAFFER -- they could take away our contract as easily as it was awarded it to us. I will not tolerate any dereliction of duty, if any of you are incapable of following instruction to the letter, then tell me now."

A deathly silence was the reply, the vacuum of quiet was suffocating, stretching time out. Francesca broke it. "Now, Sister Kelly, fetch me the sample's label, so I may mark it."

Kelly nodded and walked around the woman, who was twitching and shaking. As her fingers wrapped around the metallic label, Francesca stepped in behind the nun. "This is the punishment for not heeding my words."

Mother Superior held the wooden bar with two hands, and brought it down on top of Sister Kelly's head. It crumpled under the impact, leaving a U-shaped divot, as the nun sank to her knees. Francesca brought the slat down again and again, each swipe swishing through the air, before ending in a solid thwack. There was the sound of breaking bone, every downward smack ending in a wet shucking sound. After fifteen blows, Francesca put a foot under the nun's body and turned her over. Kelly's face mask had been split in two, the human features divided evenly; a coating of green slime was sprayed over the neutral skin tone. Beneath the torn vestige was the brown insectoid head of her true form. One of the eyes had burst, a cornucopia of ruin and desolation.

Kelly's snout snuffled at the air. Francesca held the wooden bar in one hand, and pointed down at her fallen kin, shouting to the roof beams. "THIS IS THE PRICE OF YOUR DERELICTION OF DUTY."

Looking back down at the insect nun, who held her hands out, not just to try and block future blows, but to beg for her life, Francesca swatted them aside and battered the snout with the makeshift weapon. A few lusty blows later, and Kelly's skull caved in, her snufflecone and the remnants of her eyeball sinking within, forming a lake of green gunk.

The nun's hands fell against the floor, fingers twitching. Francesca cast the wooden bat onto the body and walked up to the third subject, a tall, well-built man. Turning the label round, she let it go to slap against the man's chest. "Well, we can feast on Sister Kelly soon enough, but we have more pressing matters, let's continue with the tastings. The next harvest location isn't going to select itself now, is it?"

A nervous echo of, "no," sounded back.

Francesca motioned for a couple of the nuns to dispose of both the brutalised remains of Sister Kelly, and the female subject from Ludlow, who was still leaking chunks of ribbed brain and blood onto the floor. "Excellent, now, let's go and see what the inhabitants of Tewkesbury taste like. I'm rather hopeful about this one."

26

In the large conservatory, modelled on a Japanese Zen garden, the two priests sat cross legged, opposite each other. Each rested on a plush cushion, a low wooden table positioned between them. Placed in the middle, on a coaster fashioned from a smoothed-down pebble, was a whisky tumbler filled with two fingers of the finest single malt that only a well-paid priest with no other hobbies could afford. Flynn and Yowder had their eyes closed, hands rested palm-up on their knees. "Reach out with your desires, Flynn."

His face a welt of concentration, Flynn's nose twitched, detecting the alcohol, his brain mapped out its distance away, its height above sea level, the weight of the glass, and he began to factor in the possible influence of the Coriolis effect.

Yowder's mouth twitched. "Excellent...I can feel your thirst as it builds inside you."

"It smells so good...I normally have to make do with the bargain basement booze."

"Silence. Centre yourself. I can sense your cravings. Reach out for it. Take the whisky. Consume it. Let it become one with you."

"No, Father, I will resist. I must..."

"Search your feelings, Flynn, you know as well as I that you cannot control your impulses. We both know that you will try to get the whisky. Drink it all down. Every last drop. It is...your destiny..."

Flynn's fingers curled reflexively. He could all but feel the heavy glass in his grasp, the sunlight trying to streak through the deep amber oily liquid. A strand of drool began to unfurl from the corner of his mouth. "Yes...yes...take your drink, and your journey to the drunk side will be complete," Yowder snapped, his hand falling behind him.

When he opened his eyes, Flynn's senses were razor sharp. Before he was even aware of his muscles moving, his hand had shot out towards the drink, fingers splayed, ready to clamp hold of the glass and bring it towards him to devour his prize. As his skin grazed the side of the glass, there was a blur from across the table, a flash of silver, an arc of pure light. At the base of the newly-formed crystal rainbow erupted a geyser of red. Flynn felt a lash of fire run up his arm, through his armpit and into his chest and pulled his hand back instinctively, which pulled the crimson fountain closer towards him.

Time slowed to a crawl. Flynn held his hand in front of him, and noted, with an odd degree of dispassion, that he was missing a finger. The little one. Not his favourite, by any stretch of the imagination, but he had always found it to be a reliable digit, handy for ear mining. In its place was a slight stump, the base of the finger having been sliced off diagonally, the wound curving down perfectly with the shape of the side of his hand. Flynn saw the white glint of bone, before it was covered in a blood jus, the pressure turning the initial spurt into a steady pumping which was slowly trickling down his arm, between his legs and onto the virginal white cushion. He dared a glance towards the table, saw the whisky, its surface barely disturbed, the last ripple blooming out to the edge. Next to it was his finger.

He chuckled. It looked like a pork chipolata, missing a blanket of bacon and twenty minutes in the oven at a hundred-and-eighty degrees. Fan assisted, of course. It was resting in a small puddle of blood, and a steel bridge ran from it to Yowder's hand, the wakizashi withdrawing as quickly as it had appeared. The gnarled priest slid it silently back within its sheath, and laid the weapon on his lap.

After a few seconds, with incredulity now the dominant feeling, Flynn sputtered. "You cut my fucking finger off, you bastard!"

Yowder nodded, and rotated his body around ninety degrees, fetching a tray which carried a handmade clay teapot and two small matching cups. Placing it in front of him, he poured out two cups of tea, and held out one for Flynn, who looked at it as if it were a grenade. "Tea?" Yowder asked.

"Are you deaf? I said you cut my finger off."

"You bastard."

"What?"

Yowder continued to hold the cup out, opening his eyes slowly, holding Flynn in a stare akin to a cobra before it strikes. "You said that I cut your fucking finger off, *you bastard.* Tea?"

"Is it going to grow my finger back?"

"I'm not sure what tea you've had before, but I'm not aware of any that have the required regenerative powers."

"Then why the fuck would I want to drink your tea?"

"Because it's the best tea this side of Hereford. Now. Don't be a baby, take the tea, drink it."

Flynn reached out with his free hand, the one with the correct allocation of fingers and thumbs, and took the cup, placing it on the table in front of him. "Thanks, anything for this, by any chance?" He held his other hand up, blood continuing to stream from the injury.

"I do," Yowder reached behind him, and pulled out a portable blowtorch, lighting the flame and holding it out.

Shrinking away, Flynn said. "I was thinking more like a cloth? A bandage? Some kind of medical gauze? I mean, what kind of nut-job has a samurai sword and blowtorch handy?"

Yowder raised his hand.

"It was rhetorical, you looney toon," Flynn lifted up a bum cheek and tore at the bloodstained cushion cover. After splattering blood over the finely-raked sand and pebbles, Flynn wound the thick cloth around his hand.

Looking down at the table, Yowder held the cup with both hands, and sipped the tea. "You're here to rid yourself of bad habits. Those you know and those you don't. I did warn you that some of my methods will seem a little extreme. From a certain point of view."

Flynn held up the blood-soaked rag. "You don't say."

"What you fail to appreciate is that these things can exact a heavy toll on you. Maybe not immediately, in fact, very infrequently is it instantaneous, instead a lifetime of cancerous decay will slowly eat away at you until one day you look at yourself in the mirror and see that nothing of you remains. That you have allowed yourself to wither away, and done nothing to stop it claiming its inevitable bounty. What kind of man would do that?"

"One who could wear gloves without having to pad a finger out?"

Yowder blew into the cup's caldera, causing steam to billow out. "A man who does not know restraint. Who does not know *the way*. You are capable of so much, yet you have allowed yourself to become a slave to something which should be no man's master. You have abandoned the light, and allowed yourself to become shrouded in darkness. We will deal with that…in time, but first we must cut out this poison. We must show you how to take control again, that you are your own master, not fermented grain or grape."

"Cut out the poison? Was it in my little finger?"

"Placed on the scales of fortune, is it not better to lose something small at the beginning, than to lose it all at the end?"

Flynn looked under the table. "Where the fuck are you getting all this from?"

Yowder placed the cup down and folded his arms. "You are here for a reason, Father Flynn, to be set back onto the path, or…"

"Or, what?"

"Or to be cast out. You must know that if you leave this place before I say, you'll be living on the streets within a fortnight, pulling off suited executives into Styrofoam coffee cups round the back of betting shops. Doing anything, to take the pain away. You'll say to yourself, just one. More. Bottle. I'd say that whilst it *is* an extreme approach, you can now confront this demon."

"What are you going to do? You can't follow me around forever, cutting off another finger every time I have a drink."

"True. But I now only have to be there nine times instead

of ten," Yowder nodded towards the cup of tea.

Flynn cradled it between his hands, took a sniff, then a mouthful, his face creased up. "I think I prefer the bargain basement whisky."

"Drink up, we need to move onto step two."

Swaying gently, Flynn waved his hands. "Before we do, I think I might need to have a bit of a snooze, I'm not feeling tip-top." His eyes rolled back into his head, and he flopped sideways.

Yowder sipped his tea, before reaching across the table and picking up the severed digit. "Now, let's go and see what lives within your mind."

27

Flynn was aware of precisely one thing: he was falling. He could feel no connection to any ground, although being immersed in complete and total blackness, there was no way he could be certain. Perhaps he was glued to a large hamster wheel? Being hurtled around at speed, this would just be like that damn priest, Yowder, the one who had all too casually sliced off one of his fingers without so much as a warning.

No, he was definitely falling. He floundered about a bit, thrashing around in the void. He quickly realised that his limbs were not in contact with anything. Yet, he didn't feel like he was accelerating. He deduced that if he was indeed falling, then he would be gaining speed rather than maintaining a nice steady rate of descent, --that wouldn't make any sense.

There was also no sound, except for the warring voices in his head having a discussion about why there were no acceleratory forces at play. Well, that, but also how losing his little finger on day one was going to purge his personal demons, and get back to smiting those who pissed off the church without resorting to kneecapping nuns.

With his mind a blur of nonsense and contradictory statements, Flynn shouted and screamed. Though he could feel the air escaping his lungs, and his throat become hoarse, he could not hear the fruits of his vocal labour. Nothing but the sensation of falling, and complete and total silence. Even when he moved a hand in front of his eyes, he could not make out the familiar form of his skin and bone. Rather annoyed with the turn of events, Flynn tried to spin, to swap axes and to at least see if he could control this freefall he found himself in.

Nothing.

This was becoming rather troublesome. He was then struck with one thought, one solitary question of doom-mongering:

am I dead?

It was possible. The last thing he remembered was surveying the blood-soaked cloth wrapped around his hand. It was likely, to a fair degree, that he had bled out. If insufficient medical staff were around - and let's face it, everything he had seen of the place so far would suggest that was the case - then it was likely that he was laying down on a Japanese Zen garden, in a conservatory, in Wales, having ruined the carefully-raked surface by bleeding profusely into it.

Flynn sought to push the thought from his mind, he was still aware in some form or another, so whatever was happening to his body, he wasn't going to bear witness to it for a little while. Perhaps he would come to, and find that he had a bionic finger? It might be a boon. The lopping-off of said digit could in fact be a new way of upgrading him to the next version of Crimson Rosary operative.

The bionic finger would undoubtedly have a laser in it, able to slice through titanium in a jiffy, liquefy eyeballs in mere seconds, and blind an airline pilot thirty-five thousand feet in the air. Yeah, this was all part of some surgical procedure to turn him into a cyborg priest. He just hoped that they wouldn't do a Robocop on him - the rather needless remake - go a bit surgery crazy, and start taking off things that could've stayed. He didn't mind having a cool laser finger, but losing his legs and having bionic ones would be overkill. His pins were his best feature, and no amount of super sweet augmentations would make up for having to finally ditch his dream of being a catalogue leg model.

His mouth opened again in a soundless scream, yet from the endless blackness, he heard his lamentations being returned to him as if someone was turning the volume up on their television. His terrified scream grew louder and louder; in the distance he saw a light, and felt himself lurching towards it. Oh great. This was it. The end. Gravity had been returned, there was a light, and not just any old illumination, *the* light. He was going to that aforementioned light, this was without a doubt, unequivocally, it. The big one. The ol' checkmate. Death. No more swanning around on earth, drinking, smoking, wishing people would walk faster. He fully imagined that within mere minutes, he'd be given his regulation harp, and commence strumming, or harping, or whatever the suitable adjective was that necessitated him playing his new instrument.

The wind streaked through his hair and beard He couldn't feel Albie within, he must already be in axolotl heaven, living it large with his kin, finally free of living within a drunkard's burgeoning facial hair.

The sound of his screaming surrounded him, threatening to squash him like he was a testicle, shorn of covering, in the vice-like grip of a spurned lover. The light sensed that it was being usurped and increased in brightness, causing Flynn to squash his eyes shut, trying to banish it from burning itself onto the back of his retinas.

What consisted of ground met him with little grace, yet there was no pain. One minute he was bordering terminal velocity, the next he had stopped completely. It felt like he was suspended from something, but he couldn't feel anything pulling on his body. Gradually, the light dimmed. Through his eyelids, he could see fine red tributaries, and some sense of normality returned, not a moment too soon. Everything of late had been really, *really* odd.

Then Flynn opened his eyes. He stared up at a ceiling, a solitary lightbulb swinging slightly from its cord while swirls of plaster decorated the roof. His body felt warm, so he wriggled and heard the rustle of a recently laundered duvet. Looking down, he saw that he was in bed, but quickly realised that he wasn't alone.

"You're not my daddy," said a boy's voice. The timbre was familiar, though lacking the key component of *demon*.

Flynn cocked his head sideways, seeing Timothy looking at him, hidden beneath the duvet. "What are you doing here? This is *my* death, get out!" Flynn yelled, pointing to the door.

The boy shook his head, his fingers grasping the top of the duvet even tighter, "no, this is my room, *you* get out."

Realising that even though he was fully clothed, he could

ill-afford to be caught in bed with a child, regardless of whether it was either his death or some kind of hallucination. Flynn slid out of the sheets onto the floor as if he had melted. He leaped up, waving his hand at the child like he was a master of Kung Fu. "What do you want from me?"

"I..."

"Yes?"

"I..."

"Yes?

"I..."

"YES? WHAT IS IT? WHAT DO YOU WANT FROM ME?"

The child's voice dropped as if someone in charge of the EQ levels had decided to add not so much as a smidge of bass, but an entire lifetime delivery of it. "I want your skull, *priest.*" The child began to float, taking the duvet with him, forming a vacant bed fort beneath his body.

Flynn staggered backwards, trying to feel for the door handle. His eyes flitted from surface to surface --everywhere he looked, shiny animal skulls looked back with empty sockets. A stack of bird skulls were piled on the bedside table, and an owl's polished cranium held an LCD display showing the time, 6:66.

Still, Timothy rose. Around a foot from the ceiling, he stopped and began to roll to one side, maintaining eye contact with the now-frantic priest. The duvet lost its hold and fell back onto the bed, leaving the pyjama-clad boy spinning slowly in the air. Though his body rotated, his head remained level, each lap bringing with it the sound of more bones breaking before they reformed anew. It sounded like someone was slowly shaking a spray can inside the boy's body.

"How did...?"

Before Flynn could complete his sentence, the boy laughed, an abyssal drone which pushed the man back against the wall and held him in place. After longer than was probably deemed necessary, the boy stopped, and O'Malley slunk down the wall, landing in a kneeling heap. "It is I, Fattori Gutso, Prince of

Puke and the harbinger of your DOOM."

"I...I...I watched you die," Flynn stuttered, his arms wrapping around his knees, pulling them to his chest.

Timothy stopped his churning, and began to right himself before floating towards the stricken priest, his bone stick arms reaching for him. "I cannot die...I was cast out of the body, but I have found a new hiding place. Somewhere warmer. Somewhere dingier." The child hovered in front of the priest, sweat steaming from his skin, reeking of vomit and decay.

Try as he might, Flynn could not shy away from the stench or the boy, now inches from his face, the confines of the room cutting off any escape. The child chuckled, and let out a sicky burp. Out of habit, Flynn said. "Pardon you."

The child began to convulse and shake, and his body began to swell. With his guts bloated and swollen, his pyjama top struggled to contain the distended form within. Timothy's face had gone white, his eyes nothing but milky orbs dotted in the centre by a single black mote. Lips, fat slimy pipes of worm skin, opened and closed, as a blue tongue, fat and searching, slurped against the corpulent skin. As the boy arched backwards there was a wet gurgling sound, and then Timothy cracked forwards, his eyes wide, black veins bubbling and coursing beneath translucent skin, his mouth forming into the end of a hose. From within came the sound of a torrent worming its way through fleshy tubing.

Just as the first droplet of spew hit the back of the throat, and was angled forward, out towards the supplicated priest, Flynn clamped the child's lips together with his thumb and forefinger of one hand, and pinched the nose closed with the other. The expected barrage of corn-laden vomit hit the blockage, and swilled against the back of the child's teeth, stripping the enamel away. Timothy's eyes, already bulging, opened still further, apertures being pushed beyond their suggested operating levels.

Cheeks began to balloon, the skin thinning as it stretched and swelled. There was a tearing sound from within, as the expansion pulled skin and muscle from bone and tendon. Two small sacks, now free of anchor at the cheekbone, were able to continue their outward stretch. As they did, the eyes, which were previously on the verge of bursting free from their sockets, were swamped by the growing skin, and retreated within, disappearing under two taut domes of ever-thinning epidermis.

Desperation took over the possessed boy, and he began to slap and kick out at the priest, trying to release the pressure and vent the building backlog of vomit. Flynn squeezed together even tighter, straining to keep the lip and nose seams from bursting.

Something had to give, the pressure was too much, it had to go somewhere.

That place was via Timothy's ears.

As Flynn held the boy's breathing apparatus, his head nothing more than a quickly-filling washing machine drum, there was a snapping sound, like someone clucking. Almost immediately, a fountain of watery green gruel was ejected from both ear canals.

Flynn stood up, the momentum of the liquid being expelled threatening to lead him on a merry jig around the room until every last psi of vomit had been expended. Like a pressure washer on maximum, Flynn staggered, punch drunk, struggling to maintain his hold, the vomit continuing out of both ears at high power. It sprayed up the walls. It smashed against the skull cairns and shattered them. Posters of cartoon characters and video games were split and torn, ragged wet flaps slopped to the ground, the carpet turning into a mulchy swamp.

Timothy's face had shrunk inwards, like his decomposition had been time lapsed, the projector cranked up to fast forward, and the operator having disappeared off on a tea break. Skin had lost its youthful lustre and was dehydrated, cracked and ragged, nought but grey cracked render, sloughed on fragile beams of skull and neck bone. Eyes sunk inside the skull cavity, puckering up into tough stones, pitted and weathered.

The boy shuddered, the velocity constant, but now, instead of the green bile, chunks of meat, bone, coagulated blood and ribbed brain were being jetted out of each ear, the blowholes widened and blown out from the force of the blast. Flynn looked from side-to-side as chunks of rancid meat splattered over the curtains and wallpaper, sliding down like thick chunks of mucus and snot.

The ejection began to slow, the liquidised puree of human construction and bile petering out, save for the odd piece of flesh or mangled organ being blown out of the boy's head like a malfunctioning water cannon.

Flynn looked down at the boy, now a withered husk, a decayed porcelain doll, the armature dissolved away and deformed. He released his hold, and the boy gasped momentarily before hitting the floor with a dull slap. Vacant sockets regarded him impassively, and the priest felt duty-bound to say something, so he mustered a feeble. "Sorry," before covering his mouth with his sleeve lest he add to the mushy soup he was standing in with some of his own internal concoctions.

Like a papier-mâché puppet, the mouth cracked open. "I'll get you…*priest*…"

With his sleeve still covering the bottom half of his mouth like an agent provocateur, Flynn stomped down on the head, which slurped as it was squished into the acidic gravy of the demon boy's insides.

The smell was beginning to seep through his clothing; he turned to the window, which was covered by gore-splattered curtains. With his free hand, he wrenched them open, revealing a large porthole beyond. Outside, he could make out two faces, both disappearing quickly from view as the circular window was revealed.

Feeling for the clasp, Flynn feverishly unwound it, yearning for fresh air. He pushed the window open, and stuck his head out into the cold night air. The priest took in a few deep breaths before he dared open his eyes. There, in front of him, was the beaming face of Habib Marwen, the sardonic grin of a zealot glaring back. Flynn looked over to where Jack Bauer was eyeing him up, he raised an eyebrow, and yelled at the priest.

"Dammit!"

From behind him, there was a click, and darkness flooded over him like a flash flood, stealing away the frustrated face of CTU's finest and his ridiculously fluky nemesis. Flynn felt his chin being tugged, gently at first, and then, into a full-blown yank forwards…

28

Flynn came to, nestled within another bed, staring into the beady little eyes of Albie, who was sitting on his chest, pulling the man's beard as hard as he could. Patting the little fellow on the head made the axolotl chirrup. After some gentle nuzzling, Albie settled down, and began to drop off, the exertion too much for him.

"I've never seen so much devotion in an animal," Yowder's familiar gruff voice came from the corner of the room.

Sitting up carefully, so as not to disturb the sleeping creature, Flynn snuggled his back into the pillows behind him, allowing him to rest and keep an eye on the renegade priest. "What are you doing here?"

Tutting, Yowder clutched a large sketchpad to his chest. "Now, before I show you this, I want you to know one thing."

"That you're a complete and total psycho?"

"Okay…two things. One, I'm a complete and total psycho, and two, charcoal is not my best medium." He flipped the pad around, revealing a familiar scene.

"How did…?" Flynn took the pad from the man, surveying the image which had been sketched remarkably well onto its thick surface. It was of a small boy, with spouts of liquid shooting out of his ears. A man, with his back to the artist, had clamped hold of the kid's mouth and nose. Behind the boy, sketched so finely that it was nigh on invisible, was the outline of Fattori Gutso, his face in mid-snarl.

Lowering the pad, Flynn saw Yowder moving his hand towards him, his four fingers were splayed, two to one side, two to the other, forming a V. "My mind…to *your* mind," he chanted, still reaching towards Flynn's head.

"What the hell are you doing? This isn't Star Trek, you know, you can't read my mind, stop it!"

Yowder's hand came to a halt, inches from the priest, who was pushing himself as far back as possible. The therapist smiled. "I know, I just love freaking people out by doing that."

"Well, don't, okay? It's just weird."

"Oh, I know, won't stop me doing it, though." Yowder stood up and paced slowly over to the window, peering outside at a group of nuns who were playing a rather lacklustre game of netball.

"So how did you draw the picture? I mean, that boy…the demon…they were all in my dream, if that's what it was? A hallucination, maybe? I don't know, how the hell were you there?"

"Are you the same as when you left?" Yowder asked, still looking out of the window, as Sister Ingrid caught the ball right in the middle of her face.

Flynn patted himself down; he saw that his hand had been bandaged by someone skilled in triage, though he was a tad disappointed not to be the proud owner of a new laser finger. As Albie fell into a deeper slumber, he began to fall off Flynn's chest, but the priest managed to put a hand under his little body and arrest his fall. In doing so, he felt something pull on the back of his own neck, to something trapped beneath the axolotl's body.

Setting Albie down, Flynn ran his fingers around his throat, discovering a necklace of twine digging into the folds of his skin. The pendant, or whatever it was, was hidden beneath the tightly tucked-in blankets. He tugged on the pinched string and pulled loose a small bone, around half an inch long, perfectly smooth and with a small hole drilled in the end, where the starchy twine looped through. "What the hell is this? Some kind of animal bone?"

"Yes. *Some* kind," Yowder replied, before applauding loudly as Sister Tammy scored, levelling the game up at eighteen-all.

Flynn gave the bone a bit of a sniff. It smelled of nothing, except a slight tinge of furniture polish. "It looks pretty new, fresh almost." The penny dropped, and he placed it against the top half of his one remaining little finger. "Remind me never to get into swapping Christmas presents with you. I'd have preferred vouchers, or perhaps a gift box of aftershave, moisturiser and deodorant, you know, something useful. But no, of course not, Mr Psycho Priest here goes and strips the skin and meat off my finger, which *he* cut off, and gives it back to me as a necklace. I dread to think what you do to your enemies."

With his rapturous applause fading, Yowder continued to watch the game. "I didn't strip the skin and meat off your finger."

"Well, I guess that's something, you're obviously growing as an individual."

Yowder turned around, his face set like a granite golem. "I flash-fried your finger, and ate it with some borlotti beans and a nice cup of sake, it was most agreeable."

"Of course you did, I mean, why wouldn't you? Food's that hard to come by nowadays that you have to lop off your patient's digits and fricassee them? Good job I had my pants on, otherwise you might've taken the old chap off and made it into a hot dog."

"Don't be so silly. I would never do that."

"Good."

Turning back to the netball game, Yowder said."I saw your winky when I removed your clothing, there's no way you could get a decent meal out of *that* anyway."

"Har-di-har-har, my word, you really *are* a card, huh? Come on, what weird reason do you have for eating my finger?"

"I was like you once, an operative in the Crimson Rosary," Yowder held a hand out and jangled his crimson rosary beads until they clacked together. "I was in the foreign service, though, not the cushy little numbers you get to go on around here. No, not me. I've fought shamen in Borneo, an entire tribe of pygmies sought to end me when I destroyed their craven idols in Bolivia. This one time, I faced off against Qzxprycatj, the apocalyptic world-ending beast atop Mount Sinai, with a band of fellow priests, solemnly sworn to protect this planet and all its sundry items." The priest tore himself away from the game going on below, and locked eyes with Flynn. "I've seen things you people wouldn't believe..."

Flynn coughed and shook the finger bone necklace. "And this is all terribly interesting, but why the fuck did you eat my finger?"

"I was in the jungles of Haiti, I had been severely wounded by a Voodoo priest. We had a falling-out over who should have the last guava for dessert one night, so we decided to settle our differences with a good old-fashioned knife fight. You know the sort, first one to die, loses. Problem was, he was infinitely better than me, so-"

"Hang on a minute."

"What?"

"Is this story going to go on a while?"

"A little, yes, I mean, it isn't going to be a long ramble, but I thought it prudent to give you some adequate degree of backstory."

Flynn shook his head. "No, thank you. I've already had to listen to one long-winded story in the past few days, I'm not sure my sphincter can stand another one."

Yowder sagged. "Oh. But it's really good."

"I don't care, the last one was okay too, but I just don't think I can bear someone else prattling on about something that frankly, I'm not that fussed about."

"But it makes the Serpent and the Rainbow look like a kids' show."

"Not interested."

Yowder cocked an eyebrow, and licked his lips. "There are loads of heaving bosoms?"

Flynn contemplated this latest revelation momentarily, before shaking his head. "Nope, not fussed. I just want to know, in a few sentences, how the hell you managed to get into my dream."

"Oh...well, long story short, as I crawled through the dense foliage, I was found by a sugar cane farmer, who took me back to his family. After a series of trials, they...look, are you sure you don't want to hear it?"

"Yes, come on, you were nearly there."

"As I lay on a bed made of straw and donkey hide, the farmer's wife asked me who had injured me. I told her...Papa Frank. She crossed herself, and started babbling on in French. Then she turned and asked me if I wanted to know how to find him, to know his darkest deepest fears. Naturally, I said yes. She asked me for the blade I had fought him with, which had tasted his flesh. I handed it to her and she peeled off a strip of skin and meat that I had managed to slice from him. Ten minutes later, I'm having a small Voodoo priest burrito. She taught me the secret incantation, and I had everything I needed to beat my foe."

The bed creaked as Flynn sat up. "Actually, I'm quite interested to hear the full story now."

"Tough, you had your chance. So, anyway, I can enter people's fugue states, I just need to eat a piece of them, and say the magic words. Then, whilst they're unconscious, I can enter their mind, find out their biggest fears, their hopes and dreams, and use it to help them. I have to say though, that with you, it was more than a dream. It would seem that this demon, Fattori Gutso, is a part of you now, not a complete possession, but a piece of his essence dwells within you. I think he has been a contributing factor in your recent travails."

"Okay, so that's pretty cool, but you could've just mentioned your little plan, I'm sure I would've agreed to you shaving a bit of me off to get some answers, you didn't have to cut off a pinky."

Yowder clapped as the game ended via a last-minute winner by Sister Brenda, before he headed for the door. "The subject can't be aware of what you're doing, it doesn't work otherwise."

"Awfully convenient."

"Quite. Now, rest, do not under any circumstances overdo it in the next day or so, your body and mind have had quite the ordeal, okay?"

Flynn mock-saluted. "Whatever you say, boss."

"Good, now-- I'll be back tomorrow morning, I hope

you're ready for round two."

"You're not going to cut anything else off, are you?"

Just before closing the door behind him, Yowder said. "Now *that* would be telling."

The door clicked to, and Flynn sank down into the pillows, his mind wrestling with everything that had happened. His stomach rumbled, interrupting his chain of thought, reminding him that he hadn't eaten anything of substance in some time. Managing to extricate himself from the straitjacket of blankets, Flynn first helped Albie back into his beardy bed, before he picked through his clothes which had been placed over the back of a chair.

Pulling his trousers on, he felt something dig into the top of his thigh. A quick rummage revealed the possessions of the priest who had met his demise at the pointy bonnet of the taxi driver. He rolled the whistle around in his fingers. It was shiny silver, with no discernible marks, and apart from the open end where you would purse your lips and blow, there was nothing else. No opening at the opposite end, nothing.

Flynn put it into his mouth and blew. He sprayed the inside with his own spit, as he increased the output of air from his lungs, but despite his efforts, no sound came out. A little irked, and feeling a tad light-headed, he threw the whistle onto the bed.

As he buttoned up his shirt, he turned back to the room, and jumped backwards, seeing a nun standing at the opposite side of the bed, the door beyond her closed. She held her hands in front of her. "Hi, it's me, Sister Erica, do you remember?"

Flynn, his chest still bare, covered up his nipples with his hands. "Erm…"

"From the coach? I was eating pie, and then you turned and looked at me, and I…"

Clicking his fingers, Flynn pointed. "Of course, yes, I remember you. The nun."

Sister Erica giggled, and ran her hands down her rather easily distinguishable clothing. "That's me."

"I'm sorry…how did you…"

"You summoned me. With the pipe of summoning."

Flynn looked at the small whistle on the bed. "Ah, that's what it is. Of course. So, what do you want from me?"

The nun stood up straight. "It is time to give Mother Superior your report."

29

"What is this place?" Padraig recoiled away from drunken patrons as they staggered past the priests, through the doorway and back out onto the streets of Knighton. A large neon sign hung overhead. "*The Last Resort*, wasn't that a song by Papa Roach?" he asked.

O'Malley shook his head. "Dear, sweet Padraig, culturally oblivious to everything, huh? It was Nickelback, I know all the songs they did. I've got all their compact discs. Big fan of the newish metal, me. Come on, follow me, and try not to stand out too much."

Padraig put a thumb under his white collar. "We're dressed as two priests, I think standing out is an intrinsic part of this get-up."

"You'll see," O'Malley winked, and after plying the bouncers with a tenner each, slinked past the line of waiting punters and into the club. No sooner had they gone past the cloakroom, and the pumping Euro techno beat had started to hammer into their crania, that Padraig realised exactly what kind of club it was.

"These ladies have no proper clothes on, they're just in their undergarments!" His eyes flitted from one greased-up lady to another. They were gyrating against poles, or bent over tables, picking up glasses and high value tips.

O'Malley grabbed hold of Padraig's arm. "Don't let their Brazilian thongs, cupless bras and lacy camisoles distract you, trusty Padraig. We're on their turf now, one wrong move and they won't find your remains until the next inhabitants of this planet drill you out as oil. Come on, we're heading to the bar."

As the pair squeezed through the undulating throng of people, Padraig saw that there were a number of other priests in attendance. Always in pairs, one was enjoying the hospitality, the other standing behind a few feet, trying not to stare too closely at an exposed nipple. But it was the *other* people that stood out. There were a group of men whose faces were covered entirely in hair, they wore expensive suits, and tufts of mane protruded over their cuffs and collars. They stood around in a semi-circle, having a natter and laughing, the noise coming out like howling wolves silhouetted by a full moon.

Another group comprised female dwarves, their legs swinging like pendulums on the high chairs whose summit they had climbed. One turned to look at Padraig; she had two flat noses, the four nostrils flared quickly, and the lady turned back to her pals, sipping on green cocktails which belched grey smoke into the air.

"Father, where exactly are we? If it gets back to the Archbishop that we frequented this…this…*place*, we could be hauled over the coals."

O'Malley chuckled. "Oh, Padraig, trust me on this one, no-one, Archbishop Tena included, is going to reprimand us for being here."

Padraig ducked under a set of leather-boot-clad legs, the owner sitting on a stairway, her legs hanging off the end. As she blew him a kiss, a tiny goat's head appeared out of her mouth. Its eyes, covered in purple mucus, blinked open, and it brayed in annoyance before being swallowed back within.

"Now that was definitely a lesser demon, some kind of familiar, Father. I should return to the hire car and fetch your holy weapons of smiting."

"Nonsense, Padraig, look, come here a minute." O'Malley put an arm around his equerry and led him to an abandoned table of half-finished drinks and an unravelled, but unsoiled condom, draped over one of the martini glasses. "See, there are some deities that can't be fully exorcised, or dispelled, okay? Either they're too far gone, have too much of a hold on their host, or quite simply, they're just too damn dangerous. So, in those circumstances, we come to an agreement."

"What kind of agreement?" Padraig struggled to tear his gaze away from a trio of women, who were spinning nipple tassels so quickly that they created a small gravity well.

"Tell me, noble Padraig, what do they like doing, these demons and whatnot?"

"Murder, mutilation, sexual deviancy, the list is quite lengthy, Father."

"And are these traits the sole reserve of demons?"

"Well no, but-"

"In fact, some of them actually invented these things. Look, over there --by the red telephone box."

Padraig craned his neck, seeing a woman in a white dress, which clung to her body as if it had been spray-painted on. The only visible strip of skin was her head, which was healthily tanned.

"That is Martina Ingolstadt, she invented the cock ring. Trust me, its existence didn't start off in such a...jovial way. One of my forebears was charged with bringing her to justice, after she had tortured and maimed the male inhabitants of Tommel in The Netherlands. Before he cast her into the void, she begged for her life, offering the priest a lend of one of her more...subtle devices. Five minutes later, and with a grin as big as the Rhine, they came up with the first such arrangement. She would stop collecting tallywackers, in exchange for the church being allowed to patent her invention."

"That sounds very wrong, Father."

"Maybe, but this place is just one of hundreds scattered around the world, in towns and villages such as this, away from the hustle and bustle of society. They get to live out their perversions, and we don't risk upsetting the ethereal balance, it's very precarious." O'Malley slapped Padraig on the back and proceeded to the bar.

"Father, that's as may be, the demons and their kind, but there some other people in this place, that don't look-" Padraig walked into the back of O'Malley, who turned around with a start. He looked past the priest and into the face of the barman, which separated in two, both hemispheres waving like kelp on the seabed; individual eyes, contained within their own pods of flesh, looked back blankly, "-human," the equerry finished.

The barman's face slapped together, the skin sealing from the bottom up, making a near-invisible join, though each side was distinctive as the left was a coral blue and the right a deep purple. "Smoke on the Water," the barman said, dryly.

"Eh?"

Pointing back at the dwarven ladies, who were feeling the varied muscles of one of the male 'entertainers', the barman repeated. "Smoke on the Water. The cocktail they're drinking, that's what it's called."

"Oh…thanks," Padraig mumbled, hoping that his eyes weren't sticking out of their sockets as much as they felt like.

O'Malley plunged a hand into his pocket, looking for his wallet. "My good man, we are not alone in this universe. Many an intergalactic traveller has been either exiled to this rock of ours, or has crash-landed. These sanctuaries of ours are perfect harbours for them. Whilst we are like children in this vast old universe, we are at the very least, gracious hosts. Ah, here we go."

Padraig felt a hand gently slap against his arse cheek, he turned around to see a woman clutching a negligee, held together by two thin pieces of ribbon. "Hey, sugar, I'm Mary, you looking for a good time?" Before he could answer, the woman pulled on the ends of the ribbon, and the silk parted, revealing three pairs of breasts, which she jiggled encouragingly.

"I…erm…"

Mary pulled Padraig in, tussled the back of his hair, and whispered in his ear. "Trust me baby, you're going to wish you had six hands."

Turning slowly back to O'Malley, Padraig squeaked. "Father? What's going on here, what are we doing?"

"Looking for an old friend."

"But she has six…boobettes…"

"Good, Padraig, go with the flow a while, okay? You work hard, it's time to play hard, if you get my meaning? Why not keep…a-*breast* of current affairs?" O'Malley winked. "I say, good barkeep?"

The barman grunted. "You're back, huh? What do you want?"

"Melina, is she around?"

Like an obstinate oyster eager to hold onto its pearl, the barman's face contracted, and his lips pursed. "She don't want to see ya, not after last time." He leaned in and shook his fist, the eight fingers balled up tight. "You're lucky I don't-"

"Tony, it's okay, I got this," a woman's voice shouted from upstairs. Both O'Malley and Padraig turned as one, and watched a woman descend the stairs slowly. Each step a ballet, she maintained eye contact the entire time, coming to a stop in front of O'Malley. "What do you want?"

O'Malley stood awkwardly, his hands in his pockets. "I…just need a word…about something…if that's okay?"

Her eyes looked him up and down. "I guess I can spare a few minutes. For old time's sake. Come on." With that, she spun on the spot and began to lead him up the stairs, her hips swinging with every level of ascension.

As O'Malley passed, he said to Padraig. "I won't be long, I'm just going to pump her for information."

"I bet you are."

O'Malley slipped a tenner in the man's jacket pocket. "Get six-pack Mary here a drink, just whatever you do, don't order the champagne."

Padraig called out as the distance between them grew. "Why not?"

"Three reasons, one: if you can afford it, the church is paying you too much, two: you'd break your holy vow of celibacy, and three: the things she would do to you might send you stark raving mad." O'Malley disappeared up the staircase.

Padraig turned around, straight into the well-stocked bosom of Mary, and offered a weak grin. "Madness might well be worth the price of entry…"

———~———

After leading O'Malley down a corridor lined with plush carpet, and walled by closed doors, Melina opened the door to room 13, and held it open for him. The walls were covered in a ruby wallpaper, matching the carpet. Pride of place in the middle of the room was a four-poster bed, with thin cotton fabric draped over the corners. The sheets were tucked in, and more cushions than were necessary were piled up at the head.

As O'Malley began to loosen his white collar, the door clicked behind him. "Well, I wasn't expecting *this* kind of reception," he turned around. An open palm met his cheek just as he finished looking at her. His head rocked to one side. Before he could regain his senses, there was another solid thwack, as she repeated the feat on the other cheek, sending his head cracking against his other collarbone. Gingerly, and wary of another strike, O'Malley rubbed his cheek, and wobbled his jawbone. "Still got one helluva mean backhand on you, Mel, you keep up with your racquetball?"

The only reply was another slap, which rocked his head to the other side. O'Malley squashed his eyes shut, nothing more came, except for a rasping of a lighter, and the crackle from someone pulling smoke into their lungs. "What do you want, O'Malley?"

Daring to open his eyes, O'Malley searched the room, finding Melina, dressed in green velvet boots, and an outfit best described as 'Sexy Robin Hood,' sitting on the edge of the bed. Jiggling his jaw so that the bone went back in where it should, O'Malley thought about taking a step towards her, but decided against it. "I need your help, we've found a body, and it isn't in our database."

Melina took in another drag; burning the cigarette down to half its length, she blew the smoke out, giving the room the appearance of a music venue where the dry ice machine had gone into overdrive. "Why me? I'm sure you could've seen another of your exotic whores."

O'Malley waved a clearing in the smoke and headed towards her voice. "They meant nothing, you're the only one for me."

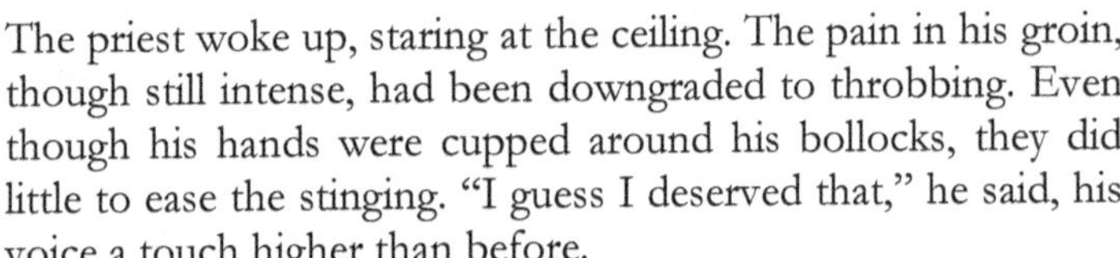

The priest woke up, staring at the ceiling. The pain in his groin, though still intense, had been downgraded to throbbing. Even though his hands were cupped around his bollocks, they did little to ease the stinging. "I guess I deserved that," he said, his voice a touch higher than before.

"Be grateful I didn't cut it off, though I would've needed a microscope to find it."

O'Malley sat up, winced at the pins and needles that assaulted his crotch, and pushed himself backwards against the bed. "Yeah, yeah, look, Mel, I know you're angry, you've got a right to be, but I wouldn't be here if it wasn't important. Please? Remember that week in Brussels? Huh? We had fun, didn't we? Me, you, all that lace --and the bucket of frites?"

Melina, now stood with her back against the door, arms folded, let her stoic demeanour soften. "Fine, what is it?"

"Some kind of insectoid, it has a giant mouth in its chest, but it has human legs, guessing it's a hybrid, but we have no idea what it is. Do you?" O'Malley pulled his iBible out and held up the phone, showing the video of the autopsy.

Melina pushed herself away from the door and watched the footage. As the priest pathologist sawed away at the nun's torso, she paused the video. "When was this taken?"

"A few hours ago. The nun, creature, *thing*, was killed this afternoon."

"It's badly burned, how did that happen?"

O'Malley sat up straighter, the pain in his balls still sending shooting pains up into his chest. "A long story, look, do you know what it is?"

Melina took the phone from the man and spooled the footage on, stopping on the nun's insect face. She passed it back to him. "I can do better than that, I can show you."

30

As the foreman held the door open, O'Malley looked up at the drab brick-and-steel-clad building. "When you said you were going to show me, I thought you meant take me to the outer reaches of the solar system. Tease me with untold sights, experience new cultures, food the likes of which my taste buds would never taste again, perhaps even a little tête-à-tête with a mysterious alien. At no time during that thought or any of the other options I considered, did I think you would take me to an industrial estate on the outskirts of Droitwich."

Melina, who had disappeared into the building already, stomped back outside, grabbed hold of the priest's shirt, and dragged him inside. As the foreman - sporting a moustache which looked like a furry caterpillar had died and been stapled on his upper lip - snorted, he tipped his hard hat, and disappeared back into the security room. "You wanted answers, and I'm going to show you. It'll be easier for you to see this here, than for me to show you on their homeworld. Unless of course you *want* to be eaten alive?"

O'Malley smoothed out his shirt. "It would have been nice to have had the option, that's all. I can look after myself, you know?"

"When it comes to *them*, erring on the side of caution is the wisest thing to do. Come on, it isn't far." Melina strutted off down the corridor, her high-heeled boots clip-clopping on the steel walkway.

O'Malley ran his fingers through his hair and followed in lockstep. After a few minutes, and a number of twists and turns, which had thrown any sense of knowing where the hell he was, he buried his nose into the crook of his elbow. Daring another breath, he took it away, before shoving it back in once more. "What is that stench? It's repellent, like damp meat mixed with mouldy nappies."

"We're nearly there, come on, don't be shy." Melina stopped in front of a set of double doors; two small windows, covered with glass smeared with handprints and old cobwebs smudged out the view of the room beyond.

Whatever was in there, it was loud. Another quick whiff confirmed that it was also the source of the smell which O'Malley feared was seeping into his pores. He was convinced that it might take a healthy application of bleach and the stiff brush to rid his skin of the smell. "Where are we, exactly? I didn't see a sign or anything on the way in, and if the sounds and smells are anything to go by, then I'm not particularly looking forward to you opening those doors."

Melina punched a four-digit code into a small panel, and took a step back against the wall. As the doors slowly opened into the room, a waft of decrepit air billowed down the walkway, O'Malley's eyes began to stream. "It's like death," he mustered, before pulling up his shirt so that it covered his face up to the bags under his eyes.

"Come on, here are the answers you seek." Melina folded her arms and began to tap her foot impatiently.

Rubbing at his eyes with his shirt cuffs, O'Malley staggered forwards, each step becoming more laboured as though an increasing number of invisible weights were being tethered to his ankles. By the time he reached Melina, he felt like a deep-sea diver, though he longed for a fresh oxygen supply that didn't test the boundaries of his gag reflex.

The sound of humming machinery gave way to another noise, albeit slightly out of place. O'Malley turned to look at Melina as he passed her, and into the threshold of the room. "Chickens?" Not quite believing what he was hearing, he continued onwards, coming to a stop against a metal handrail, which bordered a suspended walkway, around thirty feet above the ground.

Melina appeared at his side. There was a gentle thump behind him, and as he turned to see the door closed shut, she pointed into the room. "Well, what do you see?"

O'Malley retched within the confines of his shirt, feeling his hot damp breath create condensation on his chest. The room was a large warehouse, divided in two. Both sides were surrounded by wire mesh, and six-inch square gaps allowed decent views of the space below and the occupants of the cages.

A conveyor belt rolled from one caged area to the next, the rollers grinding a tedious drone, a hopper dumping straggly chickens onto them with a constant regularity. After watching for a few seconds, the delivery of the sickly birds and the rollers blended together, the surprised noises of the animals falling in between the squeak and chatter of the machine.

The birds themselves were of poor quality. The few feathers they had, clung to emaciated bodies as if they were glued on in an act of kindness. Their beaks had been clipped, and little flat triangles pecked away at the rubber conveyor, trying to snack on small flecks of sustenance, which were nothing more than dried skin and broken claw. Some of the more mobile ones, after being deposited on the belt with a squawk, tried to walk back the opposite way, to the hopper and apparent freedom. The speed was set marginally faster than their legs could carry them, and they ended up walking on the spot momentarily, before ambivalence or blind acceptance made them stop and give in to the fickle mistress of poultry fate.

Within the large cage, people dressed in white NBC suits, complete with breathing apparatus and thick black rubber gloves, worked in tandem. Via a roller door, one person would wheel in another pallet loaded down with cages of near-lifeless chickens. After stopping, the next in the chain would merrily pick up the helpless animals by whatever body part they could get their hand around, and sling them into a giant metal drum. Another would wind the drum slowly, causing the birds to whirl round at slow speed. After a few rotations, they would lift the drum upwards, which deposited them into the hopper itself. Each person carried out their roles with a bored efficiency. The delivery of the chickens was never interrupted.

The roller door opened, and another person with another pallet laden with lame birds would appear.

"Chickens? Some kind of food production factory then? They don't look like they have much meat on their bones, what can they possibly make out of them?" O'Malley asked.

Melina pointed down to the other caged area, where the conveyor belt did a sharp left turn, and ran past larger individual cages. These ones were made of sturdier metal, and thicker bars kept whatever was in them, safely contained. "They get delivered to *them*."

O'Malley ventured down the walkway, clutching the handrail as he did, vertigo made his head spin. As he followed the conveyor belt, keeping pace with the latest batch of emaciated poultry, he strained to see what was waiting for them at the end. He stopped dead, looked back to Melina and said. "More chickens? But those ones are massive! Look at the tail feathers on that one over there, it's an absolute monster!"

Melina sauntered down towards him. "Are they chickens? Look again."

Standing on his tiptoes, O'Malley struggled to get a decent angle on the inhabitants of the other cages. As he strained his Achilles, he watched as the lead chicken passed the first cage. A clawed hand shot out from the bars, grabbed hold of the chicken, which let out a strangled 'BA-CHIK', its eyes bulging out of its head before it was yanked inside. There was a crunch, audible even above the noise from the conveyor belt, followed by a burp.

One-by-one, as the hapless birds struggled to stand on their weak legs, they were snatched up by clawed hands, covered in feathers, from the caged inhabitants.

A bell tolled on the first cage; another person, dressed in the same garb as the chicken-deliverers, cautiously pulled the cage backwards on a trolley. Like a choreographed dance troupe, as soon as the cage was wheeled out of position, another was pushed in its place. Another clawed hand, more eager than the others, shot out, snatching chickens, managing to gather two scraggy ones in a single feathered fist.

"Come on, you can see better further down." Melina led the way, heading past the conveyor belt which completed the circuit, depositing the few surviving chickens back into the first caged area. They were afforded no respite, as they were then dumped back in the hopper, continuing the cycle forever onwards.

The back half of the second caged area was laid out like a communal shower room. White tiles, fouled by all manner of muck, stretched out in a large rectangle. The person connected the front of the cage to a large square hole, and after pulling up the cage door, jiggled the container. O'Malley gulped, waiting for whatever it was to be revealed.

The hands came out first, adorned with downy feathers that almost covered the long fingers which had squeezed the chickens' bodies so forcefully just moments earlier. The torso followed, ambling out like a monkey, its legs bowed and deformed. The thing shuffled out of the cage, which slammed shut behind it. The portal to the tiled chamber closed, and the person wheeled the vacated cage away.

"Is it some kind of ape? An albino chimpanzee?" O'Malley asked.

"Shhh, look."

The creature smacked its fists against the closed door, before grunting and bounding to one of the corners. It turned and looked up at the gantry. "My god..." O'Malley said. Its face, though covered with white feathers, flecked with blood and spattered with stringy veins and meat, was like a giant fly. It had a small snout in the middle of its face, which puckered with every sniff, its eyes, a swarm of smaller eyeballs formed together into one, looked up, unblinking. Its chest rose and fell, before a mouth, an upside down semi-circle of smooth lips, parted, revealing two rows of mountainous teeth, a forbidding range of enamel. It chewed idly on a tough piece of chicken skull before tipping backwards and closing up.

"It's one of those things, from the boot of the car. The nun, or whatever, but it looks different, why is that?" O'Malley asked, unable to take his eyes off the beast. Its belly was distended, it sat on its feet, not caring about comfort or function. Its mouth opened up, and its fingers picked strips of flesh that were caught between its fearsome incisors.

"They're called the Kaihoro, a race of insectoids that live on a planet which orbits twin suns, far beyond this system. They have two redeeming features, one, the obvious thing, is their mouths, which can chew through obsidian and gloom rock, they are voracious. Second, is that the queens have a rather unusual method of procreation."

"This sounds ominous, did they get jiggy with some humans or something?"

"Of a fashion --before they produce a clutch of eggs, they must feed for two days straight. Up until they were able to travel in space, they feasted on their own kind. Whole colonies of Kaihoro would be bred purely so that they could be devoured, and allow the continuation of their species. Then, one day, a queen managed to stow away on a ship which was surveying their home planet. Long story short, it ate the crew and began to create its eggs, only when they hatched, they had adopted some of the genetic material of the visiting creatures.

"Shortly after, their scientist clade made a breakthrough and they were able to venture out into the universe. One day, they stumbled across a small backwater planet populated by slightly developed monkeys, and, well, developed a taste for them."

O'Malley let his shirt fall down. "You're talking about us, aren't you?"

Melina nodded. "Instead of having their usual six legs, the batch of babies adopted your bipedal method of traversing, and a few iterations later, they were born with hands. All the while, they maintain their own genetic key, the giant mouth and face always remains, it is other facets and appendages that they seem to adapt.

"Anyway, the queen who made this batch was captured, and after some breeding, her brood was put to use in other ways."

"Ahhh, I see, kinda answers the ancient question."

"What's that?"

"Which came first, the chicken or the egg? From the looks of it, it was the chicken. So, let me get this straight. The queen had already picked up the human body parts through her mother, and through eating the chickens, picked up some of their genetic make-up, yeah?"

"Correct."

O'Malley looked down at the creature, which had lifted itself up off the floor, its spindly legs holding it inches from the ground, its hands pressed against the tiles in front of it. The creature began to grunt and howl. "Okay…I suppose the obvious thing is, why chickens? Why did we start merging the Kaihoro with chickens?"

Melina pointed at the creature, who was rocking back and forth, still supported doggy-style on the floor with its limbs. "It was more out of accident than design. You see, they have one other unusual feature."

There was a loud gurgling, followed by a series of deafening splats. The creature, anchored in place, shuddered as its hind quarters quivered and pulsed. Beneath it, propelled out of its sphincter at force, were discs of perfectly-formed meat. The creature continued discharging the waste for a minute and a half. When it finally ended, the relief on its face was palpable. After wiping sweat from its feathered brow, it turned and sniffed its waste, before recoiling and padding to another corner, this one a good degree more sanitary. It nuzzled up with one of its brethren, and began to fall asleep.

Cautiously, a factory worker entered the tiled area, and swept up the droppings into a large plastic bag. As they did so, another person, armed with a crackling cattle prod, kept one of the Kaihoro at bay. Its chest mouth snapped shut, growling as it was zapped and prodded. Collection complete, the pair scurried out the way they came in.

"I don't get it, why are they collecting its poop?"

Melina smiled. "The Kaihoro can process all manner of meat, even if it's nothing more than skin and bone. Once a number of leading fast food restaurants found out about their…talent, they set up this facility to help mine the animals that they ordinarily couldn't get anything from."

O'Malley's face dropped. "You don't mean…"

"Yes," Melina nodded, "this is how they make chicken nuggets."

Looking down at the creature as it snored, O'Malley asked. "So why nuns?"

"Let me tell you of the Tale of Sister Cecelia, saint, saviour, syphilis sufferer, sous chef, and synonymous with alliteration sycophants…"

31

The Kaihoro found your planet by accident, after they turned left at Venus and ended up crash-landing south west of Maidenhead. Their spacecraft were ramshackle affairs. Lacking any necessary engineering skills, they would cobble together anything and everything they found, usually after eating, and pooping out, the unfortunate owners of the aforementioned starships.

These were purebred Kaihoro, six legs, small stubby wings which evolution had yet to delete from their genome, and, of course, that giant mouth of theirs. They were much like your young spawn, always putting things in their mouth first, before trying anything else.

There were six in total, scouts sent out from their homeworld. This was back in the days when they had just started to realise the possible applications of merging their DNA with other species. Problem was, and still is, that the universe is a big old place, and the number of inhabited planets, at least with anything worthy of consideration of assimilating into your genetic design, is pretty small. To use a human saying, it's a lot like trying to find a sewing machine in a hay stack.

Is that right?

No matter, I think you understand. So, after flattening a disused dairy farm milking shed, the Kaihoro sprung free from the wreckage. Realising the craft was damaged beyond any attempt they could make to repair it, they decided to transmit an SOS in the hope that another craft of their kind was in the vicinity to come and pick them up. It was a long shot, but it was all they had.

After sending the distress signal, they knew that they had some time to kill, so after playing a game of tentacle-shell-claw, the loser stayed behind with the perished vehicle. The others went off in search of food, and, in the highly likely event that they would be stranded on the blue and green rock, a permanent settlement they could call their own.

The five insectoids came across a small village named Dorney. On the surface, it had everything they needed. Water to aid the spawning process, and a wide variety of lifeforms to consume. It was this curiosity that almost became their downfall.

There was a farmstead, owned by the Lovatt-Snooks, they had recently converted from arable to a petting zoo, and were in the process of stocking their pens with two of every animal that people considered 'cute.' Cute in Kaihoro passed for tasty-looking.

The five Kaihoro had already worked their way through the rabbits, pigs, and llamas, and were tucking into a family of boar, when the farmer, Tim Lovatt, started his nightly rounds. As is their custom in the countryside, he was armed with his shotgun in case there was an errant fox or ne'er do well, slinking around his prized possessions.

Tim found the pooped-out rabbits first, and after finding his other animals turned into piles of meat plop, happened upon the Kaihoro. As they were unable to communicate except for a series of really annoying clicks and whirrs, Tim opened up with both barrels, coring one of the scouts and winging another. Having never seen projectile weapons in action before, the Kaihoro prostrated themselves in front of the farmer, concluding that their great and uncaring god, Chikki Wattu, was displeased with them and had sent an avatar to deliver forth his terrible vengeance. This enabled Farmer Tim to eject the spent cartridges and start to reload.

As they prayed and clicked, Tim offed another at close range, taking its head clean off. It would seem that Tim bore an uncanny likeness to crude cave paintings of the paramilitary wing of Chikki Wattu, because even with their colleague's brains and guts being sprayed over them, they continued to pray, hoping that perhaps if they just paid homage a little faster it would help their cause.

It didn't.

Managing to postpone his shock and surprise at seeing exactly what it was he had just blown apart, Tim decided that it would be best to continue with the cull, operating very much on a shoot-first, psychologically process the events later basis.

Just as he was about to ventilate the head of another Kaihoro, who was quite clearly unarmed and posing no threat whatsoever, there was an issue with Beryl, the apparently-stillborn pony, who had in fact been revived by the geese and confined to one of the closed stables. The poor thing was deemed unworthy of being petted by children —on account of her terrible skin conditions, halitosis, and head horn, yet she somehow managed to effect escape and charged at Tim, who was oblivious to his impending doom.

Beryl met Tim at speed, connecting the soft fleshy cushions of his buttocks with her deformed bony head and pointy horn, which caused him to pitch forward into a somersault. As he landed, his finger squeezed the trigger, which, with the barrel having found its way to the base of his neck, led to Tim inadvertently decapitating himself.

The Kaihoro, with the threat of imminent execution removed, stood over the headless body of the farmer. One-by-one they realised that their entire belief system was a pile of rubbish, predicated on an outdated feudal caste system, a lack of knowledge about the meaning of life and a number of cave drawings which, when they thought about it, had probably been drawn by one of the Chikki Wattu worm priests for the single purpose of enslaving them.

The worms, all male, had been ruling over the female Kaihoro for as long as their entwined histories had been recorded via the somewhat shaky medium of rock illustrations.

As this revelation hit them, they grew angry, and a determination to get back to their homeworld, and tell the other Kaihoro the truth, became their sole concern. As they clicked and whirred amongst themselves, they heard a slurping sound, and looked across to Tim's body. Tucking into the ragged stump of the farmer's neck was Beryl, her scabby white mane dripping with blood.

Having never tasted this kind of animal before, they each crouched down by a limb, and took a bite. Needless to say, they were WOWED. Never before had they tasted something which had the potential for versatility. They passed pieces of the farmer around, ensuring they left offerings to their saviour, Beryl, who was quickly losing interest in feasting on her one-time owner, and regretting her moment of impulse which had resulted in her becoming half an orphan.

The Kaihoro ate every morsel, leaving nothing but the farmer's neatly folded clothes. They had long since departed by the time Tim's life partner came out an hour or so later, checking up on her errant fella and the coterie of fluffy animals which she was convinced would make them a tidy sum. After finding Tim's bloodstained clothing, Anna, along with her friend, Felicity, resorted to drinking a bottle of homemade rhubarb gin to help ease the pain. A few hours later, and a little worse for wear, the pair resolved to track down Tim's murderers and hoist them atop the nearest lamppost by their necks.

By the break of dawn, the Kaihoro had worked their way through the east side of Dorney. The population now consisted of piles of defecated human meat, neatly-deposited in the corners of pantries and outdoor toilets. Their rampage only came to a halt when the lead Kaihoro, called Tikka Blerwer, suffered acute indigestion and suggested they should all have a bit of a rest and continue with the buffet later. Unfortunately, they chose to rest in the cellar of the village pub, The Tawdry Hun.

Anna and Felicity rounded up the remaining villagers into a sizeable posse. After pointing out what had become of their neighbours and inbred family members, they didn't bother to seek out the local constabulary, mainly because he had already been eaten. Instead, they, gathered pitchforks, rifles, and flaming torches. It was the middle of the day, though, and the sunlight did lessen their impact somewhat, but the yokels insisted.

Tradition is tradition, after all.

Following the trail of crapped-out people, they laid siege to the pub, convinced that the perpetrators were Dutch spies. They trusted few, and still hadn't recovered from the events of the Raid of the Medway in 1667. They delivered an ultimatum in broken Dutch, which meant little to the Kaihoro.

Although they had never seen a firearm before Tim had so keenly introduced them to one, they knew about fire. So even though the torches didn't really illuminate anything, they sure as hell scared the bejesus out of the insectoids, who knew their time was up.

Sensing that they had little to lose, Tikka Blerwer convinced the others that if they were going to go out, they should do so in a blaze of biting and snapping of giant maws. Plus, she had developed a taste for spines and the marrow within, so was sure that she could at least rip a backbone or two out, before they were set ablaze and burned to death. As she teetered by the cellar door, ready to lead her sisters out to their certain death, there was a coughing behind them. Out of the gloom came Sister Cecelia, sipping sherry, and singing a soaring sea shanty about swimming, snarling sharks. At first, the Kaihoro contemplated eating her. As they circled the nun, she swayed, slightly sozzled from the sauce.

With first dibs won, Tikka opened her giant mouth and went to rend the woman apart, but instead of fearing the insectoids, she soothed its side, softly stroking the sentient's snuffling snout. Tikka stopped. What was the dinner doing? Cecelia spoke succinctly, words the creatures could not discern. She pointed to the hatch, and wagged a finger. "Sweet sorrow shall you see, should sanctuary that way you scurry. Safer still to sit straight and allow Sister Cecelia to secret you with some skill. Savvy?" She held aloft three habits, and after some coaxing, managed to get the Kaihoro into their disguises.

In a quick training montage, she showed them some rudimentary basics on walking on two legs, fashioned veils for each, and hurried to the cellar door. She pushed it open and marched them out, each hidden beneath the habit and veil. The villagers, either too enraged to see past the feeble disguise, or too stupid, bought Cecelia's story and let them leave.

Tikka led the survivors back to the spaceship, where, fortuitously, a passing ship, working for the Galactic Association of Fine Food and Exotic Refreshments --or GAFFER, had heard their plaintive cry, and came to help.

After telling the GAFFER their story, and spending a lot of time discussing the wonderful taste and texture of humans, they were offered a lift back to their homeworld, with the prospect of working together on some future culinary projects.

Sister Cecelia was never heard from again…some say that she was taken back to the Kaihoro homeworld as a God, revered as one, and lived out the remainder of her years in luxury. Others say that Tikka served her as the main course as thanks to the passing GAFFER representatives for saving them.

One thing is sure. The Kaihoro went home, and there was an uprising. The previous ruling class of the Chikki Wattu worm priests were overthrown and enslaved, their tyranny at an end, the female Kaihoro now reigning supreme. With the help of GAFFER, they were given bigger and better ships, and charged with finding new and more lavish meats.

In particular, the blue-and-green rock was earmarked for investigation. Every year, on the anniversary of their crash landing, a delegation of Kaihoro, specially bred with humans, would land on the planet. Dressed in the vestments their forebears were smuggled to safety in, they would choose a nondescript village and pick it clean, taking home an assortment of meat products, which they sold to GAFFER, and on the open market. A promise was made…as soon as they were able to, and had the means to do so, they would return en masse. Earth would become a farm world, humans the cattle.

———————～———————

O'Malley gulped. "That's disgusting. Hang on…you've known about this? All along?"

Changing gear, Melina settled back into the middle lane and nodded. "Of course I have, what being in the galaxy *hasn't?*"

"And you've not told me or anyone else?"

"Why would I?"

Looking out of the window, as fields sped by, O'Malley fidgeted in his seat. "So…have you…you know…eaten any human?"

"Yes."

"What do we taste like? Are we any good?"

Melina veered back into the fast lane. "Didn't really think you were anything to transmit home about, I found human to be rather bland."

O'Malley retched. "Urgh, that's gross, I've never eaten human…or alien for that matter."

Laughing, Melina yanked the car back across two lanes of traffic, and rested a hand on the priest's knee. "I think you *have* tasted alien before, remember?"

"I knew you were going to bring that up, sooner or later."

"So, go on, what *did* alien taste of?"

"If I had to liken it to anything, it was like licking a nine-volt battery."

"Enchanting. Anyway, the Kaihoro became agents for the GAFFER, though they have always had a particular soft spot for the delicacies of earth."

"Where are we going?"

"They will have a base somewhere, we need to find it quickly."

O'Malley looked out of the window, as they overtook an estate car at speed, the children in the back looking at them with a mix of fear and adulation. "Where would they be?"

Melina bashed the horn, before undercutting a white van, drawing alongside to give the driver the finger. "I would imagine they would need to be somewhere they can blend in, after all, a group of nuns is quite conspicuous. It isn't as if they could just stay anywhere, is it?"

"True. I know, we should go and see my old mentor, if anyone knows where large groups of nuns congregate, it would be him."

"Fine, but we need to be quick, the Kaihoro are quick to anger, and slow to forgive. It would only take one thing for them to stop their small-scale operation, and ratchet it up to a full-blown invasion. I just hope that no one antagonises them before we can either get to them, or they've completed this year's harvest. Otherwise this planet, and everyone on it, would be nothing more than potential appetisers."

32

Flynn shirked the hand from his shoulder. "Get your fucking mitts off me." The nun went to put a hand on him once more, the priest held up a fist. "Go on, do it. I fucking dare you." She stopped and moved away. Flynn straightened out his jacket. "One more thing, the next one of you fucking penguins who calls me a worm, is going to be eating their meals through a feeding tube for the foreseeable future."

Erica looked at him, her head at an angle. "That is illogical, we do not require feeding tubes to gain sustenance."

The priest walked past her and down a corridor, which opened up into a large stone courtyard. At the far end, beneath a walkway, he saw Mother Superior sitting at a table, sifting through a mountain of paperwork. She picked up a cracker, and began to slather lashings of Chipping Camford compote on it. "Enough of this, we do not have time to bicker," she shouted.

"Agreed. I think I've reached a breakthrough in my therapy."

Francesca pointed to the opposite side of the table. "There."

"There's no chair, do you want me to stand?"

"Well, of course I do. You don't think I'd allow *you* to sit down at the same level as me, do you?"

Flynn rolled his eyes and stopped to take in the sights. It was a hive of activity; nuns were scurrying from ground-floor rooms, laden with cardboard boxes, all stamped and sealed. They walked in perfect lines, each foot stepping into the footfall of the nun in front of them. They were well-drilled, and, regardless of the bulk of their load, bore their burden with no complaint.

"You ladies have been busy," Flynn muttered. In the centre

of the room, was a tall rocket, with fins sticking out of the base. "Wow, this is cool, didn't know this was a museum, too."

Francesca stood up. "How dare you, this is a state-of-the-art Groccken T12, the GAFFER gave this to us, it's only been on the market for five tetracycles. I'd hardly say it belongs in a museum."

Flynn stood before the rocket, running his hands up and down the smooth surface as he strolled around the metal cylinder, craning his neck up to the roof, trying to take it all in. The nuns were all walking to the opposite side of it. Finally completing a lap, he saw that the women were stacking their packages into the rocket. "Handy, put all your stuff in there, suppose it stops it being piled up in your rooms."

The nuns continued to work, ignoring the priest tottering around where they were loading their samples. As soon as they deposited their load, they bowed and crossed themselves before heading back to the store room, ready to collect more for shipping. Francesca continued to pore through the latest profit and loss printouts.

With the women seemingly occupied, Flynn ambled across to the rocket's cargo bay, and, after checking that no one was watching, pried open one of the boxes. Picking a jar from its reinforced packaging, he read the label. "One-hundred-percent free range and organic. Pickled eyeballs." With another quick glance around, he cracked the jar lid open, the acrid smell of vinegar assailing his nostrils. Peeking inside, he saw perfectly round eyeballs bobbing up and down within the liquid, and looked at the label again, checking for a typo. "Pickled eyeballs, blue…okay…how did you get onions to look like this?" Flynn looked around for an answer, but no one was there. The first of the nuns reappeared from the stock room, and the shipping centipede resumed its cycle.

Flynn dipped a finger into the vinegar, poking one of the eyeballs, which sunk, before rising to the top once more. "They are divine," Francesca's voice, close to his ear, made him jump.

"Jesus, you scared the crap out of me."

"I don't suppose you have been allowed one before?"

"I've had normal ones, you know, but nothing this fancy. It's amazing the detail you've gone to. Guess you lot make all this and sell it at Farmers Markets and the like?"

Francesca's mouth formed into an O, before she regained composure. "I'm surprised one of your kind knows about markets, I think we need to tighten up what you can and can't do. The revolution should've put a stop to some of these liberties you used to take for granted."

"Eh? Revolution?"

"Fine, go on then, you may have one. Your crass stupidity has broken the seal anyway, it's not as if we can sell that now, is it?"

"Ah, I'm sorry, didn't really think, just these look really lifelike. Bit of an odd one though, it's not Halloween for ages."

"Do you want one or not?" Francesca snatched the jar from the priest.

"Yeah, I'll give one a crack." Flynn dug his fingers into the jar, and, after a little bobbing - the little sods kept rolling away – he finally managed to pick one out. In the palm of his hand, and free of vinegar, the priest took a closer look. It was indeed expertly crafted, he could even make out the fine lines that looked like veins, the attention to detail on the iris was second to none.

Francesca fished one out and held it out to him, Flynn tapped the eyeball he was holding against hers. "Cheers me dear," and slung it in his mouth. He bit down with his back teeth, the surface as tough as a pickled onion should be. After applying a smidge more pressure, there was a crack, and a wave of thick gloopy fluid flooded from within. "Mmm, it's like a mini crème egg or something." As the liquid ran over his tongue, a second wave of taste hit.

It had the consistency of albumen, and his taste buds recoiled as hints of clove trickled down his throat. His lips puckered at the sharp taste. Desperate to get the experience over with, he crunched and chewed as quickly as possible. Each bite made the onion taste more leathery, and no matter how much he crushed the thing down, it remained stringy and tough. Flynn pinched his nose and fought to swallow, his throat resisted at first, but finally the mush was admitted entrance into his guts.

Francesca smiled. "It is an acquired taste, and plainly not for the likes of you." Her brow furrowed as she pointed to the bandage. "Have you damaged your prosthesis?"

Flynn twisted his hand. "This? Don't worry about it, long story, bit of an extreme session with one of the therapists here. I'm beginning to think that I should've gone for the long game. Tell me, Sister-"

"Mother Superior."

"Oh yeah, Mother Superior, what's your speciality?"

"Acquisitions," Francesca replied sternly, waving for Sister Wanda to come forward.

"Yes, Mother Superior."

"This worm has had his prosthesis damaged, please remove it and get a replacement."

Wanda nodded and stepped forward, and Flynn held up his hands. "Seriously, what did I say about the worm thing?"

The nun placed her hands on Flynn's shoulder and forearm; her hold was firm. Pushing down, she tried to pull and twist the arm, which went back as far as it could go before Flynn let out an annoyed, "OWWW."

Francesca placed a hand on Wanda's arm, urging her to retreat. She yanked up Flynn's sleeve, revealing a hairy arm and a tattoo of Boyzone. The two women gasped. "You're…you're…no worm," Francesca said.

"Finally! I've been telling you people to not call me that, it's about damn time you listened."

The Mother Superior whispered in Wanda's ear, who bowed and jogged off to the conveyance line of nuns. As one, they stopped, put down their boxes and began to converge on the priest, who looked around for an exit. "So, if you're not a worm, then you're one of *them*, cattle. Human. Food."

"Eh? Have you been on the cooking sherry?"

The nuns had formed a semi-circle behind him, creating a

barrier of black and white like the deadly Emperor Penguins. Flynn walked into them, and staggered forward, trapped between a nun and a hard place. He narrowed his eyes towards Francesca. Her habit twitched, and as he saw a sliver of pink tongue run along the divide, his mouth fell open. "What the hell are you?"

Francesca held the eyeball between her fingers and threw it into the air, the thing spinning upwards until gravity claimed it and it began to fall. As it did, Francesca's chest mouth snapped open, revealing rows of dagger teeth and an anxious waiting gullet. The eyeball disappeared into the vacuous maw, which closed slowly, showing the Mother Superior's human face last, with a devilish grin affixed. She looked the priest dead in the eyes. "Hungry, always hungry. Why do all the cattle ask us that?"

Flynn looked down at the box he had ripped open, and thought back to the recent taste sensation. "My god…they're real?"

"Of course they are, my lovely. Freshly plucked and rounded from the annual harvest this afternoon, all ready to be sent off-world, to the finest patrons the universe has." She leaned in, looking into the priest's eyes. "Oh, look, what a wonderful pair of blue eyes you have. We're two short in this jar, I think I know where we can get some replacements from."

The decision to flee came suddenly, the choice to go out swinging an instinctive one. He turned to his right and cracked Sister Roberta with a vicious uppercut. The nun took off the floor a few inches and flew backwards, crashing into the table, sending reams of paper everywhere. Flynn let his fists fly, and, after some wild swings, had taken out another couple of nuns, enabling him to form a small avenue of escape.

In the distance, he could see the doorway he'd come in through, and bolted for it. As the exit grew larger, he knew what he had to do: get back, find Yowder and the rest of the security priests, and put these nuns down, or whatever the hell they were. His legs were pumping away, his arms swinging, trying to exert every ounce of speed. The door was only around ten feet away now, he had made it.

He reached out a hand, but before he could grab hold of the handle, he felt something jab into his neck. All he could do was manage to slap a hand against it, as if he'd been stung by a wasp, before his entire body went rigid and he collapsed to the floor. He slid, face down, his momentum coming to an abrupt end as he smacked against the wall.

For a few seconds, he could see nothing except the contour of the stone slabs beneath him, then the world spun as he was turned over. Francesca's face came into view, looming over him, other nuns crowding around above her, including a couple nursing their faces, whose skin looked as though it had come loose from the skull beneath. Mother Superior chuckled. "Why are you running away? You may not be grade A meat, but I'm sure we can turn you into a little something for our journey home."

33

Somehow, he had been made to stand up, do an about-turn, and march quite merrily to a large metal room, one floor down. After coming to an abrupt stop, Flynn tried to inject some movement into his limbs, but, try as he might, nothing was responding to his internal commands.

One of the nuns, referred to by the head honcho as Sister Ophelia, was busying herself behind him. Unable to see what the woman was up to, the sounds of metal clanging against metal, saws being revved up and blades being sharpened were not helping the various scenes of torture being played back-to-back on a matinee performance in his mind, just for him.

What the hell had happened? How could they have taken away every single movement? Flynn tried to wiggle his toes, then reviewed the decision, instead trying to move one toe so minutely, that it would barely constitute movement.

No dice.

Perhaps his hopes were too lofty. No matter, toes are for pros, there had to be something he could do to prove he was in control. To his rear, something heavy thudded against the floor. He heard a swish of polyester as the nun bent over, followed by a few solid thunks as she padded whatever it was she had dropped into the palm of her hand. She let out a happy sigh, and continued with her noisy preparation.

Now trying to stymy the image of having his fingers broken one-by-one, and the bones pulled out through the tips, leaving his hands ready for filleting, Flynn retreated inwards. What could he do? Something surely had to be under his control.

Blinking?

No.

Flaring his nostrils.

Nope.

Slightly moving one finger against the one next to it.

Nada.

Allowing a thread of drool to slip from his lips and fall onto his shoes.

FOR THE LOVE OF GOD!

That was one of his all-time favourite things. Nearly every night he had woken up in the early hours, turning straight over into a cold wet patch of dribble on his pillow. It had gotten to the stage where it was almost involuntary, just the merest hint of rest and he would burble spit out of his mouth. If he couldn't even do *that*, then his number was well and truly up.

"Well now, *worm*, let's get started," Ophelia appeared in his eyeline, pushing a trolley weighed down with implements, most of them shiny, and some beyond even the bounds of his fertile imagination. There was a generator in the middle of the gurney, with a variety of power tools wired up to it. Some had been improvised. A circular saw head had teeth which could cut through time itself. Or so his brain figured.

The trolley castors squeaked and strained under the combined weight of the tools of his impending bloody disassembly. As the nun came to a stop, Flynn felt something inside of him loosen; a padlock jimmied open, a Pandora box, in this instance, a Flynn-box, being opened by inquisitive demonic fingers.

+Priest, you must do something to prevent your destruction+

Who the hell are you?

+I'll give you a clue, you buffoon, do something to spare us from our collective DOOM+

Oh great, this guy again, Mister Puke himself.

+Hey, it's the *Prince* of Puke, *actually*, I didn't spend my time murdering my way through the demonic bloodline to be dismissed as a mere commoner. I thought you realised that the vision you experienced showed you the truth?+

You mean, that was real?

+It's no wonder I bested you, *priest*, the other one is

infinitely more capable than you+

Why I oughta…wait a minute, why aren't you wearing me like a morph suit? Poor little Timmy an ill fit?

+I have not possessed you entirely, *priest*, you ingested me, I cannot control your feeble body that way+

That sounds pretty nasty.

+I currently possess your tonsils, imagine the havoc I could wreak+

Erm…you're not too au fait with human physiology, are you?

+No…I normally feed on people's bad emotions, get a rise out of them and then ascend, this is a little strange+

Really? This is a tad much for me, if I'm being honest.

+I too am in a peculiar situation+

So why have you taken so long to announce your arrival? It's been three months.

+I was waiting for the right time to reveal myself+

You what? You're not the bloody Sith, you know.

+Who? So, the tonsils, what do they do exactly? Are they in charge of anything important?+

Ophelia pulled on a pair of thin latex gloves, taking her time to ping each finger so that the material clung to her skin. After what seemed an age, she started to go through a number of items. First off, she picked up an angle grinder, whirring it into life and holding it in front of Flynn's face. Despite looking into the spinning metal, he couldn't feel the backdraft on his skin.

+Forget I asked, this nun is actually going to take you apart, I thought it was just one of your weird church games+

"Maybe save this for when I've flayed you," Ophelia turned off the tool and laid it down. She rooted through the objects and picked up a hammer and chisel. "You humans always seem to have too many bones, perhaps I can liberate some of them before I get to the good bits." She ripped open Flynn's shirt, and felt for the end of his ribs. She placed the chisel where rib met breastbone and pulled the hammer back.

+I hope this doesn't hurt me too+

Ophelia stopped as the hammer connected, doing nothing but letting out a tiny crack. "Oh no, no, no, that will keep for later. I think I need to do what Mother Superior requested of me." Dumping the hammer and chisel back onto the tray, she spun around, holding a dessert spoon.

+**She's going to eat you like sorbet, I think she might be mental**+

She's not going to eat me. Not with that.

+**What else could she possibly do with the spoon, priest?**+

"This is the spoon of plucking."

+**Ahhh, of course, the whole eye thing, good choice**+

You're not helping.

+**You want my help, mortal?**+

That would be terrific help, would you mind?

The nun's chest mouth breathed out onto the surface of the spoon; before slurping shut, Ophelia rubbed the cutlery on her tunic. "Now, let's get those ocular orbs of yours out of there, and tidied up, we have a quota to meet."

Any time now.

+**I am trying, *priest*, the hold over us is total. It transpires that I am not able to affect much in these small fleshy sacks**+

For fuck's sake…

+**Do not take that tone with me, mortal! If you had let me possess you properly then I might have been able to help**+

To aid with the sense of impending dread, Ophelia began to cackle out of both mouths. After that, she turned the spoon so that she could gouge away better, rested one hand on the side of Flynn's head, and began to move the spoon in slowly, making sure that the priest could see it the entire time.

My mother always said I had beautiful eyes.

+**Soon, you'll be able to see one up close. I'm pretty sure this nun will show you your eye when she pries it from your…I mean, *our* skull, she has that cray-cray look about her**+

The nun began to press the spoon into the bottom of his right eyelid, Flynn could see the silver handle lead up to the woman's still-cackling face. Beneath the evil laughter, Flynn heard a rustling, as if something was pushing its way through a gorse bush. Ophelia angled the spoon up, and as she did, Flynn saw a tiny pink hand, the fingers near-melded together, grab hold of the base of the metal bowl. As Ophelia went to push the spoon of plucking within, and have a bit of a root around, trying to sever the muscle that held it in place, she felt resistance. She put her other hand behind the spoon, and leaned into it. Another tiny pink hand grabbed hold of the spoon, balancing out the application of pressure.

The cackling had given way to a snort of annoyance. Ophelia pulled on the spoon, heaving Albie from Flynn's beard, who hung from the handle like he was about to start doing monkey bars on an assault course. The nun's face dropped, even its giant chest mouth sagged open. "I don't believe it, how can it be?"

Albie growled, turning his hands to face out the same side and spun around like a gymnast working the high beam. With an allez-oop, the axolotl vaulted through the air, managing a seven-twenty flip before landing neatly on top of the spoon bowl. Ophelia lowered the spoon, and went to grab the creature with her free hand. "I thought your kind were all dead."

+I did not know you were already possessed by underling demons, you are proving to be quite the welcoming host, I shall invite many of my kind around to par-tay inside your fetid skin wrapping+

There was a whining sound, growing in volume, until it reached a shrill pitch. "Oh no, you don't, you vile creature," Ophelia managed to wrap her fingers around Albie and began to squeeze. Flynn could just make out the amphibian's eyes bulge, imbued with an internal red glow.

The nun's face was twisted in rage, before a focused lance of red light hit her smack dab in the nose. A small wisp of black smoke rose from the impact site, coupled with the smell of burning rubber. The nun was frozen, her face twitching and vibrating. There was a whoosh, and the beam flashed with intensity, burning through the nun's head and hitting the back wall, scoring it.

Ophelia stood there, the centre of her face cored through. The red beam stopped, Albie's eyes receded back into his skull, and he edged to the back of the spoon, bounced up and down a few times, and disembarked with a double twist and pike, landing expertly on the priest's head. Flynn looked through the gaping hole in the nun's head, at the wall opposite. Finally, Sister Ophelia collapsed to the floor, the spoon shooting off under the trolley.

+Impressive, most impressive, that demon is exemplary+

It's not a demon, it's Albie.

Flynn's vision wobbled, his legs momentarily turning to jelly as control of his body was restored. The priest fell to his knees, taking in deep breaths and flexing his hands, checking he was still intact. Flynn turned to see Albie sitting on his shoulder, holding a foot-long twig thing in his little paws. The axolotl held it out to him. "Aww, thanks, little guy, you saved my life back there!" Flynn patted Albie on the head.

"It is my pleasure, Flynn of the cloth, I am glad to have been of assistance."

Father Flynn's mouth fell open, no words escaped, but he did drool over his shoe, a few moments later than intended, admittedly, but he felt some small degree of gratitude that his body was his own again. He wiped his lips with his sleeve. "You…you…you can talk."

Albie bowed. "Of course I can. It's not that difficult, you're a long way down the evolutionary scale than I am, I was quite taken aback when I landed on this planet and found out that you still had game shows."

Flynn sat down on the floor, pushing the dead nun away with his feet. "So what are you? Who are you? Where did you come from?"

+He is a denizen of the underworld+

"No, he's not."

+I bet you…YOUR SOUL+

The axolotl placed a slimy hand on Flynn's cheek. "My name is Cachoonga Burpp, I came here when I fled my homeworld, the distant planet of Bellch."

"You fled your world, why?"

Albie crawled down the priest and walked over to the nun. After hauling himself onto the dead thing's chest, he pushed his hands under the white habit and began to pull the thick skin back, revealing a brown hide beneath. The axolotl continued to peel away, scratching and tearing at the clothes and mask, until the nun's true form was laid bare.

"That is one ugly mother…"

+I would do it. Over and over again until there was nothing left of its corporeal form+

"Of course you would, Fattori, this is not information that surprises me."

Albie passed the face mask to the priest, who turned it upside down. "Wow, this thing is better than what they have in the shops."

"These are presents from the GAFFER, a galactic-wide federation which preys on the tastiest of species. This thing, and her race, the Kaihoro, want nothing except to turn the inhabitants of worlds into wonderfully-flavoured delicacies, or to add them to their genetic code. They are parasites."

"You don't say, they seem a bit far out."

Sitting down on the insectoid's chest, with the still-rising smoke as a backdrop, Albie continued. "They came to my homeworld, flying the flag of peace, asking if they could meet our leaders and organise an interplanetary sports competition. We are peaceful people, and extremely competitive, so naturally, the hierarchy agreed. This was our downfall.

"As soon as the delegation arrived, and talks began over whether to include crazy golf, communications across our world were blocked. An invasion fleet began to land, and in no time at all, they had enslaved the population. It turns out they had been visiting us for many years. The reports about small settlements disappearing overnight was not down to arguments turning to violence over bowling scores, but *them*." Albie pointed at the Kaihoro, the top half of its body revealed, its face a ruin.

"We were so blind. All those years they had been working out how best to prepare, cook and serve us. They said we were a taste sensation, and that we were going to be up for an award. We were herded into camps, and slowly, but surely, they began to boil us in batches for two sun cycles. After that, we were deboned, skewered, and, after being seasoned, roasted. Still alive. Our species cannot reproduce very quickly, and in no time at all, we had all but been wiped out. One day, they came for me, one of the last remnants of my kind. I managed to escape, and stole one of their ships.

"They caught up with me and disabled my craft. Thinking me dead, they left me adrift in the cold dark of space. Yet I did not die. I fell into hibernation, not caring if I lived or died. I awoke one day to find that my capsule had been breached, yet I still lived. Would my torment ever end? I shouted to the blue sky. Crawling through the smashed window, I found myself in a field of orange and brown. I had crash-landed on your planet, and when some humans found me, they did as the Kaihoro had done with my kind, they incarcerated me. Until you saved me."

+Got to say, that is a cool story, little demon+

"Okay, so that's a bit weird, terribly sad, but cool. Why didn't your species use your laser beam eyes when you were invaded?

Albie blinked. "I did not get my powers until I landed on your planet, I guess your atmosphere metabolised within, and gave me these wondrous gifts."

"This sounds terribly familiar…are you sure your homeworld is not called Krypton and your name is Kal-El?" Flynn asked.

"Positive."

"Good enough for me, so, we need to stop them, there's no telling what they could do," Flynn got to his feet, still a little wobbly.

+We need to teach these nuns a lesson, we cannot let them turn you all into dinner. This displeases me and my kind+

"You're all heart, Fattori. Look, the plan remains, we get back, get Yowder and anyone else, then we storm this place and kick their arses."

Albie laid a hand on the priest's foot. "Flynn of the cloth, put me back into my sanctuary, I am unsure if I can be of much use during this battle, but if I can, I will. My homeworld and all of my beach volleyball team must be avenged, regardless of the cost."

34

After pounding away on the door to Yowder's office for a good five minutes, Flynn decided that in the face of possible extinction, a quick dose of door brutality was called for. A few meaty kicks later, the wooden frame splintered, and the door swung inwards, smacking against a tall metal filing cabinet.

"What the hell, man?" Yowder's voice came from the back of the office. His chair faced the far wall, and he sounded a little peculiar.

Flynn tried to close the door as best as he could, but the splintered wood stopped it being closed fully. He shoved it as far back as it would go, then speed-walked across to Yowder's desk. "Why didn't you let me in? I was banging away for hours."

"I told you not to exert yourself, you shouldn't be here, kicking in doors. You should be resting. Many challenges still to go, you have."

Grabbing hold of the back of Yowder's chair, he spun it around, and the priest made a "weeeeeeee," noise as he was flipped to the front. "That was pretty cool, man, can you do it again?" Yowder looked up with a big grin, his eyes hidden behind a large pair of mirrored sunglasses.

"I don't think you fully appreciate the situation."

Yowder went to stand, wobbling as his arse lifted from the chair cushion, before he resigned himself to falling, slumping back down as quickly as he had tried to stand. "Whatever, I don't think *you* understand the situation."

"Are you drunk?" Flynn went to wrestle the sunglasses from Yowder's face, who resisted, the pair resorting to slapping each other's hands. The elder priest ducked under a lazy swipe, and caught Flynn round the face with an open palm, the slap reverberating through the room. Victory --of sorts-- won, Yowder pushed himself back, holding the sunglasses firmly against his head. The chair hit the wall, and he juddered to a halt.

"Look, Yowder, I need your help, those nuns up at the other building, they're...I don't know what, aliens? Mad mental women, who want to turn humans into a variety of food products and sell us to the universe."

"And you were asking me if *I* was drunk?"

"I'm telling the truth!"

"Why don't you stop your gills vibrating, and then we'll talk, like men. Human men."

"Gills?"

"Yes, they're vibrating. I've tried to ignore it, but between that, your waving tentacles and the virulent mutant kelp writhing around your feet, my patience with your shifting form has reached breaking point."

Flynn looked down, the carpet tiles remained as static and staid as they had always been. A few iffy stains aside, the only way they were writhing would be if they were infested with a colony of silverfish. The priest furrowed his brow. "What have you taken?"

"Nothing."

"Define nothing."

"What is this, the Spanish Inquisition? I told you to stay in your room. More trials tomorrow. Important trials. *Very* important trials. Bigly trials. But no, here you are, smashing my door in, trying to steal my sunglasses, oozing all over my beach, jabbering away about hungry nuns."

"You're off your nut, aren't you?"

"Maybe."

"Well, this is just effing marvellous isn't it? In the hour of need, you're off your balls. You were supposed to help save us, to lead us into the light, not leave us in the dark hungry mouths of those damn nuns."

Yowder inched forwards in his chair. "Okay, so I may have tried the efficacy of the narcotic ahead of tomorrow's trial. If anything, you should be thanking me, the last thing you want is a bad trip, eh? Especially given your current cephalopod leanings."

"But I'm not…okay, fine. So, what have you taken?"

"Some may call it Lysergic acid diethylamide, others LSD, me? I call it the gateway to realisation."

"You were going to suggest we both get high?"

"That's about the size of it."

"After you cut my finger off and lectured me about drinking?"

"Are you still bitching about that? Come on, man, you need to let go of the past, move on. That's, like, rule number twenty-three of therapy. Or something."

Flynn marched over to the window and pulled the blinds open. He wheeled Yowder across to the window, and pointed at the large rotund building. "You see that? In there are things masquerading as nuns, they are going to take over the world and turn us into squeezy tubes of human meat sauce. I need your help."

"I don't think I'm going to be of much use, I'm off my gourd. Come see me tomorrow, this is some good shit, we're gonna have a whale of a time…" Yowder raised and lowered the sunglasses at speed, marvelling at the swirling kaleidoscope of colours cavorting in front of him.

"Those damn women…alien…things will be gone by morning." Flynn fell to his knees; raising his hands up to the heavens, he bellowed. "Who will help me rid this planet of those turbulent nuns?"

The door crashed open again. "I will."

Both priests turned around, looking to the doorway at the newcomer. Flynn rolled his eyes. "For fuck's sake, anyone but you."

O'Malley waltzed into the room, hands on hips, a swagger in his gait, a smug grin fixed on his face. "The enemy of my enemy is my friend, what say you, Father Flynn?"

"I say you're a wanker. What the fuck are you even doing here? Why is it, that every time I have something important to face, you swan in, trying to take the credit? You're as welcome here as the morning-after pill sacrament at Sunday mass. Why don't you take the hint, and piss off?" Flynn walked over to the doorway.

"Hold it, sunshine, you're not going anywhere," O'Malley blocked the exit.

"Move out of my way, or so help me…"

O'Malley shimmied left and right, stopping Flynn from escaping. After a few seconds which bordered on utter embarrassment, the pair stopped and glared at each other. O'Malley looked past Flynn. "Master Yowder, the situation is indeed grave, Flynn speaks the truth. The nuns up there are indeed aliens, hell-bent on transforming the human race from sentient creatures into the latest galactic taste sensation. We need your guidance now more than ever."

There was a groan from the chair as Yowder sagged down. "I told this one, I ain't going anywhere, I'm on the start of a wonderful journey inside my own psyche, if I don't come to tomorrow morning, sparked out in a field, my legs shaved, face painted, and with a slight twinge of shame, then I'm nothing. NOTHING."

"Then help us, tell us what we must do, how do we beat them?" O'Malley pleaded.

Yowder clicked his fingers. "Of course, this must be the final trial that the prophecy spoke of."

"Final trial? Prophecy? I've only had one other trial before it, and that involved you lopping my finger off and conducting some kind of voodoo ritual."

"Hey, kid, I told you it would work fast, I'd say two trials was pretty damn fast, wouldn't you?"

"I guess…"

Yowder sprung off the chair and teetered across to the man. He slung an arm around him, pulling Flynn in close. "This trial will be the making of you, then you could come back, and complete your training, oh, the things I have to show you, the wondrous activities I have in store."

Flynn folded his arms. "Like what?"

Spinning Flynn around, Yowder sprayed his arms wide,

painting an imaginary vista. "I'll teach you how to lift rocks…"

"Big deal."

"With your mind, woooooo," Yowder squeezed Flynn closer.

"Yeah right."

"That's not all, you'll lift a rock, with your mind, whilst doing…a handstand."

"Okay, so that is pretty cool."

"I knew you'd like that." Yowder began to do a weird little jig, leaping from imaginary stone to imaginary stone, hoping not to step into the bubbling molten magma on either side of the rocks. "Plus, we'll go down to the Forest of Dean, and you can carry me round like a backpack! All the while, I'll impart arcane knowledge to you, tell you wondrous things which will blow your mind."

"I think I'll pass. Once I take care of those nuns, if I take care of those nuns, I think it'd be best if you just sign something for the Archbishop saying I'm all better."

There was another crash at the doorway. "Duke, you must stay on, complete your training."

Flynn turned to face the voice. "Padraig? Of course…quite apt that we're at Saint Judas, when there's one stood right in front of me."

Padraig shook an umbrella, before resting it against the filing cabinet amongst the shards of wood from the near disintegrated door. "I did what I had to, Duke."

"You lost your right to call me by my first name when you sold me out, you'll refer to me as Father Flynn."

"Yes, yes, if you don't listen to me, you'll listen to your old equerry, Padraig, you must come back and complete your training. I see it now, the path ahead, you are the chosen one," Yowder pawed at Flynn, who shook the priest off.

"If we don't stop those nuns now, there won't be any training!"

Padraig held his hands out. "Father Flynn, I did what I had to, you were going too far, that boy…he didn't have to go out that way, you could've saved him."

+His soul was pitiful, barely worth the effort, I should've taken the inane grinning woman, she looked feisty+

O'Malley stood in between the pair. "Look, Flynn, I'm not here to steal your glory, I'm here to stop them. We can do that. Together. If you go back and try to take them on your own, it's madness. Madness, I tell you. Let us put aside our differences and kick those nuns back to where they came from. We can do this, you and I..."

Flynn rolled his eyes. "Fine." The others cheered and pumped their fists. "But we do this my way."

O'Malley held his hand out. "Those cannibal nuns from outer space won't go down easy, we'll only get one shot at this."

"Cannibal? I thought you had to eat your own species to be a cannibal?"

"There's so much you don't know, we can discuss the semantics another time, every moment we dally, they grow bolder. As you say, if we're not quick, they could escape, and we'll have to wait until next year."

"Bullshit. This ends today." Flynn grabbed O'Malley by the wrist and shook fiercely.

"So, what's the plan, Flynn?"

35

The full moon lit up the car park, the priest's footsteps crushing the shingle with every step. In the distance, a short way up a driveway, stood the cylindrical building, the top tapering to a rounded nub and jutting into the bottom of the moon. Flynn bum-puffed a cigarette, the cherry now a stick of glowing ember. "Which one is yours?"

"Just up ahead," O'Malley smoothed his hair back, using copious amounts of Dapper Dan to slick his mop down. He came to a stop as Flynn kept on walking. "Hey, it's here."

Flynn began to laugh. "That's it? They gave you a Fiat 500? Jeez, you must've pissed off all manner of people to get that."

Opening the boot, O'Malley began to rummage around. "It's a hire car. My one got…requisitioned. It was this or nothing." He pulled a Roman gladius from its hilt, and held it to the light. "Lux aeterna," O'Malley said in a deep booming voice - not his own. The sword made a WHOOMPH sound, and the blade erupted in flame. "We shall cleanse the pantheon in fire, and this land of those devilish witches."

"Calm down, Matthew Hopkins, you ain't no Witchfinder General, you know."

O'Malley, still holding the flaming sword aloft, pouted. "Padraig, hurry up and take a picture, will you? It'll look good on my Instagram."

The equerry, already balancing all manner of items under his armpits, struggled to open his iBible. After dropping the umbrella onto the floor, he managed to take a suitably heroic shot, and began to upload it on the priest's behalf.

"Will you put that bloody thing out? We're supposed to be incognito, if one of those nuns looks down here and sees some priest brandishing the fiery sword of Brutus, they're gonna know that we're about to storm their compound and kick the shit out of them. Or die trying, at least."

"Good point, well made," O'Malley conceded. "Lux obscuritas," he bellowed in his ridiculously booming voice, the sword gutting immediately, the steel returning to its solid form.

Flynn was rifling through the various weaponry, ignoring the mace of Windoo, and the morning star of braining, and smirked as he wrapped his hands around something. "What's this, then, O'Malley? Doesn't look church-certificated to me."

There was a whirring and buzzing sound. O'Malley, having sheathed the sword, turned around to see Flynn brandishing a nine-inch dildo, which had been switched on, and looked as though it was trying to escape the clutches of the priest. His cheeks reddening, O'Malley snatched it away, and desperately began to try and deactivate it. Finally, the sex toy fell silent, the embarrassed priest shoving it into a rucksack. "I…erm…don't know how that got there."

A cough made Flynn jump. "Well it's definitely not mine," a woman's voice said.

With his hands up, ready to Kung-Fu-chop any potential assassin, Flynn stood his ground. "Who the hell are you?"

"Melina, I'm an acquaintance of that one." She pointed to O'Malley, who was nose-deep in a tub of Vaseline.

"Phew, I thought you were one of those nuns in Friday casual dress, trying to get the drop on us. Are you going to help?"

Melina shrugged. "I wasn't planning on it. I'm ambivalent to your current plight, if I'm being honest with you."

"Of course, I don't blame you, the odds are stacked against us." Flynn rooted around some more, before smacking his palms against the boot. "Dammit, there's not much here, we should have shotguns for this deal."

"How many are we dealing with?" O'Malley pressed the button on the switchblade of justice, before cursing that the edge was dull and lifeless.

"Thirty, maybe even forty, at a push."

O'Malley pushed aside the shurikens of Peckham. "You're right, we should have shotguns for this."

"If only the security priests hadn't been sent off on a course on riot control, we could've used their help right about now. As it stands, we only have one thing going for us, and that's the element of surprise. Though any minute now, they could find out what I did to that nun in the basement who was going to slice and dice me, and then the game is gonna be up. Think, goddammit, think…" Flynn rested his head against the boot, his eyes flitting to the front of the manor house, where a pair of nuns were reeling in the sprinkler system for the night. "Wait a goddamn minute…I've got a plan so cunning, that they're going to add this to the Crimson Rosary training manual. O'Malley, Jugs, here's what we're going to do…"

Melina folded her arms. "Did he just call me, Jugs?"

36

Sister Alicia patted the blackjack of bludgeoning against the palm of her hand. Hearing a rustling, her head snapped towards the noise, her eyes trying to pierce the hazy murk. The perpetrator, a feral iguana, looked at her, chewed some more on a nice verdant leaf, before bounding back into the foliage. "And don't come back," Alicia warned, shaking the weapon at the bush.

She slipped her hand through the leather strap, and began to twirl it around her wrist. "You'll take someone's eye out with that," Sister Leah warned. Moving out of possible hitting range, the nun began to pace up and down the path.

"I thought they would've sent the main delivery up by now, GAFFER won't be pleased if it's late," Alicia said, narrowly missing catching herself with her flailing blackjack.

"Mother Superior said she had some last-minute additions before they could blast off, and that we should make sure we have no more pesky intruders."

From the bottom of the path, the sound of crunching gravel forced the pair to stop and look. As one, they moved together, forming a barrier between whoever it was and the door which led to the nun's sanctum. "Halt, who goes there?" Leah demanded of the night, squinting to try and resolve the blurry shapes into something recognisable." These masks are no good, I can't see anything with them on," she whinged.

The crunching grew louder and louder, a pair of high pitched voices were bickering, drowning out a bassier speaker, joined with the sound of skin slapping skin. The singular voice complained, then fell silent. "Fellow sisters, we found this…worm trying to get back to the main building, he must've escaped our clutches."

From the gloom, two nuns materialised, and in between

them, Father Flynn, his hands bound, struggled and moaned. "We fear he was trying to raise the alarm, so we apprehended him, and will deal with him…inside."

Alicia began to tap the blackjack against her hand. She exchanged a curt nod with Leah and the pair split, allowing a tiny avenue to open towards the closed door. "Who is that? Identify yourself, or we will be forced to bludgeon you into submission."

The oncoming nuns turned their heads and exchanged a hissed conversation, before one turned back. "Tis I, Sister…Melanie…now, be quick, let us in, we do not have much time to spare." The trio came to a stop in front of the two guards. With Alicia blocking the way, Leah began to circle the small party, sniffing the air as she made laps around them. Coming to a standstill behind the new arrivals, she looked at her partner and shook her head gently.

"Pray tell, fellow sisters, we will grant you entry if you can give us the password," she said, slipping the blackjack off her wrist, and into her hand, gripping the handle tightly, eyeing up which one she should bludgeon first. She decided on the false worm, it should go down easily enough, she could then try and get one of the fake nuns.

"Erm…is it iva?"

Alicia frowned. "What? Iva?"

The lead nun looked up, her face showing off a dusting of stubble on her chin, a hand disappearing into her tunic. "Yes, I've a surprise for you." Before Alicia could indulge in some good old-fashioned beatings, the blatantly fake nun pulled a large meat cleaver from the inside of her clothing, the steel head as large as a dinner tray. Revealed to the world, O'Malley hefted the cleaver above his head, and with all his might, swung downwards.

It caught Alicia in the middle of her head, the edge continuing on its path, slicing through the insectoid as if it were nothing more than a single-ply sheet of tissue paper. The two halves of Sister Alicia stood together for the briefest of moments, before peeling apart, landing on the ground with a gentle slap and a healthy spurt of green blood.

Leah took a step back, trying to take in what had just happened. Before she could act, the worm had turned to face her, his hands free of bondage. With a deft flick of his wrist, a long thin blade slid from his sleeve, the hilt perfectly coming to rest in his palm. As Leah went to open her mouth to raise the alarm, Flynn rammed the stiletto blade of bastardry through the bottom of her jaw. The blade pushed through the skull with ease, the point breaching the back of the cranium, and stuck up in the air as though Leah was wearing an old First World War German Pickelhaube. With her mouth open, Flynn could see the blade, smeared with green goo, running vertically through the nun's head. With both hands on the hilt, he rotated the blade around at speed, turning the interior of Sister Leah's head to a gritty paste. The nun fell slack, and he discarded her lifeless body onto the floor.

O'Malley shook the blood from the cleaver, and before stowing it back on his person, he patted Flynn on the back, who shirked at the unexpected human contact. "You're right, that was cunning."

"Come on, let's get this over with, these past few days of sobriety have been far too much for me." Flynn wiped the blade on Sister Leah's habit and pushed the door open.

37

Melina, Flynn and O'Malley crept into the room, the door clicked behind them, sealing them inside. They stood at the edge of the square stone courtyard, the rocket still sitting plum in the centre. Steam rose from the bottom, coiling around the metal tube like ghostly ivy, trying to get a foothold on the silver trunk. Mother Superior Francesca stood by it, her back to the intruders, clapping her hands and shouting orders to the cadre of nuns.

The aliens were milling around, packing the last of the boxes into the rocket's hold, ensuring it was stacked to perfection, so that the contents would survive take off and retrieval. Others carried spare nun uniforms, and chewed on strips of human jerky, eager to get off this rock and onto their next assignment.

Flynn hid behind a wooden column; beckoning the others to do the same, he waved them into a mini-huddle. "Look, we need to take them from different sides, sure, they have the numbers, but we have one thing on our side."

"Surprise?" Melina asked.

"Surprise," Flynn agreed, "and holy weapons."

"Two things, then?" O'Malley said.

"Fine, yes, two things, surprise, holy weapons and a grim determination to save our planet. Shit. Yes, yes, I know, three things. Come on, let's get this over with, before it descends into farce. You two split up, one over there, the other over there. When I give the signal, start chopping up those bitches. I'm gonna take care of the Queen Bee." Flynn reached up the inside of his shirt, and pulled out a small, double-headed axe.

O'Malley and Melina nodded in approval, and were beginning to split up, when the priest stopped. "What is the signal? How will we know when to attack?"

Flynn gave a big shit-eating grin. "Oh, trust me, you'll know. Now go, get in position, we don't have much time --and I need a wee."

The pair crouched down and hopped from cover-to-cover, working their way round so that they could trap the cannibal nuns with a classic pincer movement. Flynn kneeled down, and began to remove his collar. Laying it down in front of him, he slowly unbuttoned his shirt. Stripped down to his vest and trousers, he poked his fingers into his beard and Albie chirruped and stuck his head out. "Hey, little fella, this shit just got real, we're about to kick off now. Whatever happens, you stay put, okay? This is on us, so regardless of what you see, and whatever happens, do not come out, okay?"

"Okay, Flynn of the cloth, I will agree to your request. Just do one thing for me…"

"Of course, anything, just name it."

Albie grabbed hold of Flynn's nose, looking him square in the eye. "Avenge my people…"

Flynn nodded and patted the axolotl on the head, who turned tail and wiggled his way back into the thicket of facial hair. Bending down to pick up his weapons, he looked skyward. "Hey, big guy, I know we haven't always seen eye-to-eye, hell, sometimes, I have called you out for being a right bastard. But if you're up there, looking down at us, well…this ain't the time for thoughts and prayers, this is the time for action. A good old-fashioned lightning bolt of smiting wouldn't go amiss right about now."

The priest looked out across the courtyard, there was a clunk above him as the roof began to peel back, revealing the star-covered velvet sky. The steam swelled like an eighties revival concert, the nuns hurrying in and out of the ethereal miasma. "You ain't gonna get a better shot than right now, Big G," Flynn whispered to the heavens.

The roof clunked once more, locking into place. Flynn huffed and spat onto the floor. "Figured as much, this is down to us, we're in control of our destinies now, not you." Father Flynn rocked the axe back and forth in his hand, getting used to the weight. "It's show time."

Flynn rolled to his right, coming up into a crouch. He pulled the axe back behind him, took aim, and let it fly.

"No, Sister Muriel, I've told you before, the toolbox goes in last. Honestly, must I do everything myself?" Mother Superior Francesca shouted. Ducking down, she felt a ripple of displaced air above her, followed by a scream, then a disconcerting gurgle. Following the disturbance, she saw Sister Muriel staggering about by the rocket, an axe embedded in the middle of her face.

The toolbox clattered against the floor. Muriel grabbed hold of the axe handle and tugged, trying to pull it free. Mustering all her strength, she managed to yank the weapon out of her face, although she took her mask and an insect eye with it. She screamed, and fell to the floor, clutching the chasm where her eye used to be. Francesca scowled. "Who threw that?"

From behind her, there was an ungodly scream. She turned to see the piece of meat they had captured earlier, sprinting toward her, brandishing a thin knife, yelling all manner of obscenities. Regaining her composure, she watched the human close in on her, before leaping up and sticking a foot out, connecting squarely with the man's nose.

Flynn's murderous rush came to an abrupt halt as Francesca's foot caught him on the schnozz. There was a crack of bone, and a spurt of blood, which soaked into his vest. He sunk to one knee, holding his broken nose, and trying to shake free the phantasmal tweeting birds which flew around his head. He had barely managed to shake off one imaginary sparrow, when a balled fist clocked him on the side of the head, sending him spinning through the air and into one of the wooden beams bordering the courtyard.

Francesca unfurled her fist, knuckles cracking, and then reformed it, taking up the drunken fist stance. "I thought you were already processed, worm, no matter, I get to take you apart myself, now."

"Not…quite…I brought some friends," Flynn gasped, as he tried to pull air into his lungs.

From either side of the arena, there were screams. Francesca turned to see the decapitated heads of her kin flying through the air. The perpetrators, dressed as nuns, were brandishing gleaming weapons, and making short work of anyone who ventured too close.

Mother Superior Francesca stood up to full height. She clapped her hands thrice, and four nuns, who had been on stacking detail, scurried to form a loose protective shell around their leader. Each reached into their wimples and pulled out a foot-long metal tube. Amongst the screams of their kind being brutalised, the four pressed down on the handle and a crackling length of purple energy shot out of each cylinder.

Upon ejection, the beams sagged, turning into lashes of barbed light, fizzing and crackling, rebelling against the oxygen of the room. Standing up, Flynn beckoned a nun forward as he spat out a wad of blood in her direction.

Francesca nodded toward Sister Ingrid, who flung her hand back, the snarling whip eager to feel the kiss of skin. Flynn edged forwards, ducking down quickly as Ingrid flicked her wrist forward, the snake of energy smashing into the wooden beam behind him. Ozone crackled from the length of purple light, inches from Flynn's face. Turning to face his adversary, he rolled beneath the beam and ran full pelt at the nun.

He managed to stab her in the guts, pulling the blade out quickly and neatly. The nun screamed in pain, but pulled her arm back, the lash wrapping around Flynn's body. His back arched, flinging his head skyward, and his entire body wracked with pain. Ingrid pushed the power button harder, and the light grew brighter, the beam thicker, the pain now excruciating. His jaw ground together, so much so that he could feel his molars crushing against each other, fissures forming within the enamel. Ingrid snapped her hand back, and he was temporarily released from his torment, although he fell to the floor on his hands and knees, gasping for air. The nun laughed, circling like a cat with a wounded rodent, baiting him, but the words barely registered, as every cluster of nerve endings fired into nothingness.

"I can't..."

+Priest. Maybe I can be of assistance+

Ingrid continued to circle and cackle. She was enjoying the sport; far too often she had to content herself with ripping apart helpless villagers or eating her own kind, there was nothing noble in it. She longed for the fight, one-sided or not, and she was going to make this last as long as possible. "On your knees, worm, I will not be denied my fun."

Flynn willed himself to stand as Ingrid cracked her energy whip and it lacerated his chest, leaving a bloody welt in its path. The nun cackled some more.

Placing a hand against the wound, Flynn doubled over, his head looking at the floor, while his body began to convulse. His diaphragm started to shake, and a fine coating of sweat sheened his body.

"Awww, Sister Ingrid, I think you've broken him," Francesca mocked, her colleagues keeping a watchful eye on the other two pugilists, who were still butchering the unarmed nuns with wilful abandon.

Flynn belched once, twice, and as the third echoed free, there was a retching sound, and he vomited. It came forth like a broken hydrant, a torrent of spew spattering the floor, the force scouring the surface. The nuns began to laugh. "Ingrid, finish him, he is putting me off my supper of lung kebab," Francesca ordered.

The nun began to circle the vomitous priest, working out an angle of attack to reduce potential splashback. Flynn upped the intensity, the liquid going from thin to thick and lumpy, and stifled the flow before letting out one last spear of puke. The tip froze as it hit the floor, forming a vertical bridge between stone and mouth. Flynn opened his mouth wide and extricated himself from the mouthguard of sick that had solidified in his mouth.

Ingrid contemplated her next move, the whip slack in her grip. Flynn grabbed hold of the top of the column of solidified puke, and wrenched it sideways, snapping it free. He held it aloft, it was rough and jagged, like a stalagmite. He turned to Francesca and winked, before his free hand worked its way to the tip of the vomit block, and began to squeeze.

A sound rang out, like fingernails being dragged down a blackboard, stopping O'Malley and Melina in their tracks. Everyone stopped being butchered for a moment, to look at Flynn. The priest shook his fingers, which were starting to grow into talons. With his fingernails as sharp as coffin tacks, he began to whittle.

The only sound was a steady beat of clacking, as a blur of fingers began to shave and shape the block of vomit. Chips and shards of sick showered the courtyard as Flynn worked like a man possessed. After a few moments of furious work, the claws receded, and he held aloft a sword, a katana, smithed from his own puke and shaped by the hand of a demon.

"My god…" Francesca mumbled, as Flynn turned the blade to show off the maker's symbol, "he's got a Fattori Gutso blade!" The nuns covered their mouths in shock, gasping and regarding each other with concern.

Flynn held the sword high above his head, double-handed. "My turn." Ingrid was still paralysed by what she'd just witnessed. She offered no defence as the priest swung the sword down diagonally, bisecting the alien nun. Completing his swing, he watched as Ingrid first dropped her whip, before the two hemispheres of her body started to separate. Her upper torso slid from atop her stomach and legs, and slapped against the floor. The priest flicked the sword, green goo splattered over the nun's dead body.

As the survivors began to muster a fightback, getting energy-based swords from crates and trying to keep the two bogus nuns in their midst from adding to the pile of limbs and heads with their own, Flynn circled Francesca and her remaining protectors. They formed up in front of the Mother Superior, hands unfurled, and regripped their whips, the purple beams spitting out sparks of ejected light.

Flynn feinted forwards, Sister Ursula falling for the ruse and sending the length of her lash into nothingness. The priest bounded towards her with one step, two steps, before sliding on his knees towards her. With the sword held aloft, he disappeared through the nun's legs as if she were the entrance to a Ghost Ride in a theme park. Ursula coughed up a wad of bubbling green blood before the two halves of her body began to split apart.

The blade had only cut through to the base of her neck, and she parted like a wishbone, her slashed organs and ravaged skeletal structure sluicing from the opening and dropping onto the floor with a loud splat.

Sister Violet barely had time to react to her other guardian's demise, as Flynn had risen up, surfing the wave of blood-backwash, and sliced her head off before she even knew that the priest was there. As her head somersaulted through the air, Flynn thrust the sword forward, spearing it through the ragged meat of the neck. He brought it towards his face, looking like he had just purchased a large novelty toffee apple. "Mmmm, she looks good enough to eat," he mimicked with the dead nun's mouth, before he flicked her head at the rocket. It bounced off it with a dull thud, disappearing into the fog that was forming at the base of the projectile.

The one remaining bodyguard, Sister Julia, bent down and picked up one of her sister's now lifeless hilts. She aimed her own energy beam at the retrieved weapon, and formed a long-chained nunchuck. Satisfied with her work, Sister Julia bellowed a war cry, and leapt at Flynn. The end of the nunchuck caught him on the temple, sending him spiralling backwards, holding his head.

Julia landed softly, and advanced quickly, working the nunchucks around her body, emitting high pitched clicks and whistles, signalling her displeasure in her native tongue. She raked Flynn's body as he fought to regain his composure, pulling his arms in close, weathering the barrage of blows assailing his body.

The nun kneed Flynn in the guts, and then shot a foot out, catching him in the solar plexus and sending him a few feet back before he collapsed down to his knees. He coughed, spat blood onto the stone floor, and wiped his mouth with the back of his hand. "Not bad…for a woman."

Julia's face dropped and she let out a keening wail. Holding the nunchuck loose in one hand, she dug her fingers from her free hand into the middle of her face. Grabbing tightly, she wrenched the mask free, leaving her insectoid features showing in the habit. Her chest mouth opened and closed, teeth clicking against each other. She discarded the human face onto the floor, her large bulbous eyes reflecting thousands of mirror images of Flynn back at him.

Forcing himself to his feet, he managed to bring the katana up just in time, as Julia renewed her attack. He blocked high and low, as she sought to either wind him or knock him unconscious. The alien screeched its annoyance and began to flail wildly, forcing Flynn back, until his spine pressed into one of the wooden beams holding up the floor above.

He ducked as the nun swung for his head, the purple chain of energy wrapping around the thick wooden block. Julia grabbed hold of the hilt with both hands, trying to wrench her weapon free. Flynn lifted himself up, so that he stood between her arms, the sword edge pressing softly against the inside of her right arm. "Time to disarm you, evil wench." He pulled the sword back, so that the dull edge hit the inside of her other elbow, then with one hand grabbing the bottom of the sword hilt, smacked the weapon to the other side. In one clean circular movement, the blade sliced through both of Julia's arms.

The insect nun screamed, her tiny mandibles opening up like a Chinese takeaway box. Julia staggered backwards, green gunk jetting from both her stumps. She looked from one to the other, as if expecting the nightmare to end. Flynn picked up one of the severed arms, and looked at Francesca. "Hey, give the lady a hand," and flung the hacked appendage at the Mother Superior who batted it aside.

Julia sunk to her knees, and Flynn walked past her on a direct path to Francesca. As he passed the supplicated nun, he jabbed the katana behind him, through the back of Julia's head, and out through the tiny mouth on her face. As the sword was pulled free, she fell forward, and smacked into the floor.

"It's over," Flynn stood a few feet in front of the Mother Superior, pointing the sword into her face. Francesca looked around, and all she could see were her butchered sisters. A hand rose up from the floor towards one of the murderous nuns, now revealed to be one of those wretched humans. Mercy was not forthcoming as the hand was batted aside, and the skull caved in with a box of corned human.

Melina and O'Malley panted, before approaching the isolated woman, each a point on a triangle. Francesca stuck her chin out. "Perhaps we can discuss some sort of treaty?"

Flynn laughed. "You must be joking. No, it's far too late for that, I think it best that we put an end to your murderous ways, you've eaten your last human. Do you have any last words?"

Mother Superior stood defiant, and straightened out her clothing. As she did, a hand ran inside her tunic. "Well…there is one thing…"

Before she could finish, there was an almighty scream from the upper floor, as a blur of black and white somersaulted over the balustrade and landed in front of the rocket, facing Melina's back. The three humans formed a line, them at one end, Francesca in the middle, and the new arrival opposite.

The figure turned around, revealing a morose sumo-like woman, her plump body rippled, visible even through her tunic. In her hand, she held a human skull, although it was larger than normal. One hand rested on the crown, the other beneath the jaw, and dead eyes looked out. The sumo gave a toothy grin, pressing a button set in between the skull's eyes, which lit up with a glowing purple hue.

"Sister Momo, my lovely, please deal with these…things," Francesca took a step backwards.

"I've got this one," O'Malley said, sauntering forward.

Coming to a stop in an en garde pose, he beckoned the sumo nun forward. "Come on then, chunky, let's see you beat me."

The nun continued to smile as her hands dropped the skull. As it fell to the floor, suspended on a rope of purple energy, she slammed her foot against the beam, causing the skull to change direction and fly out horizontally. It smacked O'Malley in the testicles before he could even try to dodge the attack. His cleaver clattered to the floor first, followed by his body, hands cupped to his nether regions, trying to feel if there was something there which could be salvaged. He lifted his face towards the still grinning nun, "not…again-"

The nun pulled her arms back, taking the skull with them. She slammed her feet into the floor, and threw her hands forward, propelling the baleful skull towards O'Malley once more. It caught him full in the face, sending his head rocking backwards against his neck. As it bounced forward, his eyes rolled up in his head and he passed out.

Melina scurried across to him, patting his cheek, trying to get some life back into him. His eyes blinked open. "Mother?" Soothing his brow, Melina shook her head, and O'Malley frowned. "Not mother?"

Flynn did the lateral splits as the skull came his way, flying into the space where his body had been. Momo heaved, and it came sailing back to her, catching Flynn on the back of the head as it did so, causing him to headbutt the stone floor. Flynn rubbed the back of his head and stood up slowly.

The nun began to circle him, twirling the skull from the end of a short lead, her beady eyes locked onto him, that gormless grin still painted on her creased face. With a speed that belied her size, she flung the skull out again, and Flynn jolted to his left as it whistled past his ear. Learning his lesson, he ducked quickly, as his opponent tugged on the leash and it careened back over his head.

The nun caught the skull in the palm of one of her giant hands. Opening the jaw of the weapon, so it looked like it was laughing at him, she pressed another button, which made two-inch spikes erupt from darkened orifices. Flynn stepped in and took a lazy swipe, Momo edged back and avoided the blow, countering by swinging the pointy skull. Flynn screamed as the jagged points raked his skin, leaving gouges across his chest. Ventilation slits had been cut into his vest, and blood was soaking into the off-white fabric, leaving train tracks of red as proof of impact.

Flynn walked backwards, so that he could feel the beam behind him once more. "How about you try that again?"

The sumo nun obliged before the words had escaped his throat. Flynn just about managed to move his head as the spiked skull slammed into the thick wood behind him, a graze on his cheek trickling drops of blood. The nun pulled on the lead, but the skull was too far embedded. Flynn smirked. "Oopsy."

Flynn dropped the sword and grabbed hold of the energy beam. As soon as he made contact with it, his fillings began to rattle inside his teeth. Spots of light bloomed in front of his eyes, and he could feel his brain pulsing within the cerebrospinal fluid that surrounded it. Fighting back the pain, he tugged on the leash and the nun tripped forwards, unable to arrest the momentum.

The sumo nun's feet continued to slip on the blood slick floor, unable to gain purchase. Flynn reeled her in like a prize turbot. As she approached, she stuck a foot out against the supporting beam, managing to stop her movement.

Flynn let go of the rope of purple energy, and shook his hands, trying to get feeling back into them. Looking into the sumo nun's face, which was mere inches from his, he said. "Well done, just one little thing." He placed a hand behind the woman's head, and slammed it into the spiked skull which jutted out from the beam. Her face was compressed between his hand and the embedded skull and its myriad of pointy metal shards. The grin on her face disappeared, and her body fell slack in his hands.

Bending down to pick up his sword, the nun remained hanging from her own weapon. "Stick around," Flynn said, before pacing towards Francesca, who clapped him mockingly.

"Oh bravo, you know, for a meat popsicle, you're awfully determined."

"No more surprises, let's end this."

"Let's."

Francesca withdrew her hand, pulling out a double-edged sword, the metal near iridescent with imbued energy.

"Nice."

"It's Sirian Steel, forged in a nebula, it was a present from my benefactor."

"I look forward to taking it from your decomposing corpse." Flynn held his sword out into the Mother Superior's face.

The pair faced off across a floor that was a shallow lake of green blood and body parts. They shouted rallying cries, then ran at each other. Yelps of pain replaced the sound of battle as they passed each other, and doubled over. Turning back to face one another, a further red channel had opened down Flynn's chest. He pried blood-slicked fingers into the wound and winced, before trying to pinch the curling skin together.

Francesca turned slower, a hand clutched to the join of her habit. Her chest mouth's lips had a laceration which exposed rancid gums and gleaming teeth. Thick globules of green blood dripped onto the floor. She held a hand out, to steady herself against the beam, trying to take in a breath. She fought to stand up. "I...I...I underestimated you..."

"I won't let you make that mistake again," Flynn promised. He held his sword behind him, the blade perpendicular to the floor.

Mother Superior nodded limply. "Fine, let's do this." Her giant mouth bit down, fighting back the pain, and she forced herself to stand up straight, sword held above her head.

The pair yelled obscenities once more, and charged across the floor. Francesca slashed downwards, but Flynn was too quick, passing beneath the blow before it could connect. As he did so, he turned the blade sideways, and sawed across the nun's stomach. Each of them came to a stop, a few steps past the point where they had met.

There was a clatter as sword hit flagstone. Flynn turned around slowly, seeing the Mother Superior standing still, head tipped backwards. She let out a wet rasping, before collapsing to her knees. The priest made his way to his fallen foe, to stand before her. She was clutching her midriff, her hands grabbing at chunks of flesh, trying to keep her guts inside. Francesca's blood-flecked face looked up at him, and offered a weak smile.

Flynn rested his sword against her throat. "Your tyranny is at an end; no longer will you turn us into food."

The Mother Superior chuckled, a horrible wet sound. "Oh you fool…" She palmed the thick crucifix that hung around her neck, twisting the metal figure's head until it was upside-down. "I think you'll find it is I…who will have the last laugh."

She pressed the head down, before collapsing backwards. Her hands came away from her body, and thick cords of lime green intestine slopped out of the deep wound, pooling around her feet. Flynn bent down and picked her head up. "What do you mean? Last laugh?"

Francesca opened her eyes, and blinked slowly. "Your pitiful planet has now been marked for harvesting…though I'll never see it…they'll sell you all over the galaxy. You'll be…farmed…till extinction."

Her back arched, pushing more of her ruptured innards out through the wide rupture, then she fell slack, eyes closed, the forked tongue lolling out of her mouth.

"Bugger."

38

"Oi, Mister Fancypants, get your arse up," Flynn kicked the sole of O'Malley's shoe. Getting little-to-no reaction, he kneeled down and hooked the man's eyelids open.

With the room coming back into focus, O'Malley batted the hand away. "Get off me." The priest pushed himself backwards against the crates, took in the scene of devastation, and allowed himself a fist-bump. "Oh yeah, guess who saves the day again? Yeah, baby-"

Flynn appeared in his eyeline, and tapped his chest with green blood soaked fingers. "Yeah, me, you've spent the last few minutes visiting Unconsciousville, population: one. See that over there?" He pointed to the still-steaming remains of Mother Superior Francesca. Her head had lolled to a shoulder, and through her rictus, insect mandibles poked through. Flynn coughed and pointed to Momo, still impaled on the spiked skull, embedded on the wooden beam. "And that one, don't forget that one, or any of the other guardians who were actually armed with a weapon."

Flynn crouched down by the slaughtered nuns, rooting through dismembered limbs. "Yep, looks like you two are the real heroes alright, you massacred a load of unarmed insect…woman…things. Bravo, outstanding work, really. I'm sure you'll earn the highest possible honour for such a heroic deed."

Forcing himself to stand up, O'Malley staggered across to his nemesis, jabbing him in the collarbone. "If it wasn't for me turning up a few months back, that demon would've used your flensed carcass as the framework for a canoe down a river of vomit."

+I hadn't thought of that, where's my Demonic notebook and pen+

"You don't have one, you idiot," Flynn blurted out.

"Eh? Of course I don't have a canoe made out of your body, you're still using it." O'Malley furrowed his brow, and rubbed some life back into his dead arm. "Are you okay? You look worse than your usual shadow-of-crap self."

Flynn picked a path through the rubbery limbs that were scattered across the floor. He wrenched the metallic armband from Francesca's forearm and tossed it across to O'Malley.

"Ooohh, shiny, did they get this from Argos?"

"Not quite, it would seem she's triggered some kind of emergency signal, said our planet has been earmarked as a new and vital stop for any foodie alien who wants to snack on some fresh meat."

"Oh."

"Yeah…oh, so, Father Fucking Wonderful, what's the plan?"

O'Malley studied the device, trying to pry open a panel on the back, only succeeding in breaking a nail. "It won't make any difference," Melina turned it over, "once the display is blank, and this one is, it means that whoever she contacted has already received the message."

"How do you know?"

Melina rolled up her sleeve to reveal a similar device, except hers was covered in a green felt, like algae. "Same model, wearables are all the rage nowadays."

"So what the hell are we going to do?" Flynn slumped against the rocket, and thumped its side, a hollow thud ringing out.

From above them there was a piercing shriek, and the trio turned as one, to identify the intruder approaching their wallowing midst. Clutching hold of the bannister rail, surveying the scene of nunicide, was Sister Caitlin. Charged with driving the nuns around on their various collections, she had been in the coach out back, trying for the last time to get the blood splatters off the upholstery. Intermingled with it was a strange white liquid, now a scabby crust, which had seeped out of the offering the worm had brought them before he had been nunhandled into the device and hand-cranked into thin ropes of minced human.

Her bony finger was pointed down at the perpetrators of the murderous violence that had been meted out to her sisters. Her eyes raced over the mutilated bodies, until they settled on Mother Superior. "You, you little…"

Flynn looked behind him on the off-chance that she was addressing someone else. O'Malley and Melina backed away, in case the nun had a death ray gun with a large area of effect. "This will not stand, you shall be punished for this outrage," Caitlin promised. The nun climbed onto the bannister, and held her arms out like she was auditioning for the latest edition of Crucifix Today. Shutting her eyes, the woman took a step forward, into thin air.

Flynn let out an involuntary yelp as the nun pitched forward. She managed to rotate a hundred-and-eighty degrees through the air, before landing smack on her back on the stone floor. There was an audible crunch of bone as they shattered on impact.

Urging the others to stand back, Flynn walked across to the stricken woman. Standing over the broken body, he looked down at her still face. Caitlin's eyes were wide open like a surprised frog, fixed onto a spot on the ceiling. Her arms, still outstretched, were palm-up, her right wrist bent at an angle that defied composition. Flynn looked back at O'Malley and Melina and shrugged, before squatting down. "Well, that really showed me, huh? Way to go, lady, kill yourself so that we don't have to worry about a sequel."

As he chuckled, the nun's one good hand slapped him on the back of his neck, pinching his spinal column at the base of his skull. "Oh, you'll see that I have one little surprise left!" Caitlin, clutching the priest in her vicelike grip, opened her mouth, allowing her insect mandibles to pick and pull at the fake skin. With the bottom half of her head now revealing her true form, her throat began to oscillate.

"Shit," Melina stepped forward, "Flynn, you might want to stop her doing that."

Flynn tried to look across to the woman, but Caitlin held him firmly, the shrill pitch growing louder and louder. He could feel liquid running from the corner of his eyes, as droplets of his blood pitter-pattered onto the Kaihoro's face, the toothy corners of her insect mouth scooping the liquid into her open maw. It seemed to act like a lozenge, enabling the thing to reach a new octave.

With her head down, Melina barged into Flynn, releasing the hold the nun had on him, and the pair fell into a heap. Shaking his head, Flynn rested on his elbows. "What's she doing?"

Before Melina could answer, the keen wailing began to ripple around the room like a shrill Mexican wave. Flynn looked across to the Mother Superior, whose mouth was wide open, emitting the same noise as the nun who had started off the screeching aria. All around the room, each nun's head, whether it was attached to its body or not, began to scream the same forlorn note, rising in pitch. On all fours, Melina crawled over to the body of the nun, every step closer, contorting her face in agony. The sound reached a crescendo, the domed room letting the note ripple around its lofty dimensions, swirling it like a sonic tornado. The bodies of the nuns began to convulse, limbs, separated from their owner, slapping against the floor as if they were fish dumped onto the deck of a trawler.

Melina pressed her hands over Caitlin's mouth, and for a brief moment, the woman was silenced. The thrashing ceased. Caitlin's eyes rolled in her head, glaring at the muffler. With a balled fist, she caught Melina under the jaw, sending the woman sprawling backwards along the floor. As soon as the hand came free, the noise belched forth once more, joined instantaneously by the other nuns. The floor was alive. Arms, shorn off at the elbow or shoulder righted themselves, so that the palms faced down on the stone floor. Fingers came to life, dragging what remained of the limb and scurrying towards the epicentre of this abyssal singular note. Legs jiggled, rolled, or scurried across the floor, all headed for Caitlin. The bodies that were intact stood on unsteady limbs, and loped off. Along the way, they bent down to pick up decapitated nun heads, their mouths agape, shrieking as one.

The mass of holy woman offal converged on Caitlin, piling on top of her as if she were the object of a playground game of Bundle! Melina cracked her jaw back into place and edged towards O'Malley, who was looking at the pile of bodies and shaking his head.

Flynn joined them. "What the hell are they doing? I thought they were all dead?"

Melina rubbed her temples. "She is a scryer, the rarest of Kaihoro, I didn't think any were left after the great purge."

"Yeah, great. How about we get a history lesson later, and settle for facts and information now, on what the fucking shrill woman is doing, and why all the dead bodies have got up and decided to have a bit of a wander," Flynn said.

The mass of nuns began to squish together, coalescing into a giant ball of black, white and green matter. "They have the ability to see things beyond this world," Melina bellowed over the din.

There were loud popping sounds every time a head or limb merged with the gelatinous mass.

Flynn grabbed hold of Melina and shook her. "As interesting as that is, I don't think that's what she's doing right now. Tell us, what the FUCK crazy lady is doing, right now."

The last of the nuns shambled into the bulging mass. The screeching remained, mouths formed on the surface of the ball belched out the dread tone, all the while the shapeless mulch of body parts contracted and swelled.

"Is it a bomb? Is she going to blow up? She looks like she's going to blow up," Flynn flinched, as a squeak of gas caused half of the nun mass to shift sideways.

"No, it's not a bomb…" Melina shrugged the priest off and looked for the exit. "We need to go…now."

Flynn pinched the bridge of his nose, stood in front of Melina, with his back to the febrile collation of life. "Why? Why do we have to go, just tell me what the fuck is going on."

The sound stopped. It was replaced by a squeaking, as if fingers were rubbing a wet balloon. This lasted a few seconds before it was replaced by a loud roar, and droplets of warm water rained down on Flynn's back. Both Melina and O'Malley began to walk backwards to the exit, the priest managing to raise a shaking finger at something behind Flynn.

"Well, you two really are-" the priest turned around, and found himself nose-to-nose with a face that was stripped of all skin. Beyond a pointed snout were two baleful red eyes, which glowed as if they were being stoked from within. Flynn gulped and took a step backwards, trying to fully appreciate what the hell was manifesting in front of him.

It looked like a pig. Yeah. A pig. At a push, it could be considered a boar. As if agreeing, the thing shook its head, and two tusks pushed their way through the skin, either side of the back of the snout. They curved down and then up, pointing towards the ceiling. Flynn tipped his head back as they grew in front of him. They were a patchwork affair, formed from pieces of spine, arm and leg bones. All crushed together and solidified.

Its mouth opened, revealing two sets of teeth, a smaller set of sharp triangles at the front, dwarfed by an even bigger set behind them. Ropes of drool slid down the enamel and onto the floor. With every step backwards, Flynn took in more and more of the creature. Its entire body was tacky, as if it had just been born. Green veins pulsed just beneath the surface, still forming and growing within the framework of viscera.

Its clawed front foot scraped against the floor, leaving deep divots in the stone. Flynn could make out a thumping organ nestled at the base of its throat, the beast's heart, at a guess. With every beat, the thing grew bigger, its features growing at the same pace. Soon, the top of its spined back was level with the first-floor walkway. Nodules of freshly formed bone glistened from their spawning.

Finally managing to remember to breathe, Flynn turned around and sprinted for the door, which was already closing behind Melina and O'Malley.

39

Melina and O'Malley were bickering with each other by the time Flynn had kicked open the door and escaped the building. They fell silent as soon as he appeared. "So, Missy, any chance you can tell us what the fuck that thing is?"

"Okay, but can we please move away from the building?" Melina nodded to the gravel path which led down to the manor house.

"Well?"

"That thing, or at least the approximation of it, is called a Bolo-Bolo, it is native to the Kaihoro homeworld, and up until a few hundred years ago, used to eat them. It was top of the food chain, it hunted them day and night, weaselling the insects out from any place they could hide in. The adults could grow twenty-feet tall. They liked two things: using their tusks to gore anything that got in their way, and eating crunchy Kaihoro."

Flynn, still speed-walking with Melina, frowned. "Wait, liked, you said liked, as in past tense."

"Yes. The Bolo-Bolo were driven to extinction."

"Let me guess, by our new BFFs, the nuns?"

"Correct. The Chikki Wattu worm priests worked out that the Bolo-Bolo tracked the Kaihoro by their smell, it's a musky scent, so they taught the females how to mask their aroma. A band of eight left to try their luck. Two days later, or dimplings, as they call them, they returned, their bellies full of Bolo-Bolo meat. Elated with this knowledge, and the hope that they might not end up extinct, the Kaihoro did what they do best."

Flynn slapped a fist into the palm of his hand. "They ate them."

"Yep, every last one of them. Unbeknownst to them, the flesh of the Bolo-Bolo was tainted, and those who ate them fell ill. Whilst the bulk of the Kaihoro rejoiced at being able to come out of hiding, enabling the Chikki Wattu worm priests to ascend to power, the afflicted insects were stashed away in a cave and forgotten about, left to die."

"So many stories…" O'Malley said, breathlessly.

Melina shot him an evil stare. "Anyway, a few months later, a group of Kaihoro approached the main hive, saying that they were the spawn of the ones that had eaten the predators that once terrorised their species. They had developed special powers, they could divine the future, sometimes, turn acid into fermented alcoholic drinks, and-"

"Somehow turn themselves into big fuck-off pig things?" Flynn ventured.

"Exactly. The science behind it is a bit murky-"

"Convenient."

"They were all thought to have died out, though, the Chikki Wattu worm priests weren't too keen on keeping them around, what with their foresight and predilection to transforming into huge hungry beasts capable of laying waste to entire temples. So, they rounded them up, under the pretence of sending them to a special party, and murdered the lot of them."

O'Malley laughed. "They couldn't see that well into the future, then, nor be that bright, if they fell for that old chestnut."

"Or, they did know, and most offered to sacrifice themselves so that a few may live, knowing that in time, the Kaihoro would overthrow the Chikki Wattu worm priests and rule the planet, with a little help from Sister Cecelia of course."

"Who?" Flynn asked.

"Don't worry, I'm sure we won't hear of her again, or discover her fate, eh?" O'Malley said aloud, to no one in particular, least of all you.

The trio stopped. Beneath their feet, they could feel a deep rumbling, as if they were wandering atop a giant belly, and the stomach within was rather peckish. Turning around slowly, they saw the gravel shifting on the path, as if it were being sieved. There was a huge crash, and the giant beast smashed through the wall of the nun's base.

"CHEESE IT!" Flynn shouted, and, ditching any pretence of altruism, began to leg it to the main house.

As Melina and O'Malley struggled to keep up, Flynn turned the corner behind the east wing of the main building and disappeared from view. The pair trotted down the hill and stood in the car park, aware of the beast behind them braying at the night sky, stamping its feet on the ground.

"Pssssst, knobheads, get over here, quick sharp," Flynn whispered.

Ducked behind the Saint Judas minibus, Flynn beckoned them closer, all the while maintaining vigil behind them, on the off-chance the beastie was looming down on their super-secret hiding place. Melina and O'Malley darted behind the vehicle just as the creature galloped down the slope and headbutted the corner of the building. The newly-renovated dining area was now rendered al fresco. The Bolo-Bolo rifled through the debris with its tusks, seeking sustenance, or something it could pound into a greasy smear.

"Where's Yowder when you need him?" Flynn asked.

O'Malley nudged him in the ribs and pointed to a distant shrubbery, where two pairs of eyes were looking out from a well-topiarised mid-section of hedgerow.

"How do you know it's him?"

"His…Johnson is sticking through the bush, he always gets a little excited when he's off his nut on LSD."

The Bolo-Bolo, realising there was nothing edible in the rubble, flicked its head towards the parked cars and began to thud along them.

"Balls, he's gonna find us…" Flynn cursed.

Sniffing the air with its dewy snout, the creature turned its head this way and that, trying to get a bead on something it could spear and hopefully toss into the air and snap in half on the way down. It could sense something behind some nearby bushes, but it got the sense that whatever was on offer was going to cost more in calories to catch than to eat.

Getting a tad irate, and seeing if it could flush out the

mammals, the Bolo-Bolo ducked and brought its head up through the bottom of a Volkswagen Golf. The alarm began to bleat in annoyance, before the creature smashed it repeatedly against the ground, showering the car park with an array of mechanical parts, and bottles of hoarded screen wash. It bucked up on its hind legs, and stamped down on the chassis until the alarm faded into nothingness and the roof was parallel with the footwell.

"Oh great…we're next," O'Malley mumbled into his handkerchief.

The beast snarled and jumped off the wreckage, parallel to the rusting minibus. It breathed in the still night air.

"No-one…say…a….word," Melina whispered.

"Hi-de-ho, camper," a woman's voice called out from the doorway to the main building.

The Bolo-Bolo snapped its head towards the sound, and let out a low growl. Slinking down as low as possible, it began to pad towards the voice. Holding their breath, the trio pressed themselves against the side of the minibus and watched as the bulky creature crept past them. As its tail swished by, Flynn darted across to the corner of the car next to where they had been hiding and peered over the boot. "Oh shit."

Roberta was still wearing her straitjacket, though she pulled at the straps with her teeth, hoping to free herself from its confines so she could give the newcomer a firm handshake. After all, that's what she did. "Hello, I'm the welcome nun. I welcome people, and I'm a nun. Duh, obviously," she chattered.

Tripping over her slippers, she missed out the bottom two steps and landed on her face at the base of the stone steps. After years of honing her technique, she managed to stand up with little fuss. The Bolo-Bolo, realising it had been discovered, tensed its muscles and stood up to full height, towering over the diminutive wriggling lady.

With a quick tug, Roberta spat out the last tricky strap and ducked down, just as the beast's tusk swung horizontally towards her. She shimmied backwards and discarded the jacket like it was a spent husk, as the spur of bone whooshed through the air.

"There, that's better isn't it? Neil always says that they give the best hugs, but he's lying."

The Bolo-Bolo, now a little irked, tipped its head back and roared.

"I know, I know, tell me about it, Mister Pig-Dog, he should know that he gives the best hugs. He's nice like that. So, I'm Roberta, the welcome nun, and you are?"

With its snout now level with the woman's head, the creature bared its teeth and snorted. Roberta winced, and wiped a sheet of thick snot from her face. As she worked to get the goo off from her glasses, she said. "Now, looks like you're a bit nasally, so you'll need to see the Doctor in the morning. One place this thing has plenty of, it's Doctors." She began to laugh as if she was having a seizure whilst sniffing.

Placing her spectacles back on the bridge of the nose, she smoothed her clothes down. "I'll just call you Scraps, you look like a Scraps. So, I don't think we've ever had a doggie stay with us before, not since the Guinea Pig incident…I'm sure you won't catch on fire, though. So, I'll just show you to your room. It's bound to be near mine, I hope you don't get any brown liquid drip-drip-dripping into your doggie bowl."

Roberta held a hand out; the Bolo-Bolo retracted slightly, before sniffing the proffered flesh. Its eyes began to water, and it backed away. Roberta began to fidget. "Where are you going? I'm the welcome nun, I welcome people, and doggies, apparently. You have to shake my hand. It's what happens."

The creature stepped back into a Toyota MR2, crushing the engine beneath its feet. "Well, I think you're awfully rude, and you know what happens to people…or doggies that are rude, don't you?" She shoved a hand underneath her dress and began to root around. The Bolo-Bolo didn't know where to look, its back foot was snagged on the plastic radiator pipes. Roberta stood up, brandishing a section of lead guttering. "If you won't play nice, I'll have to bash your head in."

Feeling trapped, the beast, still on its haunches, pulled back, before exploding out like a steampunk-infused battering ram. Its head connected with Roberta and she was propelled back up the stairs and through the open doorway. There was a loud smash as she clattered into the reception desk. As various items settled after the fall, she whimpered. "Okay, Scraps, consider yourself welcomed. I'm going to have a lie down now. Tell Neil not to touch my stuff…night night."

Flynn sunk to the floor. *Are you gonna do something, Mister Vomithead?*

+I've done all I can, that sword took all the puke out of you. It takes a while to build up good quality vomit to make a sword as good as the one you left up there+

Oh yeah.

+Bloody ungrateful if you ask me+

"Fear not, Flynn of the cloth, I can assist you."

O'Malley wrinkled his nose, and pulled his fist back. "Flynn, don't move, there's a Portuguese man o' war coming out of your beard. Either that, or your face has prolapsed."

"Wait!" Flynn shouted.

The sound of metal squeaking against gravel rang out.

"Urgh…it's got a proper face and everything. Disgusting, I'll just slug it in the jaw, hold still."

"Shall I incinerate him?" Albie asked.

Flynn lowered O'Malley's fist. "It's okay, he's a friend, of sorts. How can you assist us, Albie?"

"I will need a cup of tea, and then I think I can be of more use." Albie plopped out of Flynn's beard and sat on his lap, pointing into the car park. "We should go now."

They all turned their heads as one, tracing the path of the webbed fingers, the Bolo-Bolo glaring down at them, its teeth clamped shut, claws digging trenches in the car park floor.

"I've said it before, and I'll say it again. CHEESE IT!"

As an engine spluttered into life, Flynn and O'Malley looked back to see Melina in the minibus driver's seat, winding the window down. "I'll keep Babe the Pig here busy, just hurry up with whatever it is you're going to do."

The minibus reversed, smacking into the beast's meaty back

hip, the impact leaving a red and green smear down the rear panel. Somewhat irritated, the Bolo-Bolo roared and turned to face the van. Melina slipped into first gear and began to rag the vehicle around.

The two priests, with their cover now doing laps around the car park and the emergency overspill arrangement out back, watched on as Melina nipped in between large stone dividers and the metal shrapnel from the various cars that the creature had either crushed already, or was taking apart as he ran roughshod over them. As she completed another pass, she honked the horn; the pair could see her gesticulate wildly as she went past, the large fleshy boar in close pursuit.

Albie yanked Flynn's sideburns. "We must go, else her sacrifice will be in vain." Reluctant to leave, and wishing there was a popcorn dispenser, Flynn nudged O'Malley, and the pair turned back to the house. With entry to the dining area a simple matter of clambering up and over what remained of the exterior wall, the operatives from the Order of the Crimson Rosary headed inside, in their quest for…a cup of tea.

40

The canteen was a muted affair; aside from the gaping hole in the wall, and the rubble strewn across the beige floor tiles, it was drab and uninspiring. A counter ran along the back wall, housing empty metal trays that were usually stacked with all manner of fried or grilled food. Flynn vaulted over the worktop, catching his foot on the till as he went, and landed on his face in an open doorway.

"And they say you were the best," O'Malley peered down at the priest, who was scrabbling around on the floor, trying to pick himself up. Albie pushed himself free from the human wreckage and wound his arm around his body, trying to stretch out the sprain.

"Piss off, can we get this done?" Flynn got to his feet, and looked around, trying to find the beverage station. "Ah-ha, over here."

Tucked behind the kitchen wall, a plastic display unit sat on a worktop. "Holy shit…look at this lot," Flynn said.

There was a screech of tyres from outside as Melina completed another successful lap. The Bolo-Bolo tried to end the chase quickly by leaping across the corner, but missed the back of the van, skidding instead into the trashed MR2, which concertinaed like an accordion. It shook its head, before resuming the chase. "Not the brightest thing, is it? All it's got to do is stay where it is, and it could probably just swat Mel as she comes around again," O'Malley pointed out.

"Look, you keep an eye out, let me know if that thing has a change of heart and decides to eat us first, okay?"

O'Malley nodded, reached under the counter for a multipack of crisps, and settled in for a stake out. Flynn stuck his fingers up behind the priest's back before ducking back into the kitchen to deal with the latest conundrum.

"Which tea is it? We have Earl Grey, English Breakfast, Afternoon tea, Camomile, Green Tea, Salted Caramel Green Tea, Red Tea, Bush Tea, fucking artisanal tea hand-picked by orphaned chimpanzees who live in a commune in Warsaw tea. Whatever happened to settling for a Tetley?" Flynn whinged. His hands a blur, he picked one of each, and turned back to Albie who was limbering up on a food preparation station.

His arms laden with more tea than it would be possible to make from one kettle, Flynn looked down at the axolotl. "Well? Do you have a preference?"

"Flynn of the cloth, I require a tea fitting of the time of day."

Looking through his collection, he replied. "I don't think I see 'End of the fucking world' tea. Nope. There's no, 'We're going to be eaten alive' tea either. A little help, if you please. I'm struggling as it is to understand how a nice cup of tea is going to help us in our current predicament."

Albie leaped through the air, and landed on Flynn's face. He tapped what constituted its nose, which was really nothing but two small holes poked in his head by whatever had created him. "Calm, Flynn of the cloth, all will be revealed. But in order for this to work, the tea must fit the time of day."

Flynn exhaled loudly, just as there was a loud clatter outside. "Go, Mel, go!" O'Malley shouted, before shoving another handful of cheese-and-onion crisps into his gob.

"Fine, think goddammit, think," Flynn mumbled to himself. He dumped the individual sachets of tea on the counter and picked through them.

"Well, it's night, so that rules out Afternoon tea," he said, flicking that variety onto the floor.

"Though it is not far off morning, so I'll keep English Breakfast," he slid the packet to his designated keep pile.

"I'm gonna have to blend something up," he looked down at Albie. "I warn you, this could taste pretty rancid."

Albie closed his eyes as his tongue flicked out of his head and licked his eyelids, before it slapped around its face, and into its nostrils, rooting around inside for hidden nose treasure.

"Though I guess taste is not high on your list, all things considering," Flynn supposed.

"So, it's summer, something floral perhaps? Hello, this seems rather jolly," the priest pressed down on a packet of Orange and Lotus Flower and added it to the keep pile.

"Though there is no way I'm using that," Flynn flicked the smoky Russian caravan tea onto the floor, "horrible stuff."

"Still need something else though…it's lacking one vital ingredient…ah, this should balance the breakfast out." Flynn went through the teabags and picked up a Snore Clear bag, made from camomile and spearmint.

"A most excellent selection, Flynn of the cloth," Albie agreed.

"Now, let's get that kettle on the go."

41

Five excruciating minutes later

"Is it done yet?" O'Malley whinged. He shoved a finger in his mouth and scraped the congealed mass of crushed soggy crisps from his back teeth.

"Shhh, a watched kettle never boils," Flynn said.

CLICK.

"See."

O'Malley turned back to keeping watch; as Melina sped by, the creature lashed out at the van, and gouged the back half of the windows completely out. "I think we'd better hurry up with that picnic…or whatever the hell you're planning on doing. Come to think of it, why it that thing doing the planning anyway?"

"Albie?" Flynn added.

The axolotl gripped hold of the mug, four strings looped around the handle. He shook it at the priest, who picked up the kettle, set the beverage container down, and filled it up. "There, what now?" Flynn asked.

Albie climbed onto the lip of the cup and looked into the liquid below, as the various tea blends swirled and began to infuse with each other. "Now…we wait."

"What the fuck?" Flynn blurted out.

Pointing inside the mug, Albie said. "It has to brew first, else it won't work."

"Of course…silly me…fine, let's give it a couple of minutes."

42

TWO MORE AGONISING MINUTES LATER

"…and…ready, so, you going to drink up your lovely cup of tea?" Flynn asked, tapping his wristwatch.

Albie nodded. "You might want to stand back, Flynn of the cloth, this will be rather explosive."

Taking heed of the creature's warning, Flynn joined O'Malley by the till, looking into the kitchen, as the other priest looked out into the car park. "This better work. On the last pass, that pig thing had taken most of the roof off. Mel's out there driving around in a goddamn clown car. I'm expecting the doors to come off at any moment."

Right on cue, the spluttering van screeched around the corner, all the doors having fallen off, leaving the woman rather exposed. "Any time today, you guys," she shouted at them. The Bolo-Bolo was panting heavily, and nuzzled the back tyre with its tusk, making it blow out. The minibus wobbled as Melina fought to get it under control before disappearing from view once more.

"Albie, whenever you're ready?" Flynn said.

Albie flexed his little hands out in front of him, wishing he had knuckles to crack. Grabbing hold of the four pieces of string, he hauled the teabags out of the mug and dropped them onto the side. "Get ready for a surprise," he winked, before leaning into the deep brown liquid and drinking deeply from it.

After a loud slurp, Albie flipped off the mug and landed on the patch of worktop which operated as a serving hatch between canteen and kitchen. He closed his eyes, stood up as tall as his legs could stretch, and reached towards the heavens. "Here it comes, I can feel it."

Flynn held onto a cupboard, daring to look upon what was

about to happen.

PARP.

Albie opened an eye, and looked behind him. "Oh dear…that wasn't supposed to happen."

The stench hit Flynn in the face, and made him gag. "Dear god, that smells awful."

"Sorry, Flynn of the cloth."

"Is that it? That's your big plan, a fart? I mean, granted, it stinks like nothing I've ever smelled before, but I was hoping for something with a little more WOW factor, you know?"

Albie sprung back over to the mug, leaned over the rim and took another slurpy gulp. His tongue clacked in his mouth with the smorgasbord of taste sensations.

PAAARRRRPPPPP.

"Jesus, that was a proper little ripper," O'Malley piped up.

"Something is missing, Flynn of the cloth, it's not working."

Flynn muttered his favourite curse under his breath, and crawled over to the worktop. He scooped Albie up, and placed him on the worktop. "Let's see what we've got here." He picked up the mug and held it under his nose. Closing his eyes, he let the steam rise up into his nostrils, tickling his nose hair as it went.

"Hmmm…oaky, yet soft, hints of bergamot, slight tang of chewing gum, and what's that? At the back? It's…it's…" Flynn's eyes burst open, "…it's hope."

+Do you want me to add some weak gruel vomit? Is that the missing ingredient?+

Flynn flung open a cupboard, and worked his way through the contents, settling on a tall frosted bottle. He unscrewed the cap and placed the bottle to his lips, holding it there.

"Flynn? What are you doing with that Martini?" O'Malley asked.

Flynn looked down at the bottle, and at his bandaged hand. "Not today." He poured a slug into the cooling tea, and slid it across to Albie. "There you go, little fella. If I know one thing, it's what alcoholic beverage works best with hot drinks."

Climbing back onto the summit, Albie held onto the lip of the mug with his webbed toes, and bent his head into the concoction.

PPPPPAAAAAAAAAARRRRRRRRRPPPPPPPPPP.

"Albie, seriously, come on, it's beginning to smell like O'Malley's mum in here."

"Hey!" O'Malley protested.

"I am sorry, Flynn of the cloth, there are two reasons why I do not drink tea. The first is that it gives me gas."

"No shit, you don't say? No-one light up in here, or we're all goners," Flynn called out.

"...and the second is..." Albie stuck his mouth into the drink and chinned it until nothing but that bloody awful sediment remained.

"Oh shit," O'Malley called out.

Tearing his gaze away from Albie --who had slumped to the worktop and appeared to be swimming upside down, Flynn looked through the hole in the wall. "Oh, balls."

The minibus had taken a helluva beating, and the steering column, realising it was not a NASCAR, but was being driven like one, locked to the right. With no windscreen, Melina was clearly visible as she waved the two priests out of the way, the van heading straight for them.

Time slowed to a crawl. First, the minibus bucked over the small pile of stonework that was the remainder of the wall, taking advantage of the opportunity to take flight. Melina tugged on her seatbelt first, checking it was secure before bringing her arms up instinctively to protect herself from the inevitable and sudden end to her little joyride.

Flynn sprung through the air, managing to meet the still-stationary Father O'Malley, as he gawped, open-mouthed, at the half-ton piece of flying junk that was heading straight for him. Flynn managed to tackle his nemesis to the ground as the bumper connected with the top of the counter, sending the till flying towards the wall.

As small change showered the cowering men, the back of the minibus tipped up, its forward motion halted. The wheels and rear axle clattered back to the ground. Melina rubbed the back of her neck, trying to look behind her.

With the adrenalin waning, normal speed was restored, and Flynn peeked over the counter. Outside, the Bolo-Bolo had come to a stop, and regarded the smoking vehicle. Its chest heaved up and down, the exertion of the chase having knackered it out. Its claws dug into the ground, and it shook its head from side-to-side, trying to rid itself of the debris it had accumulated in the laps of destruction.

"Get out of there, Mel!" O'Malley screamed.

Melina tugged at the seatbelt, pressing down on the button, the length of fabric holding her in place. "I can't…it's not…"

The Bolo-Bolo took in a deep breath, flexed its claws, and started to pad towards the scene of the crash. "Mel, please, you have to get out of there, *now.*" The priest scurried over the counter and the front of the van, and began tugging on the seatbelt.

"It won't come out, what will we do?" O'Malley shouted at Flynn.

Brushing away a solitary tear, Melina cupped O'Malley's face. "It doesn't matter, go…just go. Save yourself."

"No, I can't, I won't, I got you into this mess, I'm going to get you out."

"It's fine, please. Just don't you dare let my hideous death be for nothing," Mel leant towards the priest, who was still fighting with the seatbelt buckle, and kissed him on the lips. The pair froze, joined together.

Heavy panting from the creature defrosted them, O'Malley looked through the ruin of the minibus to see the monster now only a few feet away from the bumper. Its eyes glowered at them, as its teeth chattered together. The priest turned back to Melina, sat on her lap, and wrapped his arms around her. "Not a chance I'm leaving you like this. We go together…"

A clawed foot lashed out at the back of the vehicle, cleaving half the van away in a single swipe. O'Malley forced his eyes shut, clutching hold of Melina as tightly as he could. He could feel the beast's breath steaming over his arm.

From behind, there came a low drone, and a blast of heat raced down the side of the conjoined couple's faces, followed by a guttural roar. O'Malley opened his eyes and saw a beam of incandescent red light lancing from the kitchen and straight into the Bolo-Bolo's right shoulder. The smell of burned meat and toasted almonds stung his nose.

Limping backwards, the Bolo-Bolo licked at its wound, before baring its teeth. The beam of light gutted in an instant, a crackle of ozone replacing it momentarily. From the kitchen came the sound of clattering cutlery and plates smashing against the floor. O'Malley looked into Melina's eyes, and stroked her cheek, before turning back.

There, standing in the doorway, was the creature that had been living in Flynn's beard, except it was no longer pocket-sized. It stood eight feet tall, having to knock a hole in the wall just so its new form could traverse from one part of the room to the other. Its eyes glowed red, before fading back to their normal cobalt blue. It strode purposefully out of the kitchen into the canteen, its body still expanding. Lashed around its neck was a length of rubber hose, it looked like it had been used on a pressure washer. As the engorged axolotl stood up to full height, a figure ducked under the lintel and sat up proudly on the back of Albie's neck.

In one hand, Flynn held a frying pan, which glowed with a coruscating blue light. With the other hand holding on tightly to the rein, he stood up on his mount. "Get away from them, you bitch!" Flynn squeezed his knees into Albie's jowls, shooting out a few red bolts of semi-automatic laser eye fire.

The Bolo-Bolo staggered back from the assault, inching backwards into the car park. Flynn patted the axolotl's head, getting a loud chirrup in return, then, brandishing the frying pan aloft, he shouted. "Albie. We ride!"

The pair sprung past the jagged remains of the minibus, O'Malley pulling off his white collar, flicking through the multitools to find a serrated blade so he could free Melina from the choking seatbelt. Albie bound towards the boar-like monstrosity, smoke still rising from the impact of the laser beam. The Bolo-Bolo swayed this way and that, instinctively wanting to pounce and attack the new arrival, eat it, with some luck. A small part of it wanted to flee, lick its wounds and perhaps snack on some of the local wildlife. Its indecision proved costly, as Flynn leant to his right, dug his heels into Albie's flank and smacked the beast across the head with the frying pan.

The blow snapped the monster's head back, cracking the top of its skull against its foremost back spine, shearing it off. Albie banked round the rear of the creature, and before it could react, Flynn swung again, making the beast's fearsome head catapult against its other shoulder. It howled in pain, turned, and headed for the outside world.

Flynn brought his monstrous mount to an abrupt stop and smoothed the patch of skin behind one of its ears. "Come on, boy, let's go kick some alien arse." Albie looked back with an alarmed expression. "I mean that thing, not you. You're one of the good guys, let's go, my trusty steed!"

The Bolo-Bolo had pulled itself outside and was looking around. Escape seemed to be the most viable option remaining, and it searched out a path to freedom. It spotted a gap between some large bushes, and bounded towards it, as fast as its injured leg would allow.

"Come on, we have to stop it getting away, this ends today," Flynn shouted in Albie's ear, as he flicked the rein and they set off after the monster at high speed.

As the Bolo-Bolo fled, spears of red laser exploded around it, and across its body. It tried to jink this way and that, but it couldn't get out of the crosshairs it found itself in. Another shot caught it on the back of its leg, sending it off course. As it approached the large bush, one of the bipedal mammals leaped out of it, clutching something to its chest, it looked like a flayed dead bovine of some kind. It lowered its head, hoping its tusks would clear a path and offer it some cover in the process.

"A little further, come on, Albie," Flynn shouted, as he held on for dear life, and dug his heels in some more. A solid beam of thick red light shot out of Albie's eyes, coalescing into a single molten lance of laser. As it struck the Bolo-Bolo just above its tail, there were two screams.

The first was from the beast itself. The light penetrated its thick dewy hide, and continued onwards, turning its organs into thick green-and-red marbled soup. The beam shot out of the creature's snout, smacked into the column supporting the entrance to Saint Judas, and obliterated it. The howl of pain ceased as the Bolo-Bolo's brain was liquefied, and its legs went limp.

Continuing on its path, momentum pushing it forward, it breached the hedgerow, with its chin creating a huge divot from the point of impact. It was at this point that the owner of the second scream was revealed. Impaled on the Bolo-Bolo's left tusk was a very naked Father Yowder. The ivory prong had gone in through his upper thigh, and he was hanging from it like a Christmas decoration from a tree.

"This really hurts," he shouted, at least informing people that he wasn't dead, which, all things considered, was quite handy. The Bolo-Bolo slid to a halt, jolting Yowder, tearing away the last vestige of skin and muscle that had been holding him on. He landed backwards on the creature's nose, and lay beached upon it, like a whale following the wrong directions to the ocean deep.

Albie slowed to a gentle trot, and Flynn hung off the rein until the axolotl had slowed down to a standstill. He dashed over to the man, who was rather nonplussed with the whole thing, shock having visited him early, and taken away the immediacy of seeking medical attention.

As Flynn approached, he saw that Yowder's leg was at a weird angle, the man himself was an ashen white and was pointing to the sky, trying to work out where Orion's belt was, and why it was called a belt in the first place. "Shit…we need to stop the bleeding," was probably the most obvious thing anyone could say upon seeing Yowder, considering that blood was being ejected from the torn arteries and veins at a rather troublesome rate. With the wound being so high up the man's leg, Flynn struggled to see how a tourniquet would work.

"Of course," Flynn clicked his fingers, and beckoned Albie across to him. "Now, I just want a tiny little bit of laser, right about there." Albie nodded and squinted, shooting out the smallest drop of fiery light.

There was a high-pitched momentary screech.

"Oh…looks like you missed, and have inadvertently circumcised him. No matter, have another go, but please, try and get the rather large gaping wound. Not the small shrunken penis, okay?"

Albie nodded, crushed his eyes closed, and let out a slither of immolation, which seared Yowder's life-threatening wound. Yowder laughed. "It smells like bacon. Why can't I wriggle my toes?"

Flynn put his arms under the man's armpits and pulled him gently to the ground. As he did, the lower part of Yowder's spine shook like a bag of rocks, the vertebrae within shattered and smashed from the impact.

O'Malley and Melina ran over, the priest covered his mouth with his hands. "My god…is he…is he okay?"

"Lost a lot of blood, can celebrate Hanukkah, still off his nut on LSD and his back is smashed to pieces. But, all things considered, he should pull through," Flynn gave an enthusiastic thumbs up.

The Bolo-Bolo grunted, the last piece of its brain not reduced to organic slag, fired up, and it opened its mammoth jaw, eager to snag at least one of the stinky mammals. "Not today, you fiend." Flynn held aloft his frying pan, just as a bolt of lightning cracked down from the heavens, connecting with the metal, and lighting him up in a proper heroic pose. Leaping up, he brought the frying pan down on the Bolo-Bolo's skull and caved it in. Acting on impulse, he kept smacking away until O'Malley put an arm around him and whispered in his ear. "That'll do, Father, that'll do."

Flynn raised the Holy Frying Pan of Lighting to the sky, and saluted the Crimson Rosary lightning satellite, a prototype from the Reagan Star Wars initiative. "Cheers, Edgar."

There was a chuckling behind him, and he looked down to see Yowder pointing to the glinting stars in Orion's Belt. "Look, there's the buckle."

Flynn and the others looked up, before he said. "My god, that's not the buckle, that's the spaceship the cannibal nuns from outer space signalled. Dammit. I forgot all about them, I thought we'd won."

Albie nuzzled the priest with his rounded nose. "Come on, Flynn of the cloth, let's finish this."

"And you're sure this is going to work?" Flynn asked, peering through the gaping dome roof.

Albie nodded. "I am sure, there is one thing in this universe at which I excel."

The pale blue sky, being slowly lit up by the encroachment of dawn, was visible through the hole in the nun's base. Albie pulled his arms behind his back, limbering up. "On my homeworld, before we were tricked, incarcerated, and eaten, I was the javelin world-record holder." Flynn patted Albie on the head, and rested on the bannister, giving him a perfect viewing spot.

In the sky, there was one star that shone brighter than the rest. It was like a pearl on a velvet cushion. Albie picked up the rocket with one hand, feeling its weight. "Are you sure? I'm certain there is another way," the priest asked.

The axolotl grimaced, gritting its little peg teeth together. "I'm sure." Albie planted his feet, licked a finger, and felt for the wind direction, which seemed a little pointless as they were stood inside a building. Flynn didn't want to bring it up and ruin his concentration, though, so he kept quiet.

With his free arm outstretched, pointing towards the glowing orb, Albie pulled the rocket back behind him. "This is for my people."

With all his might, he hurled the metal dart. It soared

through the air, propelled by strength, conviction, and revenge, and supported by three gold medals from the annual athletics games on his homeworld.

43

The debris was still tumbling through the outer skin of the earth's atmosphere, creating a free firework display for the northern hemisphere as the helicopters of the Order of the Crimson Rosary buzzed over the distant treeline. "Better late than never, I suppose," Flynn grumbled.

Yowder squeezed the priest's hand tighter. "Thank you…"

"What for?"

"For covering me up. I can't stand the feel of fabric against my skin. The last thing I'd want when the rescue squad turn up is for me to be lying here stark bollock naked." Yowder tugged on the hem of the tartan blanket, making sure it covered up his saggy testicles.

Flynn nodded towards the stump where Yowder's leg had once been. "Are you going to be okay?"

Yowder slapped what remained of this thigh; a few burnt flakes of skin and meat fell onto the gravel. "I'll survive, could've been a whole lot worse. Plus, it's going to help you out in the long run."

"How so?"

"I've still got to complete your therapy, there's less of me now, so I'm going to be lighter to carry round the forest." Yowder allowed a grin to break the stoicism of his face.

"You were serious about that?"

Yowder's smile faded as quickly as it had birthed. "Deadly serious. I've got some moves which may help you, when you're back out there. A little something I picked up from the Jigglebooty clan of Sierra Leone."

"If Archbishop Tena lets me, that is." Flynn looked to the corner of the house. A Blackhawk helicopter lowered towards the ground, black-clad operatives jumping from the cargo bay and bringing their weapons up, scanning the area. Their white collars were visible even from a distance. They called out curt commands; one squad disappeared into the building, through the breach, whilst another began to approach the group still sat on the verdant lawns of St Judas.

"Hey, Flynn," O'Malley called out.

Flynn nodded a thanks to Yowder and stood up, turning around to face his fellow priest. "What do you want, O'Malley?"

For a few seconds the pair glared at each other, before O'Malley extended a hand. "Friends?"

Flynn shook O'Malley's hand. "Acquaintances," the pair laughed.

Donning a fresh pair of mirrored sunglasses, O'Malley wrapped his arm around Melina's waist. "Well, if you don't mind, I'm going to get the debrief over and done with, Mel and I have got lost time to make up for. Is that okay?"

"Of course, just don't be going and stealing my thunder now, you hear?"

O'Malley snorted, and put on an air of mock-offence. "Me? Would I do that to you?"

"Let's not test the boundaries of our new-found relationship just yet."

"Until the next time you screw up, I'll be seeing you." O'Malley gave a brief salute before walking off arm-in-arm with Melina, waving towards the approaching fast reaction squad, though their title was something of a misnomer. The operative relaxed his Holy Trident of Spalding and spoke into his throat mic, bidding the pair forward for a pat-down.

The sound of a mobile phone ringing broke the still air. Flynn sought out the source, and saw Padraig speaking into his iBible, still clutching that damn leather holdall to his chest. After a few quiet sentences and some nodding, he headed across to Flynn, red-faced. "It's…erm…for you…Father."

After losing his look of surprise, Flynn took the phone. "Hello?"

"Flynn! Good work, I've seen the initial reports provided by Padraig and the on-site team. Looks like you've pulled off quite the coup."

"Thank you, Archbishop…though I had some help, I couldn't have done it on my own."

"Tish and pish, consider yourself reinstated forthwith, just please, lay off the sauce a bit, please? For the church? For the Order of the Crimson Rosary?"

Flynn flexed his bandaged hand, and nodded towards Yowder. "A friend helped me realise that some things are best enjoyed in moderation."

"Excellent, now, if you think you're up to it, I've got a demonic spawn infestation, down in Torbay. I know you've just been through hell and back, but I need my best man on the case, are you interested?"

Flynn's chest swelled with pride, and cigarette smoke. "You bet your shiny moisturised arse I am, your Grace."

"Excellent, you know what you need to do, I look forward to your report on both matters. Tena, out."

Closing up the iBible, Flynn handed it back to Padraig who shied away. They stood there for a few awkward seconds.

"That was-"

"How have you-"

The pair spoke at once, over each other. Padraig held his bag tighter and bowed his head slightly. "Go on, Father, after you."

"How have you been, Padraig?"

"Okay, Father, look, I'm sorry, about before? I didn't want to…just…you gave me no choice."

Flynn slapped a hand on Padraig's back. "I know, old friend, I know. Say, do you have the Volvo around here?"

Shoving a hand into his pocket, Padraig held up a key fob and pressed a button.

BEEP BEEP.

"I certainly do, Father."

"Do you think you would mind working with me again, Padraig?"

The man's face lit up with joy, and his eyes began to well up. "It would be an honour, Duke…I mean, Father Flynn."

"Go fire the old girl up, we've got some evil to return to sender."

Padraig quickstepped to his car, as he opened the driver's door, he called out. "Father, I've got some mini sausage rolls in the back. With chorizo, just how you like them."

+He is a strange one+

You can talk, Prince of Upchuck.

+One day, I will spread from the jail of these fleshy sacks at the back of your throat, and bring you your DOOM! But until then, I will help you where I can. My demonic kin are good fun to squish, you can count on me+

Flynn waved a medic across to Yowder and gave the man a thumbs-up, before heading over to Albie, who was sitting on a wall, looking up at the pyrotechnic display still going on above them. Even over the first strains of daylight, the multi-coloured trails were spectacular.

"You did it, you saved us and avenged your people. Thank you, Albie."

The creature sat there, still fixated on the fizzing lines of nuclear fuel raining down on the planet. He turned to Flynn. "Then why do I still feel so empty, Flynn of the cloth?"

"You've been through so much, even when you landed here, you were imprisoned. You just need to process everything, come to terms with your survivor's guilt and the new world you find yourself in." Flynn gestured towards Yowder, who was being poked and prodded by the medic. "There's someone here who can help. Sure, his methods are a little out there, but he gets results."

"Thank you, Flynn of the cloth, one day, when I am at peace, I would like to work with you again. It has been an honour."

Flynn gave Albie a hug, before standing up and beginning to walk towards the revving Volvo. He stopped, turned, lit a cigarette, and said. "When that day comes…I'm gonna need a bigger beard."

Cast

(In order of appearance)

Father Flynn

Eryk Lagaste

Padraig

Niall O'Riordan

Derek

Tom Peters

Meredith

Aneka Ilstrom

Timothy

Ben Killian

The Voice Of Fattori Gutso

Alesandro Del Chieri

Father O'Malley

Brad Humperdump

Sister Wilma

Betty Mahon

Gilbert

Dirk Latte

Sister Beryl

Tina Carmichael

The Voice Of Albie
Jim Yoo Chan

Archbishop Tena
Nigel Kilpatrick

Chris Hall
Guy Jones

Jennifer Hall
Mary Swaffinkel

Mother Superior Francesca
Nina Engelmann

Ian 'Scotch' McRae
Charles DeSmith

Dylan
Ufe Abeniko

Mack
Michael Popswatch

Dwayne
Kurt Bemmie

Cagoule
Jim I Wuz

Dick Hawkins
Paul McFeeney

BILLY
Nathan Ranger

HANNAH
Elisabet Gomes

FOREST CANNIBAL NUN
Rose Tilley

LEE-ANNE
Lisa Thompson

LILY
Missy Templeton

SISTER OPHELIA
Tracey Savage

EDDIE
Ron Fish

TREVOR
Rusty Beauchamp

DAVID HUGHES (PHIL DE HOLE)
Ken Wakaku

FATHER O'HANRAHAN
Petr Canacek

SISTER ROBERTA
Rita Wurlitzer

Father Yowder
Patrick Tellman III

Melina
Victoria Sanchez

Sister Cecelia
Jo Taylor

Sister Momo
Pat St Angela

Sister Caitlin
Mary Bevan

Animals Provided By
Dabbi Animal Sanctuary
Pom as herself
Quina as Albie the axolotl

Spanish Localisation Specialist
Gabino Iglesias

Special FX
Chainsaw Guts

Writer Support
Debbie Bradshaw

Supplies By
Sainsburys
Rowden Arms

Technology Provided By

Samsung
Apple
Jawbone

Edited By

Linda Nagle

Cover Art By

Adrian Stone

Published By

EyeCue Productions
Sinister Horror Company

Design By

EyeCue Productions

Directed By

Rusty Beauchamp

Written By

Duncan P. Bradshaw

Written On Location At
Casa Bradshaw
Chippenham, Wiltshire. UK.

SOUNDTRACK

THUMPER - Raging Speedhorn
EXIT MUSIC (FOR A FILM) - Radiohead
METHOD MAN - Wu-Tang Clan
TALK SHIT, GET SHOT - Body Count
STALKER - Fuck Buttons
REAL LOVE - Asend & Ultravibe
EAT YOU ALIVE - Limp Bizkit
VIOLINS & HAPPY ENDINGS - dEUS
THE RUNNING FREE - Coheed and Cambria
I WANT YOU SO HARD (THE BOY'S BAD NEWS) -
Eagles Of Death Metal
FIRE, FIRE - Heaven's Basement
THE ONLY LOONEY LEFT IN TOWN - Carter The
Unstoppable Sex Machine
MLADIC - Godspeed You! Black Emperor
FUTTERMAN'S RULE - Beastie Boys
GOLDEN DAWN - The Grid
YA MAMA - Fatboy Slim
STILLBORN UNICORN - Mongol Horde
CALL TO ARMS - The Defiled
FIRE WATER BURN - Bloodhound Gang
AIN'T NOBODY PERFECT - Being As An Ocean
RABBLE ROUSER - Enter Shikari
DEVIL IN A MIDNIGHT MASS - Billy Talent
THEME FROM GUTBUSTER - Bentley Rhythm Ace
SOMETHING GOOD - Utah Saints

All incidental music by Ketamine Theremin and FEED

BONUS MATERIAL

THE DARTH PLAGIARIST ENDING

STARTS FROM THE END OF CHAPTER 37

THIS WAS THE ORIGINAL ENDING
REPLACED BY WHAT YOU'VE JUST READ
KNOWN AS THE DABBIDAH ENDING

WARNING:
UNEDITED, MAY CONTAIN ERRORS.

38

Picking his way through the massacred nuns, and lopped off body parts, Flynn took care to not fall over. He held his chest with one arm, trying to let the skin knit together again and begin to heal. Resting against a crate were Melina and O'Malley, still in their holy women tunics. Melina mopped the injured priest's head with a strip of cloth, soaking up the blood and sweat, he tried to fend her off, but his feeble attempts were ignored.

"Is he okay?" Flynn stood over the survivors.

"He will be, did we do it?" Melina asked, helping O'Malley to his feet.

Flynn shook his head. "This lot of nuns are defeated, but the Mother Superior managed to send some kind of signal off-world. I think our troubles have only increased."

Melina pointed to the rocket. "Whatever received that signal is in low orbit, waiting for this. They'll need to verify the message first. Then they'll head off into hyperspace to the GAFFER central distribution hub, where the harvesters will be fired up."

A nun, with one arm missing and dried green blood flaking from her skin gasped and reached her one remaining hand up towards Flynn. The priest pressed his foot against the woman's throat, pinning her to the floor. Holding the sword above her head, he drove it down through the alien's skull, impaling her against the floor. Her fingernails scraped against the stonework as they contracted, rigor mortis setting in immediately. Flynn let the sword remain upright, as a crude memorial. "Then we're fucked?"

O'Malley stumbled across to a crate and sat down. "Ahhh, that's better." He looked at the rocket, which was still belching steam, a series of red lights blinked on the guidance fins. He clicked his fingers. "Well, why don't we send them their delivery? Just one loaded with a little extra punch?"

"Of course," Melina jogged over to some glowing metal canisters, as tall as a goat. "These are fuel cells, with some tampering, I could rig these to blow, but-"

Flynn butted in. "There's always a but, I'm guessing it can't be done via a timer or automated trigger, that someone will have to go up with it?"

"How did you know?"

"Call it a lucky guess, and way too many Hollywood films with the exact same situation." Flynn looked from Melina to O'Malley. "Okay, fine, I guess this could be the final part of my therapy."

Melina had pulled off a panel from one of the fuel cells, and was rewiring it. "Eh?"

Flynn stuck a hand in the air. "Please, miss, pick me, pick me! I said I'll do it, I'll go up in the rocket, I'll detonate your little IED, don't think I've got much planned for...you know...the rest of my life."

Pushing himself up, O'Malley staggered across to the priest. "Bullshit, I can't let you do this, I'll volunteer for this one-way ticket to KABOOM-Ville."

"Of course you will. Look, O'Malley, I appreciate the gesture, but let's face it, you're the main star of the Crimson Rosary, you always have been. I'm the joke, the has-been. It's cool, I don't mind, least this way my legacy will be something other than my drinking record in the chapel bar," Flynn play punched O'Malley on the shoulder, making the man wince.

"Do you know why I always try to upstage you, Flynn?"

"Because you're a monumental bellend with an inferiority complex?"

O'Malley chuckled, and clutched his ribs. "Not a bad guess. You were always the one who got the best gigs, you know? That possession you went to, you know...the *one*? They sent *you*, not me. I only turned up when things got out of hand."

+Ha ha ha, you were a terrible opponent, priest+

"And look at me now," Flynn held his arms out, displaying his battered and bloodied form. "I'm an alcoholic, with self-destructive tendencies. I'm a wash out. A section nine. Let me have this one, let me make up for the fuck up that I am."

"I outrank you. You know that I could just order you to stand aside?"

Flynn stuck up his two fingers. "You're a wanker, O'Malley, but you're not a complete bastard, you know this makes sense, you know that this is the only way that this can go down."

O'Malley stood up, he held out his hand. Flynn studied it, before wrapping his fingers around it, the two men gripped tightly, and exchanged a near invisible nod. "You know, Father Flynn, you can be my wingman, any time."

Flynn smiled. "Bullshit, you can be mine." The two men embraced, Flynn pulled O'Malley closer, and whispered into his ear, they separated and the unsteady priest nodded.

"It's really good that you too have got this little bromance going, but it doesn't matter."

"What do you mean?" O'Malley and Flynn asked as one.

"Well, I know for a fact that although one part of you is six inches tall - under certain conditions - the rest of you isn't."

The two men looked at each other, then at their crotch, before staring at the woman. "What do you mean?" O'Malley asked,

Melina beckoned them away from the rocket, a few feet back, she pointed to its peak with a pair of pliers, the silver tip appearing as a twinkling star against the night sky. "See up there? That's the guidance system, neither of you can fit in there. Only something really small can get in there and control it manually. It's the Kaihoro failsafe, to make sure that their own equipment can't be used against them in the way that we're planning to."

Flynn smacked his fist against his palm. "Dammit. Then we are all royally screwed."

There was a rustling sound from the priest's face, Albie stuck his head out from the wiry hair. "Flynn of the cloth, perhaps I can be of assistance?"

"Erm…Flynn, you have some talking pink snot crawling out of your beard," O'Malley edged away, looking for a weapon or large tissue.

Melina put an arm around him, and shook his head. "No, he's a friend."

"No…not you, Albie, I saved you from those cultist knobheads so you could have a better life. Not to pilot a rocket which is nothing more than a giant bomb into a spaceship orbiting the planet, which isn't even your own. You deserve better, you deserve to live," Flynn pleaded.

Albie climbed out of the thatch, and sat on Flynn's shoulder. "You avenged my people, Flynn, and you saved me. I'm the last of my kind in this universe, and I…"

"What?"

"…I…"

"Shhh, it's okay, little fella, what is it?"

The axolotl, tears being held back in the corners of his eyes, looked up to the man who had been his home for the past few months. "I don't want to go out like a bitch."

"He makes a good point," O'Malley added.

"Please, let me do this for you, let me do something to thank you for giving me these last few months, our adventures, the things you let me do to you."

"Eh? What things?"

Albie shrunk backwards. "Oh…nothing…just when your throat swells up in a few months' time, and there's a chirping within…just promise me that you'll look after our children."

"WHAT?"

Albie ran a slimy paw down Flynn's cheek. "Tell them about me, tell them what I did. But most of all…tell them to live."

"What did you do to me exactly?"

"Shhhh," Albie pressed his greasy hand against Flynn's lips. "You didn't think I was just sleeping in there did you?"

"I feel a little violated to be honest…"

"Oh, Flynn of the cloth, thank you…you've taught me so much. Now, go, live, keep this world safe so that our mutant offspring have a future, safe from the hungry mouths of the Kaihoro. You have to let me go."

Flynn held out a hand, which Albie jumped onto. The priest walked to the rocket, and held his hand against the cool metal surface. The axolotl scurried across the palm of the priest's hand, and using his blend of natural oils and scum, began to climb up the rocket. As he got to the refuelling pipe, Albie looked down. "I have been, and always will be…your friend, Flynn of the cloth."

"And the little critter that took advantage of me when I was unconscious," Flynn shouted back.

The axolotl's chin bulged up like a balloon, and let out a burp. "In time…I hope you can forgive me for that. Now…I must go."

Flynn waved the little creature off, Albie disappeared from view, as he pulled open a small access panel, and closed it behind him. "Quick, help me with this," Melina nudged the priest in the ribs, nodding towards the modified fuel cells.

As the steam continued to broil and build, Melina and Flynn stuffed the fuel cells inside of the cargo hold, having to take a number of the boxed up food items out, to make room. "How will he…you know…set this lot off?"

Melina closed the cargo hatch up. "One big jolt and this lot will go up like the end of the world. Don't worry, your little friend knows what to do. Come on."

39

With O'Malley slung between the shoulders of Melina and Flynn, the trio pushed the door open, and scuttled down the path, back towards the main building. Amidst the crackling of their feet on the gravel, there was a groundswell building behind them. A low growl turned into a loud WHOOSHING sound, as the rocket booster jets fired up.

Getting to the car park, the three of them collapsed to the ground and rolled over, looking back up the hill to the nun's base, silhouetted against the violet night sky. The main doors of the manor house opened up, Yowder and Padraig ran out towards them, checking on the extent of their injuries.

"Well?" Yowder asked. "Did you pass the trial?"

Flynn rested on his elbows, panting, he pointed to the open roof at the top of the small hill. "You could say that."

A corona of yellow and orange haloed the cylindrical stone building, the rocket, a spear of silver in the dawn sky appeared from the glow and smoke, lancing steadily upwards. "My god…" Yowder stuttered.

The rocket pitched slightly, a ball of immolation behind it, propelling it upwards. The glint of silver slowly faded, leaving nothing but a small yellow sphere, its glow diminishing with every second. Then it was gone. Nothing remained but the bruised sky, even the stars blinked out, wary of what would happen next. The nun's base was delivered back into darkness.

Silence reigned. Each of the onlookers held their breath, afraid to be the first to break the spell of solemnity.

Just as the first wave of doubt was born, there was an explosion of light above them. A second moon burst into existence for the briefest of moments, a wide yellow eye looking down on the inhabitants of this blue and green rock, surveying them. Then, like paint being dipped into crystal clear water, the glow dissipated, leaving the moon as the sole beacon in the dawn sky. Its brief sibling nothing but a golden smudge, fading slowly away.

As the sky regained its normal hue, with a pale blue band of light on the horizon, heralding a new day, streaks of orange, red and silver fell back to earth. Like a firework display from the heavens, light clawed at the dark, tearing it asunder.

There was a screeching sound, and a startled yelp from the main driveway, Flynn stood up, and dusted himself down. A yellow vehicle skidded around the corner, coming to a stop a short distance away from the small congregation. The interior was full of smoke, and blinking lights. O'Malley got up and yelled. "Hey, that's my car."

The door opened up with a hiss, smoke rolled out, and Ian stepped through the miasma. He was wearing a silver jumpsuit, tight fitting, and not particularly flattering. He checked his watch, and stormed across to the group of people eyeing him up. Pulling up his silver lensed sunglasses, he tapped his watch. "Exactly on time. Good. Good."

"What have you done to my car? That was a gift from the Vatican itself," O'Malley, ignoring his wounds, raved at the taxi driver, who blanked him and stood in front of Flynn.

"Come on, we have to go, there's more to be done," Ian grabbed hold of the priest's elbow and tried to drag him away.

"Woah, steady on there, I ain't going anywhere. I need some kip, some new clothes and a cup of tea, ideally with some biscuits," Flynn shook himself free.

Ian pouted and put his hands on his hips. "Look. It's the nuns. They're back."

Flynn laughed. "Look, we just killed them all, if you don't believe me, go and have a look up there. I don't know what you're after, but I'm done. Okay?"

"Not now. Then. You know, in a bit," Ian waved his hands about.

"That's great, but I'm going to have a lie down," Flynn patted the man on the back and headed towards the reception.

"It's about your children," Ian shouted.

Flynn stopped dead. He shook his head and looked over his shoulder. "Fine. You know what, I'm going to regret this, but let's just go. I don't think I can take one more long-winded story. None of this really makes sense anymore."

Ian guided the priest to the car, Yowder shouted out after them. "No, you must come back, you must finish your training. There's this cave that I need you to go into. It's dark, perilous and only you can gain entrance to it."

"That doesn't sound right, Yowder. Thanks for your help, but I gotta go," Flynn waved his hand, and got into the passenger seat of the car. As the door closed automatically, he looked at the interior. The dashboard was fully digital, showing an array of dates, and futuristic looking dials, behind him was a transparent box, two thick wires ran through the body, arching off into the bowels of the vehicle, they glowed pink and orange.

"You took care of the cannibal nuns then?" Ian asked, fiddling with a multitude of switches.

"Yeah…looks like you were right. How did you know?"

Ian turned to face the priest. "I did try telling you after we hit the priest. Dynynbwtya Lleian. Do you know what it stands for?"

Flynn wiped the spit from his face, required by the Welsh speaker to roll the absurd number of L's. "No, but I guess you're going to tell me."

"Man-eating nun, or close enough to it."

"Of course it does…stupid me. So what happens now?"

"Brace yourself, Father, where we're going…it's going to be a bit of a surprise," Ian began to flick various buttons, and twiddle dials.

"Where? It better not be Kidderminster, I fucking hate Kidderminster," Flynn grabbed hold of the seatbelt and clicked it closed.

Ian looked at the priest, with the most maniacal of grins. "Oh no, we're going…back to the future."

Flynn scowled. "But I haven't been *to* the future in the first place, how can I return somewhere I've never been to?"

"Oh…true…that's a bit annoying, I've been looking forward to saying that for a while now," Ian looked a tad dejected, as he smacked on the lid of the temporal engine.

"So, really, where are we going?"

Ian pulled down his sunglasses. "The year 2139, the nuns…they're back, and of all the possible futures I went to, there was only one outcome. The human race was turned into cereal bars. Then I found out about an ancient prophecy…and…well, without spoiling things for any potential stories that might come after this one, why do you think I'm here?"

Flynn shrugged. "You know what? I genuinely don't care, let's just go."

Managing to pull off a wheelspin, Ian skidded around the car park, lining the modified Popemobile up with the long drive, and the open stone gateway beyond. "Let's go." With a screech of tyres, the car sped off down the gravel track, fire belching behind it, the tyre tracks channels of brimstone and sparks. As it zoomed beneath the archway, the vehicle blinked out of existence, leaving nothing but a spinning hubcap behind.

Padraig shook his head and folded his arms, he leant over to Yowder. "I can't believe he's gone, he was the last best hope we had."

Yowder kicked at the stones by his feet. "No…there is another…"